Praise for *Truth Be Told*

"*Truth Be Told* is exceptional and a must-read. Murray tackles topics such as AIDS, infidelity, God, drugs, atheism, and politics in such a way that when you close the book not only do you feel satisfied, but you feel like you can jump over any hurdle that may be in your life."

—Ericka P. Thompson, *The Indianapolis Recorder*

"I found myself touched by the characters and know that there won't be any dry eyes when readers come to the close of this very profound spiritual journey."

—Wayne Jordan, editor in chief of Romance in Color.com

"Victoria Christopher Murray is back! Once again she's given us a fast-paced novel about people of faith who must face real-life challenges."

—E. Lynn Harris, author of
What Becomes of the Brokenhearted

"*Truth Be Told* is a truly enjoyable story. The unforgettable characters lend an air of reality to this emotional and engaging read. Her latest is sure to please fans and resonate long after the last page is turned."

—Jacquelin Thomas, author of *Soul Journey*

"*Truth Be Told* dishes a healthy dose of pure drama as it careens down a path plagued with infidelity, desperation, greed, and a series of consequences, which can only be overcome through grace."

—Patricia Haley, bestselling author of *No Regrets* and *Blind Faith*

Also by Victoria Christopher Murray

Grown Folks Business
Truth Be Told
Temptation
Joy
Blessed Assurance (contributor)

A Sin and a Shame

Victoria Christopher Murray

A Touchstone Book
Published by Simon & Schuster
New York London Toronto Sydney

TOUCHSTONE
Rockefeller Center
1230 Avenue of the Americas
New York, NY 10020

This book is a work of fiction. Names, characters, places, and incidents either
are products of the author's imagination or are used fictitiously. Any resem-
blance to actual events or locales or persons, living or dead, is entirely coinci-
dental.

TOUCHSTONE and colophon are registered trademarks of Simon & Schuster, Inc.

Designed by Jamie Kerner-Scott

Manufactured in the United States of America

ISBN: 0-7394-7014-0
ISBN 13: 978-0-7394-7014-5

A Tribute to My Father

It happened again.

During the middle of writing this novel, my father, Edwin Christopher, passed away suddenly. I didn't think life could be this brutal. This is the second time, while trying to write a novel that exalts God, that I've lost someone so close to me. And like the last time, grief wrapped its arms around me and I knew that I would never survive. How could I? How could I survive—losing the first man I ever loved? The man I've loved longer than any man in my life? The first man to make me feel special, told me I was a queen, convinced me that I could do anything. My father had many successes and achievements in his life, but I know the most important to him were that he loved God without reservation, loved his wife for more than fifty years, and loved his daughters unconditionally. He gained the respect and admiration of all who knew him and the many who just happened to cross his path. My sister, Cecile, said it best—Edwin Christopher was a man of solid character and all of his daughters just wanted to be half the woman that he was a man. It seemed too cruel that God would take him away from us. After all, he hadn't been sick. Just went for a walk one Monday morning . . .

And then it happened again.

God showed up. Well, that may not be the correct way to say it, because God was always there. He never left—even though there were more than a few moments when I questioned Him. My father's passing had obviously been a mistake; the first mistake He's made in all of eternity, and it had to be with my dad. For the first time since coming to know God, I was mad. At Him!

But then I heard the voice of God. And I listened. There was no reason to look at this as a loss. I had gained so much just by having Edwin Christopher as my father.

And then it happened again.

I was comforted and I was healed.

So, this is a tribute to my father—my earthly one and my heavenly one. Thank you, Daddy, for being such a tremendous father. I was always so proud to be your daughter—to look like you, walk like you, speak like you. I will always love you and you will always be my daddy.

And thank you, Heavenly Father, for your long-suffering love. In spite of myself, you keep on loving me, and keeping me, and holding me. I would have never been able to walk through these months without you. And I would have never completed this novel without your constant nudging that in spite of life, your will must continue to be done.

A Sin and a Shame

Prologue

This was not the way Jasmine had planned to spend the night before her wedding. Her fingers squeezed the toilet's edge as she crouched over the commode, her knit dress hiked high around her hips.

Celebratory sounds drifted into the bathroom from outside. The cheers continued, the toasts kept coming—all without her. It didn't matter. It wasn't like she had many friends or family there to celebrate with her. Tomorrow, her sister, Serena, godbrother Malik, and their two assistants, Gabriella and Tina, would be sitting alone on the left side of the church if they kept with tradition.

At least her fiancé was loved and respected enough to fill the church with hundreds who would see her fantasy come true. Even now, she anticipated the "oohs" and "aahs" that would ring through the sanctuary when the oversized doors of City of Lights at Riverside Church opened and everyone saw her draped in the fifteen-hundred-dollar designer dress. Then there would be the horse-driven carriage that would carry her and her new husband to the reception at Tavern on the Green.

Jasmine took another deep breath, and pushed herself up. But her stomach rumbled and she sank onto the toilet seat.

"Jasmine?"

She almost groaned at Gabriella's Spanish accent. Jasmine didn't like her. Just put up with her because Malik wouldn't have it any other way.

"Jasmine?"

"I'm in here, Gabriella."

"Are you all right? You've been gone for a while."

"I'm fine," Jasmine said, not rising. "I'll be right out."

"Are you sure?"

Jasmine closed her eyes. *Leave me alone.* "I need a moment."

She heard the door swing open then close, muffling the joy from the party and returning her to her silent sanctuary. All she wanted to do was rush home and collapse into bed, but that couldn't happen. Any minute now, her fiancé was liable to start banging on the door, wondering where was his "darlin'."

She stepped outside the stall and wobbled across the Italian tiles. Grabbing a tissue from her purse, she dabbed at the perspiration on her forehead. She kept her glance away from the mirror. Didn't want to look into her eyes. Didn't want to see the question because she already knew the answer.

Finally, she allowed herself to glimpse at her reflection.

"Am I pregnant?" she whispered to her image. She had to fight to keep the tears away. Fight as hard as she did to keep the nausea away.

"Oh, no," she cried. "Oh, no. Oh, no. Oh, no!"

Chapter 1

Jasmine swung the designer dress in front of her as she gazed into the mirror. "Can you believe this is a size six?"

Serena leaned against the silk pillows stacked against the bed's headboard. "I can't believe you bought all these things," she said to her sister. "How are you going to pay for this?" Serena motioned toward the bags and boxes strewn across the room.

"You didn't answer my question," Jasmine said, fixing her eyes on her reflection.

"You didn't answer mine."

Jasmine faced her sister with raised eyebrows. "Why are you worried? Dad left us—"

"Not enough for you to be going off like you're Oprah."

Jasmine sighed. That was what was wrong with Serena. She lived life in the middle. She lived in a middle-class neighborhood, with a middle-class job, trudging through her middle-class life. But there was nothing "middle" about Jasmine. She lived outside of the box where she knew all the abundant blessings could be found.

"Can you believe this is a size six?" Jasmine repeated, turning back to the mirror, this time with a silk pantsuit draped in front of her.

A slight smile crossed Serena's lips. "You do look good, girl."

Jasmine smiled too. She'd worked hard to lose twenty pounds and get in top shape for her mission.

Serena sighed. "Wish I could do that."

"I thought you'd joined Curves."

Serena waved her hand in the air. "Girl, I'm a Curves dropout. The women there were looking at me like they wanted me to really exercise. I pretended I had to go to the bathroom, and snuck out the back door."

Jasmine laughed. "Well, you should take up running, like I did." She didn't mention that along with her almost-daily sixty-minute runs, she'd spent hundreds of dollars on laxatives in the last three months.

Serena said, "I ain't running nowhere. I've decided that I am perfectly fine in my size eighteen." Serena squinted as her sister primped in front of the mirror. "Seriously, Jasmine. I'm worried about you."

"No need. I'm just preparing for my new life in New York. I plan on having much sex in the city and I've got to be ready."

"Girl, you need Jesus," Serena said, holding a Bible above her head. "That's why I bought you this."

"I've already got one of those."

"You can't have too many," Serena said, as she tucked the book inside the nightstand drawer. "With the way you're acting, you need Jesus all around you."

"I don't know what you're talking about. You, of all people, know how much I love God."

"And I would know this how?"

"Like you never noticed who was sitting next to you every Sunday the last two years."

"Honey, there are plenty of unsaved folks parked in pews all across America."

"Well, I'm not one of them," Jasmine said, thinking how she'd changed since she'd asked Jesus into her heart. Not only was she in church every Sunday, but she had even remained celibate her first year in Florida. Almost 365 days—and she had counted every one of them. "I gave up a lot for the Lord."

Serena laughed. "What did you give up?"

Jasmine faced her sister. "I gave up married men. I may not be all holy like you, but I'm making progress."

Progress indeed, Jasmine thought. Two years ago, she'd made a list of promises: Besides swearing to never again have sex with a married man, she vowed to never miss a Sunday service. And, she pledged never to tell a lie—if she didn't have to. She was living the Christian life and was pleased that she'd kept her commitments to God.

Serena sighed. "I pray for you, girl. I pray every day."

"You don't have to worry. All I'm doing is getting my groove back."

Serena shook her head. "That's why you bought all these clothes? To have sex?"

"No, silly. The clothes are an investment."

Serena glanced around the master bedroom of the condo her sister had just purchased. "I thought this apartment was an investment."

Jasmine shook her head as if she was tired of explaining this. "I'm investing in my life. These clothes are going to help me find my next husband."

Serena moaned.

"You can groan if you want," Jasmine said, now holding a black knit mini dress in front of her. "By this time next year, I'm going to be Mrs. Somebody Important."

"Why is getting married suddenly so important to you?"

Jasmine had asked herself that question so many times. It wasn't that getting married was important. It was that she'd been single long enough, and it wasn't like she was getting younger. It was time to settle down—again.

"I just want to be married. And you know how I get when I want something."

Serena peered at her sister and Jasmine could almost hear her thoughts.

Jasmine said, "I'm fine."

Serena kept her stare on her sister for a bit longer. "I hope so," she said before she stood and, with her hands, pressed the wrinkles from her jeans. "Well, Big Sis . . ." Serena slipped into her down overcoat.

Jasmine held up her hand. "I told you not to call me that anymore. I don't want you making a mistake around anyone." She returned to admiring herself in the mirror. "Remember, I'm thirty now."

"Oh, Lord." Serena looked up at the ceiling. "Forgive me, Father, for calling on you like that, but this child needs some help." She returned her glance to Jasmine. "How are you thirty, when I'm thirty-five, and you're almost five years older than me?"

"Not anymore."

"Please."

"I mean it, Serena. I'm thirty now. Look at me," Jasmine said, sweeping her hand down her side.

"You need to look at your birth certificate."

Jasmine waved Serena's words away. "Like anyone is going to ask to see that."

"What about your driver's license?"

"I'll think of something. Your job is to just remember that I'm thirty."

Serena held her hands up. "Whatever. Listen, what time are we leaving for church tomorrow?"

"Malik said he'd meet us at the hotel at ten-thirty. We're going to take a cab uptown."

"Uptown?" Serena grinned. "You got the lingo down."

"Honey, I'm a New York City girl for real."

"Whatever you are, I'm outta here," Serena said, sliding into a pair of gloves. "I want to pack tonight so I can make the three o'clock train. If I miss that one, I'll have to wait until seven. And I want to get away from this cold, girl. A week in New York in January is enough for me."

Jasmine laughed at her sister, the Florida girl, wrapped snuggly in a white down coat, looking like the Michelin man. "You're still going to take the train home?"

"Yeah, I like the ride."

"You only like it because it's free."

"Duh, who doesn't like something free? Jerry didn't work at Amtrak all those years for nothing," she said, referring to her husband who had passed away six years earlier.

"I don't understand you. We've got all this money from Daddy's insurance policy. Why don't you fly? Take one of those cheap flights from New York to Florida."

Serena shook her head. "I'm fine. It only takes twenty-four hours and I'll get a lot of reading done." She shrugged. "I love the train."

"You love being cheap. Besides, I thought you'd be rushing home to see Carl," Jasmine teased.

Serena rolled her eyes. "I'm not rushing home to see anyone."

But Jasmine didn't miss the smile that lit Serena's face. Since her husband passed away, Serena hadn't shown interest in anyone. But a few months ago, Jasmine had invited one of her coworkers, Carl Cosby, to church. She had no plans of introducing Carl to Serena—until she saw the way the self-proclaimed nerd kept glancing at her sister. It was a casual introduction that Jasmine expected to go nowhere. Her sister had made it clear that her focus was on God, her children, and work. But then, Serena accepted Carl's invitation to dinner.

Jasmine had been thrilled. She prayed that Carl could bring her sister some happiness.

"Anyway," Serena continued, "you may think I'm cheap, but we'll see who'll be calling who for a loan in a year."

"I'll lend you money if you need it," Jasmine kidded. "I'll be married to a rich man by then."

"Whatever. Anyway, give me a hug."

"I'm going with you."

"You're still staying at the hotel? I thought you'd want to sleep here tonight with all your new clothes since your bed arrived today."

Jasmine wrinkled her nose. "No way," she said, looking around as if the room disgusted her. "Look at these walls. Who ever heard of a purple bedroom?"

"It's not purple, it's plum."

"It's ugly. I don't know what that girl Sheila was thinking," Jasmine said, referring to the woman who had sold her the Upper East Side condo. "The woman has no taste." Jasmine grabbed her purse and full-length mink from the bed. "My decorator will be here on Monday with the painters and a week from today, this place will look like someone with class lives here." She slipped into her coat and then linked her arm through her sister's. "Okay, hon, where should we go for dinner?"

Serena shook her head as she looked her sister up and down.

Jasmine said, "Don't say anything about my new coat. Just tell me where you want to eat."

Serena rolled her eyes. "I saw a diner on the corner."

"Honey, you need to recognize where you are. Ain't no diners around here."

"Well, wherever we go, I don't want to spend a lot of money," Serena said, as they stepped into the carpeted hallway lined with gilded mirrors.

Jasmine sighed. Her sister was getting on her nerves with this useless chatter. Their father had left them almost a million-dollar insurance policy. Sure, they had to split it, but it was tax-free money. Jasmine wanted to make sure her father's passing a year ago was not in vain. His money was being used well.

Along with the apartment, she had a closet full of new clothes, a high-profile job, and enough optimism to fill Yankee Stadium. She'd made the investment; now all she had to work on was getting the return.

"Don't worry about dinner," Jasmine said. "I'll pay."

Serena crossed her arms as they entered the elevator. "I'm telling you, a year from now you're going to be calling me."

"You got that right. I'll be calling you and inviting you to my wedding." Jasmine pressed the button for the lobby. "Just make sure you call me your little sister," she said, as she slid her Chanel sunglasses on her face.

"Lord, help her," Serena mumbled.

But Jasmine ignored her sister's grumbling. The wheels in her head were spinning. She was a thirty-year-old New York City girl on a mission.

Chapter 2

"This is too early," Jasmine whined.

Serena peered through the floor-to-ceiling windows of the West Side Regency Hotel lobby. She pulled her coat tighter as if she could already feel the barely-above-freezing temperature.

Jasmine said, "I need something to wake me up."

"I need something to warm me up." Serena shivered as she watched the yellow cabs and other cars speed by. There wasn't a pedestrian in sight.

A moment later, Jasmine grabbed Serena's hand and pulled her toward the glass doors.

"I'm not going outside until Malik pulls up in that cab," Serena yelled, causing eyebrows to rise among the elite hotel's patrons.

"You want something warm. Look over there." Jasmine pointed across the street.

It took a moment, then Serena smiled.

The cashmere-coated doorman opened the door for them. "A friend is coming to pick me up," Jasmine said to him, shivering as the frigid air rushed inside. "Please tell him we're waiting over there." She motioned with her chin.

She didn't wait to see if the doorman agreed. The sisters dashed across the street, ignoring the car horns that blared at them. Seconds later, they settled into the warmth of Starbucks. The coffee shop was swarming with Sunday regulars layered in thick clothing and balancing bulky Sunday newspapers underneath their arms.

"This was a good idea," Serena said, as she stood behind a blond man clad in a velour jogging suit and knitted cap.

Jasmine surveyed the crowd. When she turned back, the man in front of them smiled. Jasmine rolled her eyes. True, she was on a husband-finding mission, but a white boy would never do.

"May I take your order?" the young man behind the cash register asked.

"A venti cappuccino and a croissant," Jasmine said.

"Ah, excuse me." She turned toward the voice; the blond man who had been openly staring at her just a moment before, smiled again. "It's not a croissant," he said with a French accent. "It's a croissan'," he added, putting emphasis on the last syllable.

Jasmine looked over her shoulder, then turned back toward the man. "Are you talking to me?"

He nodded and stepped closer. "You said croissant, and that's not the correct pronunciation. The *t* is silent."

"Are you talking to me?"

The repeat of her question erased his smile, still he nodded. "I was trying to help you," he said, as the barista called Jasmine's name.

Jasmine sauntered closer to the man. "So you're helping me? With my pronunciation."

His smile returned and he nodded again.

Jasmine picked up her drink, tucked the bag with the croissant inside her tote, and said, "Well, pronounce this." She lifted her right hand and stuck her middle finger in his face.

The coffee shop filled with laughter as the man stood still, shocked for a moment, before he rushed away.

Jasmine turned to Serena. "Have they made your drink

yet?" she asked. "We've got to get to church." She turned away and strolled toward the door.

The wind whipped across Riverside Drive.

Serena jumped out of the taxi and dashed up the multi-dozen church steps before Jasmine and Malik were able to slip from the car. As Malik paid the driver, Jasmine glanced at the Gothic building with its twin towers that flanked several stained-glass windows; the sturdy structure looked as if it had been standing for centuries.

"It is too cold out here," Malik, her six-foot-seven god-brother said, as he slipped his arm through hers before they raced up the steps.

Jasmine loved being with Malik. He'd been the one to make her two years in Pensacola bearable when she'd moved there from Los Angeles. She and Malik had been close growing up, but lost touch when he'd left California as a high school freshman to attend boarding school at Piney Woods in Mississippi. Jasmine had kept track of Malik, at first through his parents; but once his family moved to Florida, only the media kept her abreast of her godbrother's rise to basketball fame, first in college at Georgetown and then in Miami where he was a second-round draft pick. When he'd first turned pro, Jasmine made an attempt to reach out, but when she never heard back, she didn't bother again.

She'd been too consumed with her own life anyway, trying to inspire her ambitionless husband. But once she moved to Pensacola, she and Malik reunited and resumed their friend-ship as if twenty years hadn't passed.

When two of Malik's NBA friends convinced him to open a restaurant in New York—a sister restaurant to one they owned in Los Angeles—Jasmine had been devastated. But within weeks, her distress had flipped to delight when he asked her to join him as the restaurant's project manager.

"I need someone to oversee the entire venture," he'd said. "With your financial expertise and business savvy, you'd be great. Are you interested?"

"Are you kidding?" she'd asked.

"I'm willing to offer you a piece of this, Jasmine. Give you a vested interest."

His statement had barely parted from his lips before Jasmine was on the Internet making airline reservations. With her father gone, there was nothing keeping her in Florida.

Malik pulled open the wooden door and the two stepped into the church's vestibule. Serena stood next to an usher wearing a suit as bright-white as his smile.

"We have to wait until the prayer ends," Serena whispered.

Jasmine took off her gloves and blew on the tips of her fingers. She peeked through the glass doors leading to the sanctuary; the church was Easter-Sunday packed. Malik had told her that City of Lights at Riverside was always filled to standing room only.

"You're going to love Reverend Bush," Malik whispered. "You'll be dying to get to church every Sunday after you hear him."

Jasmine doubted Malik's words; all the Sundays she'd spent in church, there wasn't a minister who could hold her attention. But still, she kept going because that was just what saved people did.

The usher opened the doors and Jasmine entered first. Drums and trumpets and saxophones blasted through the church as if it were a concert hall. She stepped into the last pew, but Malik took her hand and led her and Serena down the center aisle. The usher smiled, just like the one at the front door, and directed them into the third row.

Jasmine scurried in, between her sister and godbrother. As she shrugged off her coat, she glanced around the capacious cathedral.

This was nothing like the small Methodist church she attended in Florida. Here, there were as many white faces as black ones among the hundreds of parishioners in the sanctuary. And the music—this was as good as a gospel show.

Malik and Serena sang along, but Jasmine didn't know the words. Still, the music made her move. Jasmine closed her eyes and swayed.

When the music softened, Jasmine opened her eyes and stood stone stiff. Only her eyes moved as her glance followed the man who'd entered the sanctuary. She watched, mesmerized, as he strutted, in his brown-stripe, single-breasted five-button suit, to the center of the altar. When he turned, he brightened the church with his smile.

Who is he?

It took everything within her not to run up and introduce herself, before a woman motioned for the congregation to sit.

"Good morning, church."

While everyone returned the woman's greeting, Jasmine silently stared.

"Do we have any first time visitors . . ."

Jasmine popped up from her seat.

" . . . this morning," the woman finished.

Jasmine prayed that the woman would ask visitors to say a few words. So she could introduce herself. So the man would notice her.

"On behalf of Reverend H. Samuel Bush and the entire congregation here at City of Lights at Riverside, we'd like to welcome you to our services . . ."

Get on with this, Jasmine said inside, keeping her eyes on the man in the brown suit.

When he looked at her, her chest poked out a bit more and her smile widened. She hoped he could see her dimples.

You are one fine man. She tried to push her thoughts to him.

When the visitors sat, the focus of her desire stood. He said, "Good morning, church."

"Morning, Reverend," echoed through the air.

Jasmine's mouth opened wide. "That's Reverend Bush?" she exclaimed, a bit loudly.

"Ssshhh." Malik admonished as he searched his Bible for the scriptures Reverend Bush gave to the congregation.

But while Malik and Serena followed the reverend's directions, Jasmine didn't open her Bible. She had no intention of taking her eyes off that man.

"In this new year of 2004, we must all begin to understand every facet of God. We must understand the difference between His grace and His mercy," the reverend sang in a bass that almost made the walls resonate. "Many a dictionary will tell you those words are synonyms. But let me tell you, saints, His grace and His mercy are very different."

Jasmine twisted in her seat.

"You see," Reverend Bush continued, "grace is getting something you don't deserve."

When I get a hold of you, you'll be thanking God for His grace.

"And, mercy is *not* getting something that you *do* deserve."

Jasmine almost laughed. *Maybe you'll be begging God for mercy.*

As the reverend continued, Jasmine followed his movements. She loved the way his hands glided through the air as if he were conducting a symphony. She loved the way he swiveled his hips, just slightly as he emphasized points. She loved the way he danced across the raised step in front of the altar. She loved him.

He's the one, her inside voice said with surety. *The man I'm supposed to marry.*

Only then did it occur to her that he could already be married. She leaned forward, squinting to see better. She didn't want to go back to that sin. But then, if he was the man whom God wanted her to be with, would it be a sin to take him away from his wife? She peered at the reverend's fingers as he gestured. No gold, no silver, no platinum band in sight.

Reverend Bush held his Bible in the air. "Understand that

as God's children, we are blessed with grace and mercy. But understand the difference and you'll begin to truly understand your blessings."

Jasmine chuckled. She understood her blessings. She'd been in New York for less than a week, and God had already answered her prayer. This was all about her blessings. That's why Malik had started attending this church months ago. He'd found City of Lights—and Reverend Bush—for her.

Reverend and Mrs. Samuel Bush. Mrs. Samuel Bush. Mrs. Jasmine Larson Bush. The synergy of those syllables sounded wonderful.

She crossed her legs and noticed the way the hem of her pants leg rose slightly. And the wheels in her head turned. Next week, she'd wear a skirt. And sit in the front row.

I'll have my man in two weeks.

She chuckled and it wasn't until both Malik and Serena stared at her that she realized she'd made the sound out loud. She covered her mouth, turned in her Bible as Reverend Bush gave another scripture. Yes, this was a day that the Lord had made. This was the day that she fell in love.

Jasmine had never been so glad to see her sister go.

She waved as Serena stepped onto the down escalator leading to Track 14. As soon as her sister was out of sight, Jasmine grabbed Malik's hand.

"Why are you in such a hurry? Let's at least wait to make sure her train takes off on time."

"I'm not going to leave the station." Jasmine looked at her watch and then glanced through the congestion of the Sunday afternoon Penn Station crowd that bumped around her. "We need to talk," she spoke above the announcement blasting through the station's speakers. She pointed. "Let's wait there."

"I thought you wanted to go to the Shark Bar."

"This will have to do," she said. Jasmine marched into

Houlihan's, past the sign that asked for customers to wait to be seated. She chose a table along the window, overlooking the end-of-the-weekend chaos.

Malik strolled behind Jasmine, shaking his head. "So," he began, as Jasmine tapped her fingers on the table, "what's set you on fire?"

For the first time since her new man left her sight, Jasmine smiled. "Our reverend."

He grinned. "I told you he was good." Malik signaled for a waiter.

"Oh, I can imagine how good he is," she said, as the waiter handed them menus. She tossed hers aside.

Malik lowered the menu from in front of his face. "Jasmine." He said her name slowly.

"Is Reverend Bush married?"

"Oh, no," he moaned, and slumped a bit in his seat. "Why are you asking me that?"

"Just answer me."

"He's a widower."

"Yes!" Jasmine slapped her hand on the table.

"No! He's not for you. Jasmine, he's a pastor."

"That makes him perfect for me." It was true, Jasmine had never considered a pastor in the past, but when she thought about it, there was no better man. Preaching had become a big business with megaministers and supersanctuaries. Networks devoted hours to preaching, healing, and moneymaking. She could be the perfect pastor's wife.

"No," he said as if the word had seven syllables. "He's not perfect for you. I know what you like."

"Obviously you don't."

Malik leaned toward her. "Believe me, I know you. Reverend Bush is not glamorous enough, not sexy enough, not rich enough—"

Those words took her smile away. "Isn't his income tax free?"

"What does that have to do with anything?"

Her smile was back. "Everything." She held up her fingers. "First, I don't know why you say he's not sexy. He is *so* fine. Second, he's the pastor of that big ol' church. If he's not making the bucks, he needs a woman like me and he'll be rolling in the Benjamins soon enough. And third, I'm not into money that much anymore," she said, and then wondered if that part were true.

Malik peered at her. "You haven't changed that much. Believe me, Reverend Bush doesn't have enough money for you."

Jasmine waved his words away. "Whatever he makes, it's enough. That suit he was wearing didn't come from Kmart. I'm telling you, he's the man."

"Besides the fact that you know nothing about him, he's a preacher, Jasmine."

"That's just what I need," she said as if Malik should have known that. "Look, being a Christian hasn't been easy for me."

"Tell me about it." Malik took off his glasses and rubbed his eyes as if the conversation made him weary.

She said, "I'm determined to make heaven my home and I know Reverend Bush can help me get there."

Malik rolled his eyes. "That's supposed to be between you and God."

"In the meantime," Jasmine continued as if Malik hadn't spoken, "I can create a little bit of heaven for the reverend right here on earth. I'm sure of it; he's going to be my husband."

"What about the fact that he's probably ten years older than you?"

Jasmine laughed. She'd be able to be forty now. "Like age matters? I'm telling you, he's the one for me."

"You've decided all of this, even without having met him?"

"Haven't you ever heard of love at first sight?"

"Yeah, but don't both people have to see each other? Reverend Bush doesn't even know you're alive."

"You're going to take care of that. Aren't you on the board or something?"

"I'm on the building committee, but I'm not going to help you."

She leaned across the table and kissed his cheek. "Yes, you will," she said. "Do you know why?"

He moaned.

"Because you love me. And you promised Dad that you would take care of me and Serena."

He shook his head. "Serena is easy. But you—"

The waiter interrupted, "Are you ready to order?"

Jasmine glanced at her watch. "Serena's train is gone by now. So, let's go."

"I thought you wanted to eat."

"I do. You're taking me to the Shark Bar." She stood, slipped her mink over her shoulders, and marched past the waiter.

Malik shook his head as he stood. "Sorry." He slapped ten dollars into the waiter's hand. "We're going to the Shark Bar."

Chapter 3

The church was as electric as it had been last week, although Jasmine wasn't sure if it was the sound from the church musicians or the sound of the harps that had played in her head since she'd jumped out of bed this morning. By the end of this day, she and Reverend Bush would have arranged their first date, and if God was on her side, it would be tonight.

Jasmine filed in behind other parishioners, who, like her, had arrived early to get the best seats. She tossed her coat across her arm and then sauntered down the aisle in her canary yellow suede miniskirt with matching bustier and jacket, her eyes fixed forward—on the front row.

Just as she passed the fourth pew, the usher put out his white-gloved hand, motioning for her to take that seat.

She pointed her finger. "I'm sitting there," she said, her eyes on her final destination.

The usher smiled. "Those seats are reserved. You can sit here."

"You don't understand," she began, leaning in close. She didn't miss the way his eyes wandered to her chest. "I'm Malik Kincaid's sister."

The usher's smile widened. "I didn't know he had a sister."

"Yes," she said with triumph. "I just moved here and this is my second week visiting your fantastic church."

"Welcome," he said. Then, he pointed to the same row that he'd shown her before. "You can sit right there."

Jasmine frowned.

"The front-row seats are reserved," he said, as if her familial connections didn't matter.

She took a deep breath, but his taut smile stopped her further protest. She turned, and a woman in a hat as wide as her hips bumped her and slipped into the last available fourth-row seat. Jasmine's eyes quickly scanned the space. The sanctuary had filled.

She whipped back toward the usher, her eyes flashing.

He said, "I can help you find a seat back there if you want."

She wanted to slap the smile off his face. Instead she stepped quickly, moving back, back, finally finding a seat in the middle of the last row, flanked by two women, who wiggled with irritation as she wedged into the small space between them.

When praise and worship began, there was no joy in Jasmine's heart. She'd spent almost three hundred dollars on her dressed-to-impress outfit and twenty-five dollars on the sheerest of hose to show off two of her best assets. Now, it was wasted.

All week, Malik had refused her pleas to make a personal introduction. When he'd gone to L.A. on Thursday, she'd decided to take care of Reverend Bush herself. This morning, she'd risen with the sun, and hurried to church confident that Reverend Bush would ask for an introduction afterward—after he'd eyed her sitting in the front pew.

Now as Reverend Bush sauntered into the sanctuary, hundreds of parishioners sat in front of her; there was no way she would be seen.

As the reverend ministered, Jasmine opened her Bible and willed herself not to be upset. This was not the end. She'd just have to create another opportunity. She didn't like it, but if there was one thing she'd learned since she'd been saved, it was that being a Christian often called for patience. How often had she heard her father, Serena, or some minister talk about God's timing?

After the benediction, she stepped outside the pew and took a final glance at Reverend Bush. She paused. The reverend stood at the altar, greeting a woman. Three others stood in line as if they were waiting to speak to him too.

Jasmine strode toward the reverend, but almost made a U-turn when the usher from earlier moved in front of her.

"May I help you?" he asked with his never-ending smile.

Her chin jutted forward. "I'm going to say hello to Reverend Bush." She braced herself, ready to barge past him, knock him straight to the ground if she had to.

"Of course," he said, stepping aside.

It took a moment for his words to register as he motioned for her to proceed to the end of the line that was now seven deep.

Her thoughts went from cursing this man out to wanting to say a prayer for him. But she kept her eyes on Reverend Bush. He oozed compassion—the way he gently touched the woman's hands. The way his thick eyebrows furrowed with concern as he listened to the woman speak.

With each step forward her heart beat faster. All week she'd planned for this. Knew the words she would say. Knew how she'd smile, tilt her head, capture him with her mere presence.

"Hello, I'm Reverend Samuel Bush," he said, holding out his hand.

Jasmine didn't miss the way his eyes quickly took in all of her. He frowned—just a bit—when his eyes paused at the gold-studded edge of her cleavage-raising bustier, and regret filled her. She hadn't thought this part through. If she was going to be a reverend's wife, she would have to be more conservative.

She took the reverend's outstretched hand. "I ... I ..." she stuttered, and tried to recall all she'd practiced. His grin warmed her; she said, "I'm Jasmine Larson. Malik Kincaid is my brother."

"Ah, yes," he said, throwing his head back a bit. "Malik's godsister. He told me you were moving to New York. How do you like our city?"

"It's wonderful. It already feels like home." She parted her lips in the fashion she'd practiced and lowered her eyelids so he could see the length of her lashes.

"Well, welcome to New York and City of Lights. I hope we'll be seeing a lot of you here."

"Oh, yes. In fact—"

"Reverend," her nemesis usher interrupted her moment. "Deacon Marshall needs to see you before the next service."

"Ah yes, Brother Hill." He turned his smile back to Jasmine. "I hope to see you again soon," he said, already stepping away.

By the time her lips parted, he was too far away to hear her. She moved to follow him, but before she could get close, Brother Hill stopped in front of her.

"What is your problem?" she snapped.

"Reverend Bush has finished greeting visitors."

Jasmine raised her chin. "I'm not a visitor," she said, trying to step around him.

"Whatever you are," he said, blocking her, "Reverend Bush is not available now."

Jasmine's glance turned toward the closed side door that Reverend Bush had gone through. Even if she were able to slay this giant standing in her path, she wouldn't know where to go. She turned back and stood square before the usher.

With his eyes, he told her he knew what she was up to.

With her eyes, she told him that she was ready to rumble.

Only Jasmine spoke. "See you next Sunday," she said, as if the two had just had an agreeable exchange.

Without moving, he said, "I'm looking forward to it. Have a blessed week."

Jasmine smiled. He had no idea that by the end of the week, his words would be prophetic. She was going to have a very blessed week.

Chapter 4

It was difficult to balance on one foot with the phone tucked between her shoulder and ear.

"I'm on my way, Malik," Jasmine said, trying to squeeze into the leg-hugging boot.

"Jasmine, this is an important meeting. You said you'd be here before eight."

"I'm doing my best, Malik."

"If this is your best, Jasmine, I need better than your best. We're opening in less than three months and I don't have time—"

She cut into his tirade. "I'm really sorry, Malik," she said, wishing she'd gotten out of bed when the alarm first rang. But fatigue had encouraged her to hit the snooze button over and over.

The past week had been beyond tiring. Between working with decorators for her apartment and the restaurant, and adapting to her new position with her more-than-demanding godbrother, her days had been too long and her nights too short. It was only thoughts of Reverend Bush that had made the week tolerable. And it was only the exhaustion that yesterday's disappointment had brought that kept her in bed far longer this morning than she planned.

"Malik, I'm walking out right now. I'll be there in ten minutes."

Without a good-bye, Malik hung up. Both knew she was at

least twenty minutes away—and that was if she could find a cab the moment she stepped outside.

Jasmine grabbed her coat and briefcase, fumbled with the lock on her door, then dashed to the elevator.

"Come on," she said, leaning on the button.

Just as the elevator arrived, Jasmine heard "Hold the elevator!" The voice boomed through the hallway.

Jasmine rushed inside, held down the Close Door button, and then watched the door slide slowly shut. Then, just as quickly, it sprang open.

The heavy fragrance of perfume wafted inside first, and then a woman followed, donned in a mink coat that swept the floor and a matching fur headband.

"You can close the door now," the woman instructed as if she'd known what Jasmine had been doing.

Jasmine pressed the button and focused on the In Case of Emergency instructions on the elevator's panel. But she couldn't resist stealing a glance at the woman.

It usually took seconds for Jasmine to assess women, but this one was difficult to judge. She stood at least a head taller than Jasmine. She was as erect and elegant as a dancer, shoulders squared, head high, with her hands—holding a small purse—crossed in front of her. Her mink, although probably several years old as revealed by the shawl collar, was obviously expensive.

Yet, at the same time, her makeup was caked on so thick, Jasmine was sure it would take a scalpel to scrape it off. And the foundation, a few shades too light for her mocha color, didn't cover the roughness of her weathered skin. But her eyebrows fascinated Jasmine the most. They had been shaved and replaced by a thick black penciled line that almost looked like an inverted *V.*

Without looking at her, the woman said, "You're new to this building."

Jasmine didn't know if her words were a statement or a

question. And she didn't know why the woman sounded angry. But she responded, "Yes."

For the first time, the woman looked at her directly. She frowned. "Yes? Is that all you have to say?"

Now Jasmine frowned, confused.

"Didn't your parents teach you any manners?" the woman blurted as if she were a teacher reprimanding an unruly student.

Jasmine's eyebrows raised. *Who do you think . . .*

The woman continued through Jasmine's thoughts. "Don't you know to say, 'Yes, ma'am,' to your elders? My goodness, you're as rude as that woman, Sheila, who used to live in that apartment."

It was because of her manners that she didn't tell the woman what she really thought at that moment. She crossed her arms and only said, "Yes, I'm new. Just moved in two weeks ago."

The woman stared at Jasmine for a moment and then one side of her mouth upturned into half a smile. When the elevator doors opened to the lobby, the woman motioned for Jasmine to exit first.

Fine, she thought, anxious to get as far away from this ornery old lady.

"Good morning, Ms. Larson."

She barely nodded at Henrikas, the Lithuanian doorman who seemed to be in the lobby whenever she came or left, no matter what the time.

"How are you today?" he asked, as he moved toward the glass doors. "Do you need a cab?"

Given that she was already late, her only choice was to say, "Yes." But not before she eyed the sleek limousine parked at the curb. She sighed with longing. "One day," she whispered, imagining the time when a car would be waiting for her.

"Did you say something, Ms. Larson?"

"I need a cab, please."

"Certainly." He closed his overcoat and then pushed open the door for Jasmine's elevator partner. "Good morning, Ms. Van Dorn."

The woman nodded at the doorman and then turned to Jasmine. "Do you need a ride somewhere?" she asked in the same tone that she'd used in the elevator.

You've got to be kidding. There was no way she was going to get into any car with this cantankerous biddy. And anyway, Jasmine could imagine what this woman drove—probably a barely moving Lincoln Continental that was as old as her coat, and that probably held the fragrance of the perfume that had overwhelmed her since the woman stepped into the elevator.

"No, thank you," Jasmine said, resisting the urge to add a sarcastic, "Ma'am."

The woman did it again—stared for a moment and then one side of her mouth curled into a smile. "You have a good day anyway," she said, still sounding as if she were pissed off.

Jasmine's eyes followed Ms. Van Dorn as she rushed through the door. The driver jumped from the limousine's front seat and a moment later, Ms. Van Dorn disappeared into the back.

Minutes later, when Henrikas waved for Jasmine to come to the cab he had flagged for her, she was still standing in the middle of the lobby with her mouth wide open.

"I'm jealous, Malik. If Jasmine had been with us when de Janeiro first opened, it wouldn't have taken two years to break even."

Jasmine tilted her head to the side, letting her bone-straight, auburn-streaked hair swing over her shoulders. She smiled as J.T., Malik's friend from his ball-playing days, licked his lips.

J.T. said, "What would a man like me have to do to get a woman like you?" He paused. "For our club, of course."

Before she could answer, Malik interjected, "Don't get any

ideas, J.T. Jasmine is with me for the long haul. She's a partner, you know."

"That's right," she added with a smile, knowing that there was a lot more to J.T.'s question. She was aware that Malik knew that too. But her godbrother was all about the business.

"Too bad." J.T. grinned. "We could make beautiful menus together."

Jasmine's glance wandered to the platinum band on his left hand.

"Well, I think that covers it all," Malik said and stood.

Jasmine packed up her computer as the friends exchanged parting words. She'd been almost an hour late for the meeting, but blessedly, Malik, J.T., and J.T.'s partner, Lamont, had used the time to bond over talk of basketball and women. Once she rushed into the conference room and began reviewing the final plan for Rio with the three men, she knew her godbrother (and his boys) were beyond impressed. She'd pulled together the budget and the timetable, and pointed out all the areas that still needed to be developed to meet the April 15 opening.

"Well, Ms. Jasmine." J.T. took her hand and brushed his lips against her skin.

Oh, brother. But she smiled because she knew that's what J.T. expected. Of the three, he'd been the biggest star in the league. And that's why Jasmine could never understand the way he dressed. She could see the suit he wore was tailored— just about sewn onto his body. But who told the curly-head pretty boy that wide-stripe suits looked good on a seven foot, three hundred pound man?

Lamont offered Jasmine a soft smile and squeezed her hand. "Nice meeting you, Jasmine." He glanced at Malik before he continued, "He was right about you. You certainly know your stuff."

Before she could respond, J.T. asked Malik, "So, you got the honeys lined up for later?"

Jasmine smirked. She may have changed, but times had not. J.T. and Lamont both wore wedding bands but obviously sub‑ scribed to the theory that "all men cheat." Two years ago, she would have been begging Malik to arrange a night for her with J.T. He was the kind of man she'd once craved—attractive, powerful, rich. The fact that he'd exchanged marriage vows with another woman wouldn't have been any kind of deterrent.

"That's my clue to go." Jasmine stuffed the laptop into the case and hoisted the bag onto her shoulder. "I'll see you in L.A., hopefully by the end of the week."

"I'm looking forward to it," J.T. said, stepping close to her. "I'll make sure you have a good time. We'll tour the city."

"No need," Jasmine said, not backing away. "I grew up in L.A." She paused. "I've seen everything there is to see."

"I can show you some things you've never seen before."

"Down, boy." Malik chuckled. "Remember, Jasmine's fam."

With his hands in the air, J.T. backed away. But his grin re‑ mained. "My bad. But you can understand, bro," he said, not taking his eyes off Jasmine. "She's—"

Malik interrupted, "About tonight, I'll give you guys a call. I have a meeting with my pastor and we can hook up after."

J.T. laughed. "Man, I cannot believe you've turned into Mr. Sunday school."

Malik shook his head, cool under the heat of J.T.'s teasing. "Don't get brand new. You've always known where I stood spir‑ itually."

"I'm just sayin'—"

"Look, I won't be long. It's going to be a quick meeting." Malik moved toward the conference room door. "I'll holla when I'm through."

Jasmine's smile was wide as she watched the three exchange the brother handshake and then J.T. and Lamont disappeared into the elevator. She was right on Malik's heels when he walked past his assistant, Gabriella, and into his office.

"That went well, Jasmine."

"You didn't tell me you were meeting with Reverend Bush," she said, closing his office door.

He hesitated for only a moment before he said, "I can tell you worked hard over the weekend. Thanks for having my back with those marketing ideas."

"Malik, please," she said, hugging the computer bag to her chest. "Let me go with you."

"Jasmine." He said her name in a tone that sounded like he was in pain. "I'm not doing this with you."

"Why not? What do you think I'm going to do?"

"Nothing . . . because you're not going with me. This is a private meeting."

"Just you two?"

"No, for the building committee."

"That's even better," she said, sitting across from him.

"The meeting is just for the committee members."

"So I'll join the committee."

"Applications are no longer being accepted."

Jasmine frowned. "You have to apply to work on a committee at your church?"

He chuckled. "No, I was kidding." His smile went away. "Jasmine, this is a closed meeting for the members to make a quick report. It's going to be in and out. All business. No social time."

"Okay, but Malik, you can't deny that I'm really good at marketing. I can give you guys some ideas."

He glanced at his watch. "I've gotta get going."

"So, you're really not going to help me?"

He closed the calendar on his desk. "Have Gabriella make your reservations for L.A. Remember, the designers are presenting their final plans tomorrow, so Thursday would be a good time to go."

She remained in her chair, even when he moved around the desk and kissed her cheek. Still, she stayed in place, not looking at him.

"Okay, you win."

She jumped up and smiled.

He held up his hands. "Not today, but I promise I'll figure out a way for you to get together with Reverend Bush soon."

She turned to stone.

"Come on, don't be mad."

She lifted the computer bag from the floor. "Only dogs get mad, Malik."

He shrugged. "Remember tomorrow's meeting," he said. "The entire staff will be there."

She didn't acknowledge his words. Just stayed in her place as he said good-bye to Gabriella. When she heard the bing of the elevator signaling the closing doors, she stood. She walked past her new assistant, Tina, and into her own office.

Like her apartment, this space was still filled with un-packed boxes. She sat at her desk, opened her compact, and checked her makeup. Then, she pulled an empty manila folder from the box of supplies Tina had given her. Finally, she tossed the strap of her purse over her shoulder.

"Malik, how long have you known me?" she asked the empty office. "You know I don't give up." She clicked off the light in her office, then waved to Tina. "I've got a few errands to run. I'll see you tomorrow."

It had been eight days since she'd first laid eyes on Reverend Bush. Not too much time in the scheme of life. But too much time for her and the reverend. It was time to get this party started.

The pointed toe of Jasmine's stiletto boot tapped an impatient beat.

The plan had been to walk into the church, march into the meeting, present Malik with important papers he'd forgotten, and then accept Reverend Bush's gracious invitation to stay.

But once she arrived, she hadn't counted on Mrs. Whittingham. The church's secretary was a short, stout, gray-haired woman who made up in her tone what she lacked in stature. Mrs. Whittingham glared at Jasmine over gold-rimmed glasses that were set low on her nose.

"I am not about to allow you to barge into that meeting," she said in a voice that was barely a whisper after Jasmine made her request known. "You are not a member of that committee. Are you even a member of this church? I've never seen you before." The woman rolled her eyes before she motioned for Jasmine to have a seat on the couch outside of the conference room.

Now, Jasmine glanced at her watch. An hour passed—time wasted.

The double-doors to the conference room finally opened and Jasmine jumped to her feet. Pairs of men and a few women strolled through the doors, still continuing their conversations. One man stopped when he saw her and Jasmine groaned inside. Her nemesis. The usher. Brother Hill. Even though his white suit was absent he still wore his welcoming smile, although Jasmine was no longer fooled.

"Jasmine, what are you doing here?"

She turned from the usher when she heard Malik's voice. Her smile widened when she saw the one standing next to him. "Hey, Malik," she said, as if she was supposed to be there. "You ran out of the office so fast you forgot these." She handed the empty folder to him and then turned toward the reverend.

"Reverend Bush, good to see you again."

"Yes." He smiled back at her and Jasmine was glad that she'd worn the black knit dress today. Although it hugged her body's curves, it was still more conservative than what she'd worn to church.

The reverend said to Malik, "I had the pleasure of meeting your godsister yesterday."

"Did you?" Malik responded, although he kept his eyes on Jasmine.

But her attention remained on the reverend. "Yes, we met right after the service. Reverend," Jasmine said, "Malik told me a bit about the building committee."

"Yes, we're excited. Our hope is that the center will become a hub for this community."

"I think that you are . . . what you're doing is incredible," she said, taking a step closer to him. "And I want to offer my services to you."

He questioned her with his eyes.

"Did Malik mention that I'm a marketing specialist?"

"No," the reverend said, as if he were surprised.

"Yes, I'm working for Malik and his new club. And, I'd love to . . . work for you."

The reverend paused for a moment, and inside, Jasmine's heart leapt at the way his stare seemed to penetrate right through her.

I knew it, she thought. Yes, he was a preacher, but he still belonged to the faction of humans that was her specialty—he was a man.

The reverend said, "I appreciate that offer, but I don't know how you'd be able to help me . . . or the committee right now."

Malik said, "Jasmine, we're still in the planning stages." He turned to Reverend Bush. "I'll call you tomorrow with those numbers." Malik placed his hand on Jasmine's elbow, and squeezed just enough to let her know he was serious. "I'll walk you outside." Malik nodded his good-bye to Reverend Bush.

"Have a good evening," Reverend Bush said and paused. "Both of you."

Her eyes widened as the reverend stepped away. She wanted to slap Malik, but that would have to wait. "Reverend Bush, I know you're not at the stage for marketing yet, but planning is always good. How about lunch tomorrow?"

The reverend swiveled around. Surprise was etched in the lines of his forehead.

She said, "I know your calendar is probably full, but you have to eat." The steps she took toward him left only inches between them. "And I have some ideas for you," she said softly.

She was sure she saw a glimmer in his eyes.

He said, "I apologize, Jasmine. Somehow I've given you the wrong impression. I don't need any ideas . . . or anything else from you."

She frowned. "But, Reverend, I—"

"Thanks, Reverend Bush," Malik said, this time taking Jasmine's hand. "I'll call tomorrow."

Reverend Bush nodded, and then with a final glance toward Jasmine, he disappeared into his office, with the ever-grinning Brother Hill steps behind him.

Malik kept his smile as he said good-bye to other committee members still lingering, but once outside, all decorum was gone.

"What was that?" he yelled.

She jerked her hand away and tightened her coat against the winter's air. "What's your problem? I brought you the folder of the plans we went over today. I thought you'd want to review them tonight."

Malik opened the folder with a smirk on his face, as if he already knew it was empty.

"Oh, well," Jasmine said not even bothering to act surprised. "I must have picked up the wrong one."

"Don't play with me, Jasmine. Both of us know what this is about."

She turned and marched toward Riverside Drive. "So what?" she asked over her shoulder. "I've asked for your help over and over."

"And you think you'll win me to your side by busting into a church meeting?"

"I waited outside that conference room for over an hour. So, I wasn't busting into anything." She stepped off the curb and held out her hand, signaling for a taxi.

He pulled her back onto the sidewalk. "Jasmine, what's going on? I thought you'd put all of this stuff behind you."

She frowned. "What stuff are you talking about?" she asked, although she knew what he meant. She was sure her sister and father had told Malik every deranged detail of why she'd left Los Angeles. How she'd become obsessed with her best friend's husband. Serena and their father had probably made it sound as if she'd been swinging from a loose branch of a crazy tree.

But there was no way Malik could equate Reverend Bush to Jefferson Blake. Reverend Bush was not married. And there was a big difference between obsession and determination.

"Jasmine, I thought you were happy here."

"I am," she said looking directly at him. "Why is my wanting to get to know your pastor such a problem? I just want to spend some time with him because I like him."

"You don't know him."

"That's why I've been asking you to help me."

"Jasmine, you're chasing the wind. Reverend Bush is not interested in you."

"And you know this . . . how?"

He sighed. "Jasmine, you're almost forty years old, way too old to be going through this. I would think you'd want to spend your time learning about the city, getting set up in your apartment, and most importantly, getting settled in your job. I need you one hundred percent at Rio."

"And I'm not going to give you any less," Jasmine said. "My social life won't interfere with my work. But just remember, Malik, it's my social life. And it's none of your business."

He softened his voice. "I'm worried about you. It's like you're obsessed . . . again."

There it was. She tried to contain her rising rage. "Let me break this down for you. I met someone whom I'd like to get to know better," she said, speaking slowly. "It happens every day between men and women, Malik."

"It happens when two people are interested in each other, Jasmine. And, Reverend Bush is not interested in you."

What was he talking about? Twice, she'd seen how Reverend Bush looked at her. Yesterday it had been a look of disapproval, but still, his glance had wandered. And today, she saw the glimmer in his eyes. She knew she could have the reverend any time and in any way she wanted him. "It doesn't matter what you think," she said to Malik. "I'm going to spend some time with Reverend Bush. One on one. Man to woman. Not. A. Big. Deal."

They stood toe-to-toe. Then Malik backed away and raised his hand, motioning for a cab. When the car eased over, he opened the door. "I'll see you tomorrow," he said as she slid into the backseat.

That was the extent of their good-bye. Jasmine gave her address to the driver and then leaned back against the cracked vinyl seat.

That was ridiculous, she thought. The way Malik had spoken to her. All because of one minor mistake she'd made in the past. She didn't know why everyone still made such a big deal over Jefferson Blake. It wasn't like she'd had an affair with her best friend's husband. It was just sex, just once. And Kyla and Jefferson were still together, living happily in that nirvana they'd created. So if they were able to move on, why was she being defined by her past?

Reverend Bush was nothing like Jefferson Blake. Reverend Bush was a free man. Grown and free. And so was she.

I'm worried about you. It's like you're obsessed again. Her sigh was filled with anger at the memory of Malik's words. As if he were some kind of doctor. As if he were qualified to give her a diagnosis.

Actually, she'd felt this way when she *had* seen a doctor. To appease her father, Jasmine had visited a psychologist when she first moved to Pensacola. It had been a surprise to her when her father had insisted. All her life she'd thought black people didn't go to shrinks—black folks went to church. God took care of anything that ailed anyone.

But her father thought it best if Jasmine turned to God—and Dr. Reade. She'd made the promise to do both. Although she went to church every Sunday, she'd seen Dr. Reade twice. Stopped right after he told her that she suffered from autophobia.

When she'd searched the Internet for the definition, she'd spent twenty minutes laughing at how that psychologist had lost his mind—and needed to lose his license.

"I don't have any fear of being alone."

"You say something?" the driver shouted over the strange fusion of sounds that screamed from the car's speakers.

She didn't bother to respond. When he eased the car to the curb in front of her building, Jasmine tossed seven dollars into the driver's hand.

"Good evening, Ms. Larson," Henrikas greeted as he opened the cab door. "I hope you had a good day."

With barely a nod, she made her way to the elevator. Every-thing annoyed her—Henrikas's grin, the clicking of her heels on the marble floor, even the glare from the overhead chande-liers. By the time Jasmine entered her apartment, she was ready to be alone.

Autophobia? I don't think so.

She tossed her coat and briefcase onto the couch, tugged off her boots, and sauntered into the kitchen. She stared at the five bottles of water that sat alone on the refrigerator shelves, then opened the freezer. A minute later, she sank onto her couch, tucked her feet under her, and stuffed a tablespoonful of Rum Raisin ice cream into her mouth. "Malik needs to stay out of my business."

This time when she slammed the spoon into the mound of Häagen-Dazs the utensil bent. Standing, she left the carton on the sofa table and returned to the kitchen. She tore open the package of cheddar cheese potato chips, and stuffed a handful into her mouth.

A sudden knock on the door surprised her. Henrikas was supposed to announce guests. *Malik,* she thought, as she moved toward the door. *He'd better have an apology with him.*

"Good evening," Ms. Van Dorn, her elevator partner from this morning, greeted Jasmine without a smile.

Shock kept Jasmine standing in place, her mouth stuffed with chips.

Ms. Van Dorn raised her penciled eyebrows. "May I come in?" she asked, even as she brushed past Jasmine. When she still hadn't moved, the woman added, "Are you going to just stand there? Where do you want me to put this?"

For the first time Jasmine noticed the red basket Ms. Van Dorn carried. Slowly she closed the door, her eyes never leaving the woman.

"Well?" Ms. Van Dorn said, as if Jasmine was making her lose patience.

"What is that?"

Ms. Van Dorn blew a breath of air. "It's your dinner," she continued as if Jasmine should have known that.

Jasmine frowned. "Dinner? For me?"

The woman shook her head and placed the basket onto the kitchen table. "Who else would I be bringing dinner for?" She faced Jasmine. "Unless you're telling me that someone lives here with you."

"Ms. Van Dorn, I don't want to be rude—"

"Then don't. Just say thank you."

Jasmine stared at the woman. Without her mink, some of her elegance was gone. In her flowered wrap dress that seemed a bit too snug, Ms. Van Dorn looked like the many older women Jasmine saw daily, strolling the city streets. But although Jasmine didn't know her story, she suspected there was nothing ordinary about Ms. Van Dorn. Not living in this building, not being carted around in a limousine, and not wearing the diamond stud earrings that glittered from her ears.

"I'm still waiting for the thank you."

Jasmine muttered, "Thank you."

Her reward was one of the woman's half smiles. "You're wel-come." Ms. Van Dorn moved through the living room as if she had an invitation. "When we met this morning, I could tell you were one of those young working women. More concerned about your career than eating." She stopped and eyed the melting ice cream on the table. "Obviously, I was right." She turned back to Jasmine. "What's your name?"

"Jasmine."

The woman was silent, as if she were waiting for more.

"Jasmine Larson."

The woman half smiled again. "Nice to meet you, Jasmine Larson."

"Nice to meet you—"

"Ms. Van Dorn. But call me Mae Frances. That's what my friends call me." Her gruff tone remained, but now her eyes matched her smile. Mae Frances walked toward the door. "One night when you're not so busy, maybe we can go out to dinner. Get to know each other better."

Jasmine nodded because she couldn't think of anything else to do.

"Speak up, child."

If she wasn't so much older, Jasmine would have had some choice words for the woman. But she only said, "Okay."

Mae Frances nodded. "Have a good night, Jasmine Larson."

Jasmine sighed with relief when the woman opened the door. She couldn't wait to dump whatever was in that basket into the trash. There was no way she was about to eat food from someone she didn't know.

But before she stepped into the hallway, Mae Frances turned back. "And don't worry about eating my food. I may be a stranger to you today, but you can trust me."

Jasmine tried not to show her surprise. Had she spoken her thoughts aloud?

Mae Frances continued, "I'm just being neighborly. We haven't had many people in this building who look like us. So, I'm just being what my mother raised me to be." She lifted her chin an inch higher. "I may live in New York, but I still have the good graces of my Southern roots. Enjoy your dinner."

For the second time that day, Mae Frances Van Dorn left Jasmine standing with her mouth open. But only for a moment. Jasmine rushed to the dining room table and pulled away the cloth covering the basket. She eyed the chicken in the plastic container, the bundle of grapes, and the small box of crackers. It was a strange combination.

She peeled off the cover of the container and the aroma of the fried chicken knocked away her concerns. She tore a wing apart, took a bite, and moaned with delight. It had been a long time since she'd tasted chicken like this—seasoned, fried, crisp, and tender.

Who are you, Mae Frances Van Dorn? The question played in her mind as she carried the basket to the sofa and feasted on the three pieces of chicken. With each swallow, her trepidation about eating food from a stranger disappeared. It didn't take long for the basket to empty, and Jasmine lay back, satisfied, still wondering about her new neighbor. But she didn't linger with those thoughts for long.

She had work to do. First, she'd focus on Rio. And then, she'd turn all of her attention to Reverend Bush.

Chapter 5

J *asmine, this looks great."*

Startled, Jasmine dropped the telephone back onto her desk. What was she thinking? She should've closed her door.

Malik entered with a hesitant grin. These were the first words he'd spoken to her since they were at church last night.

He dropped a binder onto her desk. "I can't believe I never thought of it and J.T. never mentioned it; that's what happens when you're computer free. But, you're right; we need a website."

"I'll get working on it." When he stayed in place, she said, "Is there anything else?"

"I know it's only been a couple of weeks, but you're doing a great job."

She waited for an apology to accompany his compliment, but when he said nothing more, she asked again, "Is there anything else?"

His eyes stayed trained on her before he shook his head and walked out of the office. She followed him, and closed her door.

She hated this tension, but if Malik couldn't accept her and Reverend Bush, that was his problem. She knew what she wanted and no one had ever stopped her from getting—or doing—what she wanted.

She thought about the plan that had come to her during the early morning hours, and then dialed the numbers to City of Lights.

When Mrs. Whittingham answered, Jasmine turned into Scarlett O'Hara.

"Hello," she drawled. "My name is . . . Kyla Blake." She paused to stop herself from laughing as she gave her used-to-be best friend's name. "I'm calling from *Christian Today* magazine."

"Oh, yes, how are you?"

Jasmine hesitated at Mrs. Whittingham's greeting. "I'm just fine this wonderful morning, and how are you?"

"Blessed and highly favored."

Jasmine wanted to gag, but kept the smile in her voice. "I'm calling because we want to do a feature on Reverend Bush—about the new community center."

"Is this a follow-up to the interview you did last month?"

What? Jasmine almost said aloud. Had she picked a real magazine who had talked to Reverend Bush already? "Ah . . . yes . . . in a way . . . this . . . is a follow-up," she stuttered. "I didn't do the interview last month, but my colleague has asked me to check a few details."

"That'll be fine," Mrs. Whittingham said as if Jasmine was her best friend. "When do you want to come in?"

"Ah . . . I'm working under a deadline and I was wondering if Reverend Bush had any evenings available this week?"

"Evenings?"

"Yes," Jasmine said quickly, hoping to erase the frown in Mrs. Whittingham's voice. "I want to interview the reverend by telephone, but I want to do it at a time when he isn't so likely to be interrupted." For good measure, she added, "You know what I mean, sugah?"

"That makes sense." Mrs. Whittingham's smile was back.

"I know how important Reverend Bush is and I know it's hard for him to make this kind of time during the day. So, when would be a good evening for me to call?"

"Can you hold?"

"Sure." Jasmine held her breath, counting the seconds.

"Well, you are blessed today. If you can call him tonight, Reverend Bush will be here in the office. He has a meeting that should end around seven-thirty. But by eight, everyone should be gone."

Jasmine had to force herself not to leap from her seat. "Do you think he'll wait there in the office for me? I mean wait for me to call?"

"Definitely. I just told him and I'll leave a reminder. Just call between eight and eight-thirty."

"Aren't you the sweetest thing. I don't know how to thank you!"

"You're more than welcome. We love your magazine and the way you bring news to the Christian community."

"We certainly try. You know what I'm going to do for you, Mrs. Whittingham? I'm going to get you a subscription to our magazine, free, of course."

"We get it here at the church, but I would love my own copy." She gave Jasmine her home address and thanked her again. "By the way, one last thing . . . ah, I apologize, what's your name again?"

Jasmine frowned. "Kyla."

"And your number, Kyla?"

She only had a second to think before she rattled off her cell number.

Jasmine hung up feeling smarter than most people, but she didn't spend too much time savoring this victory. She called the rental car company and arranged for the car to be driven to her.

The next hours were filled with shuffling papers and thoughts of tonight. It would only take this one time. She'd be charming, he'd be smitten. They'd be together.

Just after seven-thirty, Jasmine picked up her purse, and the envelope and folder she'd prepared, then turned off the light in her office. As she pressed the Lower Level button on the elevator, she thought about how someday she'd tell Reverend Bush just what she'd gone through for the two of them to be together.

Jasmine maneuvered into the church's parking lot. As expected, the lot was empty—except for a green Land Rover and a white Impala. Jasmine grimaced. She'd only expected to see one car. But then she shook her concern away. Even if the car belonged to Mrs. Whittingham, there would be nothing she could do to mess up her plan.

Jasmine turned off the car, looked around the parking lot, then lifted the envelope from the passenger seat. She pulled the knife from the packet, and wondered for a moment if she'd need a larger one.

When she stepped out, her eyes scanned the lot once more before she knelt down and with a quick jab, stabbed the tire, then twisted the knife before she pulled it away. Within seconds, the air fizzled, and the tire began to shrink. She waited a few minutes more, then returned the knife to the envelope, reached into the car for the folder, and rushed to the church.

She was surprised when the door was locked; she rang the bell.

"Jasmine?" Reverend Bush said as he opened the door.

She was pleased—even in the dark, he recognized her. "Reverend Bush." She stepped inside. "How are you?"

"Just fine," he said, and his frown deepened. "What can I do for you?"

"Actually, I'm here to give this to Malik. He left important papers behind again."

The way the reverend's lips turned slowly upward and ended somewhere between a grin and a smirk, let Jasmine know that he didn't believe her. "Malik's not here," he said in a you-know-this-already tone.

She frowned. "He's not? He told his secretary he had a meeting with you."

Reverend Bush shrugged. "Not tonight. He was here last night, remember?"

"Wow." She lowered her eyes. "I don't know . . ." She paused. "Oh, well." She turned toward the door. "Thank you, Reverend." She smiled inside when she saw his frown return. Like he expected more from her. Like maybe now, he believed her story. "Have a good evening," she said and moved as if she was anxious to get away.

When she placed her hand on the door knob, he said, "Wait."

She almost laughed. It wasn't even going to take the flat tire to get his attention.

"How did you get here?" he asked. "Do you need to call a cab?"

Those were not the words she wanted to hear, but still, she was encouraged. "No, I have a rental. I had to run some errands for Malik."

He peeked into the parking lot. "Okay, I'll stay here while you walk to the car."

"Thank you, Reverend," Jasmine said, turning away from him. "Have a good night."

She could feel his eyes on her and even in the night's winter air, she slowed her walk, added more swivel to her step. She'd thought he'd walk her to the car, discover the flat tire with her. But whichever way it went down, they'd spend the rest of the night together.

As she approached the car, she slowed even more, careful to put surprise in her body language. "Oh, no," she whispered, and leaned next to the car. She stayed, kneeling, even though her knees began to ache. Behind her, she heard the reverend's footsteps on the concrete.

"What's wrong?"

"I have a flat tire," she cried out.

Reverend Bush peered at the flattened rubber. "Looks that way."

"I must have run over something."

Even in the dark, she could see him squint. "I can't imagine what would cause a gash like that."

"Guess I should call the rental company," Jasmine said. "Or some kind of auto club." She paused and looked up at him. "Or something."

He glanced at the tire once again. "Okay, come on back inside." He took her hand, pulled her up. When she stood, he was so close—his lips just inches from hers.

She saw it again—the glimmer in his eyes.

Seconds ticked past before, with a turn and a cough, Reverend Bush moved away. But there was triumph in her smile and victory in her step as she marched behind him.

In her head, she reviewed the next phase—how she'd make the call, then they'd sit and sip coffee. They'd wait. And talk. And in the end, he'd know the best parts of her. She was almost skipping when they walked into his office.

"May I use your phone?" she asked, slipping her coat from her shoulders. She smoothed her plum-colored suit over her waist.

"Hold on." He motioned for her to take a seat as he picked up the telephone. "Brother Hill, can you come into my office?"

In the silence that followed from the moment Reverend Bush hung up until Brother Hill stepped into their space, the reverend's words still hadn't connected. Nothing registered until Brother Hill appeared. His smile switched to a smirk when he looked at her.

"Brother Hill, Sister Jasmine has a flat tire. Can you help her change it?"

"No problem."

Their exchange moved faster than she had time to think. Brother Hill asked, "Is your car in the lot?"

She nodded. When he gestured for her to follow him, she did.

Think, Jasmine, think.

The deacon paused at the door and took a coat from the rack. "Of course, there's a spare in the trunk?" he asked in a tone that told her he suspected this was no ordinary flat tire.

She wanted to slap that smirk from him. "I would think so." She crossed her arms. "But I don't know. It's a rental."

"Give me the keys." She dropped them into his hand. "Wait here."

Her eyes followed as Brother Hill stepped outside to the car and knelt by the back tire. With the cold of the night, she was sure he'd work fast.

I should have taken out the spare.

But there was still time. When Brother Hill popped open the trunk, Jasmine took a deep breath and returned to the reverend's office.

"Thank you so much, Reverend," she said as she stood at his opened door.

"Not a problem," he said, looking up from papers scattered on his desk. "Brother Hill will take care of you."

She nodded. "Would you happen to have any coffee or tea?"

He shook his head. "No, Sister Whittingham cleans up everything when she leaves. Sorry."

"That's okay," Jasmine said entering his office and settling into a chair.

But before she had the chance to lean back, the reverend said, "Sister Jasmine, would you mind waiting outside? I'm sure Brother Hill will be finished in a few minutes and I'm expecting a call."

"A call?" she said.

"Yes, I have an interview I have to do."

No, you don't.

"I'm preparing for that now."

Still, she sat in place.

"Sister Jasmine?" He stood and came around his desk. "Would you mind waiting in the lounge?"

She nodded and stood.

Think, Jasmine. Think.

He escorted her to the couch in the outer office, then peeked out the window. "It doesn't look like it'll take Brother Hill too long," the reverend said. "It sure is cold tonight."

"I can call Triple A so he doesn't have to be out there."

"No, Brother Hill has it under control." He glanced at his watch. "I'm sorry, Sister Jasmine, but I've really got to prepare for this call."

How could she tell him there would be no call? What could she say to get him to focus on her?

But she stayed, sitting silently, as he stepped into his office. And closed his door. And left her no closer to him than she was fifteen minutes before.

Think, Jasmine. Think.

She didn't have a plan when she finally stood and marched to his door. But she'd figure out what to say when she was inside. There was no way she was going to waste this time, especially not after the charge that had shot between them in the parking lot.

Her hand was still in the air, preparing to knock, when she heard Brother Hill behind her.

"Sister Jasmine, your car is ready."

Like all the other times she'd come face to face with Brother Hill, Jasmine wanted to curse him out. How could he change a tire so quickly?

She smiled, hiding her frustration. "Thank you so much…Brother Hill."

He took off his gloves and blew on his fingers. "It's cold out there."

She said nothing. Didn't think it was a good idea to tell him that she wished he'd frozen to death.

He said, "Can I give you some advice?"

Still, she kept silent.

Brother Hill spoke as if she'd invited his words. "You need to set your sights on someone else." He paused and looked directly at her. "Reverend Bush is not interested in you."

She crossed her arms.

He continued. "Do you think you're the first woman who has thrown herself at the reverend?" he asked with a chuckle in his voice. "Women like you run through this church like the A train. There's another one coming along in a few minutes or so."

"You have a lot of nerve talking to me that way," she hissed.

He raised his eyebrows. "Talking to you what way? Like you were a woman hurling herself at a man who's not interested?"

Jasmine was tempted to reach for the glass paperweight that sat on Mrs. Whittingham's desk and knock his squat behind silly. She rolled her eyes and brushed past him. As she paused to close her coat, he opened the door for her.

"Have a good night, Sister Jasmine," Brother Hill said. As she took the first step outside, he added. "And try not to run over any more knives."

She whipped around and he held up her knife. She opened her mouth to deny his accusation, to rant about his nerve, rummaging through her personal property, but then she grabbed the knife, turned, and marched toward her car. It didn't matter what he thought. If he said anything to Reverend Bush, she would deny it. She had the knife. It would be his word against hers. And with the way Reverend Bush looked at her tonight, she knew he'd take her side.

Brother Hill was still standing at the door as she screeched from the parking lot. The first thing she was going to do when she became Mrs. Samuel Bush was get rid of Brother Hill. He was going to have to leave City of Lights. Find some other Christians to harass.

Just that thought brought back her smile.

"Okay," she said aloud. "This was just a little setback." And really, there was nothing to be upset about, especially when she recalled the few moments she and the reverend shared. The way they stood close. The way their lips almost touched. Her plan was well on its way.

She was almost at her apartment when her cell phone rang. She looked at the number, rolled her eyes, but clicked TALK any-way.

"Hey, Serena. What's up?"

"Hey, yourself, you don't sound like the happy New Yorker."

"Had a long day."

"Well, I was calling to check on you. How's it going?"

Jasmine sighed as she pulled the car to a stop in front of her building. She could see Henrikas peeking through the door. "It's okay, just a lot of work."

"What's wrong?"

"Just . . . a lot of work. How're you doing?" Jasmine asked, eager to take her thoughts away from Reverend Bush.

"Well, I have some news. Carl and I made it official. We're a couple."

Jasmine turned off the ignition with those words.

"Serena, that's great. It's about time you got some."

"Oh, it's not like that," Serena said in a school teacher's tone. "We've just committed to dating, but we're going to do this God's way."

Jasmine laughed. "When was the last time God went on a date?"

"Oh, you got jokes. I'm just saying that we're going to date the way God intended."

"Oh, so no sex, huh? Too bad."

"No sex, no kissing. We won't even hold hands if we feel it getting out of control."

Jasmine opened her mouth wide. "How can you call it dating if you're not even going to kiss?"

"I'm not going to try to explain this to you. You know what God desires from us."

"Yeah, but He also knows that we're all sinners," Jasmine said, tucking her purse under her arm as she reached for her briefcase. "I know He doesn't expect us to remain celibate for the rest of our lives."

"Whatever. I didn't call to get into this. Just wanted you to remember that you have a sister who loves you very much and who is praying for you always."

"Thanks, sis. I need those prayers."

"Well, you got them. Call a sistah sometimes, okay?"

"Kiss my nieces for me and tell Carl I said hello." Jasmine was sure the next time her sister called, it would be to cry over losing the first man she'd been serious about since her husband, because Jasmine knew there wasn't a black man alive who would date without sex.

Jasmine shook her head. Her sister and her rules. *She'll learn,* Jasmine thought. *That Christian stuff doesn't work in today's times. All you can hope for is to go to church and try to stay saved.*

Jasmine motioned for Henrikas and he rushed from the building.

"Ms. Larson, I didn't recognize you."

"Can you pull this into one of the visitor spaces? I have to return it in the morning."

"Sure, one of the guys can do it."

In the elevator, Jasmine chuckled again as she remembered her sister's words. *Not even kiss?* If anyone besides Serena had told her this, she would have still been laughing. But she knew her sister was serious. Serena lived life on a different plane than most when it came to God.

Maybe that was a good thing. Maybe being chaste gave Serena a direct line to God. Well, if there was anything Jasmine needed right now it was effective prayers.

By the time Jasmine stepped into her apartment she could feel her sister's prayers, because there was already another Reverend Bush plan brewing in her mind.

Chapter 6

This time, Jasmine was a Jamaican.

"Mrs. Whittingham, my name is Patricia Jones and I'm Malik Kincaid's new assistant."

"Oh, hello, Ms. Jones. What can I do for you?"

Jasmine leaned back on her couch. "Malik asked me to call the reverend and find out something that he needs for a report he's submitting to Bill Cosby." Jasmine lowered her voice. "You know Malik is trying to get . . . ," she paused for a moment, "Bill Cosby to attend a fund-raiser for the building committee."

"No, I didn't know that," Mrs. Whittingham gushed.

"Well, it's still quite a secret, so I would greatly appreciate it if you didn't repeat this."

"Of course not."

"Thank you, but I needed to speak to Reverend Bush about something that Malik wants me to put into the proposal for Mr. Cosby."

"What do you need? I'll find out from the reverend and get back to you."

"Reverend Bush isn't in right now?"

"He's here, but he's working on a project and I can't disturb him."

"Mrs. Whittingham, this is very important. Malik has to

get this program on Mr. Cosby's calendar right away." When the secretary stayed silent, Jasmine added, "I wouldn't insist normally, but this is one of the first projects Malik has given me and I would hate to go back to him and tell him that I couldn't complete it. I promise I won't take more than a minute of his time."

Mrs. Whittingham hesitated and then said, "Hold on a moment."

Jasmine was surprised at the way her heart pounded. "I'll put you through, Ms. Jones," Mrs. Whittingham said when she got back on the line. "And," she lowered her voice, "I didn't say a word about Mr. Cosby." She giggled.

"Thank you." First, there was the sound of dead air and then Reverend Bush's greeting.

"This is Jasmine Larson," she said, losing the accent.

"Jasmine?"

"Yes, and please don't be upset, Reverend," she said quickly, careful to add a bit of trembling to her voice. "The only reason I told Mrs. Whittingham I was someone else was because I knew she wouldn't put me through. But this is important."

"What is it, Sister Jasmine?"

"I . . . I need to talk to you. I don't know if Malik told you, but my father recently passed away."

"I'm sorry to hear that."

"And I've been having nightmares and difficulty sleeping."

"You looked fine last night . . . and the night before that."

She heard more behind his words and wondered if Brother Hill had told him about the knife.

"I was fine . . . I mean, I'm fine during the day. It's just when I sleep at night . . . or try to sleep." She paused. "My pastor in Florida had been working with me. I was much better when he counseled me, but since I've been in New York, I've tried to handle this on my own," she quivered. "But it's not working."

"So you want a counseling appointment?"

"Yes." *Preferably as soon as possible,* she wanted to add.

There was a long pause and then, "Sister Jasmine." Reverend Bush sighed as if he were weary. Then suddenly, he said, "You know what? I think it would be a good idea for us to talk."

She sat straight up.

He continued, "In fact, I have some time this afternoon. Would you be able to get here by four?"

She paused. She'd wanted a later appointment, one that would lead from the church to a restaurant, to her apartment—or his place. But she'd figure that part out later. "I'll be there at four," she said, keeping the tears in her voice. "And thank you. I really need this." She added another sob before she clicked off her phone, and stretched her legs onto the coffee table. She dialed another number.

"Tina, I'm working on a project and don't want to stop right now, so I'm going to work from home."

"Did you forget the meeting with Malik? He wanted to go over the Web companies with you."

"What time is that?"

"At four. He wanted to handle this before you went to L.A."

She hesitated for just a moment. "I'm sorry, Tina, but I really can't make it this afternoon. I'll send Malik an e-mail and explain."

"He's in his office—do you want to talk to him?"

"No," she said, knowing that she could fool Mrs. Whittingham and Reverend Bush, but there would be no way she could trick her godbrother. "He'll keep me on the phone forever. Don't worry, I'll handle Malik."

She hung up, and tossed the phone onto the table. In a few minutes, she'd send that e-mail. Make up some new project she was pursuing for the club. Then after that, she would turn all thoughts to the reverend.

She ticked off a to-do list in her head. Get a manicure and pedicure. Purchase new lingerie. Select the most fabulous outfit to wear. Something simple, but sexy. Something conservative, yet revealing. Something definitely easy to take off. Lastly, she'd pack for her trip to L.A. because she didn't plan to be home in time tonight to do it.

She hated to leave New York right after this first date with Reverend Bush, but in a way, it was good. It would leave him wanting more of her.

Jasmine jumped from the couch. The chase was fun. But now it was time for the conquest.

Jasmine saw her scorn and could almost hear her growl when Mrs. Whittingham opened the church door, but she ignored the attitude.

"I have an appointment with Reverend Bush," Jasmine said.

"I know you do."

Jasmine shrugged off her coat, and felt Mrs. Whittingham's stare.

"Is there something you want?" Jasmine asked, her tone filled with disdain.

"I *want* you to know that I don't appreciate what you did this morning . . . Ms. Jones."

Jasmine laughed inside. She was so tempted to tell Mrs. Whittingham what she really thought of her wide hips, but she already had her victory. And if Mrs. Whittingham didn't watch out, she'd be going the way of Brother Hill. Once she and Reverend Bush were a couple, Jasmine had no intention of accepting any kind of attitude from anyone.

"Sister Jasmine, thank you for coming," Reverend Bush said, pulling her away from her thoughts.

She jumped from her seat, pleased to see his smile. But she was careful to keep her cheer inside. The plan was to first get the counseling she needed, and then get the man she wanted. "Thank you, Reverend." She lowered her eyes, made her voice sad.

"Oh, brother," Mrs. Whittingham growled just loud enough for Jasmine to hear.

Jasmine wanted to choke the woman, but instead she followed Reverend Bush into his office. She snuggled into the
chair, but right away sat up straight when she noticed that
Mrs. Whittingham had followed them.

Reverend Bush said, "Mrs. Whittingham joins me for all of
my single counseling sessions," he explained. "It's in our church
policies, but we didn't get a chance to go over those with you."

There was no way she was going to allow this. "But Reverend Bush, what I have to say is . . . private. I don't feel comfortable sharing—"

"I can assure you," Mrs. Whittingham said in a tone much
softer than the one she'd used to speak to Jasmine just minutes
before, "this is standard. I have a degree, and although I don't
do any counseling, I am bound to the same rules of ethics as
Reverend Bush."

"Still . . ." Jasmine began, shaking her head. She blinked her
eyes several times, as if she were trying to press back tears.

"Sister Whittingham," Reverend Bush began, keeping his
eyes on Jasmine. "Maybe this once we can do this. Let me
meet with Sister Jasmine . . . alone."

His secretary frowned. "Are you sure, Reverend?" she said,
her voice filled with warning. "We don't want any problems."

Jasmine made up her mind. Getting rid of Mrs. Whittingham would be her first order of business.

The reverend nodded. "I'm sure Sister Jasmine won't give
us any problems."

"Of course not, Reverend," Jasmine said and then turned
her glance to Mrs. Whittingham. She had to fight to keep her
smirk away.

The church secretary stood, glared at Jasmine once again,
and then took her time strolling from the room.

"You can close the door, Sister Whittingham," the reverend
said.

Mrs. Whittingham opened her mouth to protest, but then
followed the reverend's instructions. She had barely closed the

door when Reverend Bush said, "Sister Jasmine, I am tempted to listen to your story, but I think it would be best if we just got to the point."

Jasmine crossed her legs. *I knew it,* she thought. At least there wouldn't be any games.

"Truth be told," he said, and leaned back in his seat, "I don't believe the reason you told me you're here."

"Oh, no, Reverend," she said, loving this exchange. "You can believe me." She smiled and edged forward. "I have been having . . . dreams."

He paused as he took in her words, their meaning. "Sister Jasmine, the only way I've ever known to be is honest. So, let me begin by saying that I recognize all your little tricks."

His words pushed her back in her seat.

He continued, "The call you made this morning—"

"I explained that. I did what I did because Mrs. Whittingham doesn't like me."

He spoke over her words. "The call you made yesterday." He held up his hands. "And don't bother denying it. I called the number you gave to Sister Whittingham when the magazine didn't call me and I got your voice mail."

What was she supposed to say? *Think, Jasmine. Think.*

"The times you tried to meet Malik here . . ." He paused and shook his head. "Sister Jasmine, these kinds of things have to stop. They're disruptive—not only to me and my work, but to those who work with me."

She took a deep breath. "Reverend, you're right. Maybe I've gone about this the wrong way, but the only reason I did all of those things was because there seems to be this hedge around you."

He nodded as if he understood.

"I couldn't seem to get to you. All I wanted was two minutes with you to ask you to lunch—"

"You asked me to join you for lunch, Sister Jasmine. You asked me and I declined in the politest way I could."

"But you had to say no because there were others around. But now," she leaned forward again, her calm confidence returning. "It's just us. We're both single. We're both attractive, at least I think you are." She paused. When he said nothing, she added, "And we both want to get to know one another."

He shook his head. "Sister Jasmine. I have to apologize. I don't know what I did to give you that impression." He stopped and made his voice stronger. "But I am not interested in going out with you."

Her back straightened with indignation.

"I don't fraternize with women in my congregation."

She exhaled. "Oh, is that the reason? Come on, Reverend." Then she asked, "May I call you Samuel?"

"You can call me Reverend Bush."

Her smile left her face, but she kept it in her voice. "If the problem is my attending services here, that can be solved. It's not like I'm a member." She leaned toward him. "You've been honest with me, so let me do the same. I feel the chemistry between us."

He glanced at the clock before he looked at her. "I don't know what you're feeling, but whatever it is . . ." He paused. "I'm not feeling it." He let his words stay in the air before he added, "So, let's make this clear—no more games, no tricks, no phone calls." He peered at her for another moment. "I hope we understand each other."

"I don't understand at all."

"I don't know any other way to say I'm not interested."

Her face heated under his glare. Slowly, she rose and turned away, determined not to utter another word.

"Hope to see you in church on Sunday, Sister Jasmine."

Without looking at him, she closed the reverend's door. She wanted to run to her car, but first she had to pass Mrs. Whittingham's desk. The woman sat, as Brother Hill leaned over her, and the two hovered in quiet conversation. Their talking stopped when she neared. She wasn't going to give them any satisfaction—she looked them straight in their eyes before she turned to the exit.

"Sister Jasmine, you have a nice day."

All she wanted to do was get away. From Reverend Bush and his cronies. If he didn't want her, fine. This was New York. The city was filled with eligible men. Men who were more sophisticated, who had more money, who were much finer, and who had much more to offer than the reverend.

Hope to see you in church on Sunday, Sister Jasmine.

Oh, yes, he would see her. He would see her every Sunday.

As she stomped to the corner, she made a vow. To make sure that the day would come when she would make Reverend Bush regret his rejection. One day Reverend Bush would be sorry that he had ever let her go.

Chapter 7

Some things were going to have to change.

Jasmine zipped her suitcase, threw her mink over her shoulders, and then rolled her luggage into the hallway. As she rode in the elevator, she thought of the list she was going to give Malik once the club opened. First, she'd need a car service. Calling for cabs had been fine—until she noticed how many people in New York had drivers.

At least I'm flying first class, she thought, although she wondered why Malik didn't have his own plane. If he had, she wouldn't be up so early.

She yawned and pushed back thoughts of Reverend Bush that had kept her tossing much of the night. She refused to yield to the feelings his words had caused. She was above that. She was above him.

"Good morning, Ms. Larson," Henrikas said the moment she stepped off the elevator. It was barely six o'clock, but Jasmine was no longer surprised to see him at every hour. "Do you need a cab?" he asked with his ever-present cheer.

Jasmine nodded. "I'm going to LaGuardia."

He nodded, but just as he opened the door, Mae Frances sauntered from the elevator.

"Good morning, Jasmine Larson." She eyed Jasmine's bag. "Looks like you're going on a trip."

Jasmine's eyes roamed up and down her neighbor. Mae Frances was wrapped again in her mink.

"Well?" Mae Frances said, exasperation in her tone as she waited for Jasmine's response. A diamond glinted from her ring finger.

"I'm going to Los Angeles on a business trip."

"That doesn't sound like fun." Mae Frances turned to Henrikas. "Put her bags in my car, please."

Jasmine frowned. "What?"

Mae Frances raised one penciled eyebrow. "You're going to the airport, aren't you?"

"Yes, but—"

"But what? Don't you need a ride? Or would you prefer to take one of those . . . cabs?"

Jasmine wasn't sure if she liked Mae Frances—not the way she talked, not the way she took control. But her curiosity about the woman was tying itself around her neck.

"Well, are you coming?" Mae Frances asked with impatience.

"Yes, thank you," she said, thinking riding in a limo was better—even if she had to ride with her.

"How are you on time?" Mae Frances asked once the car pulled from the curb. "Do you have a few minutes to spare?"

Jasmine hoped this woman wasn't about to take her on some drive through the city. "My plane leaves in about two hours, but I like to get there early."

"No problem." Mae Frances said to the driver, "Starbucks, Gerald Davis." When the car stopped, Mae Frances said, "I hope you like this place."

"Yeah, I do."

"Good. My treat." Mae Frances opened her purse. "Get whatever you like," she said as she pulled out her wallet, "and bring me back—" She stopped. "Oh, shoot. I forgot to stop by the bank."

"No problem." Jasmine opened the door. "I'll get it."

"Thank you," Mae Frances said, then asked Jasmine to buy her a venti coffee and two pastries. "I have a sweet tooth," she added.

In minutes, Jasmine was back, and Gerald sped toward the airport. "Thank you, Mae Frances. I really appreciate this."

Mae Frances' smile was so warm it disarmed Jasmine. "I told you the other night, I'm just being neighborly."

Jasmine sipped her latte. "I have to admit, I've never had a neighbor quite like you."

Mae Frances leaned back and laughed so loud, it startled Jasmine. "You're not the only one in our building who feels that way. I'm sure for years some of those old fogies have held meetings trying to figure out how to get rid of me."

"How long have you lived there?"

As fast as it came, the woman's laughter went away. "Sometimes I feel as if I've lived there as long as that building is old." She sounded as if she was weighed down by years. "My husband and I settled there in nineteen sixty-four. I was the first Negro to live in that building."

The word made Jasmine flinch, but she said nothing at first. Wondered why Mae Frances had said "I."

"Wow, that's forty years."

"I was a young bride." Mae Frances sounded gruff again. "My husband had his medical practice on the first floor of the building when he first started."

A *doctor?* That explained the limousine, the mink, the diamonds that she sported.

"What kind of doctor is your husband?"

Her eyes flared, then softened. "Let's talk about you. Where are you from?"

"I was born and raised in Los Angeles, but I just moved here from Florida."

Mae Frances nodded. "And your family?"

Jasmine's face stretched with surprise. She was the one who was supposed to be doing the questioning. Still she answered, telling Mae Frances about her parents and Serena. And the next question came; Mae Frances asked if she were married. Then asked where she worked. The queries continued until the car eased in front of the Delta terminal. Only then did Jasmine realize that Mae Frances knew much about her, but she hadn't uncovered too much of anything about her neighbor.

"Well, Jasmine Larson," Mae Frances began once the driver stepped from the car and opened the door. "Have a nice business trip."

"Thank you again."

The woman nodded. "By the way," she began, "how did you like the dinner the other night?"

The memory made Jasmine smile. "It was great. Thank you for that too."

"Then we can have dinner together when you get back. My treat since you treated me this morning," Mae Frances said, holding up the Starbucks bag.

Her first instinct was to say no, but then she looked at Mae Frances sitting so regally, head held high, back pressed against the seat. And when she peered a bit closer, there was something in the woman's eyes that Jasmine hadn't seen before. Sadness, loneliness, she wasn't sure. "Dinner would be nice, Mae Frances." She stepped from the car and took her bag from Gerald.

Mae Frances pressed the button, lowering her window. "Let me know when you get back."

Jasmine paused for just a moment. "Yes . . . yes, ma'am."

Mae Frances's eyes widened. She leaned back and laughed. Jasmine could still hear her laughter, even as she turned into the terminal.

Chapter 8

Jasmine was on top of the world.

That's the way she felt as she gazed out the tenth-floor window overlooking Doheny Drive. At first, Gabriella had booked her into a no-name hotel in the Valley. But she'd changed that. That was not the way she was going to return to Los Angeles.

The ringing of the phone interrupted her thoughts.

"Ms. Larson, your car is here."

"Thank you," she said to the concierge.

With a quick glance in the mirror, she smoothed the black dress over her hips, grabbed her shawl, and gave a smile of thanks for the warmth of a Los Angeles winter.

In the elevator, she once again dismissed thoughts that had plagued her all day. The thoughts that tried to convince her she'd been a fool with Reverend Bush. It didn't matter because she was already over him. Already looking forward to the pay-back that would be oh, so sweet.

Before she took a step from the elevator, a voice greeted her. "You look wonderful as always," J.T. said.

"I thought I was meeting you at de Janeiro."

His lips slipped into a smile that looked more like a leer. "I was just about to come . . . up to your room."

In spite of herself, she chuckled. "The concierge called. My car is here."

He reached out, gesturing for her to hook her arm through his. "That would be me. Did you think I was going to let you walk into the club by yourself? If I have my way, you won't be alone at all tonight."

Jasmine took his arm, although she was not about to take his offer. Not even Reverend Bush's rejection was going to make her go back to bedding a married man.

She slipped into one of the many Town Cars waiting in front of the Four Seasons. As the car accelerated down Wilshire, J.T. chatted. "The salsa contest begins sometime between nine and ten; we just go with the crowd. But this contest put us on the map."

When the car turned onto the 405 Freeway, it was difficult for her to focus on J.T.'s words. Her thoughts took her to the past, her years in Los Angeles. Her life with her ex-husband, ex-lovers, ex-friends.

J.T. said, "We thought we'd attract the thirty-, forty-year-olds who were outgrowing hip-hop. But you'll see as many twenty-year-olds in the club as anyone else." He rested his hand on her leg.

With a smile, she slid away from his touch.

"Don't you like me, Jasmine?" he asked as if he were offended.

But Jasmine knew his tone was just a ploy. He was playing the same games she once mastered. "You're married."

He raised one eyebrow. "And?"

She matched the look on his face.

"I'm not talking about divorcing my wife," he said.

She chuckled under her breath.

"I'm just saying that since we're going to be working . . . closely together," he slid across the seat until he was almost on top of her, "we should make the best of this relationship."

"I agree," she said before she pushed him away. "And I promise you. This is going to be a good *working* relationship."

He leaned back against the seat and laughed. "You're a

hard one. I can't say that I've had many turn me down." He shook his head. "I would never have taken you for one of those kinds of women." She frowned, and he said, "I don't mean to offend you, but you look like a woman who knows how to have a good time. Like a woman who goes after what she wants."

Jasmine chuckled. If he only knew. "And you know all of this just by looking at me?"

He nodded. "It's a compliment, really. You just don't seem to be someone who plays by the rules."

"I don't. Not anyone else's. But I do have my own rules."

He looked at her for a long moment. "I don't give up easily."

Jasmine gave him a smile and was relieved when his cell chirped. As he barked orders into the phone, Jasmine turned back to the window. The car whizzed by the Getty Center as they navigated north on the freeway.

She'd been surprised when she'd first learned de Janeiro was in Thousand Oaks. When she'd lived here, she never ventured far from the city's excitement. It seemed L.A. life had changed.

The limousine eased off the freeway and two blocks later, slowed. De Janeiro shone in bright lights that illuminated the entire width of Ventura Boulevard.

J.T. slid out and took Jasmine's hand. He held her as they maneuvered through the Thursday night crowd that swarmed outside.

At the glass doors, J.T. shook hands with the linebacker-looking man standing in front of the velvet rope. They stepped inside, and the club was brilliant with excitement. Salsa music bounced off the orange walls of the massive room. The club was packed with women clothed in bright tops and flowing skirts, and men with festive shirts and black pants. A few suits were sprinkled through the crowd.

The gleaming parquet dance floor was empty, but almost all the small round tables that surrounded the perimeter were filled with patrons sipping colorful concoctions and snacking on finger foods from the evening carte du jour. The circular bar that commanded the center of the room was crammed with customers.

"I'm going to the back," J.T. said. "Need to check on a few things," he yelled over the music. He was so close, his lips grazed her earlobe.

She shivered.

"You can hang out here," he said, then paused, "or you can come with me."

His lips, his hands, his invitation made Jasmine remember Reverend Bush. His words. His rejection. Then, she imagined how J.T. would feel—on her, in her.

"I'll wait right here," she said, pointing to the bar.

He chuckled. Like he knew something she didn't. Like he knew she wouldn't last for long.

She scooted onto an empty round stool.

"Hey, Art," J.T. yelled to one of the bartenders. "This is Jasmine. From Malik's club. Take care of her." The bartender nodded and she ordered a Coke, no ice.

When she turned around, J.T. had already begun his passage toward the back, pausing every few steps to bask in the admiration of his fans.

Jasmine sipped her Coke, swung the bar stool around, and surveyed the space. She felt like she was in the middle of Ipanema. From the beach murals on the wall to the palm trees that filled the space, no one could have convinced her that she was not in South America.

Her glance paused at a group of men in suits, standing in a small circle. One turned to meet her eyes, and raised his glass toward her. When she realized she was staring, Jasmine turned away from the familiar man.

Her mind scanned her memory. He wasn't someone she'd bedded. Although there'd been many she'd shared her body with, she remembered every man.

Behind her, a voice wrapped in silk said, "Hello."

She didn't have to turn to know who it was. She felt him—
and the voltage he carried. She smiled her hello, then said, "I
know you, don't I?"

He laughed. "That's supposed to be my line."

A current flashed between them and the way his eyes
shined told her he felt it too. She couldn't stop staring. "Where
do I know you from?"

He sipped the golden liquid in the glass he held. "That's
what I'm trying to figure out," he said, looking at her through
narrowed eyes.

"I used to live in Los Angeles. Maybe we went to school together."

He shook his head. "I just moved here a few years ago." He
paused. "So, you don't live here now?"

She shook her head. "I live in New York."

His glance inched up her body. "Too bad."

Jasmine's eyes wandered to his left hand. Long, manicured,
bare fingers curved around his glass. She held out her hand,
eager to touch him. "I'm Jasmine Larson."

He laughed. Took her hand. "Jasmine. What are you doing
here?" he asked, still holding onto her.

She frowned. "We do know each other."

"Well, not really." He leaned in closer. "But we've met." He
dropped her hand, and took another sip of his drink.

She frowned. "Well?"

"I'm Brian. Brian Lewis."

It took a moment. "Jefferson Blake's best friend."

"Yup, and you're one of Kyla Blake's best friends."

"Used to be." She looked down into her almost empty glass
and took a final sip.

"That's right. You slept with her husband and she ran you
out of town." He chuckled.

"I don't think so." She did not share his humor. "How are
Doctor and Mrs. Blake?"

He shrugged. "You know them. Living their perfect life."

He took the empty glass from her and placed it on the counter. "Let me get you another one. What are you drinking?"

"Just Coke, no ice."

He raised his eyebrows. "That's all you want?"

She bit her lip. "For now."

As Brian got the bartender's attention, she used the time to study him. She remembered now—Dr. Brian Lewis. They'd met years back at Jefferson's fortieth birthday party. She'd been impressed and had tried then to get his attention. But as she recalled, he only had eyes for Alexis Ward.

Her eyes narrowed at her memory of Alexis, Kyla's other best friend. Her archenemy.

Brian handed Jasmine a glass. "Let me know when you want something more," he said with a smile.

"So," Jasmine began. She glanced at his hand once again, this time checking for a tan line on his ring finger. "I guess things didn't work out for you and Alexis." Satisfaction filled her tone. When she'd left Los Angeles, Brian and Alexis had been quite an item. It did her heart good to know that not even the gorgeous Alexis could hold onto this man.

He asked, "You remember Alexis?"

"Of course. She was Kyla's best friend, remember?"

"Still is. She's also my wife."

Jasmine was glad her back was against the bar's counter or she would have fallen off the stool. "You married her?"

He chuckled. "Well, yeah. Why not? She's smart, funny, gorgeous."

Jasmine held up her hand. "There is no need to give me a litany of Alexis Ward's attributes."

"Alexis Lewis," he corrected her.

She took another sip of her soda, wishing for a moment that it was mixed with a bit of rum. "So, if you're so happily married, where's your wife?" Before he answered, it occurred to her that Alexis could be here too—lurking in the background, readying to jump out and ruin her day.

"My wife is home."

His tone made her twist her entire body toward him. He stood so close she could feel his heat. "She lets you go out and play without her?" Jasmine whispered.

He turned his glass upside down, finishing what was left. "I'm not that kind of cat. I do what I want to do."

Jasmine slid one leg off the stool, brushing against Brian as she moved. "And so," she asked, "what is it that you like to do?"

His tongue grazed his lips, but before he could answer, J.T. interrupted, "Hey, Brian. What's up, man?"

They exchanged greetings and Jasmine stepped to the side, studying Brian once more. Even in the darkness of the club, she could see the sharp angles of his jaw, the square shape of his chin, the fullness of his mouth—lover's lips. She licked her own as she tried to remember what kind of doctor he was; she'd ask once J.T. left them alone.

She took another sip of her drink. Yes, there were a couple of things she wanted to remember and new things she wanted to learn about Dr. Brian Lewis.

J.T. finally turned to her. "I have some things I need to go over with you."

Brian's glance moved between them. "You know each other?"

"Yeah," J.T. said and put his arm around Jasmine.

She wanted to dodge his embrace, but she was pushed against the bar. "J.T. and I work together. My godbrother and I are opening a similar club in New York and I'm here to check out a few things."

Brian's smile returned. "How long are you here, Jasmine?"

"I was supposed to go home Saturday morning." She twirled the glass in her hand. "But I can stay longer . . . if there's a reason."

J.T. looked between the two and frowned. "Jasmine, we need to talk before the contest begins."

Brian pulled a card from his wallet. "Call me if you decide to stay an extra day . . . or night."

She glanced at the ecru linen card. "We'll see," she said, although she'd already made up her mind. She would be going home on Sunday. When she looked up, he smiled. She thought, *Maybe I'll stay until Monday.*

J.T. placed his hand on the middle of her back and nudged her away. When they were alone, he said, "How do you know Brian?"

"He's an old friend."

"He's married."

"I know."

"Thought you didn't mess with married men?"

Jasmine shrugged, but said nothing. She didn't. But this was the man who had exchanged vows with Alexis Ward.

She couldn't hide her smile as she looked at Brian's card before she tucked it into the zippered compartment inside her purse.

For hours, *J.T. kept* her occupied—watching the dance contest, talking to the winners, mixing with the customers. But even as she worked, her eyes were on watch for Dr. Brian Lewis.

"So, is there anything else you want to see?" J.T. asked, leaning into Jasmine.

"No, I'm just going to walk around for a bit, okay?"

"Yeah, all right." He turned into the waiting clutches of a trio of spandex-adorned women who had been shadowing them all night.

Jasmine was happy to pass J.T. to the roving ménage-a-trois. She'd completed her tasks, now it was time for fun. She strolled through the club still packed with partiers, dancing and drinking as if they didn't have anywhere to be in the morning. But after checking out every inch of the space, she accepted that Brian was gone.

"J.T.," Jasmine said after she'd scoped the entire club. "I'm going to head back to the hotel."

"Sure you don't want me to go with you?" he asked, even though the women were still clinging to him as if they were appendages.

"No, but thanks for everything."

He chuckled. "I've got to give it to you, Jasmine. You're living right. Call me later if you feel like doing a little wrong." He pulled away from the women and walked her to the waiting car.

She slid into the back, then waved as the car pulled away from de Janeiro—and her thoughts were already on Brian Lewis.

She wasn't really surprised that Brian had married Alexis. For years, she'd watched men swoon at that woman's feet. And she'd watched Alexis pretend none of that attention mattered. But Jasmine had never been fooled. Alexis was just like her. Just waiting for the right man with the right money.

It seemed that Alexis had her hand in the jackpot.

The thought would have angered her, except that she recalled the way Brian's eyes devoured her as if she were his favorite dessert. And she could still feel the charge that sparked between them the entire time they talked. Perhaps Miss Alexis didn't have it all.

She pulled out his business card, and stared at his name. She wondered if she should call tonight, or just wait until morning.

The message light was blinking when Jasmine stepped into her hotel room. She kicked off her shoes and picked up the telephone.

"Jasmine," Malik began on the voice mail, "I left details with a Gayle Conners at the front desk. Change of plans. I need you back in New York tomorrow. I'll explain in the morning. Call me before you get on the plane."

By the time he spoke his last word, the smile that had accompanied her thoughts of Brian Lewis faded. She called the front desk, got the details of her return trip, and then sank onto the down comforter. She could pretend that she'd never received the message, but by morning, Malik would be blowing up her cell until he confirmed that she was on that plane.

With a sigh, she stood and found Brian's card in her purse. Her fingers caressed the raised letters of his name, then she tore the card into tiny pieces. As the paper bits floated toward the waste container, Jasmine said, "Consider yourself lucky, Miss Alexis."

Chapter 9

J asmine *covered her mouth*, but she couldn't stifle the yawn as she rolled her bag toward security. She'd just fallen asleep when Malik called.

"Yes, Malik, I'll be on the plane, but what's the emergency?" she'd asked.

She'd been shocked when he told her he needed her for a dinner meeting with the Web designers.

"Malik, you can handle that," she'd said, already trying to imagine how she could piece together Brian's business card.

"I don't know a darn thing about computers. I need you here with me."

He'd gone on to remind her that the club would be opening in two months and they were already behind.

Now, as she waited at the gate, she leaned against the wall, silently begging the attendants to start loading the plane.

"It's pretty early to be at the airport, huh?"

Her gaze moved toward a man standing next to her. He smiled. She didn't. She hated people like him—those who had no difficulty stretching their lips into a grin before the sun even began its daily ascent.

Jasmine pretended she hadn't heard him. She wasn't even thinking about starting a conversation. In her mind, her trip to New York was already planned. First, she would sleep straight through to Chicago. Next, she would crawl to her connecting flight and then repeat the process, not opening her eyes until she landed in New York.

"We are ready to board Flight Sixty-seven to Chicago. Our first-class passengers can board at this time."

The announcement was barely finished before Jasmine was handing her boarding pass to the attendant. And not many more minutes passed before she was in her window seat, eyes closed.

"Today must be my day."

She peeked through one eye, and groaned. The same I'm-happy-even-before-the-crack-of-dawn man who'd tried to add cheer to her morning in the boarding area smiled at her. She pasted a get-out-of-my-space sneer onto her face and closed her eyes.

"I guess it's early for you," the man said. "I get the message."

Obviously, you don't.

"This will be a good flight to catch some shut-eye," he continued as if she were listening.

If you don't shut up . . .

"I'll probably try to do the same," he inserted as if she cared.

Jasmine squeezed her eyes shut even tighter.

"Hey, do you want—"

Jasmine rose up in her seat. "Would you mind?" she snapped.

He grinned. "I was just going to ask if you wanted one of these." He offered her a pillow.

She didn't want to take it, but sleep would come easier if she did. She tried not to snatch the pillow from his hand. "Thank you."

Before he responded her eyes were closed. By the time the plane took flight, Jasmine was fast asleep. But soon, she was startled from her rest. With widened eyes, she listened. It sounded like a saw scratching against wood. She peeked out the window, half-expecting to see a wing falling off, or the engine falling out.

She heard it again. The saw and the wood. She turned. To the man next to her. The one who couldn't stop talking. The one who was now sleeping. And snoring, sounding like a lumberjack with a point to prove.

She twisted toward the window, trying to find that comfortable space again. But the sounds of the saw and the wood tortured her, keeping her from rest.

She sighed loudly, hoping to wake the man.

Nothing.

She turned and pushed her elbow into his side.

Nothing.

She hit him again with hopes to rouse him or hurt him.

Nothing.

Now she wished she'd stayed awake and talked to him. Anything would have been better than this misery.

She raised her finger to the passing attendant.

"May I help—," before the woman could finish, the man let out a snore so loud, it startled them.

They both stared at him for a moment before Jasmine begged, "Any chance I can change seats?"

There was sympathy in her eyes. "There are no more seats in first class, but there are a few in coach," the attendant offered.

"No," Jasmine said as if she had never sat anywhere beyond row three in an airplane. "How long before we land?"

The attendant twisted her lips as if she hated to give Jasmine this news. "In about three hours."

Three hours. Well, she'd just sleep on the connecting flight.

Jasmine grabbed her *Essence* from her briefcase and flipped through the pages, but not a story could keep her attention. Her mind was on Brian Lewis. As she skimmed through the magazine, she pretended that he'd stayed at the club last night. Imagined that they'd left de Janeiro together. And wished that she had never thrown away his card.

◆ ◆ ◆

The moment the jet hit the ground, the man awakened.

"Wow," he said, twisting out of his sleep. "I must have been tired."

"Must have been," Jasmine mumbled.

"I was knocked out."

"I wanted to knock you out," she grumbled.

"Huh?"

She said nothing.

As he grabbed his suitcase from the overhead compartment, he asked, "Did you sleep well?"

She glared at him. "Can't say that I slept at all."

"Oh." His tone made her believe that he knew why. Like he knew he'd tortured thousands of passengers before. And that made her angrier.

She tossed the blanket onto the floor, and stood.

He said, "You're in a hurry?"

"Yes."

"Well, have a great time, wherever you're going," his words floated over her shoulders as she rushed away.

She marched toward her connecting gate, but she moaned the moment she arrived at B-7 and she read the ticker message. The counter was surrounded by passengers.

"How late is this plane going to be?" one man asked.

The Delta employee shrugged. "I don't know. All I know is there's a mechanical problem."

"Well, I don't wanna get on no plane that ain't working," an elderly woman said before she wobbled away.

Jasmine waited, tapped her foot until she stood alone. "I really have to get to New York. Isn't there anything you can do?" Jasmine asked.

"The flight is delayed," the woman repeated the same words she'd spoken to everyone else.

"I know that," Jasmine said. "But isn't there something you can do?"

The girl raised her eyebrows. "What? You want me to

go out there with a hammer and nails and fix the plane myself?"

"What she means," a voice said over Jasmine's shoulder, "is do you know how we can get on another flight?"

Jasmine started to turn, wanting to ask what was this *we* stuff, but she kept quiet. If this stranger had a plan, she wanted to know it.

"Yes, that's what I mean," she said before she looked at the one who'd spoken.

Punishment was the only word that came to her mind when she realized it was the man who had given her that snoring symphony. She wanted nothing to do with him, his favors, or his snoring.

The man said, "I'm a Premier Executive member of Delta." He spoke with a smile. "Maybe you can get us on another flight."

There was that *us* again.

The attendant rolled her weary eyes and shrugged. "You can go to Customer Service."

"Thank you." He turned to Jasmine. "Come on. I've got some connections here in Chicago." He reached for her bag, but she tightened her grasp around the handle. With raised eyebrows, he said, "I can get us on another flight. Or would you rather stay here for another hour or three before they decide to cancel this flight completely?"

She considered taking her chances. But then she remembered Malik and his desperate call.

I can't believe I'm doing this, she thought as she followed him.

"I fly a lot," he said. "This happens way too much, but I know what to do."

What am I doing? This man could be a terrorist.

"With God's favor, we'll be in New York in no time."

His words made her pause. *God's favor?*

As he spoke to the woman at the Customer Service desk, Jasmine stood to the side. Studied him.

Although she liked the dimples that were carved deep into

his smoked-almond-colored skin, he was not her type. The slight gap between his front teeth made his smile endearing enough, but his opened jacket revealed a bit of a skin roll that hung heavy over his pants. And if she were wearing her normal heels she'd be looking him straight in the eye. Definitely not her type.

"Did you hear me?"

She'd been staring, not listening. "What?"

"Give me your boarding pass."

She handed him the card and stepped closer to the counter.

"Okay," the woman said, tapping into a computer. "You're going into Kennedy instead of La Guardia and that flight leaves," she paused and looked at her watch, "in fifteen minutes. You two need to get moving."

Jasmine nodded, relieved.

"And congratulations again." The lady giggled as she handed the man two boarding passes.

"Why did she congratulate us?" Jasmine asked trotting beside the man.

He grinned. "I told her we were getting married."

"What?" Jasmine stopped walking.

"You'd better come on, wifey," he said. "We don't have much time."

She hurried behind him. "Why would you tell her that?"

"She could only find one first-class seat. But when I explained that we were on our way to our wedding, suddenly there was a flight with two seats—both first class," he huffed, the slow run taking his breath away.

Jasmine wasn't sure whether to be relieved that she wouldn't be spending hours in Chicago, or to cry because she'd be sitting next to him.

"I hope you don't mind my saying that, Jasmine."

"How do you know my name?"

"Don't you think I should know the name of the woman I'm going to marry?" When she didn't smile, he said, "Your boarding pass."

It wasn't until they were settled and the plane's door had closed that Jasmine said, "Thank you."

He gave her one of his high-voltage smiles again and then handed her a pillow and blanket. "Your turn," he said. "I promise to stay awake."

As much as she fought it, she smiled.

When the plane reached cruising altitude, an attendant stopped at their seats. "Congratulations." She beamed.

He smiled; Jasmine frowned.

"We heard you're off to New York to get married."

"Yes," he said, taking Jasmine's hand. "We are so happy."

Jasmine looked down to where his fingers entwined with hers. The band of his watch glittered. When she looked back at him, she noticed the fake diamond in his ear. It was so small, she wondered why he bothered. Her frown deepened. She hated costume jewelry.

The stewardess said, "Let us know if there is anything we can do for you." She grinned as if she were really looking at about-to-be newlyweds.

"Okay, since we're pulling this little charade, don't you think we should introduce ourselves?" Jasmine whispered.

He shrugged and melted her again with his smile. "I know all I need to know. You're Jasmine Larson, and if you let me help you with your bags when we land in New York, I'll have your address or phone number from your luggage tag. I only need one to be able to find you."

"How do you know I live in New York?"

"I don't, but that doesn't matter. You could live in Alaska and I'd still find you. I've got skills."

She couldn't help it; she laughed. "Since you know my name, shouldn't you tell me yours?"

He leaned onto the seat divider bringing his smile closer to her. "Do you want to know now or should we wait for our first date?"

She laughed again. *Like that would ever happen.* "You're sure of yourself, aren't you?"

He nodded. "I'm loaded with confidence."

"Tell me your name now," she said. "This way, I'll know it's you when you call."

"So, you *are* going to give me your number."

"No, you can use those skills you talked about."

He laughed.

"So, what's your name?" she asked.

"Hosea." He paused and glanced over his shoulder. "I'd shake your hand, but we're supposed to know each other."

"Nice to meet you, Hosea."

"So, Ms. Jasmine, are you returning home, or are you going to New York for something else?"

She looked at him for a moment, wondering if he was the reason for her fading exhaustion. "I live in New York, but I'm actually rushing back for a meeting."

"Sounds like my story."

"What is it that you do?"

"Well, let's see," he said, then paused. "I'm in television."

Television. She almost laughed. She could look at him and tell what he did "in television." Probably sold TVs at Circuit City.

She pulled the blanket over her. "Let's make a deal."

"What's that?"

"If I get to sleep on this flight, I'll give you my number when we land."

He smiled. "Done deal."

Even though she wasn't as tired anymore, she closed her eyes. She'd give him her number—or at least seven digits that she'd choose arbitrarily.

She snuggled into the leather seat and allowed her mind to take her into slumber.

Chapter 10

Jasmine couldn't believe she was actually getting up for church. She'd been only an hour late for the Friday meeting, but she and Malik had talked with the Web designers until well past midnight. Then on Saturday she'd spent the day providing the company with all that they needed. By the time they'd left the office last night with promises to have the first drafts within a week, Jasmine had walked out right behind them, exhausted from work and jet lag.

Today should have been a day of mindless television with catnaps in between. But instead, Jasmine swung her legs over the side of the bed, determined to keep that long-ago promise to God never to miss church. How else would she get on God's good side? An almost perfect attendance record had to be a plus when He looked at her whole balance sheet.

But today, church had little to do with God. Today, was about exacting revenge. Reverend Bush was going to be sorry that he hadn't seen just how right she'd been for him.

With the reverend still on her mind, she flipped through the hangers in her closet. Her choice had to be on point, something to appeal to his conservatism, yet something to remind him that he was a man—who had just missed out.

She chose a navy suit that ended right above the knee, and then slipped into a pink satin camisole that cut low into a deep

V onto her chest. She chuckled as she imagined Reverend Bush trying to keep his eyes on her face when she greeted him in the after-service reception line.

Within the hour, her taxi stopped, just as Malik jumped from his cab.

"Hey," she greeted her godbrother. He took her hand as they entered the church and together, they sauntered down the aisle. Brother Hill welcomed Malik with the same smile he gave to everyone, but when he looked at her, she saw something different. The way he jutted his chin forward and returned her smirk, she knew he felt he'd had his victory. Last week, she wanted to pimp-slap him. But today, it didn't even matter.

When the choir began to sing, Jasmine stood and swayed with the rest of the worshippers. She could feel Malik's quick glance when Reverend Bush walked onto the platform, but she stayed focused on the praise singers. She'd have to tell Malik that she no longer cared about that man. She was sure she'd still be married next year; Reverend Bush just wouldn't be the man standing by her side.

"Now, everyone, I have a special surprise today," Reverend Bush said as soon as the choir sang their last note. "I cannot tell you how pleased I am, how excited I am."

It wasn't until this moment that Jasmine realized this wasn't going to be as easy as she'd expected. The sound of his voice brought back his harsh words. The sight of him brought back the desires she'd held.

"With the exception of my birthday two years ago, it's been a long time since I've shared the pulpit with anyone in my family. But today is a new day." He chuckled.

"Amen," someone shouted.

The reverend continued, "Today, someone is back. Back in New York. Back in the pulpit," he sang the last words.

"Hallelujah," another voice rang out.

"What's he talking about?" Jasmine whispered.

Malik shrugged.

"I could stand here for hours and tell you the virtues of this man." He laughed. "But that would take too long and like any good meal, I'd rather go straight for the meat." Most of the congregation joined in his laughter. "Brothers and sisters, join me in welcoming my son, Minister Hosea Samuel Bush."

The cheers were instant and deafening. While most around her stood, Jasmine sat, and tapped her hands in light applause. So, his son was visiting. She had to keep her yawn inside.

Then she heard him. Heard him before she saw him.

"Hello, City of Lights," his voice boomed from the podium.

The cheers grew louder. The drummer drummed, the pianist played a few chords.

Slowly Jasmine stood.

When the clapping ceased, the reverend's son said, "I cannot tell you how happy I am to be back. And I'm here to stay, ready to stand by my father's side."

The applause began again, but Jasmine couldn't do anything more than stare. After minutes of keeping her eyes trained on the speaker, she was sure. It was him. The man who had helped her at the airport. The man who snored. The man to whom she'd given a bogus telephone number.

Reverend Bush was back at the altar. "Now I know my son won't tell you what's been going on," he said, still beaming. "But I can brag on him. Some big things are happening," he exclaimed as he clapped his hands. "You already know that he's become a licensed minister while he's been in Chicago. And he's going to be heading up the Teen Outreach Program for us with our new community center."

Choruses of "Amen" and "Hallelujah" rang through the sanctuary.

Reverend Bush continued, "But the Lord has opened up a bigger door. Hosea was selected by NBC to host *Bring It On,* the new hip-hop Christian talk show."

Applause exploded through the sanctuary again.

I'm in television, the explanation he'd given to her on the plane, rushed back to her.

The words that were spoken now from the pulpit floated over her, past her. Nothing connected. Only her eyes worked. She stared at Hosea and today saw his tailored suit that looked as expensive as the one his father wore. And in the pulpit, he didn't seem to be as overweight as she remembered. She recalled the glint of the gem in his ear and the glimmer of the stones on his watch. Probably not rhinestones, like she'd thought the other day.

Jasmine slowly took her seat, but her mind continued to move, calculate, evaluate. Hosea Samuel Bush. He *was* in television. And he was a minister. And he was Reverend Samuel Bush's son.

Her glance moved between the two men. She would never have thought he'd have a son that old, although she didn't know his age. But age—what did it matter? She could be any age she needed to be.

Jasmine crossed her legs and smiled. How poetic was this justice? This had to be God's way of letting her know she was on the right mission: she was supposed to be married—to a pastor—with the last name of Bush.

As the service continued through the offering and the sermon, Jasmine kept her eyes on Hosea Samuel Bush. As he spoke, she listened, needing to glean all that was important to him. As he sat, she watched his movements, his gestures, his eyes.

And when he looked into the congregation and blessed them all with his smile, her affection grew. By the time Jasmine stood with the rest of the congregation for the benediction, she was sure. This was the day she'd fallen in love—for real, this time.

Chapter 11

*J*asmine's eyes were on the prize.

She stood alone in the reception line, glad that Malik had rushed to a meeting right after the benediction. Gave her time to focus on the reverend's son, without any questions from her godbrother.

She still couldn't fathom this. Even though she'd watched him for two hours, it was hard to believe: Hosea Bush was Reverend Bush's son. And the new host of *Bring It On*. This program was the talk on all the entertainment shows. It may have been pegged as a Christian show, but it was the hip-hop factor that had everyone interested. Hosea would be hosting the show with Triage Blue, a P. Diddy protégé, and Magdalene, known as a hip-hop princess with an inspirational twist.

She wasn't yet in front of him when his eyes met hers. At first, recognition, then confusion, next surprise. By the time his smile was back, she was holding his hand.

"Remember me?" she asked, fluttering her eyelashes.

"How could I forget?" He paused, widening his smile. "What are you doing here?" She noticed that he was still holding her hand. "Did you come to welcome me back to City of Lights?"

She shook her head. "I just started coming here and was surprised by Reverend Bush's announcement this morning."

"So that's why you're here. I would've thought you'd come to apologize for giving me that bogus telephone number."

Silently, she cursed, but aloud, she said, "What are you talking about?" She frowned as if she were confused.

"Uh, son," Reverend Bush interrupted. "You have a line of people waiting." Although Reverend Bush kept his welcoming expression, his eyes told Jasmine that he was not pleased with whatever she was doing.

"Jasmine, can you wait for me?" Hosea asked.

"Sure." She was glad to have the time—to come up with some story about that fake telephone number.

Jasmine sank into the front pew and watched Hosea greeting, smiling, chatting as if he were used to that position. Almost a half an hour passed before Hosea whispered to his father and then motioned to her. Even from feet away, Jasmine could see Reverend Bush's concern. She hoped that Hosea wouldn't see it too, but then again, it didn't matter. There was nothing the father could do. The son was a grown man.

Her smile was waiting when he walked over.

"So, we meet again," he said.

"I'm glad."

"Are you?"

"Of course. I enjoyed talking to you on the plane."

His laugh was so infectious she laughed with him. Finally he said, "I tried to call you yesterday."

She was too proficient in the game to even blink. "Really?" She tilted her head. "I didn't get any messages."

His smirk told her that he was willing to play along. "I didn't leave one."

"I wish you had. But this must be fate. We were supposed to meet."

He nodded and his eyes seared through her. The intensity of his glance swept away her smile. Finally, he spoke, "I don't believe in fate. But God's divine intervention . . . that's something different."

His words were as strong as his glance; after only seconds, she had to turn away.

"So, are we going to get together?" he asked, breaking the silence, easing the tension.

"I'd like that," she said, facing him again.

"What about now?"

She raised her eyebrows, surprised at his offer. Over his shoulder, she watched Brother Hill whisper to Reverend Bush and then both of their glances turned toward her and Hosea. "Are you sure it's okay with your father?"

He turned toward the men. "Oh, I forgot." He grinned. "You make me forget things." He laughed again. "So, let's do it this way." From his wallet, he handed her a card. "Call me later and we'll set something up."

"Okay, and let me give you my number too."

He held up his hands. "No, we tried that. This time it's on you."

That was fine with her. He was just making her plan easier. "I'll call you tonight."

He took her hand into his. "I'm looking forward to it." He lifted her hand to his lips, then suddenly turned it over, kissing her palm. Sparks charged right through her and she hoped he couldn't see the way she shook.

She stood in place until Hosea strolled to his father and Brother Hill, and the three men walked from the sanctuary.

It still took a moment for Jasmine's legs to steady. Finally, with slow steps, she walked from the church. *What just happened?* she asked herself. She still trembled at the way his lips felt against her hand.

But by the time she stood on the corner and flagged a cab, Jasmine had gained her composure. She reminded herself that this was her pursuit, her game. And very soon, Hosea Bush would know that too.

Chapter 12

It *couldn't have been* more than thirty degrees outside, but thoughts of Hosea warmed her. She'd asked the cab driver to let her out on Sixty-third Street, wanting to walk the rest of the twenty blocks. The fresh air helped her think, gave her time to work through the plan.

She'd walked only one block before a car eased to the curb and stopped.

"Hello, Jasmine Larson."

Everything made her smile today. "Mae Frances."

"Why are you walking? It's too cold. Get in."

This was not what she wanted. But Gerald was already out, opening the back door. She slid inside.

"Are you heading home?"

Jasmine nodded, and eyed the glass in Mae Frances's hand.

"I didn't know you were back from your trip," Mae Frances said.

"I came back on Friday." Brian's image flashed through her head. But she shook that vision away. The only man she wanted in her mind's eye was Hosea.

When Mae Frances saw Jasmine glance at her glass again, she said, "Just a little something to take off the chill. Do you want a drink?" Mae Frances motioned to the mini bar along the side of the car.

"Oh, no," Jasmine said.

Mae Frances eyes narrowed. "So, you're one of those?"

Her words took Jasmine's smile away. "One of those what?"

"Health nuts. Thinking it's not good to drink. But I tell you, there's nothing wrong with a little wine." She held up her glass as if she were making a toast.

"Oh, I'm not a health nut," Jasmine said. "I'm a Christian."

Mae Frances stared. Then leaned back and laughed. "Now, I would have never pegged you for one of those." She paused and took a sip of her drink. "A Christian, huh?" She shook her head.

Jasmine's eyebrows raised and Mae Frances held up her hand. "Don't get offended. I just never thought that word would come from your mouth."

"Okay," Jasmine began through narrowed eyes, "so what are you? Catholic?"

Mae Frances laughed again. "Isn't that the same thing? Christian, Catholic, Protestant, Baptist, hypocrite. All the same, right?"

Jasmine folded her arms across her chest, pushed back her feelings. "So what are you?"

"If you're asking what religious group I belong to, I can tell you I'm not one of those narrow-minded charlatans. I don't belong to any group. Unless you call atheism a religion."

It took a moment for Jasmine to say, "You don't believe in God?"

"Not. At. All."

She didn't know what to say. Jasmine thought every black person believed in God—especially someone as old as Mae Frances. Even during her wildest days when she didn't want any part of church, Jasmine knew God existed. Had always known. From the first time her mother and father told her.

"I guess I offended you," Mae Frances said. "I didn't mean to do that."

"You didn't." Jasmine shrugged as if Mae Frances's words

meant nothing. But she couldn't explain why sadness washed over her. "I'm just surprised. I don't understand how someone can say they don't believe in God. I mean, all you have to do is look at everything around you."

"Child, that's how I know there ain't no God. Please." She waved her hand in the air as if she were erasing Jasmine's words. "If there were a God, there wouldn't be all this home-lessness and disease and death in the world. If there was a real God, people wouldn't be killing one another in His name." She paused and finished the rest of her wine. "I'm telling you, if there is a God, then He needs to be fired because He's sure doing a piss-poor job."

The words shocked her, but Jasmine said nothing. She didn't know what to say, but she knew what she felt—pity. If Mae Frances didn't believe in God, what did she believe in?

The silent minutes that rested between them seemed longer and Jasmine released the breath she'd been holding when the car stopped in front of their building. She wanted to jump out and run, far away from this woman. But she waited as Gerald opened the door, and together, she and Mae Frances stepped into the building.

"Good afternoon," Henrikas greeted them.

While Mae Frances paused to question the doorman, Jasmine rushed to the elevator. But quickly she realized there would be no escape.

"Hold the elevator," Mae Frances called out. Once the door closed behind them, she asked, "So, Jasmine Larson, does this mean we're no longer friends?"

"No," she said. But it wasn't like Mae Frances was a friend; she was just a neighbor with some good chicken and a limou-sine.

"Good, because I think the best friends are ones whose opinions differ." As they stepped from the elevator, she added, "And maybe I can teach you a thing or two about that God you believe in. Turn you in the right direction."

I don't think so, Jasmine thought. She may not have been the best Christian, but she certainly knew what she believed. All she had to do was look at how her life had changed since God had become part of it. She was in New York and she'd met the man she was going to marry. No one could change her mind about God. She paused at her door and turned to her neighbor. "Thanks for the ride."

Before Mae Frances could respond, she wobbled, then fell against the wall.

Jasmine ran to her side, helped her to stand. "Are you all right?"

It took a moment for Mae Frances to nod. "Yeah."

"I'll help you inside. Give me your key."

"No, I'm fine." Seconds later, Mae Frances pulled her body erect, like nothing happened. "It's just the wine. Probably had a bit too much." She took the few steps to her door slowly, and inserted the key. "Thank you, Jasmine Larson." Then, she was gone.

Jasmine waited a moment, then stepped into her own apartment. Her thoughts stayed on Mae Frances, and her words about God. And all over again, she felt sorry for the woman.

She lay on her bed and clicked on the television. As a Lifetime movie played mutely in front of her, thoughts of Mae Frances faded—making room for ones of Hosea Bush.

With her eyes closed, she imagined. Took herself to next year at this time. Having a new husband. Living a new life. Being in New York couldn't be any better than this.

Jasmine was eager.

Not so much for the man, but for the plan. But it was only because she would never show it that she waited until ten to make the call; he needed to believe that her day was filled with more than just thoughts of him. He answered on the first ring.

"Talk to me, Jasmine," he answered.

She couldn't help herself; she smiled. "How did you know it was me?"

"It was either you or my pops since you're the only two people who have this new number. And, I just hung up from him."

"It could have been your father calling back."

"True, but I was sure it was you. Because I knew you'd call; you weren't going to mess up this good thing twice."

She laughed and, not for the first time, marveled at his confidence. Hosea didn't fit the physical attributes of what a woman would call fine. Being kind, he was average, pleasant enough to look at. But there was something in the way he walked, even more in the way he talked that made this man as attractive as any she'd known.

"So, did you spend the day with your father?"

"Yeah, Pops and I hung out. He's glad that I'm home."

Jasmine wondered what words of wisdom Reverend Bush had given his son—about her. Would he tell him about her pursuit? Would Brother Hill provide insight into her psyche with his flat tire theory?

But she kissed those concerns good-bye. If Reverend Bush came close to mentioning her name in a not-so-flattering vain, she was ready with an answer that would make him look like a jealous old fool. And Jasmine knew in just a few weeks, what the senior Bush might say wouldn't matter. Hosea's nose would be so wide open that he'd surrender all rights to his father's inheritance to be with her.

Jasmine giggled.

"What's so funny?" Hosea asked.

Her thoughts had taken her far away. "I was thinking who would have thought we'd ever be talking like this."

"I thought it! Remember I asked for your number, but you gave me some fake—"

"Okay, okay."

"So, you admit it?"

"Yes, and I'm sorry."

"I guess I could forgive you. A woman like you probably

has all kinds of guys asking for her number. But you really hurt my feelings." He sniffed playfully.

"Well, I want to make it up to you. Let's have dinner."

"Just what I was thinking."

"At my place."

"Not what I was thinking."

Jasmine frowned. "I'll have you know I can whip up a mean meal."

"Darlin', I'm sure you have many talents. But that's not the way I roll. We'll go out."

Jasmine wasn't sure how to play this. The plan was to get Hosea to her apartment, seduce him, then return him home begging for the next time. He needed to remember this first date, this first time.

But this twist also worked. She'd learn the depths of his pockets and how deep he was willing to go for her.

He said, "How about next Wednesday?"

Jasmine frowned. Hosea was moving as if this plan was his. Her timetable was sooner, like tomorrow. But he was talking ten days away.

He explained, "I've got a busy couple of weeks. I'm going out of town with my pops to one of his friend's church's anniversary and then when I get back, I'll be swamped with meetings. You know the drill—producers, sponsors. The whole TV thing."

"That TV thing has got to be so exciting." She tried not to gush, but it was difficult. It wouldn't be long before Hosea was known throughout the country and she was going to be part of all of that.

"At first, it was pretty cool," he said. "But over the past weeks, it's clear that there's more work than glamour in this. Anyway, let's save this talk for dinner." By the time he told her that he'd call next week to finalize plans, he'd made her laugh again and again.

She hung up with a grin and then pulled back her cheer. This was still a mission. She couldn't lose control. Had to keep her eyes, and every other part of herself, on the prize.

Chapter 13

osea had said, "Just wear jeans," when he'd called last night to confirm. "Be ready for a night of surprises."

She wanted to be annoyed that he hadn't called her in the week that passed. But when he mentioned "surprises," that had made her beam. Although she didn't know what to make of his pronouncement to "just wear jeans." After the big deal he'd made about not having dinner in her apartment, she'd expected to stroll into one of New York's premiere restaurants—certainly not wearing jeans.

Maybe it's because he's been in Chicago, Jasmine thought. Maybe casual clothes were okay there, but this was New York. She'd have to school him. Actually, that was just one of the lessons she was prepared to teach.

Even though her days had been filled with long hours working with the designers for Rio, at night she'd allowed herself the luxury of dreaming. Her plan had now moved to her wedding: the gown, the reception, the gifts. All of the images made her dizzy with excitement. The son, with his potential, far surpassed the father. From what she'd discovered on Google, NBC had big plans for Hosea Bush. And so did she.

But before they got there, much had to be done. Her number-one charge was to get him into bed, love him until he begged for more. Then, she would go about changing him, creating the man she knew he could be. The extra pounds would have to go. A visit to the dentist would fix those bottom teeth that were just a tad crooked. By the time she finished, he would be a fine specimen. And it would begin tonight.

Jasmine took a final look in the mirror. She had followed Hosea's directions and put on a pair of jeans—designer ones. But it was the silk tunic and her mink that would get them into the restaurant if anyone denied them access. And if she had to, she'd throw out Malik's name.

Jasmine was drunk with anticipation as she flagged a cab. Years from now, she and Hosea would talk about this, their first night together. She had no doubt, the next hours were going to be spectacular.

Spectacular was not the word.

"You sure you're all right with this?" Hosea asked.

Jasmine nodded, because she wouldn't be convincing if she spoke that lie aloud. She kept her lips pressed together. Here she was, in the dead of winter, in the middle of Manhattan, standing on the corner of Fifty-ninth and Columbus Circle. The last rush-hour pedestrians dashed by, covered in weighty overcoats, heads bowed, on their missions to get anywhere quickly.

But as others scuttled past, Jasmine and Hosea stood in front of a corner stand, complete with the yellow awning, the smell of freshly baked pretzels and chestnuts filling the air.

"Thanks," Hosea said to the man as he grabbed the cardboard tray filled with three hot dogs.

She could not believe this. Her first hours with the man she'd chosen as her husband were going to be spent eating hot dogs on a New York City street.

"Let's sit over there." Hosea motioned with his chin toward a park bench.

The heels of her Manolo boots clicked against the concrete

as she hobbled toward the bench. She paused before she sat, eyeing the wood for stains or stray dirt that would mess up her mink.

"Wait a sec." Hosea handed the tray to Jasmine, dumped the backpack he'd carried onto the bench, and pulled out two stadium cushions. He adjusted them in place, and motioned for her to sit down.

She sat, looked around, and wondered what she was doing here.

He sat, grinned, and handed her one of the wax-paper-wrapped hot dogs. "Are you sure you're all right with this?"

She nodded, but this time, she didn't even bother to look at him. She was beyond annoyed, and in her mind she told him so. But her wits kept her silent. A lesser woman would have huffed away, telling Hosea to lose her number. But she was Jasmine Larson. She never forgot the ultimate objective.

"This is my favorite part of the city," he said before he took a bite that consumed almost half of his hot dog. "I love these things," he said, holding up the half that was left as if it were an offering to God. "And I love this place," he added. His eyes scanned the park behind them. "I thought this would be fun since it's been warm."

"You call this warm?" Jasmine pulled her coat tighter.

"You don't see any snow on the ground, do you?" He chuckled and placed his hot dog on the carton. This time when he reached into his bag, he grabbed a blanket. He whipped it in the air like a bed sheet, then rested it on Jasmine's lap. "I didn't think you'd need this until later, but maybe this will help." He paused. "Better?"

She hated the cold. Hated sitting on the park bench. Hated eating hot dogs and calling it dinner. But the way he looked at her, his face filled with concern and hope—this part she loved.

"Yeah. Thanks." But her smile turned upside down as he stuffed the other half of the oversized frankfurter into his mouth. Then he unwrapped the second one as if it were a Christmas gift.

"You don't like yours?" he asked when he noticed her staring.

"It's okay." She took a small bite.

After a moment, he said, "Okay, let me explain. I spent hours trying to think of something for us to do . . ."

You actually thought this through.

He said, "I was thinking no one else had ever taken you out like this before."

She couldn't help it; she laughed. "You got that right."

"So, see, at least part of my plan worked."

She stopped her chuckles. *Plan?*

He said, "At least I'm making an impression. I want you to always remember this first time."

She thought about how similar his words were to her thoughts.

He asked, "So, are you from New York?"

"No," she said, then paused. She wasn't ready to give him much more. First, she wanted to know the details of his life. Then, she'd arrange her life's résumé to be his perfect wife. But she continued, "I'm from Los Angeles, although I made a short two-year stop in Florida. I've only been here about a month."

"So, I guess you haven't seen much of the city."

She shook her head. "Work has taken up most of my time. Not that I would know where to go, because I know about two people here."

"Well, now you know me. I'll show you the city and everything that makes New Yorkers sing right along with Frank Sinatra. That'll be our second date."

Her eyebrows raised high. "Confident, aren't you?"

He leaned in closer. "I knew you'd go out with me all along. Even if you did try to mess with destiny and give me that bogus number."

She laughed, even as he shoved the last of his second hot dog into his mouth. He asked, "Do you want another one?"

She shook her head, and glanced around again. They hadn't been sitting long, but the crowd had thinned as the hour approached seven. As the nighttime wind stirred around Fifty-ninth Street, Hosea packed the cushions and blankets, took her hand, and led her to the corner where the aroma of chest-nuts roasting on the open fire filled her.

As they waited at the curb, she asked, "Where are we going now?"

He shook his head. "I told you this would be an evening of surprises. Can't tell you a thing."

The words had barely left his lips before a horse-driven car-riage stopped in front of them. The man, covered in a black overcoat and wearing a top hat, nodded.

"Right on time," Hosea said.

Jasmine glanced at Hosea before he helped her climb the high steps. For the weeks she'd been in New York, she'd watched men and women snuggle close as wagons dragged by horses carted them around the city. It was a tourist activity that she couldn't wait to do—but not now. Not in February when the barely-thirty-degrees day had quickly turned into frigid winter night.

Hosea sat next to her and this time, when he reached into his bag, he withdrew two blankets, resting one on her lap and the other he sprawled across her shoulders. "Okay, Franklin," he said once they were settled.

The carriage lurched forward, then steadied as the horse trotted. "Are you warm enough?" he asked.

Surprisingly, she was. "Yeah."

He laid his arms across the top edge of the seat. She waited for his embrace, but when he didn't move, she leaned back, resting on his chest, snuggling close.

For long minutes, they stayed quiet, absorbing the flavor of the city.

"It's so good to be home," Hosea said.

"How long have you been away?"

"About ten years. Right after I graduated from NYU." His sigh was full of memories. "But I'm back and ready to begin this phase of my life. And I want to do it in the only place I've ever really called home."

Silently, she calculated. Ten years after college, that would make Hosea thirty-two, thirty-three. He was a bit younger than she expected, but she could be whatever age she needed to be.

She said, "You sound like you're really excited about being back."

"I am. This city means a lot to me. It's where I learned about love—from my parents, from God. It's where I learned about family."

"It's where your new show is going to be."

"Yeah, but that's work." His tone dismissed her words. "All that's really important is family, friends, and living and loving every day. I want to create the kind of life my mom and dad had."

When his father was the object of her affection, Jasmine never wondered about his wife. But now, she wanted to know about Hosea's mother.

"Tell me about your mom."

He stiffened. Waited, then said, "What does every man think about the woman who gave him life? I don't even have the words to describe her, except to say that she was wonderful and I loved her so much. I was devastated when she passed away."

"Had she been sick?"

He shook his head. "No, died suddenly my last year in college. From a blood clot." He paused as if he needed a moment to continue. "It took a while for me to recover. I was pissed at my pops."

Hmmm. She filed that information away.

"That's why I went to Chicago. Wanted to put as many miles between me and my pops as my bank account allowed." He chuckled. "Only got me to the Windy City."

"You've been there ever since?"

"Yup, thought I could hide from Pops and God." He chuckled again. "I didn't see Pops often, but God," he shook his head, "He never went away. Before I knew it, I was working with one of my pops' seminary buddies in Crystal Lake. Became a minister and then ended up hosting that TV show."

"Christian Times," Jasmine said, glad that she'd Googled him.

"Yeah." She heard his smile. "So you know a little something about me?"

"A little something-something," she kidded. "Would you have come back to New York if you didn't have the TV show?"

"Definitely. I was on my way back. God just opened this door with NBC." He paused as the carriage rounded the corner. "I need New York. I need to be closer to my pops and strangely enough, this is where I feel closest to my mom. When I'm here, I feel like I saw her yesterday."

"I just lost my dad." Those words were out before she could stop them.

"Are you okay?"

She nodded. "Coming to New York was good for me. Gives me a chance to start over."

"I want to start over here too." He paused, and added, "Just like you."

When she rested her head on his shoulder, it wasn't part of her plan. She'd expected him to put his arms around her this time, but still he didn't. Not that it mattered—with the plans she had for him, he'd be holding her soon enough.

For long minutes, the urban hum entertained them: cars honking, pedestrians chatting, engines revving, music blasting—the melody of New York.

She asked where he lived. He told her that he was staying in one of the houses that his father owned on Long Island. "Haven't had time to look for a place," he said. "Need some time to think about where I want to be in the city. But the most important question," he said, "is where do you live?"

She smiled, knowing what those words meant.

At the entrance to her building, Hosea jumped from the carriage, then lifted Jasmine down. She took her time getting her balance, wanting to keep his arms around her.

He followed her into the lobby, but when she looked behind her, the carriage was still at the curb.

"It's too cold for your friend to wait out there."

"He's fine. He knows I won't be long."

She chuckled inside. She didn't know what he expected, but her plan called for Hosea not to leave her until the dawn's early light.

At the elevator, she said, "I had a great time," really meaning her words.

"I'm glad."

It was supposed to be his cue, but when he didn't kiss her she wasn't surprised. He'd already shown that he preferred to display his affection in private.

She stepped inside the elevator; he didn't follow and her expression questioned him.

"I'm going to say good night." He looked around the lobby. "I think you're safe."

Her forehead creased with confusion. "You're not coming up with me?"

"No, definitely not. I only planned to drop you off, make sure you got to your door safely."

"That's it?" she asked, then lowered her voice as Henrikas turned toward them. She stepped from the elevator and pulled him to the side. "Did I do something wrong?"

He shook his head. "Why would you ask me that?"

"I thought we were enjoying each other and—" She stopped and both of their minds finished her sentence. Took them to the same place.

"Oh, no," he said so strongly, she stepped back a bit. "That's not how I roll."

This had to be a joke. But as seconds passed and he stood

stoic, her eyes narrowed. She held up her hands as if she were surrendering. "Enjoy the rest of your evening, Hosea." She stomped into the elevator. Didn't turn back. Just pressed the Close button until the doors obeyed.

Turned out that the son wasn't that different from the father.

"Maybe," she talked to herself, "this is a sign to leave these Bush men alone."

Still, her mind replayed the evening. Remembered the times they'd talked and the even better moments when they didn't.

When she reached her apartment, an emptiness that she hadn't experienced with the senior Bush blanketed her. But before an hour had passed, Jasmine traded the sadness for determination. Accepting defeat was not part of her DNA. "I just need another plan," she said. She would come up with something because she would never give up. She lived to play—and win—this game.

Chapter 14

The moment *she stepped* out of the meeting, Tina said, "Jasmine, you have a million messages."

"Oh, no," she moaned. "Who's calling now?" A mental checklist of the calls she was supposed to return was already lodged in her mind. This morning, her desk had been piled with urgent messages from construction workers, suppliers, and designers. And she even had a few from people already requesting invitations for the opening.

"It's not business," Tina whispered as she scurried behind Jasmine. "You've gotten a million calls from Hosea Bush!" She spoke his name as if he were a star.

With her eyebrows raised, Jasmine turned to Tina.

"He's called every ten minutes or so, even though I told him I would give you the message as soon as you were free."

"Did he say what he wanted?" Jasmine asked casually, although she felt her heart beat speed up. She had tossed all night, wondering why their evening had gone astray. Wondered if the senior Bush had said something to thwart her plan.

"All he said was that he wanted to talk to you. So," Tina said, and then sank into one of the chairs, "you know Hosea Bush."

"Yeah," Jasmine said.

"I love him," Tina gushed. "I watched him on cable and I can't wait for his new show. He's so funny, which is one of the reasons why I think he's so sexy. And he's so compassionate. And he so loves God," she panted. "And another thing," she lowered her voice, "he's not that hard to look at."

"I'll call him." Jasmine sighed as if that was the last thing she wanted to do. When Tina stayed in place, Jasmine added, "Would you mind closing the door on your way out?"

Tina stood. "I hope he comes to our opening. I'd love to meet him. He's single, isn't he?"

He's mine, Jasmine wanted to scream.

Once alone, Jasmine leaned back in her chair. She was relieved that he'd called. And so soon. And not once, not twice. She counted the sheets. Eight times.

She couldn't help her smile. He regretted missing out on the promise their night had held. He'd probably dreamed about what could have been.

She picked up the phone.

"I'm glad you called me back," he said after they exchanged hellos. "I was thinking that maybe you wouldn't after the way we left each other last night."

She said nothing.

"Anyway," he continued, "do you have some time this afternoon? Your assistant said your day was full, but I just need ten, fifteen minutes."

It surprised her again, that he was the one making the moves. It was her plan, but at times, it didn't feel that way.

She glanced at her desk. There was another stack of calls she had to return. In an hour she was supposed to be on-site with the club's designers, and give a final interview to the woman she hoped to hire as the club's floor manager.

But her most important project was on the phone.

She said, "I can meet now."

"Great," he sounded relieved. "Do you want me to come to your office?"

"Definitely not," she said, having no intention of dealing with the eyes and ears there.

It took no time to determine to meet at the meeting place of all quick meeting places—in thirty minutes they would meet at Starbucks on Twenty-third and Sixth.

Jasmine settled at one of the small tables jammed into the back of the coffee shop. She took a quick sip of her latte, then waved when Hosea rushed through the door. He bypassed the order line and made a beeline straight to her.

"Hey, you." He squeezed her hand.

It felt comfortable, natural, the way he greeted her. As if he hadn't left her last night wondering if they'd ever share the same space again.

He scanned the shop, packed almost to capacity even though they were in the between time, the hours between the morning dash and the lunch rush.

When he turned back to her, she whispered, "Don't worry. No one will be listening to us. This is New York and everyone in here is up to their cappuccinos with their own problems."

He chuckled. "You've figured out New Yorkers, huh?"

She shrugged. "I thought I did . . . until I met you."

The smile he'd worn faded and he leaned forward, his face just inches from hers. "I had a great time last night."

"It didn't seem that way."

"I'm sorry if you got the wrong impression, but I did enjoy being with you." He leaned back, took a deep breath as if he were inhaling strength. "There's something you need to know." He stopped again. "I'm living a sanctified life."

She frowned. She'd only heard two types of people use that word—ministers, and anyone who sang along with Sly and the Family Stone who "felt sanctified" back in the day. She had a good notion which group Hosea identified with most, but still she asked, "What does that mean?"

"I'm celibate. And I plan to stay that way."

Of all the things she'd imagined, "I'm celibate" were not the words she expected. She thought he was going to tell her that he prayed three times a day, or attended church every other night. But celibacy? She said, "Are you saying, you're . . . a virgin?"

He shook his head. "Can't say that." His eyes glazed over as if he harbored memories that held regrets. "But that's the way I'm living now. And it's been a couple of years, so I'm not about to mess up. I'm just going to wait."

"Oh."

When Jasmine said nothing more, he said, "I bet you haven't heard too many men say this before."

Men, no. Women, yes. She'd heard these words a lot from Serena, who was always talking about living holy. But these words from a man? She couldn't believe there were men who were celibate by choice.

As she sipped her coffee, she completed a quick scan of Hosea. Besides the few extra pounds, there was nothing wrong with him. So it was difficult to match those words with this man. Why would a healthy, able-bodied, apparently heterosexual man make a conscious decision not to have sex?

"So," she began finally, "you're celibate and you're waiting. Waiting for—"

"My wife."

The way he looked dead into her eyes put a lump in her throat. *This is my plan, my game,* she reassured herself.

He said, "When I find my wife I want to offer her a piece of me that no one has had." He shrugged and added, "At least no one has had in a long time."

Any other man, in any other place, would have been buckled over by now, laughing hysterically, waving his hands wildly, yelling, "Gotcha" through his chortles.

Then it occurred to her. Her eyes narrowed. "Does this have anything to do with your father?"

"Yes, with my Father in heaven."

"Oh, please," the words escaped before she could stop herself. "I mean," she began again, "do you really think God expects you not to have sex?"

"No, I think He expects that I will have plenty. And I plan to." He grinned. "Right after I get married. But for now, I'm trying to live my life so that it's pleasing to God."

Jasmine took another sip of her coffee, but inside, she chuckled. This man sounded just like her sister.

He asked, "So are you interested?"

"In what?"

"Courting."

She couldn't help it—she laughed.

"I'm serious," he said, although he smiled with her. "I'm not interested in casual dating, but courting, that's different."

"I've only heard old people use that word."

"Too bad, because we young folks should be the ones using it. Courting is just dating with a purpose, and that's what I want." He paused. "I'm interested in getting to know you better. I wanna see where this might lead."

She raised her eyebrows. "Are you saying you want to marry me?"

"No."

That word pushed her back against the chair.

"What I'm saying," he continued, "is that I'd like us to date . . . with a purpose."

She was glad for the little bit of coffee left in her cup that allowed her to take a long sip. She needed time to decide the best way to play this.

But before she could respond, Hosea pushed back his chair. "Think about it," he said as he stood.

She put down her cup. "Wait."

He shook his head. "Take time—think this through. Decide if you can do this." Before she could move, he leaned over and whispered, "This is another one that's on you. I'm not going to call, but if you're still interested, call me." Then, he was gone.

It took a few minutes, but slowly, her smile came. She was on the verge of victory. He was already moving toward marriage. This had been entirely too easy.

As she buttoned her coat, then stepped outside, she thought about how different this was from her plan. Sex had always been her surefire way to win. But it really didn't matter—the prize was still the same. And the truth was, she knew she could have Hosea Bush in any way and at any time she wanted.

She was almost trotting as she rushed back to the office. Actually, it was better this way. She'd have time—before she got him into bed—to fix him, mold him into the man he should be. An image of Brian Lewis flashed through her mind, and the thought stopped her dead in the middle of the street.

"Watch it," a man growled as he bumped into her.

"I'm . . . I'm sorry," she stuttered and stumbled. Regaining her balance, she shook away the vision. She didn't need, didn't want anyone else. Everything she had needed to go into making sure that in a year, Hosea would have achieved his purpose, and she would be his wife.

Chapter 15

S he was still in charge.

And Hosea needed to know it. That's why Jasmine decided she would wait before she called him back. Not call for two days, make him sweat.

But all the pins and needles seemed to belong to her. Even as she tried to stay distracted all day with the club's designers and contractors, she'd rushed to the phone every time her cell rang. But not one call came from Hosea.

Now, Jasmine half-smiled at Henrikas as she entered her building and waited for the elevator. She glanced at her watch and sighed. It was barely seven. Tonight would be more difficult than the day had been. But making Hosea wait was part of the plan.

She needed something to focus on, anything to fill these Friday night hours.

When the elevator doors opened on her floor, she stood frozen for a moment staring at the sight of Mae Frances slumped over at her door. She ran down the hallway.

"Mae Frances?" Jasmine called out. "Are you all right?"

Her neighbor moved as if she were trying to nod and pull herself up at the same time.

Jasmine noticed her keys on the floor. "Let me get you inside."

"No, I'm okay," Mae Frances insisted, finally standing straight. "I don't want you in there ..."

Jasmine frowned. The woman had to be delirious. She opened the door and then helped Mae Frances into her apartment.

"I said ... I was ... okay." Mae Frances slowly lowered herself onto the couch. Her eyes were like foggy glass.

Jasmine dropped the keys on the table, then eased the coat from Mae Frances's shoulders. "Were you going out?"

Mae Frances shook her head. "No, coming in."

"What happened?"

She shook her head. "I went for a walk. I'm just tired, I guess."

Jasmine wondered why Mae Frances was walking anywhere. She herself would never be caught on foot if she had a driver.

"Okay." Jasmine helped her stand. "Let's get you into the bedroom." Once there, she asked, "Do you want to undress?" She eyed the snug wrapped dress that she'd seen Mae Frances wear often.

"No." She settled on her bed and Jasmine sat next to her.

"I don't want to leave you alone. What time will your husband be home?"

Mae Frances's eyes became clear. "He doesn't live here anymore."

Jasmine sat up straight. Stared at her neighbor. "I'm going to make you some tea, Mae Frances."

"No." But her protest was weak and she closed her eyes.

Jasmine sat with her for a minute more, just watching. When she stood, she decided to make the tea anyway.

She stepped into the front room and, this time, noticed Mae Frances's home. Old was the first word that came to mind. In its day, most of the massive furniture was probably fashionable, and perhaps expensive. But that day had passed, and now the extra long brown velvet couch and oversized wooden chairs and tables just seemed dark. And heavy. And old. And the apartment smelled like a twisted mix of old and Mae Frances's perfume.

In the kitchen, Jasmine opened the cabinets and gasped. The shelves held only a single box of rice, salt and pepper shakers, and an almost empty bottle of hot sauce. The refrigerator was almost as bare: a jug of water, a half an egg carton, and a jar of jelly.

Slowly, Jasmine closed the door. What was going on? Surely, this woman who wore minks and sported diamonds had food somewhere. *Maybe she eats out all the time.*

On the counter, Jasmine noticed two bottles and picked up one. This wine couldn't have cost more than two dollars.

Jasmine shook her head and then crept back into the bedroom. She took a small blanket from the edge of the bed and covered her neighbor.

Then she left.

Jasmine considered this heavy lifting.

She carried the four shopping bags that the grocery clerk had just delivered to her, to Mae Frances's door. She knocked. Knocked again. A minute passed before she turned the knob. The door was unlocked, just as she had left it.

"Mae Frances," she called softly. When there was no answer, she took the bags into the kitchen, then walked back to the bedroom. Three hours had passed and it seemed as if Mae Frances hadn't stirred a bit.

Stepping quickly, Jasmine returned to the kitchen and stocked the cabinets with her purchases. It had been a long time since she'd visited a grocery store, but she'd walked through the aisles, filling the basket with items that seemed easy enough to prepare. Within minutes, the shelves were stocked with cans and boxes. The freezer was packed with chicken and fish. The refrigerator was filled with yogurt, milk, and cheese. This shopping expedition would feed Mae Frances for a couple of weeks.

At her neighbor's bedroom door, she stood for a moment. *What is going on with you?* As she watched her, a new thought came to her mind. She rushed into her own apartment. From her nightstand, she grabbed the Bible that Serena had given her.

When she returned, Mae Frances had shifted, kicked the cover to the floor. Jasmine laid the Bible on the bed table then adjusted the blanket once more.

In the kitchen, she tore a single sheet from a pad by the telephone, scribbled a note, turned off the lights, and then locked Mae Frances's door behind her.

When she settled into her own bedroom, the clock surprised her. It was almost eleven. No wonder she was exhausted. But what was even better was that she hadn't had a single thought of Hosea. And she wasn't tempted to call him now; she had no energy left. Her eyes were shut tight before her head touched the pillow.

Chapter 16

The knocking was insistent.

It took Jasmine a moment before she grabbed her robe, then stumbled through the dark to the door.

When she opened it, Mae Frances stomped inside carrying a shopping bag.

"What time is it?" Jasmine asked before she flipped on the light. She peered at her neighbor, still wearing the same dress that she'd left her sleeping in.

"I am not a charity case."

"I didn't say that you were." Jasmine tried to focus her tired eyes.

"Well, what do you call what you did last night?"

I call it helping a neighbor, she said inside. This wasn't exactly the reaction she'd expected.

Mae Frances said, "I'll have you know that I just didn't have time . . . to go shopping . . . yet."

Jasmine crossed her arms, stared. But in moments, she saw it—in the way Mae Frances held her head high and her back straight. In the way her chin jutted forward, and her eyes stared.

Jasmine softened and said, "I know you didn't have time to shop, Mae Frances. But I was in the store picking up a few things. And I thought I'd do the same for you. I was just trying to be . . . neighborly, I think that's the word you used when you brought me dinner a few weeks ago."

Mae Frances pressed her lips together.

Jasmine shrugged. "Look, next time you go shopping, just pick me up a few things, okay?"

Mae Frances nodded. "I'll do that." She placed the grocery bag on top of the kitchen table. "And I don't have any need for this."

Jasmine thought about the bare cabinets she discovered, and she wanted to beg Mae Frances to accept her gift. But then she realized that Mae Frances had only brought over one bag. She had to have kept a few items.

"Did you hear me?" Mae Frances said in the gruff tone that she hadn't used in weeks. "I don't want this."

"Okay."

"And may I have my keys, please?" She held out her hand and Jasmine dropped the key ring into her palm. Mae Frances nodded, then marched past Jasmine to the door. But before she stepped outside, she turned back. Smiled. Said, "Thank you, Jasmine Larson."

Jasmine sighed when she turned toward the kitchen. She strolled to the table, looked inside the bags, frowned at first, then shook her head. She reached inside and found the single item—the Bible.

I have no need for this. She remembered Mae Frances's words, as she fondled the leather cover.

"At least she kept the food," Jasmine said as she turned off the living room light and returned to her bedroom. She tucked the Bible back into the drawer, but she had no plans of giving up. She didn't know how, but one day, that Bible would belong to Mae Frances.

Chapter 17

Jasmine couldn't figure out why her hands shook.

Maybe it was because this was the beginning of the second phase and she had to get it just right.

"Talk to me."

"Hi, it's Jasmine."

"Great to hear your voice."

She didn't mention how great it was to hear his. He didn't need to know that.

"So," he said, "I guess you called to talk."

"Yeah, like you said, I took the time to think."

He inhaled. "So?"

She hadn't planned on discussing this over the phone. Really wanted to meet in person. Give him a chance to look at her, see what he'd be missing and change his mind.

She said, "Do you have time for lunch?"

"No need for lunch."

Her eyes widened with surprise.

He continued, "I gave you my position; now I want to hear yours. Just give it to me, Jasmine. Straight, no chaser."

She took a deep breath. "The truth is, I really want to get to know you, Hosea. But I can't say that I understand what you're suggesting. Courting?"

"It just means that we'll date. But we'll date in God's way.

Jasmine, I've spent a lot of years trying to live my life the way I thought it should be. And now, I want to spend these years living my life the way God wants it to be."

"So what does that mean?"

"Well, we'll go out, but it won't be physical. Won't get phys-ical."

Jasmine closed her eyes, shook her head.

He continued, "I'm not into self-torture, so we'll have a good time, but leave it at your front door. No touching, no kissing."

Her eyes shot open. "No kissing?"

"That's the plan," he said. "That's the way I think God wants it."

She bit her tongue, needing to do something to stop her protest. She'd been in enough of these discussions with Serena to know that she wouldn't be able to convince Hosea this wasn't right. Words would not convince him. Only action. She'd think of something.

"Well, it's not what I expected," she said. "But I'm willing to try."

"All the way?"

She smiled. "Well, if you mean marriage, I understand—"

He interrupted, "I'm not talking about marriage. I'm talk-ing about how we get close to that point. We can only do it as two people—one man, one woman. No one else." He paused, letting her take in his words. He continued, "From today for-ward it's just you and me and us trying to figure this out. Don't need a third party."

"If you're asking me if I'm seeing anyone else, I'm not."

"And I'm not either. So let's keep it that way. I don't want to start anything that doesn't have the chance of finishing. So are you up to this?"

It's already finished, Hosea. "I'm more than up to it."

"Are you sure?"

"I said yes. How many times do you want me to say I'm fine? Are you trying to run me away?"

He chuckled. "Far from it. Just want to make sure that you're sure. So," he took a breath of relief, "we should celebrate and make this official. Now, let's talk about lunch."

"Great." She paused. "But this time, can we do something besides the corner of Fifty-ninth and Pitiful?"

He laughed. "Are you saying you didn't enjoy our last date?"

"I'm just sayin'—"

"Okay, so maybe I won't win an award for first-date-of-the-year, but today is different. How does 'Twenty-one' sound?"

Jasmine's eyes widened at the mention of the fabled mid-town canteen. "That would be wonderful," she cooed.

"Be ready in twenty minutes."

For "21," she'd need a couple of hours. "You're kidding, right?" She jumped from her bed. "You have to give me more time, Hosea."

"Listen to you, making demands already." He chuckled. "I'll meet you in your lobby at noon."

She glanced at the clock and didn't wait for his good-bye. Just hung up and rushed to her closet. In an hour, she'd be going to the legendary speakeasy that had turned into one of the finest restaurants in the country. This sealed it—Hosea Bush was definitely the one.

Chapter 18

*J*asmine *felt like his* wife already.

It had begun yesterday when she and Hosea stepped into "21." The maître d' greeted them as if Hosea was a regular. That was the first time Jasmine held his arm tighter.

As they dined over the jumbo shrimp with fresh horseradish sauce for her and the citrus poached lobster with coconut rice for him, Jasmine tried to keep her eyes on her prize. But it was difficult when Magic Johnson, Susan Lucci, and Barack Obama were sitting in the same room.

She'd enjoyed the food. The ambiance. The company. The money Hosea was spending.

After they shared tiramisu, Hosea had surprised her with tickets to the Broadway show *Make Me Hot* and then they'd strolled hand-in-hand through Times Square. When they stopped and admired the jewels in the world-famous diamond dealer Sachs Jewelers, she squeezed his hand tighter.

A bit after seven, he escorted her home, leaving her with just a hug, and plans to pick her up for church in the morning. It was not the way she wanted to end the evening—too early, no action—but she would play it his way, for a little while.

Now, the next morning, as he held open the door of his Armada and took her hand as she slid out, she definitely felt like his wife. She had dressed appropriately, in a tan mid-calf-length suit that was suitable for any corporate meeting.

Holding hands, they stepped across the church's parking lot to the symphony of good wishes.

"Hey, Hosea, great to have you home."

"Congratulations, Hosea."

"We're proud of you."

With the kind words came the curious stares. But she kept her head high. Walked straight, moved tall. Strode like the minister's wife she was born to be.

"Hosea," Mrs. Whittingham exclaimed when they stepped inside the church's side door. Then the secretary saw Jasmine. She frowned, sighed, said, "Ms. Larson, what are you doing here?"

"She's with me," Hosea spoke.

At first, the secretary's face crinkled, then cleared with understanding. She lowered her head, and pretended that she did not see what she just saw. "Your father is in his office," she said to Hosea as if Jasmine wasn't there. "Just go on in."

He nodded. "Would you mind waiting here?" he asked Jasmine.

"Not at all." She giggled when he lifted her hand and kissed her fingers. Made just enough noise for Mrs. Whittingham to look up. The grimace on the woman's face told Jasmine that the arrow she'd aimed had hit its mark.

Jasmine sat on the couch and with her eyes, dared Mrs. Whittingham to speak. Triumph was in her heart as she flipped through a magazine.

A few minutes passed and the reverend's door opened. Father and son strolled close together, heads bent, as if their conversation was too deep for others to hear.

Hosea looked up. "Pops, I wanted to introduce you to my friend, Jasmine Larson."

A miscellany of emotions scrolled across the reverend's face. Looking straight into her eyes, the reverend said, "Actually, son, Sister Jasmine and I have met."

"Yes, we have," Jasmine said returning his stare. She was better in this game than he could ever be. She reached out to him. A beat, and then he took her hand. "Good to see you again, Reverend Bush," she said, as if she hadn't been trying to get him into her bed.

"I figured you guys had met in passing," Hosea said, standing by her side. "But I wanted to make a formal intro, Pops, since I invited Jasmine to come with me to church today."

"Well, that's great. Anytime one of God's lost sheep can hear a message, it's a good thing."

"Amen," Mrs. Whittingham said.

Jasmine didn't know which one she wanted to slap first. But instead, she took Hosea's hand into hers. And smiled at Reverend Bush. Then turned her smirk to Mrs. Whittingham.

"Pops, let me take Jasmine to her seat and then we can walk out together."

Reverend Bush pressed his lips as if he was trying to hold words inside. Finally, he said, "I want to go over a few things with you, son." He turned to Mrs. Whittingham. "Would you mind taking Sister Jasmine . . . to where . . . our special guests sit?"

Jasmine was sure the woman gagged. She squeezed Hosea's hand, and then followed Mrs. Whittingham into the sanctuary. As she moved in front of the altar, she could feel eyes watching, hear whispers.

"You can sit here," Mrs. Whittingham said in the same tone she would have used if she'd told Jasmine to lay in front of a speeding train.

"Thank you." She spread her mink along the top of the pew and then sat. Crossed her legs. Held one finger in the air and motioned for Brother Hill.

His glance ricocheted between Jasmine and Mrs. Whittingham. The secretary gave him a slow nod, then marched away.

"I'd like a program," Jasmine demanded.

He wore no smile as he handed her a bulletin. He stayed,

standing over her, not understanding. "That will be all," she dismissed him with a wave of her hand.

She never looked at him again. Just kept her eyes on the bulletin and away from the many glances she felt on her.

When the music played, she looked up. When Reverend Bush walked in, she smiled. When Hosea followed, she stood. She sang along with the praise team. And she swayed, and clapped, and thanked the Lord for all of her blessings.

Hosea glanced at her. Grinned. Winked.

She beamed. This was the way life was supposed to be.

She was the picture of demure.

· With her ankles crossed and her hands resting in the center of her lap, Jasmine waited patiently as Hosea stood at his father's side, greeting parishioners.

But even as she sat, her mind was spinning, swirling with thoughts of moving her plan into full force.

Hosea turned toward Jasmine, wiggled his fingers. She waved back and wondered what he'd look like naked. Then, a vision of Brian—nude—marched through her mind. She frowned; shook her head.

"You look intense. What are you thinking about?" Hosea asked.

She blinked, not realizing he had stepped over to her. "You."

He bobbed his head as if her words were music. "That's what I'm talking about." Holding hands, they strolled to the side door. In the foyer that separated the sanctuary from the church offices, Brother Hill stood with Reverend Bush, as Mrs. Whittingham jotted notes. Other deacons and a few of the ushers huddled in the space, snacking on the spread of fruit and pastries that graced a long table against the wall.

"Do you want something to drink?" Hosea asked, as he picked up a small bottle of orange juice.

She shook her head.

"Okay, I'll be ready in a sec. Need to check a few things with my pops since we won't be staying for second service."

Jasmine wandered past the reverend and Brother Hill, eyed the food, before she turned back to Hosea. In the service, she had studied her man as he stood with his father. They shared similarities: the tailored suits, the shining shoes, their shaven heads that gleamed. At the same time, they were walking exclamations of their generations—while the father wore a simple gold watch, the son glittered. From the diamond stud in Hosea's ear to the jewel-encrusted watch on his wrist, he blinged success. It was those differences that she loved about the son.

"Darlin', I've got to check something out with Brother Hill. Give me a few."

"Sister Jasmine will be fine," Reverend Bush said as his son walked away. Then, Reverend Bush motioned toward his office. "Would you mind joining me, Sister Jasmine?"

Without a word or a smile, she followed him; marched into the office as if she belonged there.

As soon as the door closed, Reverend Bush said, "I thought we agreed you were going to stop these games."

Jasmine lowered herself into the chair. "What games are you talking about, Reverend?"

"I told you. I'm not interested in you."

She raised her eyebrows. Chuckled. "Does it *look* like I'm interested in you?"

She could see the heat rise beneath his skin. "What do you want?" he asked.

She was tempted to tell him that she wanted—and would get—his son. But she stayed silent.

"What do you think my son would say if I told him about the things you've done?"

She didn't allow a beat to pass. "I would deny anything you said."

Now, he chuckled. "And who do you think he'll believe? His father or a . . . woman he's just met."

Jasmine let his question rest in the air. His lips twisted into a crooked grin, as if he were in charge.

"Reverend Bush, I have no doubt your son will believe you over me." She paused. "But before he does," she leaned forward, rested her arms on his desk, "I can cause enough dissension and doubt to create havoc between you and Hosea."

Her words wiped his smirk away.

"The best that would happen," she continued, "is that Hosea would resent you. Wouldn't trust you." She paused. "But the worst thing . . . Hosea just came home and it would be a shame for him to want to get away from you . . . again."

"Are you threatening me?" He glared.

Her look was just as fierce. "No more than you're threatening me." She pushed back, softened her tone. "Reverend Bush, I'm not playing games. I met your son and didn't even know who he was."

His expression said she was a liar.

"I don't want to be your enemy," she continued. "But I'm not afraid of you." She cocked her head. "So maybe we can call a truce. Start all over."

He contemplated her words. Smiled. "I'd like to start all over . . . but I don't trust you." This time, he leaned forward. "I won't let you hurt my son."

"I don't plan on doing that."

He stared at her more. "Don't think I'm concerned with your threats. My relationship with my son can withstand any truth."

Although his words made her heart pound, she shrugged as if she was willing to test that theory.

"If I see any reason to warn my son about you, I will."

She wanted to exhale, but refused to let the reverend see how his words had made her sweat. "I can accept that," she said, working to keep her voice steady.

She felt as if she were on fire, under the glare of his stare. "I'll be watching you, Sister Jasmine. That's a promise. And if there is anything that stinks, I'll smell it."

A knock on the door prevented her response. "Pops, is Jasmine—" Hosea stepped into the office. "There you are." Hosea looked between his father and his woman. "Everything all right in here?"

"Definitely," she said quickly and stood. "Just getting to know your father." She turned to Reverend Bush. "Thanks for the talk. I heard everything you said."

She waited as father and son exchanged good-byes, although all she wanted was to grab Hosea and run far away. But it wasn't like she had anything to fear. The reverend said he'd be watching—so what? Her slate was clean and would stay that way. She'd make sure of it.

Chapter 19

De Janeiro was bumping.

The walls of the massive room reverberated with the music and couples swarmed the dance floor swinging and swaying.

This trip had been a last-minute decision.

Tonight, Jasmine and Malik were going to judge the salsa contest, and then meet tomorrow with de Janeiro's chef. At first, the plan was for only Malik to come to L.A., but then he invited her.

"You should join me," he'd said to her on Monday.

"I don't think so," Jasmine said, as she eyed the stack of papers on her desk. "I have way too much to do." Besides, she thought to herself, things were just getting started with Hosea. She needed to stay in the city, keep an eye on her investment.

On Tuesday, when Malik asked again, right as she was running out the door for a late dinner with Hosea, she repeated that her workload mandated that she stay behind.

But on Wednesday, she'd told Malik, "I think it would be good if I joined you in L.A. tomorrow."

"What changed your mind?"

She'd shrugged, pretending this was nothing more than a woman's prerogative. She wasn't about to tell her godbrother about the images that had danced through her dreams after

Hosea had once again dropped her off—alone—last night.

Now, as she stepped inside de Janeiro, it took only seconds for regret to set in. What was she doing here when her desk was piled high with work? Why wasn't she home focusing on Hosea?

J.T. greeted Malik and Jasmine the moment they entered, and she stood to the side as the friends exchanged greetings. It didn't take long for Jasmine to tire of their chatter, and she rounded the bar, away from them.

"A Coke, no ice, please," she ordered.

"That'll be four dollars," the bartender said when he returned with her drink.

A voice came from behind her. "I got that."

Her hands shook and she took her time picking up her glass. Took even more time turning around, and focusing on the image that had made itself at home in her mind.

"We meet again," Brian said.

She nodded and brought the glass to her lips, giving herself time to scan every bit of him; he was better than any of her dreams. "Hello, Dr. Lewis," she finally said.

He chuckled. "Why so formal? Aren't we friends?"

"Are we?"

"I would like to think so. But then, I could be wrong. I gave you my number, but never heard from you." His gaze unbalanced her.

"I lost your card."

He laughed. "That's a good one, Jasmine."

She smiled and tried to eject the naked vision of him from her mind's eye. "I *really* lost it, and I came all the way back here so that I could get . . . another one."

His laughter continued. "I doubt that."

She laughed with him. *If only you knew.*

"So, when's your New York club opening?"

"In a couple of weeks."

He leaned forward, rested his empty glass on the bar,

brushed against her. She held her breath, taking in his scent. She didn't recognize his fragrance. Only knew that she liked it.

He asked, "Does that mean you'll be spending more time in L.A.?"

"Why do you want to know?"

He ordered another Amaretto Sour before he said, "Because I want to know how much time I have." She frowned, and he added, "To make my move."

In another time, that would have been her cue. To make *her* move. But she had changed. Didn't sleep with married men anymore.

But this is Alexis's husband.

"What kind of move are you talking about?" she flirted.

He paid the bartender for his drink, then took a sip. "Where are you staying?"

Thoughts swirled in her mind. Thoughts of Hosea. Thoughts of her plan. Thoughts of celibacy. Thoughts of her wedding.

The thoughts of Alexis made her say, "At the Four Seasons."

"Under your name?"

"Yes."

"Alone?"

"Of course."

He handed her his drink and then he disappeared into the crowd.

"There you are," J.T. exclaimed. "Thought we'd lost you."

She said, "No, I was just . . . trying to find . . . some aspirin." She slipped Brian's drink onto the bar.

Malik frowned. "What's wrong?"

"I think it was something I ate on the plane." She held her stomach. "I don't know, suddenly, I'm just not feeling well." She eyed the front door. "I feel like I'm going to throw up."

"Do you want me to take you to the hotel?" Malik asked.

"No, I'll get our driver. But I do think I need to leave. With all the work I have I can't afford to be sick."

J.T. said, "Aw, come on," and smirked as if he didn't believe her. "You can hang in there for an hour or two." He picked up the glass that she'd put down and sniffed. "Amaretto Sour. Maybe this is what's made you sick."

"That's not mine," she snapped.

Malik said, "Jasmine, if you're not feeling well, go on back. I can handle this tonight. What about the meeting tomorrow?"

"I'll be there. Thanks, Malik. I'm sorry."

"Just take care. I need you healthy in the next few weeks." He took her hand. "Come on, I'll walk you out."

"No," she almost shouted, then lowered her voice. "The car should be right out front. I'll send him back for you." She kissed Malik's cheek, then half-waved at J.T., not wanting to look at him.

Outside, she located their car, knocked on the window to alert the driver, but at the same moment, a BMW SUV swerved to the curb. The passenger door swung open as Brian leaned across the seat.

Jasmine waved her driver away, then hopped into Brian's car and closed the door, a second before someone called her name.

For the entire thirty-minute ride from the club to the hotel, everything inside of her said that Brian was just curious—just wanted to know what it would be like to be with her since his best friend had risked his marriage for her.

That should have been enough to make her turn back.

But she didn't.

Now, those thoughts were gone. Now, all she could think about were Brian's kisses. And his hands.

It started in the elevator, from the moment the doors closed. She tasted his lover's lips and they hadn't broken their embrace—not even when the elevator first stopped on her floor. Finally, they separated—for moments only—to stumble to her room.

Then they became one again, kissing, groping as if neither had done this before. They ripped their clothes off; the pieces created a path from the door to the bed. Little time passed before they were naked.

No words. No emotions. No love.

Just sex.

Tongues, lips, arms, legs moved with urgent passion. He panted. She groaned. Her head was spinning, but she couldn't capture a single thought. Couldn't concentrate on anything except for the lean mass of bulging muscles that lay over her. Couldn't feel anything except for the parts of him that were pushing her to the edge.

It didn't take long for her to cry out and Jasmine fell against Brian's chest. They both gasped for air, as if they'd just completed a marathon, and it took minutes before their breathing rhythm was normal.

Jasmine closed her eyes and thought of Brian's wife, and all the times Alexis had made her feel less than adequate. She wondered how Alexis would feel if she could see Jasmine now. Jasmine wanted to stand and cheer. Payback was beyond wonderful.

And then she remembered Hosea.

Chapter 20

Somewhere between sex and sleep, God brought revelation. And with this revelation, came shame. No matter how many magazines she flipped through, how many CDs she listened to, how many pages she read in her novel, Jasmine couldn't escape the smothering guilt. It was with her when she left the message for Malik that she was returning to New York early, stayed with her through the three-thousand-mile plane ride, then lingered throughout the night. Even now, almost twenty-four hours after she'd returned home, she couldn't flee from the memory.

"Thank you for making this for me so quickly," she said to the woman who owned the delicatessen a block from her apartment.

"No problem. Have a good time with that special man, whoever he is." The woman grinned.

That's my plan. She rushed outside, took a deep breath, and then pressed a speed dial on her cell.

"Talk to me."

"Hey, sweetie."

"I've been promoted to sweetie. I like that." Hosea laughed. "Good to hear from you, darlin'. Just get back?"

"Kinda," she lied. There was no way to explain that she'd returned last night and hadn't called. Hadn't wanted to risk him hearing her betrayal in her voice.

She said, "Please tell me you haven't made plans for lunch. I want to see you."

"Actually, I have a date—"

"Oh, no."

"With my pops," he continued. "But, no problem. Just join us."

There was no way she could break bread with Reverend Bush. Not ever, but definitely not now.

"I'll be watching you." The memory of his words made her tremble. "Hosea, I had something special planned for us."

"Great. So, here's what we'll do. Lunch with my pops and then dinner, just you and me."

She blew a loud breath.

He said, "Darlin', I can't cancel with the reverend. It's business, actually."

She looked at the seventy-five-dollar picnic basket she'd just purchased. "Okay, but I don't want to interrupt, so call me when you finish."

He chatted for a few minutes more, before he hung up. She sighed. She had so wanted to see Hosea. Needed to see him. And put her arms around him. And, hug him until she expelled Brian Lewis from her mind.

Now what was she going to do? She needed to talk. Explain to somebody that she wasn't crazy. But as she strolled past Henrikas, she realized her options were few. Malik was a man—wouldn't understand. And Serena would flip when she realized that Brian was Jefferson Blake's best friend.

Jasmine dug inside her purse for her keys, but then, she turned toward Mae Frances's apartment.

Not giving herself time to change her mind, she knocked. When Mae Frances opened the door, Jasmine said, "I know you're probably still upset with me."

"Why would you say that, Jasmine Larson?" Mae Frances motioned for her to come in.

"Because of what happened last weekend. I want you to know that I didn't mean anything by buying that food."

"You said that already. I understand."

"Good, 'cause I need a friend right about now."

Mae Frances smiled. Sat on the couch and then patted a space next to her.

Jasmine said. "And I brought this," she held up the basket, "for us to share."

Mae Frances took her smile away. "I told you, I'm not a charity case." Her gruffness returned.

"Will you stop it?" Jasmine said, her tone on edge. "I just spent a fortune on this for me and the man I want to talk about. But he had plans and I didn't want to throw all of this away."

Mae Frances kept her face stiff.

"You know what?" Jasmine bounced up. "Just forget it." She stomped toward the door.

"Where are you going, Jasmine Larson?"

She whipped around. "Back to my place, because I'm tired of this. I just want to be your friend, Mae Frances. I'm not trying to insult you, but that's all I seem to do."

In the passing seconds, her smile returned. Mae Frances stood and walked into the kitchen. "Come back in here," she demanded. "And bring that basket with you."

Jasmine waited a moment before she followed.

"What do you have in there?" Mae Frances peeked under the top. She grabbed the bottle of sparkling cider. "So this man you want to talk about—he doesn't drink either?"

Jasmine knew where this would lead, and she didn't want any part of that conversation. "No, the cider's for me. All I can say about him is that he's a wonderful man and I know he's the one."

Mae Frances smirked. "Wonderful and man cannot be used in the same sentence," she said as she stacked the pieces of fried chicken in the middle of the table. "But anyway, how do you know he's the one?"

"I just know it."

When Mae Frances raised her eyebrows, Jasmine knew that she expected a better answer. But how could she explain? Yes, Hosea was supposed to be the pawn in her plan, but somehow he had become the king. It was the way he looked at her, and spoke to her, and treated her. It was the way he made her feel whenever they were together—like *she* was the one. "I just know that I like being part of his life. And I think he's starting to feel the same about me."

"So, if everything is so wonderful, what do we have to talk about?" Mae Frances held up a piece of chicken, but Jasmine waved the food away.

"This may take a while," Jasmine said.

"I've got time." Mae Frances broke apart a wing and took a bite.

She began at the beginning; told about meeting Hosea and the dates they'd had. Although she gushed about their times, the way Mae Frances's eyes danced with amusement let Jasmine know that her neighbor was less than impressed.

"And then I went to Los Angeles." She wasn't sure how much she wanted to say here. Should she tell her that she actually slept with Brian? But then she remembered—Mae Frances was an atheist—nothing would shock her.

"You did what?" Mae Frances exclaimed when Jasmine told her about her sexcapade two nights before. "If your new man is so wonderful, why did you go all the way to L.A. to jump into bed with a man you barely know?"

"I don't know," Jasmine said, leaving out the part about Alexis.

"Isn't your new man satisfying you?"

Jasmine raised her eyebrows at the question, but then she was the one who started this conversation. "We haven't had sex."

"Why not?"

Jasmine leaned back to get a better view. Mae Frances had

to be at least in her sixties, yet she sounded nothing like the older women she'd come in contact with. Nothing like the women in the church in Florida who had so much to say about what she wore and how she talked, and what she should and shouldn't do.

Mae Frances selected a chicken leg this time, but before she took a bite, she said, "First, this . . . wonderful man doesn't drink, and next, you're telling me you two haven't had sex." She took a bite of the chicken. "What is he, a Christian?"

Jasmine folded her arms.

"Oh, Lord," Mae Frances exclaimed in between her chews. "He is, isn't he? You'd better stay away from that man."

"Why?" Jasmine frowned. "I told you I was a Christian."

"Yeah, but it's much worse when a man says it. Women usu-ally mean it, but with men, it's just a trick to get into your panties."

"It's not a trick; I told you we haven't had sex. And he's ac-tually a minister."

Mae Frances leaned back and laughed. "Now I know you're in trouble. Listen to me. I know ministers—Jasmine Larson. I'm speaking from my own matrimonial experiences, so I'm telling you, stay away from that man."

"Your husband is a minister? I thought he was a doctor?"

"He is. But his parents," she chuckled bitterly, "my dear de-parted husband's father is a big-time Baptist minister." She made a face and pushed away her plate as if the food now sick-ened her.

Jasmine covered Mae Frances's hand with hers. "I didn't know your husband had passed away."

"He didn't die!" Her angry voice returned. "I said he de-parted. He left me a long time ago." Her eyes became like glass and she stared at the wall. "Couldn't stand up to his par-ents. Just became too much for him when every week they called with a new scripture to support their view that God didn't approve of interracial relationships. Told their pure son that being married to a Negro wasn't the Christian way."

Jasmine covered her opened mouth. "I'm sorry."

Mae Frances faced her. "What are you apologizing for? I'm not sorry. I said good riddance and I've had a wonderful life ever since."

Wonderful life? Jasmine tried to keep her eyes away from the cabinets that she'd found empty and from the furniture that looked as if it might not make it through another season.

"So tell me about this Brian man in Los Angeles." Mae Frances spoke with cheer, as if her past was now forgotten. "He's not a Christian, is he?"

"I don't think so." Jasmine said no more.

"Then he's the one you should be with," Mae Frances said. "What's stopping you?"

Jasmine shrugged, and regretted that she'd shared this with Mae Frances. Although her sister would have blown two or three gaskets, she now wished she'd called Serena. She needed someone to tell her how wrong Brian was. Not someone who validated who she used to be.

"Well, I'm telling you, Jasmine Larson, with the way men are, you shouldn't really care. Just go after what you want."

Jasmine stared at the woman.

Mae Frances continued, "You don't need to care or worry about no one else. If it feels good, then do it. Because when it comes down to it, only you can make yourself happy."

Suddenly Jasmine leapt from her chair. "I forgot. I have to . . . run into the office . . . for something."

Mae Frances looked at her knowing she wasn't telling the truth. "Today's Saturday."

"Yes, but it's something that I'll need for Monday."

She nodded as if she understood. "Then you'd better get going. Thank you for sharing with me, Jasmine Larson." Her voice was soft, sad. Sounded as if the past really wasn't forgotten.

Jasmine dashed into her apartment and tried to pray away

the picture that had come to mind as she listened to the bitter words of her neighbor. She squeezed her eyes shut, pushing away any thought that Mae Frances sounded so much like the old part of her.

"Lord, please forgive me," she said, and then wondered if it really worked like that. She'd heard ministers say that's all you had to do, but, "please forgive me" didn't feel like enough.

"Lord, please help me," she added.

Images of Brian rushed into her mind. She shot up, sat straight.

"No!"

But even as she protested, she remembered him. Remembered his lips. His hands. The feel of him. She squeezed her legs together.

"It will not happen again."

She had to see Hosea. He had to help her—make sure that she never went back to who she used to be. Make sure that she never became Mae Frances.

Chapter 21

Jasmine sat on the bed's edge for a few minutes before she picked up the phone and dialed.

"Talk to me," Hosea said as soon as he answered.

"Hey, sweetie."

"Darlin', I'm on my way."

"Hosea, I'm not feeling well. I don't think I can make it to church."

"What's wrong?"

"I think my resistance is low since I've been working all these long hours." She squeezed her eyes shut, trying to push back the image of the sprawled sheets. Trying not to see, feel, Brian Lewis.

"That trip to L.A. probably didn't help."

Her eyes shot open. "What . . . do you mean?"

"It's a long ride and then to come right back, it's exhausting. My darlin' must be tired."

She let out a long breath. "Yeah, you're right," she said, hoping her heart would return to its normal beat. "So, you don't mind?"

"Nah, take care of yourself. But I've gotta tell you, I'm beginning to wonder if you're avoiding me. First dinner last night, now church." He chuckled, but she didn't laugh with him. Couldn't laugh at the truth.

Yesterday, she was sure all she needed was to see Hosea. But when he'd called and said that his father wanted to join them for dinner, Jasmine wanted to throw up. She'd lied—told Hosea that she'd been called in for an emergency work meeting.

But this morning, she *had* awakened sick. Sick with the thought of how she was going to face Reverend Bush. She'd heard stories of ministers who could see things—look at a person and know what was going on in their life.

I'll be watching you.

She shuddered at the memory of the reverend's words. Suppose he possessed that gift?

Hosea said, "I hope this is just a twenty-four-hour thing. You've got to be one hundred percent for tomorrow." When she was silent, he said, "Don't tell me you've forgotten."

Still nothing.

"It's your birthday and I have something special planned."

She knew for sure that Brian Lewis had messed her up. Forgetting her birthday—or Valentine's Day, or Christmas—it just didn't happen.

"I'll be okay by tomorrow."

"I'll call when I get out of church. If you're up to it, I'll bring you something to eat."

"Okay," she said. She tossed the phone onto the nightstand and lay across the bed.

Missing church this morning made it official. In just three days she'd broken her three promises to God; sinned in ways she had vowed she never would.

She stood and looked into the mirror. "It was just one time," she reminded herself. "It'll never happen again."

But as she returned to her bed and pulled her knees to her chest, she knew that making a vow—to herself or to God—didn't seem to mean too much anymore.

Chapter 22

This *morning, Jasmine awakened* with a smile. Her dreams had been filled with thoughts of Hosea and all that he had planned for her today. Even now, she recalled his call last night.

"Just checkin' on you because I don't want a thing to interfere with your birthday," he'd said.

"What do you have planned?"

"Don't worry about it."

Inside, she'd moaned. She prayed this wasn't going to be another disaster-at-Fifty-ninth-Street date.

"I know what you're thinking," he said before she could question him more. "But, haven't I more than made up for that minor, little, tiny date mistake?"

For the first time since she'd returned from Los Angeles, she'd laughed. "Okay, but you've got to tell me something. What time should I be ready? What should I wear? Where are we going?"

"I'm the host of *Bring It On,* not *Twenty Questions.* Relax. You be you and let me be me.

"But . . ."

"This is all you need to know, darlin'. By midnight tomorrow, you'll be calling all your girlfriends telling them just how wonderful Hosea Bush is."

She hadn't bothered to mention that she had no friends, but that didn't dull her excitement then, and she wasn't going to let anything dull it now—not even work.

She called the office, told her assistant that she wasn't feeling well, retrieved her messages, and then sank deeper under the bed covers as she flipped through the morning shows. It had been a long time since she'd allowed herself the luxury of staying in bed past seven, but she needed this time. Even though the cloud of guilt had lifted, it had left her exhausted. She needed this time to prepare for tonight.

The ringing phone grabbed her away from *Good Morning America*, and when she checked the caller I.D., she snatched the handset.

"How did you know I was here, sweetie?" she asked as soon as she answered.

"I called the office; Tina said you were sick." Hosea's voice dripped with concern.

"I'm fine. Just wanted to stay home and bask in the anticipation of our evening."

"Well, I hope I'm the first to wish you a happy, happy day."

"Yeah, you're the first," she said. She kept her grin, even though this would be the only call she'd get—at least until Serena got home from work. "Thank you." She paused and softened her voice to almost a whisper. "But can you do me a favor, sweetie?"

"Aw, darlin', when you talk like that, all I can say is, whatever you want."

"Please give me a little hint—what time, what to wear. Give me something," she whined.

He laughed. "I'm going to hang up now, darlin'. Enjoy your day."

He was gone before she could moan more, but before she could dial him again, her concerns were interrupted by a knock on her door. Sure that it was Mae Frances, Jasmine stayed in place, not wanting to face her neighbor. But when she heard the knock again, she rushed to the living room. Maybe Mae Frances needed her.

"Ms. Larson?" A thirty-something-year-old black woman with spiked hair wearing a winter-white coat greeted her when she opened the door. Behind her, two younger men, both dressed in jeans and leather jackets, balanced boxes piled high in their arms.

"Yes?" She wondered why Henrikas hadn't called. She'd have to talk to him to make sure he announced all her visitors.

"My name is Leslie Winslow," the woman said. "I'm a personal shopper with Lord and Taylor. We have a few packages for you."

Surprise kept Jasmine in place. But the woman marched past her, followed by the men.

She asked, "What is all of this?"

"Mr. Bush wanted to make sure you had everything you needed for tonight. Where can we put these?" she asked, pointing to the boxes.

"Right here," Jasmine said with the cheer of a child at Christmas. The boxes tumbled onto the couch and Jasmine didn't wait. She ripped the top off one package. The strapless, tea-length black lace dress made her gasp. "This is gorgeous."

"That's a Calvin Klein. It's Mr. Bush's favorite, but he wanted to give you a choice. So we brought several outfits."

With glee, Jasmine tore through the packages. There was a floor-length cream satin sheath from Vera Wang and a red two-piece from Oscar de la Renta. Each dress had matching shoes and a purse.

"I cannot believe this," Jasmine said as she laid each outfit across the couch. "How did he know my size?"

"I'm one of the fashion consultants on his show, and after working with him for a few weeks, I can tell you that Mr. Bush has his ways." Leslie laughed. "When he wants something, he gets it."

Those words made her happy. "I can't decide," Jasmine said.

"You don't have to. I'm leaving everything here so take your time. Then, just send back the other two."

Leslie motioned to the men who'd sat silently. "Here's my card. Call if you have any questions."

Once alone, she lifted the black dress, and searched for a price tag. There was none. She inspected the other two. Same thing.

Jasmine giggled, and with the black dress in hand, ran into her bedroom. In front of the mirror, she held it against her. "So, this is your favorite, Hosea." She twirled like a dancer. "Well, if it fits, then it's my favorite too."

With care, she laid the dress on the bed, and slipped from her robe. Then, she stopped. She really should call Hosea, thank him, tell him that now, she absolutely loved him. But, she flung that thought aside. That could wait until after she had a chance to see how fabulous she looked.

Not bad for a third date, she thought. And she knew that her plan was working.

"Wow."

Jasmine beamed. "You like?" She spun so Hosea could get a 360-degree view.

"You're gorgeous."

She stopped spinning and took in all of him. His charcoal shadow-striped tuxedo was exactly what she would have chosen for him.

Without a thought, she threw her arms around his neck. "Thank you," she said, enjoying the feel of him. "Hosea, this dress is fabulous. I've never had such a wonderful birthday."

"And we haven't even begun." He stepped further into her apartment. "This place is nice." He bobbed his head in approval, then looked at his watch. "We gotta get moving."

A limousine waited in front of her building and it took Jasmine a moment to realize that the car was for them. Inside, he held her hand as the driver pulled into traffic. "How am I doing so far?" Hosea asked.

All she wanted to do was kiss him. All she did was smile. "If the night ended now, I'd be happy."

He laughed. "We have a few more hours." Only minutes passed before the car pulled into a long line of limousines. "Don't," Hosea warned before Jasmine could ask. Their car stopped in front of a glowing-like-it-was-the-middle-of-the-day Metropolitan Museum of Art. A tuxedoed man greeted their car, and then they followed other formally dressed couples up the museum stairs. More hosts guided them to the Sackler Wing where Hosea checked her coat and they were directed to the reception line.

"You've got to tell me something," she whispered. "What am I going to say if I don't know what this is?"

"Okay." He chuckled. "This is a special benefit for the museum. My pop's a member of the President's Circle. But the benefit Chairs are old friends of the family, so I thought we'd start our night here."

"Hosea," the petite, bright-blond woman exclaimed. Jasmine stood aside as the woman air-kissed Hosea's cheeks. "It is so good to see you. How is your father?"

"And why is he not with you?" the lanky man standing next to the woman asked.

Jasmine knew nothing about these people, but she could tell they reeked of old money. The lilt of their speech. The design of their clothes. The gestures they made. Their ancestors were probably the first off the *Mayflower*.

"My dad sends his apologies," Hosea said. "He's working."

"I'm going to have to give him a call. He does much too much of that." The woman laughed.

"Speaking of work," the man jumped in, "it's good to have you back in New York. We lunched with your father a few weeks ago and he is so very excited about your show."

The woman turned to Jasmine. "And who is this lovely lady, Hosea?"

Hosea introduced Jasmine to Charlotte and Lovell

Hollingsworth, but the line behind them didn't allow for further chatter. Hosea took her hand and led her into the room where a harpist played a soft melody and waiters wandered through balancing trays with flutes of champagne and designer desserts.

"Do you have any sparkling cider?" Hosea asked a passing waiter. The man nodded, then stepped away. "I'm sorry," Hosea said to Jasmine. "Do you want champagne?"

"No, I don't drink. Not that I think it's wrong, it's just not for me."

He smiled and she did the same—inside. She'd planned that response. Scored points, she was sure.

As they strolled through the exhibit, Jasmine was surprised at the number of patrons who greeted Hosea, asked about his father, congratulated him on his show. Reverend Bush was obviously more than a common pastor, and Hosea was more than a talk show host. The Bushes had elite New York connections.

An hour later, Hosea led her back to where their car waited. "Now on to our second adventure."

When the car stopped again, Jasmine peeked through the windows. Lights shined bright from the Garden State across the Hudson River when she stepped from the car. The whispering wind stirred, but Jasmine didn't feel the cold. Her eyes were on the helicopter sitting just feet away.

It was only because he nudged her forward that Jasmine moved. Excitement made her tremble as she climbed the metal stairs and then strapped herself into her seat.

"You wanted to see New York," Hosea yelled above the revving engine. "Sit back, darlin'."

Jasmine held her breath as the helicopter swept down the Hudson River. Almost immediately, she was face-to-face with the Statue of Liberty and then they swooped over Wall Street. As they soared over Manhattan, Hosea pointed out the monumental skyline: the Empire State and Chrysler buildings, and the

United Nations. They whizzed over Central Park, before swinging north and sharing a perfect aerial view of Yankee Stadium.

Fifteen minutes after they began, the helicopter hovered,
then touched ground.

"That was amazing" were the first words Jasmine said when
they settled back into the limousine.

"Now, are you hungry, darlin'?"

By nine o'clock, they were seated at A Quiet Little Table
in the Corner.

"I've never heard of this place," Jasmine said as she slid into
her cushioned chair. Curtains surrounded their table, just like
every other one in the restaurant, giving each party privacy.

The waiter handed them menus, but Jasmine put hers
down.

"Why don't you order for me, sweetie."

He smiled; she'd pleased him again.

First, they shared an oversized salad, and Jasmine asked,
"Did you always want to be a pastor? Like your father?"

Hosea chuckled, shook his head. "Not at all. Although I
was always proud of my pops and the way he turned City of
Lights around, I didn't want to do anything that would have
me standing in some pulpit."

"But you turned out to be a minister anyway." She continued her fact-finding mission.

"Not my will, but when God says it, it is. When I graduated
from college and went to Chicago, I worked for a newspaper—
Blessings."

"A Christian paper?"

He nodded. "But, it was only because that was the first
offer I got. If anything else had come through, I wouldn't have
been there. After mom passed, I didn't want anything to do
with God. But if someone was willing to pay me . . ." He
shrugged. "I had no problem taking the loot."

"So, how did you get from the newspaper to television?"

"I went from columnist to editor to a small cable show that

was a spin-off of the newspaper. And then the show blew up. Next thing you know, NBC came knocking."

She shook her head. "An overnight success. You know you're incredibly lucky."

He took her hand. "I know I'm incredibly blessed."

Dang, Jasmine thought. She had to remember to use the right words.

He continued. "All that happened is that I finally let Jesus take the wheel, and the blessings flowed. But enough about me." He leaned toward her. "I want to know about you. What do you want?"

"I don't know," she said before she sipped her sparkling cider. "I just want to be happy."

"Is your family still in Los Angeles?"

Again she sipped, gaining time. She wasn't ready to divulge too much; she wanted to know more about him—to become what he wanted.

She said, "My mom passed away years ago."

His lips drooped and he took her hand. "So, you've lost both your parents?"

She nodded sadly. "It's been hard, but I do have my sister."

His smile returned. "Tell me about her."

She gave him the details of Serena, staying as close to the truth as she could, knowing one day they would meet.

"I've always wanted a brother, or a sister. I think that's why I really want to have children now. Lots of them."

Jasmine kept her smile, although his words almost made her choke on her cider. Lots of children? At her age, she wasn't even sure she'd be able to get pregnant at all. But even if she was able to have a child, she had no intentions of having more than one. Today was her fortieth birthday. How many children did he expect her to pop out?

"So, Serena's been married, but what about you?" he asked, after the waiter had brought their dinners. "Why weren't you ever married?" He paused. "Or were you?"

She stuffed her mouth with her pasta and chewed slowly. She hadn't expected this question, wasn't ready with the answer. She scrolled through all she knew about Hosea. If she was going to be his wife, there could be only one answer.

"I don't know why I've never been married," she lied. "I guess I'm just waiting on God."

His smile told her that she'd scored one hundred points. "That's the only way to do it." He squeezed her hand.

Her mouth opened wide when the waiter surprised her with a piece of raspberry cheesecake holding a single candle in the middle.

"Now, I know a man isn't supposed to ask," Hosea started as he took a bite of the dessert, "but—"

"I know you're not asking me how old I am?" she interrupted, placing her hand over her chest in mock indignation.

He nodded. "Although it doesn't matter to me. You could be one hundred, and I'd still ask you out to dinner tomorrow."

She smiled because she was ready. She'd been expecting this question. "I'm . . . thirty-five . . . today."

"An older woman."

She kept her smile although her heart began to pound. Had she gone too high? She'd almost said thirty-two, but thirty-five would be easier to keep track of. "So how old are you?"

"Thirty-three."

Close enough, she thought.

He asked, "Does my age bother you?"

She shook her head and took his hand. "Not at all. If you were one hundred and asked me to have dinner with you tomorrow, I'd say yes."

He laughed. "So, who's older, you or Serena?"

That was not a question she expected. At thirty-five, she and Serena were the same age. She couldn't say they were twins.

"Uh," she hesitated. "I'm older," she said deciding to keep at least that part true.

"Are you two close?"

"Yeah, Serena's a great sister. She's always looking out for me."

"Is that why you left L.A.? To be closer to her?"

The memory of her escape from L.A. tore through her mind. "Something like that," she said. "But I wanted to ask you something about the museum," she added, needing to get away from talk of Los Angeles. "I was on the board of the Cultural Arts of Florida, and I'd like to become involved here in New York."

"Really, darlin', that's wonderful."

Jasmine had no idea if there was a Cultural Arts of Florida, but it worked. Hosea chatted, and she nodded as if she was listening, but her mind was far away.

This day, and night, proved it. She was going after the right man. Hosea knew how to live. Knew how to play. This was the life she wanted. And the way Hosea looked at her in between his words confirmed that she was on her way.

Chapter 23

B y *the time the* first employees sauntered into Kincaid Enterprises, Jasmine had been working for three hours. She'd just approved the final menu when Malik strolled into her office and closed the door.

"Hey," she said, not able to hide her joy. It had stayed with her, even after Hosea ended their spectacular night by escorting her to the elevator, handing her a single white rose, kissing her cheek, and promising to call first thing the next day. She'd floated into her apartment, then the ringing telephone had brought her out of her fairy tale.

"It's first thing tomorrow," Hosea said the moment she answered. She'd glanced at the clock. It was midnight. He continued, "Just wanted to tell you how wonderful this night was for me." He hung up before she spoke a word.

Memories of the night rocked her to sleep, and were still with her when she awakened before the sun made its debut. With an energy that she hadn't had in months, she jumped from her bed and rushed into the office.

"Looks like you've recovered," Malik said, before he lowered himself into a chair.

Jasmine frowned.

He said, "Last time I saw you, you were buckled over in pain. I think you said it was your stomach."

"Oh." She'd forgotten. Last Thursday, Los Angeles, Brian, all seemed like light years in the past.

"So, what's up?" Malik asked.

Jasmine looked at the pile of folders on her desk. "I'm catching up on everything—"

Malik held up his hand. "Not talking about work. Talking about how you're feeling. You told me you were sick in L.A., remember?"

"Oh, that. It turned out to be . . . nothing."

"I guess that's why you rode off with Brian Lewis."

Her eyes widened, and all the possible lies she could tell jogged through her mind.

"Don't bother denying it. J.T. saw you."

"Brian gave me a ride to the hotel," she said, trying to keep a smile.

"Just dropped you off?"

"Yes."

"So, why did I see him stepping out of your room in the middle of the night?"

She wanted to tell him that he hadn't seen what he saw. But she didn't feel like going through that line of dialogue.

"Jasmine," Malik said leaning forward. "Brian Lewis is married."

She stayed silent.

"And don't tell me you didn't know. J.T. told me you've known Brian—and his wife—for years."

Her first thought was that it had to be a man who spread the rumor that women were gossips. Because J.T. was better at this than any woman she knew. Her second thought was to ask Malik why he was all up in her business. But the sensation of cotton balls stuffed inside her mouth kept her from speaking.

"Jasmine, I thought you were past this. You're always saying that married men are not an option for you."

"You're right," she said contritely.

His face spread with surprise as if that was not the response he expected.

"Malik, I didn't plan that. It just happened. But I can promise nothing will happen with me and Brian again."

He twisted his lips in doubt.

"I mean it, Malik," she said with as much sincerity as she could. "I've met someone and I'm not willing to risk this relationship."

It took a moment, but he exhaled. And smiled. "Okay." He paused. "So, who's this new guy?"

She waited a beat. "Hosea Bush."

His smile was gone. "Oh, no, Jasmine," he groaned.

"Malik, this is real."

"How can this be real? Last week you were in love with Hosea's father."

"I wasn't really in love."

"*I* know that. But I couldn't convince you of it."

"Look, you were right and I was wrong."

"And now you're wrong about Hosea Bush."

"I'm not. Malik, when I met Hosea, I didn't have any idea who he was. I like him because of him."

"He's not even your type."

"You don't know my type," she said, trying to hold back her anger. "And anyway, I'm not doing the pursuing. He came after me."

Malik stared before he asked, "What can I say to get you to drop this?"

"Nothing."

He exhaled a long breath.

Jasmine said, "Malik, Hosea is different. That's why I know nothing will happen with me and Brian again."

He rolled his eyes and she could imagine his thoughts: Reverend Bush, Brian Lewis, Hosea Bush. If she were outside looking in, she'd be thinking the same thing. But she knew her heart. It wasn't that she was in love, but she was certainly— after yesterday—in deep like. And her heart was open to much more.

He sighed. "I hope you know what you're doing."

"I do."

"I don't want you to get hurt."

"I won't."

He stood. "I made a promise to your dad that I would take care of you. That's all I'm trying to do."

"I appreciate that."

"You're a hard one."

"I'm not trying to be."

He left her office without another word.

Alone, she exhaled. It was careless, the way she'd handled Brian. But it was certainly a great warning. If Malik could find out, then one day, Hosea could too. There would be no more risks. From now on she had two missions: Hosea and Rio. And both missions would be accomplished.

Chapter 24

J asmine felt like a five-year-old.

She stomped into her apartment, threw her purse onto the floor, kicked off her shoes and tossed them across the room.

"This isn't working," she screamed and punched one of the pillows.

She didn't remember a time when she couldn't get a man to do what she wanted. But Hosea wasn't susceptible to her womanly wiles. He was moving this relationship forward his way, like this was his plan.

From the outside, it looked like the two were in the center of a whirlwind romance. For the last four weeks, even though Hosea's schedule in preparation for his September premiere was as frenzied as hers, he always found moments to steal her away for quick lunches, romantic dinners, or just strolls through Tribeca, SoHo, and Harlem.

Even in those in-between moments when they couldn't spend time together, Jasmine had no doubt that she was close to his heart. He showed her, through the single rose that waited at her door when she returned home from work at midnight. Or by the voice-mail messages that were on her machine before she even arrived at the office. Or even with the lunches that he had the caterers from his set deliver when he suspected she wouldn't take time for a break.

And then today, he'd shared one of his favorite Sunday adventures with her.

"New York street fairs are the absolute best," he'd told her. "You're going to love it."

So, after church this morning, she'd rushed home, jumped into jeans, and then they'd spent hours wandering up and down thirty blocks on Second Avenue, browsing through old books, tasting a bit of every kind of food, shooting hoops, and shaking their heads at the long lines that had gathered around the psychics. They laughed at the street clowns entertaining the children. They cheered as young performers sang and danced across the center stage.

To her, today had been one of their best times together—until the cab that carried them home stopped in front of her apartment.

"Hang here, chief," Hosea said to the cab driver. "I'll just be a couple of minutes."

"Fine, but the meter will keep running."

When they were standing on the curb, Jasmine put her arms around Hosea. "I had a great time, just like I always do with you."

"Glad to hear that, darlin'. But let me get you inside before I have a forty-dollar fare." He nodded toward the cab and laughed.

She dropped her hands to her side. Stood straight, as if her stance would help. "I want you to send him away," she whispered. "And then . . . come upstairs with me."

First, he stared. Then, he sighed. And she was reminded just how many times she'd extended—and he'd declined—this invitation.

"Why do we have to talk about this again?" he asked.

Annoyance was in his tone, but she didn't care. Her irritation was far beyond his.

Jasmine said. "Aren't you attracted to me at all?"

He rolled his eyes. "What do you think? I'm not blind."

Although he lowered his voice, he stayed stern. "But this is not just about me. This is about you and me and the way God wants us to live."

She took a breath to stop from screaming that she was sick of God being his excuse. The Lord couldn't possibly expect celibacy from grown folks in today's times.

But she'd told him all of that before. Tonight, she was ready with new ammunition. "Okay, I understand your view, but what about the other side?" She took his hand and led him away from the blare of the passing traffic. "Aren't you curious? What if we're not compatible?"

He frowned. "Not compatible? We've spent almost every day together. We're compatible."

"I'm talking . . . sexually." She'd lowered her voice, even though there were few passing pedestrians. "Suppose we go through all of this and then we're not compatible in bed."

He'd kept his voice as soft as hers. Placed his hands on her shoulders. "If we believe God and trust Him, and if He tells us we're supposed to be together, then He'll make sure that we're compatible in every way. God knows what He's doing. He doesn't make mistakes, Jasmine."

"Hey, buddy, are you coming?" the cab driver called.

"Yeah." He turned back; kissed her cheek. "Trust me, Jasmine. You're going to see that I'm right."

He dashed to the cab, and she had smiled when he waved. But in her head, she'd called him a fool.

Now, as she sat in her apartment, she wondered what she was going to do. This was why sex was so important. If she had bedded him by now, she'd be picking out linen and selecting a china pattern. But with Hosea, no sex meant he had the power.

She stood and walked to the window. To this point, her plan was flawless. He was falling for her; he'd told her so many times. Neither had used the L word, but she knew even that wasn't too far away.

It was an ideal relationship—except she needed sex. She needed the release. She needed the control.

Somehow, some way, she was going to get Hosea into bed. Because if she didn't, no one could ever hold her responsible for what this madness might make her do.

Chapter 25

T he sand tickled her toes.

Jasmine and Hosea sauntered, hand-in-hand, along the Fire Island coastline. She inhaled the ocean's scent and then sighed.

"You okay, darlin'?" he asked.

"I'm better than okay."

He smiled his approval, and they continued their stroll to the rhythm of the water's waves.

Today had been another one of Hosea's surprises. He'd called this morning and told her they were going to spend the day celebrating Rio's upcoming opening.

"But it's not all good, darlin'," he'd said. "I just found out that I have to be in Philly Thursday and won't be at the club with you. So, I'm doing a little making-it-up-to-you now, and I'll have a little somethin' for you when I get back next weekend."

She'd been disappointed, but she couldn't stay in the sadness for long. Not when she looked back over the past weeks and all that he did to make her feel wanted. He did everything—except satisfy her sexual needs.

Jasmine still hadn't been able to change any part of his mind—or persuade any part of his body—to have sex with her. And she was still trying to find a way to be content with that. She told herself that she didn't need his physical love when every day, he lived his love for her. She had him—emotionally, spiritually, mentally. All she needed to do was believe, that was enough.

"Are you ready to eat, darlin'?" he asked, nudging her from her thoughts.

She nodded, although she could have stayed at the edge of this paradise forever. On the boardwalk, they rinsed the sand from their feet, then strolled to the waterside restaurant Tête-à-Tête. They were seated at a booth that faced the ocean and where a sandy-haired, surfer-looking waiter took their orders. For the next hours, they shared their food, a calamari salad and a seafood stew. And shared conversation, their dreams and goals.

By the time Hosea escorted her into her apartment building, she was ready to beg for his hand in marriage.

She kissed his cheek. "Thank you for another beyond fantastic day." She turned toward the elevator, but he held her hand as if he couldn't let go.

"Jasmine," he started and then hesitated.

"What's wrong?" She wasn't sure what was behind his stare, but his intense gaze made her heart thump.

He said, "I can't end this day without letting you know how much you mean to me."

She opened her mouth, but he placed the tips of his fingers on her lips, stopping her.

"Just saying your name makes me smile. I don't know when it happened, but you've stolen my heart." He'd turned her hand, kissed her palm, let his lips linger in the center of her hand. And then he left.

Jasmine stood in place, watching him as he sauntered away. She stayed right there until she couldn't see him anymore.

Inside her apartment, even though the sun had set hours before, she didn't bother to turn on any lamps. She didn't need light as she stripped from her clothes and sank into bed. His words were still with her when she closed her eyes, and it was his words that lulled her into a heavenly sleep.

Chapter 26

The club was bustling with the sights and sounds of last-minute preparations.

The staff rushed around, security completed their walk-through, and Jasmine shouted out instructions to all. In less than an hour, Rio would be open.

She walked to the center of the space that just twelve weeks ago was nothing more than four walls of cold concrete. But now, *Premiere* magazine called the two-level club "the jewel of downtown," and declared that tonight's opening would be "the best celebration in lower Manhattan post 9/11."

Jasmine had worked hard for that review. The last weeks had exhausted her. Contractors, designers, and planners had hounded and pounded her until there was little left. But what work had taken away, Hosea restored.

Days had passed since their time on Fire Island, and still, she kept the words he'd spoken in her heart, pulling them to her consciousness whenever she needed to be reminded that she shouldn't do anything to risk winning this prize.

"I'm getting so close," she said to herself.

"Uh, oh. I've been working you too hard if you're talking to yourself." Malik strolled toward her. "You look fantastic."

She grinned. This was only the second time that she'd worn the dress that Hosea gave her for her birthday.

"You don't look bad yourself." She straightened his tie. "So, are you ready for your big night?"

"Tonight belongs to you too." He glanced at his watch. "We don't have much time before the doors open." He watched as staff still hustled through the space. "Are we ready?"

"Definitely. But even if we weren't, we still have time. Only the countriest of country folks would show up right at nine."

"What's up, my people?" J.T. swaggered toward them with a woman hanging from his arm that Jasmine knew was not his wife.

Jasmine glanced at her watch, then looked at Malik and smiled. "Showtime," they said and laughed together.

The music was blaring.

Jasmine climbed to the second-level lounge. This may have been an invitation-only event, but both levels of Rio were packed as if it were New Year's Eve. Still, the upper floor gave her a bit of a reprieve from being the welcoming hostess. Her cheeks ached from her smiles that greeted everyone and her mind was bored with the useless chatter that came from every guest.

Still, she was pleased. Three hours into the night, drinks were flowing and food was devoured as if Rio were already a first-class night spot.

She glanced over the rail and watched the couples on the lower-level dance floor, before she turned toward the bar.

"Hey, Stu, I'll have a Coke, no ice, please."

"Sure thing, boss."

When he returned with her glass, a voice behind her said, "I got that."

Her heart raced and the memory that belonged to him rushed back as if they'd been together yesterday.

When she faced him, she said, "Put your wallet away, Brian. I'm part owner, remember?"

He grinned, nodded, and then looked at her as if she were naked. Without taking his eyes from her, he said, "Nice club."

She sipped her soda, and, wished that this time, her glass was full of ice. *"What* are you doing here?"

He shrugged. "I hadn't been to New York in a while and when J.T. told me about the opening, I thought I'd surprise you." He paused. "And I know you're surprised since you forgot to send me an invitation. My feelings were hurt."

"I'm sure that's not true."

He leaned in close and when she inhaled, the smell of him reminded her of the feel of him. "I've missed you."

"I'm sure," she paused to clear her throat, "that's not true, either."

"Where are you staying?"

Her hands began to shake and she rested her glass on the counter. "At my apartment," she said with as much steadiness as she could gather.

"Where do you live?" he whispered even though the music blared loud enough to make the walls vibrate.

"I can't—"

"I know you can't . . . leave right now. But we have all night." His lips grazed her ear.

She took a step aside, needing the space between them. "Brian, I'm involved with someone."

He finished what was left in his glass. "So am I. By the way, Alexis sends her good wishes."

Jasmine knew *that* wasn't true and she wondered what was his game. Why would he mention his wife?

"Enjoy the rest of your evening, Brian."

He chuckled. "Oh, I plan to." He rested his hand on hers and a charge surged through her veins, igniting a fire within her.

Even in her four-inch stilettos, she dashed away, praying that distance would be her medicine. Cure her of the thoughts, the memory, the desire.

Downstairs, she mingled with the crowd, but she couldn't hide. Brian stayed with her, in her mind. The way he talked, the words he spoke. The way her skin tingled at his touch.

Her stomach churned; her head ached.

"Jasmine, you don't look so good," J.T. said. "Don't tell me you're sick again." He chuckled.

She stared at him and then glanced at the two women who held his arms. "I'm just tired." She peeked at her watch. It was almost midnight. How was she going to share the same space with Brian for four more hours?

"Hey, I've been looking for you," Malik yelled over the music. "This is going great."

She nodded.

"Jasmine's not feeling well," J.T. told Malik.

He frowned and Jasmine knew he was remembering the last time she'd told him that.

"This time, I really don't feel well, Malik," Jasmine said, now feeling nauseated. "I'm going to check on everything and then get out of here."

After a moment, his face creased with concern. "You're shivering."

She hadn't noticed; she didn't know why she was shaking. She certainly wasn't cold. She could still feel the heat of him. "I think it's just all catching up with me. The long hours, no sleep, the music—" Her fingertips massaged her temples.

"Well, there's really no need for you to stay. Gabriella is working with Stacy and Tina is here too if we need any extra help. Where're your things? In the office?"

She nodded.

Within minutes, he returned with her jacket and purse, and then walked her to the front door.

"Jasmine," Stacy stopped them before they stepped outside. "We've run out of—"

Malik held up his hand. "I'll handle it."

"They need you in the kitchen," Stacy said.

"Go ahead, Malik," Jasmine said. "I'll catch a cab." She peeked through the glass. "They're lined up out there." She waved good-bye, then once outside, welcomed the fresher air. Already she felt revived. This was all she needed—to get away. Leaving now was going to keep her happily-ever-after alive.

Jasmine motioned for a cab. When the yellow car stopped, a hand came from behind her and reached for the door.

Please, God. No.

"Want some company?" the voice whispered.

She couldn't look back. Didn't need to. She could smell him, feel him as he pressed against her. She slipped into the car, hoping that he wouldn't follow, then praying that he would.

Brian slid in beside her, but still, she didn't look at him. Even after she gave the driver her address, she kept her eyes away. She didn't want to look. Didn't want to see the evil that had found its way to her tonight.

Lust and lunacy.

It was that bizarre blend that had her in bed with him again. And like the last time, it started from the moment they entered her building. She'd hurried past a frowning Henrikas as Brian followed. The elevator doors had barely closed, before they were in each other's arms. His hands, his lips, every part of him made her remember what she'd tried so hard to forget.

Inside her front door, no time was lost as he ripped her dress from her body, and then stripped everything else away until she stood before him, naked. He stood, still clothed, and with a swift unzip of his pants, took her there, pressed against the front door until she screamed.

Inside her bedroom, she took control. Undressed him and then told him what to do. Made him pleasure her in the ways she'd fantasized in her dreams.

Inside her mind, sanity returned—almost two hours later.

Jasmine collapsed onto the bed before the ringing phone startled her. She glanced at the clock. It was after two.

"Let it ring," he said.

She grabbed the telephone.

"Ms. Larson, Mr. Bush is on his way up." Henrikas's ac-
cented words rushed through the handset. "I thought—"

She slammed the phone down and jumped from the bed.
"You've got to go," she screamed.

He frowned, made no moves.

"My boyfriend is downstairs."

He sat up slowly.

She yelled, "You need to get out of here."

"You need to calm down. I don't want to be caught either.
But how do you think I'm going to get out without him seeing
me?"

She couldn't breathe deep enough to get oxygen to her
lungs.

He said, "Just close the door. I'll wait in the bathroom. And
you get rid of him."

He was the one she wanted to get rid of, but the ringing
doorbell stopped her words. Brian slid from between the
sheets and when he stood, his nakedness almost made her forget her mission. He motioned for her to answer the door and
then he crept into the bathroom. She grabbed her robe, closed
the bedroom door, then rushed to the front. She took a breath
before she greeted Hosea.

"Hey, darlin'."

She swallowed the stone lodged in her throat. "Hi. What
are you doing here?" she asked, barely opening the door wide
enough for him to see her.

"I stopped by the club to surprise you. Malik told me you
left sick." He frowned. "I was worried."

"I thought you weren't coming back until tomorrow."

His frown deepened. "Yeah, but I came back tonight. Just
to see you." He paused. "Is something wrong?"

"It's just that I'm surprised." Her fingers combed through her tousled hair. "I was feeling a little sick, but I'm better now. Came home . . . and got right into—"

Before she could finish, the door across the hall opened and Mae Frances peeked out. "A lot of talking going on out here for the middle of the night."

Jasmine cringed as Mae Frances, wrapped in a tattered robe, stepped into the hallway. With her arms crossed, she glared at Hosea. "So, you're Jasmine's preacher man, huh?" she sneered.

"Yes, ma'am." Hosea smiled, and then reached his hand toward hers. When she stayed in place, he said, "I'm sorry to disturb you." He nudged Jasmine's door gently, forcing her to step aside, and he walked past her into the apartment. "Is that the woman you've—" He stopped.

Jasmine's eyes followed his glance and she almost lost everything inside of her when he bent over and picked up her dress. Her bra and thong fell back to the floor from the tangled mess.

"Isn't this the dress—?"

"From my birthday," she finished. "I wore it, didn't mean to leave it there." She snatched the dress. "It's just that when I got home, I got undressed . . . so quickly."

He glanced at her silk underwear that still lay at his feet. "I see," he said, picking up the items and handing them to her.

Tears burned behind her lids. She wanted to hug him, hold him, but she stayed away. Didn't want him to smell another man's scent on her. "I'm sorry." Her voice quivered as she placed the clothes on the couch.

"What are you sorry for, darlin'? Sorry I found out that you're a bit messy?"

The first tear flowed and she nodded.

"Ah, come on. It's just that you're not feeling well." She held her breath as he reached for her. When he touched her, she sobbed, making him step back quickly. "What's wrong, Jasmine?"

"Nothing. I'm just . . . sick . . . and tired."

"Well, then, we need to get you back to bed. Do you want anything to eat?"

She shook her head. "If I eat anything, I'll—"

He held up his hand. "I get it. What about some tea? You get in bed and I'll bring it to you."

"No," she shouted her protest. Then, lowered her voice. "I just want you to go."

He reared back at her words.

"I mean, I'm glad to see you, but I'm tired."

He looked at her for a moment longer, then shrugged and turned toward the door. But before he stepped outside, he said, "I should just wait until you fall asleep. I'll stay out here and—"

"No. If you're here, I won't sleep and—" She had no more excuses. Just prayed inside that God would pour out His mercy right about now.

"Okay, I know when somebody's trying to get rid of me."

"It's not because I don't love you," she said before she could think. It was never in the plan for her to say that first. It was never in the plan to mean those words—so soon.

He turned, paused, stared, as if he were waiting for her to take it back. Then, he grinned. "I feel the same way, darlin'." He kissed her forehead. "Get some rest and call me as soon as you wake up. Malik said the offices are closed tomorrow, right?"

She nodded.

"Good, then stay in bed all day. I'll bring you breakfast, lunch, and dinner."

It had been hours since she'd smiled. "I'd like that."

She watched until he disappeared inside the elevator. She closed her door. Exhaled. A moment later, Brian stepped from her bedroom, fully dressed.

"I thought he'd never leave."

She glared at him. Wondered how someone she despised so much could make her feel so good.

"So, that's your man?" He slid his jacket over his shoulders. "I didn't believe it when you said you were involved." He grinned. "Seems like you have a good thing going."

She hated that he was the one to remind her of that.

He buttoned his jacket and then stepped toward her. "I had a good time . . . again. Thanks . . . darlin'," he smirked.

She wanted to slap him, but instead opened the door, wanting to just get rid of him.

He said, "I'll see you again soon."

"I don't—"

Before she could finish, Mae Frances's door opened again. "I thought you two had gone inside." Then, she squinted at Brian. "You're not the preacher man."

Brian laughed. "Your man's a preacher?" Then, he faced Mae Frances. "No, the preacher man just left." When he turned back to Jasmine, he leaned over, and let his lips linger on hers for a long moment.

As much as she wanted to pull away, she didn't.

He stepped back, and his fingers traced the curve of her jaw. "Like I said, I'll see you soon." He disappeared into the staircase.

Mae Frances was still holding her stance, but her glare had turned into a grin.

"You got them coming and going!" She shook her head. "Hmph. There must be something to this Christian thing." She closed her door and Jasmine could still hear her laughing when she closed hers.

Chapter 27

Rio was a hit.

The accolades poured in, from celebrities to the media. After just a week, the buzz was that Rio was the place to be.

But Jasmine found little reason to celebrate. Her emotions were waging war. First, she wondered when her plan had morphed to love. There was no denying the way she felt, especially every time she saw Hosea. She was intoxicated with love, but guilt stole her ecstasy. And then there was the fear when she wasn't with him that somehow, he—or his father—would find out about Brian.

It didn't help that every time she entered her building, she was reminded of that night. Henrikas continued to open the door and greet her the way she always did, which just thickened her shame.

But even more than the shame she felt with Henrikas, there was the disgrace she felt with Mae Frances. No one could ever accuse her of being a Holy-roller kind of girl, but surely she didn't want to do anything to push people away from God. Especially not after the sermon that Reverend Bush had preached last Sunday.

"As Christians, we have a responsibility to God. When we tell someone we love the Lord, they will watch us. See how we talk, see how we walk. People will get all up in your business, even taking notice of who you're hanging out with."

It was at that point in the service that Jasmine felt the first pang when the image of her in the hallway, first with Hosea, then with Brian, came to her mind.

"Once you profess to be a Christian," Reverend Bush had continued, "once you ask the Lord into your heart, your responsibility is to bring people to Him, not turn people away. Make no mistake, we all will be held accountable. Especially if you've done anything to push someone away from God."

Jasmine had wanted to run from the church. That's exactly what she'd done to Mae Frances—probably pushed her away from God for good.

Since last Sunday, she'd wanted to talk to her neighbor. Needed to explain that what Mae Frances saw wasn't who she was. It had taken eight days to build the courage, but on Saturday morning, Jasmine decided that she couldn't go back to church on Sunday—couldn't face God—if she didn't take care of this.

She still wasn't sure what she would say when she approached Mae Frances's door. When her neighbor appeared, her smirk said that she remembered that night.

"Jasmine Larson, what can I do for you?"

"I . . ." She stopped. Couldn't think of the right words. "I . . . was going to the store to pick up a few things," she said, hoping God would count this as repentence. "Do you want anything?"

Her smirk went away. "No, thank you." Her chin jutted forward. "I have plenty of food."

"Okay, well . . ." Jasmine turned away. "See you later."

But she'd taken just two steps when Mae Frances said, "Actually, I do need a few things."

With a smile, Jasmine turned back. "Wait here," Mae Frances said, leaving Jasmine in the hallway. A few minutes later she returned. "I made a list."

Jasmine tried not to show her shock when she glanced at the paper filled from top to bottom with items.

"Let me give you the money." Mae Frances dug through her purse, searching. She didn't look at Jasmine when she said, "I must have forgotten to go to the bank."

"No problem. I'll pick these up and you can pay me later."

Mae Frances stood straight, pushed her shoulders back. "Thank you, Jasmine Larson."

Guess I got some shopping to do, she thought as she turned toward the elevator.

The moment Jasmine stepped off the elevator, Mae Frances's door opened.

"I'll see you next time," a man said, and then both of them appeared in the hallway. The man nodded as he passed by Jasmine.

Staying in place, Jasmine's eyes followed the tall, ruggedly handsome man as he strolled down the hall; she kept her stare until he was gone. With raised eyebrows, she followed Mae Frances into her apartment.

"Thank you, Jasmine Larson," her neighbor said, as if a good-looking man hadn't just walked out of her place. She took the shopping bags from Jasmine and motioned for her to sit. "I'll put this away and then I'll join you."

Jasmine smiled. She didn't know Mae Frances had friends like that and she couldn't wait to ask a few questions. She wandered through the living room pausing at the mantel. She lifted one of the silver frames that sat on the shelf and peered closer as if she'd missed something. The frame was empty. Just like all the others.

"I thought you'd like some tea," Mae Frances said, carrying a silver tray with a teapot and two matching cups. She sat, crossed her ankles, and spoke as if she were hosting a small party.

"Thank you." Jasmine lowered her eyes as she joined Mae Frances and took a sip from her cup. Her frivolous thoughts of the man were gone. She took a breath, hoping that her words would not offend. "Mae Frances, there're some things I don't understand."

"Like what?"

Jasmine glanced again at the fireplace. "Your pictures over there."

Mae Frances straightened her back even more. "Sometimes I wonder why I bother with you."

"What?" Jasmine's voice was full of attitude.

"Why are you always in my business?"

Jasmine glared at Mae Frances, sitting tall, defiance in her eyes. And then Jasmine saw more. Pride etched in the lines of Mae Frances's scowl.

With a breath, Jasmine inhaled a bit of calm. "That's not what I want to do. I just care about you."

Her penciled eyebrows rose. "You care?" she said as if those two words were the butt end of a joke. "Why?"

Jasmine opened her mouth, then stopped. *Why?* She wasn't sure, but she knew that in these months she'd come to care about the woman who wore diamonds and minks, rode in a limousine, yet her cupboards were as bare as her photo frames. "I care because I like you, and I believe that if I needed you, you'd be here for me."

Mae Frances blinked, "Thank you for caring, Jasmine Larson," she said softly. Then, the defiance returned. "But I'm fine."

"I know you are. I just want to know how I can . . ." She paused, took a breath. "Does your ex-husband help you—"

Her laugh was loud and long. "Help me? Oh, yes. He's the reason that I'm living off of Central Park and not in it." Her laughter continued. "Look around. Can't you tell that the great Dr. Elijah Van Dorn is helping me?"

"Mae Frances, I'm just asking because—"

"Because of the empty cabinets. Because my furniture and clothes look secondhand?" Mae Frances stood, wandered to the mantel, and stared at the blank frames. "I am fine, Jasmine Larson."

"Okay. But I was thinking, we could call someone, if you ever need help."

Mae Frances's eyes flashed with fire. "Like who? Some charity? Or the government? Are you talking welfare?" she said with an insulted inflection.

"No, not welfare. But my church, my pastor, we have programs to help seniors—"

Her laugh, even louder this time, stopped Jasmine. "Church?" She paused, and then added with a sneer, "It's because of church and your God that I'm alone." She pushed her shoulders back. "I would rather live in the park, and eat from the trash, than get involved with your church."

Jasmine frowned. "Mae Frances, God is not responsible for what your husband did."

"I know that. I know they were just using the name of some nonexistent being. But I'm telling you I won't have anything to do with a church, where people claim to love in the name of some image they can't see, but then they stab you straight in your back. Some even take the knife out, show it to you, and stab you again. Oh, no." She waved her hands. "No church, no God."

"My church isn't like that. At City of Lights, we're not one way inside and another way outside."

"You're not?" The ends of her lips curled into a grin. "Well, what do you call that stuff I walked into last week in the hall? Hmph. You got men coming and going at the same time. You're just like all the rest of God's children."

Jasmine clenched her teeth so tightly that her jaw ached. "I was just saying—"

"And I'm just saying," Mae Frances interrupted, "keep that church crap to yourself."

Jasmine glared at her; wondered why she cared. "Fine." She stood and stomped all the way to her own apartment.

"Forget you, Mae Frances!" Jasmine yelled to her walls. She bounced onto the couch and clicked on the television.

But as she flipped through the channels, her eyes misted. And then, a tear fell. Mae Frances had hurt more than her feelings. She had hurt her heart with the truth. Jasmine just prayed that God wouldn't hold this one against her because if He did, she couldn't imagine what her punishment might be.

Jasmine snatched the phone. "Hello."

"Hey, darlin', you sound upset. What's up?"

She sighed. "Nothing."

"Come on. Don't make me go through all of this. I gotta run to a meeting, and I don't want to spend all this time asking you over and over. So just tell me now, and then I can spend the rest of the time telling you how much I miss you."

Jasmine chuckled, but her humor went away as she told Hosea about her conversation with her neighbor, carefully excluding Mae Frances's last comments. "I've just never met anyone who talks about God the way she does," Jasmine concluded. "Isn't that blasphemy?"

"Darlin', there are a lot more people like Mae Frances than there are like us. Just be patient. You'll win her over."

"I don't think anyone will ever make Mae Frances change her mind."

"Remember what my pops preached. Just by watching your walk, she can come to see who God really is."

The image of the hallway scene returned and Jasmine shuddered. "Whatever," she said, needing to get away from those thoughts. "Anyway, who's your meeting with?"

"Actually, my pops. We're going over some items for the Teen Outreach Program. But I'm calling, darlin', 'cause I wanna know what you got going after church tomorrow. Any plans?"

"Just planning on being with you."

"Then add one more to that list. We're going to have lunch with my pops."

Jasmine sat straight up. "Lunch with Reverend Bush?"

"You know, we're gonna have to do something about that. You can't keep calling my pops Reverend Bush."

She wanted to tell him that she didn't want to call his father anything. Never wanted to talk to him at all.

For months, she'd done all she could to stay far from the reverend. If Hosea stayed for the second service, she made work-related excuses to get away. And she'd deftly changed the subject anytime she felt Hosea approaching any discussion of the two of them spending time with his father.

Hosea interrupted her thoughts with, "Maybe you should just call him Pops."

He laughed. She didn't.

"Aw, come on, Jasmine. Don't let Mae Frances get you down."

"I won't," she said. Her neighbor was a good cover. Now, she wished she could use Mae Frances to get out of this invitation. "Lunch with your father? Tomorrow? I don't know. I still have so much work to do."

"What work do you have to do after church?" She could hear his frown. "Are you trying to avoid my pops?"

"No, it's just scary meeting the folks, you know?"

"That would make sense if you didn't already know my father. But you know what kind of man he is. And he's been asking me to arrange this for some time." When she still said nothing, Hosea added, "I promise I won't let him chew you up and spit you out." He laughed.

"That's not funny." She shivered, imagining the sight. She could see Reverend Bush, with Rottweiler fangs. And she, a mangled mess at the end of lunch.

"Stop being so serious. After ten minutes with Pops, you'll be wondering why we didn't do this before."

Jasmine remembered the last time she spent ten minutes with the reverend. *If there is anything that stinks, I'll smell it.* After what she'd done, how was she going to sit across the table from the man who'd spoken those words?

"So, I was thinking we'd have brunch at Tavern on the Green. Okay?"

No was not an option. "I guess."

"Great, and you'll see. It'll be fine."

Jasmine couldn't wait until they'd said good-bye. For the next hour, she sat, staring, silent, wondering how she would ever get through lunch with the man who just by looking at her had the potential to make her dreams come toppling down.

Her stomach stirred, and Jasmine had a feeling that after tomorrow her life would never be the same again.

Chapter 28

*J*asmine had yet to exhale.

She hadn't while she slept, nor while she dressed. Nor while she sat in the front pew, and dreaded (for the first time ever) the end of the service. Even now, as she waited in the church's lounge, she felt as if she were suffocating.

"Darlin', are you ready?"

She wanted to tell him no, that she would never be ready to break bread with his father.

"Of course she's ready, son." Reverend Bush's lips rounded into a smile. But she wasn't fooled. His eyes said what his lips didn't—that he was still watching, just waiting, already knowing that she would fall.

Reverend Bush said, "I have a meeting with Brother Hill right after, so I'll take my car."

"Hey, why don't we just have him come with us?"

No, her insides screamed. Reverend Bush. Brother Hill. She'd be dead before they'd taken their first bite.

Reverend Bush shook his head. "He has plans, and besides," he turned toward Jasmine, "I really want us to spend the time together. I want to know Jasmine the way you do."

It was time to lie. Time to come up with some excuse. But even as Hosea chatted as they sped down Central Park West, Jasmine couldn't think of a single reason to get away. All she could do was wonder if she would still have a relationship after Reverend Bush spent these next hours asking questions, studying her, and finally somehow discovering that she had been unfaithful to his son.

She trembled at that thought. "That's impossible," she whispered.

"What'd you say, darlin'?"

She hadn't noticed that they'd arrived.

"Nothing." She eased from the car and breathed deeply, inhaling courage. This was just her imagination. There was no way the reverend could look at her and see Brian. She would just be her normal, charming self and conquer the father's heart the way she had the son's.

Inside Tavern on the Green, Hosea spoke to the waitress while Jasmine stood to the side. "So we finally get the chance to spend some time together, don't we, Jasmine?" Reverend Bush said when he stepped through the doors.

"Yes, *Hosea* really wanted this." Not me, she almost added.

He grinned as if he knew something she didn't. In silence, they both remembered her pursuit, his rejection, her threats, his promise.

"Well, I wanted this too," he said. "Wanted the chance to talk. Get to know the person that you really are."

His grin stripped away her confidence and gave her another vision: Reverend Bush, talking. Asking questions. Getting answers. Then, he'd receive a revelation from God. The reverend would rise to his feet, point his finger, and shout that she had been exposed. And then, he would reveal every one of her secrets.

By the time Hosea joined them, she needed to hold his hand just to stand. She moved on shaky limbs as they followed the hostess to their table.

I'll never make it, she thought, as the scenario she'd imagined played over in her mind.

"Jasmine?"

"Darlin'," Hosea stopped her and her thoughts. "That woman over there just called you."

Jasmine followed Hosea's glance and froze. She wanted to blink and with that motion, like the TV genie Jeannie, make the woman disappear.

"So, that *is* you, Jasmine. What are you doing in New York?" Alexis asked.

She wanted to ask her the same thing. But her lips wouldn't move. All she could do was stare at Alexis Ward Lewis—the only person on earth that she could say she hated.

But as much as she hated Alexis, she kept her gaze planted on her and not on the man who shared her table. With Hosea and Reverend Bush by her side, she couldn't face the man who made her do things she didn't want to do.

"So, what are you doing in New York?" Alexis repeated.

"I . . . I live here," Jasmine said. "What are you doing here?"

"We came for a convention," Alexis said.

"Hello, I'm Hosea Bush," he said, turning toward Alexis once it was clear that Jasmine had no plans of making an introduction. "And this is my father, Reverend Samuel Bush."

Jasmine wanted to slap Alexis, the way she smiled at Hosea. But those thoughts went away when Brian stood.

"This is my husband, Brian Lewis. You remember him, don't you, Jasmine?"

Brian said, "Of course Jasmine remembers me."

Although she kept her eyes away from him, she could feel his smirk. He shook hands with Hosea, then the reverend. He saved Jasmine for last.

"How have you been, Jasmine?"

"Fine. We really—"

"So, you guys are friends of Jasmine's?" Hosea asked as he put his arm around her shoulder.

"Friends is a stretch," Alexis said. "But we've known each other for many years."

The hostess interrupted, "Would you like to be reseated? I can arrange a table for five."

"No." Jasmine's protest was so loud, others around them paused their conversations. She lowered her voice, "We'd prefer to keep our party to three." She faced Alexis. "Good seeing you," she said as if the three words were one, and then she rushed the hostess forward. She had to get to a chair before she collapsed.

At their table, she fell into her seat. Could this day be any worse?

Reverend Bush said, "They seem like nice people. How do you know them?"

You can do this, Jasmine.

"Met them when I lived in Los Angeles."

"I thought you lived in Florida."

"I did. Right before I came to New York. But I was born and raised in L.A."

"I didn't know that," the reverend said as if he thought there was some kind of secret in her words.

Reverend Bush looked at Alexis and Brian. "We should invite them to church."

"No!" When Reverend Bush and Hosea both looked at her with raised eyebrows, Jasmine added in a lower voice, "They're here for a convention. I'm sure they won't be here next Sunday."

Reverend Bush nodded. "True." When he glanced again at Brian and Alexis, Jasmine crossed her arms. *What is he looking for?* she wondered. And then when he faced her with a stare that burned through her skin, she remained stoic, as if she weren't about to die.

The time passed with conversation, but little of it from Jasmine. She heard Hosea speak, saw his father's lips move, but she was not connected. She tried to smile, and chat, and keep her eyes away from Alexis and Brian. But every few seconds, her glance strayed to their table. She watched as they ate and held hands. She cringed when Brian leaned over and kissed his wife. And in her mind, that image faded, and she replaced Alexis with herself. And Brian's lips were over hers. And his hands were again bringing her pleasure.

"Are you okay?" Reverend Bush frowned at Jasmine.

Her hand paused in midair. She hadn't noticed that she was fanning herself. "I'm fine. Just a bit hot in here."

She looked at Alexis and Brian again and begged God to make them go away.

God granted her prayer, and the couple stood. But she had no time to celebrate when the two turned their way.

"We wanted to say good-bye," Brian said when they paused at their table. To Jasmine, he added, "It was good seeing you. Hey, give us a call if you're ever in L.A." To his wife he said, "Honey, give Jasmine one of your cards so she can get in touch with us."

The way Alexis rolled her eyes, Jasmine knew Brian would pay later for that request. But still, Alexis rummaged through her purse.

"That's a good idea," Hosea piped in. "Jasmine's in L.A. on business quite a bit."

"Really?" Alexis stopped her search and peered as if Jasmine's itinerary needed to be her business.

"I won't be there anymore," Jasmine said to Alexis. "Now that my club is open," she turned her glance to Brian, "there's no reason for me to return to Los Angeles."

"Well then, I guess you won't need my card." Alexis half-smiled. "Honey, we really have to get going."

Good riddance, Jasmine thought as the others exchanged good-byes. She breathed with relief until the reverend said, "Seems like you're better friends with Brian than Alexis."

"No," Jasmine protested and prayed that his words hadn't come from a vision. "I'm not friends with either of them," she responded, keeping her glance on the barely touched lobster omelet on her plate.

As Hosea and his father continued their chatter, Jasmine said nothing. Silence kept trouble away. There was little chance of a conviction if she offered no evidence.

And her silence gave her time to wonder. Wonder about Brian. Wonder about his games. Wonder why he wanted to play when he had so much to lose. Just like she did.

When the waiter came to clear the table, Jasmine offered her plate, with no more than two bites taken from her omelet.

"You weren't very hungry, were you, darlin'?" Hosea squeezed her hand.

She shook her head.

"Seems like you have a lot on your mind," Reverend Bush said.

"Oh, no, that's not it, Pops." Hosea laughed. "Darlin', don't be mad, but I've gotta tell him. Pops, Jasmine was nervous about having lunch with you."

"Really? And why would you be nervous, Jasmine?"

She said, "It's just that in-law thing," before she could think.

Reverend Bush raised his eyebrows. "In-law?" His glance volleyed between Hosea and Jasmine. "Son, is there something you haven't told me?"

"No," Jasmine said first. "I meant it's hard to meet anyone's parents."

"Oh," he said in a "thank God" kind of tone. "But it's not like we're meeting for the first time," Reverend Bush continued.

"That's what I told her, Pops. She sees you every Sunday."

"Yes, and when Jasmine first came to City of Lights, she tried very hard to get me to have lunch with her," he said to Hosea. Then to Jasmine, "So, I'm surprised this bothers you."

Hosea frowned. "Really?"

It took a moment to force the lump away so that she could speak. "Yes," Jasmine said, looking straight at Reverend Bush. "I wanted to be part of the church's building committee."

"Is that what you wanted to be part of?" Reverend Bush asked.

She wanted to just cry. "Yes, I had some great marketing ideas for you."

"Is that what you had for me?"

"Pops." Hosea laughed. "Stop teasing Jasmine. She's already not feeling this."

"I'm sorry, son." The reverend chuckled. "You know how I am." Then he said to Jasmine, "Sorry you've been uncomfort, able. Maybe we can start over. Do this another day."

I hope not, she thought. As Hosea paid the bill, she could feel his father's eyes. But she kept hers away from him, just waiting, until she could leave, and breath. Her legs were Jell-O when Hosea took her hand and led her from the restaurant.

"Thanks for lunch, son," the reverend said.

"I'm glad you got a chance to hang with us."

Reverend Bush turned to Jasmine. "See you soon."

"Definitely," she said before she hurried into Hosea's car.

Hosea jumped in beside her. "See, that wasn't bad, was it?"

She smiled, said no, and didn't bother to tell him that if he didn't get her home quick, the carpet of his new SUV would be flooded with remnants of the little bit of food that she did eat.

In front of Jasmine's apartment, Hosea said, "I'm not feeling too well." He tapped his chest. "Feels like heartburn."

"Do you think it was something you ate?"

"I don't know." He leaned across the console and kissed her cheek. "I'll catch you tomorrow, okay?"

"That's fine," Jasmine said, more than ready to put an end to this day. She didn't add that his father had made her sick too.

Four hours later, the afternoon sun had long ago departed, and Jasmine had done nothing more than change into an over, size T-shirt and park in front of the television. Inside her mind, images played like a Broadway production. Images of Brian and Alexis. Images of Brian alone. Images of Brian naked.

"Why am I doing this?" she screamed to the television. She didn't even like Brian, but it was the love that she had for the way he felt—and the way he made her feel—that kept her obsessed. He was a demon who'd taken control of the worst part of her.

"Never again," she told herself, as she watched a woman in a Lifetime movie beg her husband not to leave. "Never again."

This time, she'd stand by her vow. There was little probability of seeing Brian. And if their paths did cross, she would fight Brian's lust and think only of Hosea's love.

With that promise, she flicked off the television, but she hadn't taken two steps before the ringing telephone stopped her.

"Ms. Larson, you have a guest," Henrikas said. He hesitated. "Mr. Brian Lewis."

She couldn't tell if the pounding came from her heart or her head.

"Ms. Larson?"

Tell him to go away, Jasmine. "He's a doctor." As soon as she spoke those senseless words, she realized they weren't much of an explanation. Her doorman had already seen her with Brian. "Send him up," she added in a whisper.

The self-berating began the moment she hung up. *Why did I do that?* she asked as she paced.

She decided that all she would do was ask questions—find out what he wanted, why he was there—and then she'd send him back to his wife.

The moment she heard the elevator, she opened her door, making sure Mae Frances did not see her visitor.

Brian swaggered into her apartment as if he was supposed to be there.

"What do you want?" she asked the moment she closed her door.

He faced her with a grin. "Like you don't know."

She breathed deeply, initiating the fight within. "You don't need to be here."

"I know. But I've discovered that my needs and my wants are usually the same." As if he had an invitation, he settled onto her couch and loosened his tie. "Nice place. I didn't get a chance to check it out last time." He stretched his arms along the sofa.

"Where's your wife?"

"At a meeting."

"Why aren't you at the hotel waiting for her?"

"Because I wanted to see you."

"Don't tell me the great Alexis isn't taking good care of her man," she said, enjoying for the moment the fact that she could have Alexis's husband anytime she wanted him.

"Oooh, your claws are showing, Jasmine."

His leer reminded her that she was covered only in a thigh-long T-shirt. "I want you to go," she said, regaining her resolve.

He chuckled. "If you didn't want me here, why did you invite me up?"

"It wasn't an invitation. I just wanted to know what you wanted."

His face stretched with seriousness. "You want to know what I want?" He stood, moved toward her.

Jasmine backed up until she was pressed against the door. He leaned forward, one hand above her, setting his trap. "Remember last time?" he whispered. "This is exactly where I took you."

She inhaled, took in his scent. Closed her eyes, remembered. "No," she panted more to herself than him. "I . . . I . . . can't do this."

"Why not?" His tongue tickled her ear.

She tried to breathe in some sense, but longing, lust, dragged her away. Every muscle betrayed her, responding instantly to his touch. His hands, his lips took her hostage again. Took her away from what she knew was right. Made her do wrong.

This time, she was the aggressor. Ripped his shirt from his chest. By the time they backed into her bedroom, he was naked. She pushed him onto her bed and didn't bother removing her T-shirt. Just took him as she was. Every emotion— anger, fear, desire—erupted inside. She blocked out his chuckles. Tried to ignore his mocking words.

"I thought you didn't want this."

She *didn't* want him. She needed him.

The telephone rang, but she was helpless to answer it. The more she had of him, the more she wanted.

She shrieked when they connected. Cursed him when he wouldn't stop. Begged him when he slowed down.

She didn't know if minutes—or hours—had passed when the phone rang again. But still, there was nothing she could do, except take him.

She rolled from the bed and pulled the T-shirt over her head. Tossed it across the room. He smiled with admiration as she stood, exposed before him. But she didn't appreciate his approval.

As they joined again, her body left her mind. Her body drank in the pleasure. Her mind gave into the pain. She tried to think about the man she loved, but she could barely remember his name.

The phone interrupted them again. And again. Finally, she grabbed it, wanting to demand that the caller stop trespassing. But when she put the phone to her ear, the voice took her breath away.

"Jasmine, are you there?" Reverend Bush said.

She pushed Brian off her. "Reverend Bush."

"Hosea asked me to call you. He's in the hospital."

"What?" She struggled to move between the tangled sheets. "Is he all right?" She trembled as she yelled into the phone.

"Jasmine, calm down. Hosea's fine. It's serious, but he's fine. We're at Harlem Hospital."

"I'll be right there." She slammed the handset onto the bed.

"I guess I'll have to get going," Brian said.

He startled her; she'd forgotten he was there. But she didn't turn to look at him. She couldn't.

"What's up?" he said as she rushed to her closet.

"My . . . friend is in the hospital," she said, grabbing a pair of jeans.

"So, you want me to leave?"

She paused, looked at him as if he had two heads. "Yes," she began slowly. "Leave. Now."

He shrugged. "Would you mind if I took a shower?"

She wanted to curse him out. "Brian, get out of my house," she hissed.

"You weren't saying that a few minutes ago."

Her silence was his clue.

"Fine," he said and then moved as if he had nothing but time. "Can I at least use your bathroom?" He didn't wait for her response. Just slipped into his pants and strolled into the lavatory.

Jasmine paced outside the door, and willed him to move faster. Willed herself to stay composed so she could get to Hosea.

Within a minute, she banged on the door. The toilet flushed, water ran, and then he strolled out as if she wasn't in the middle of a crisis.

"I guess I'll be going."

She said nothing. Escorted him to the door. He paused, leaned over as if he wanted to kiss her. She turned away.

"Catch ya later."

The first tear came the moment she slammed the door. When she scurried toward her bedroom, her cries were faster. With everything in her, she wanted to get to the man she loved. But Hosea would have to wait.

She rushed into the bathroom, turned the Hot knob to full blast, and then shrieked under the heat of the shower's water. The man she loved would have to wait until she burned another man's scent off her skin.

Jasmine dashed past the information desk, and security guard, then navigated through the halls of Harlem Hospital.

On the eleventh floor, the nurse's station directed her to Room 1127. She took a deep breath before she entered.

"Hey, darlin'," Hosea said the moment she opened the door. His voice was weak, but his eyes were alert, wide, smiling.

As she'd dressed and then offered a cab driver double to get her to the hospital in ten minutes, she had imagined every scenario that could take Hosea away from her.

But although he was prostrate, dressed in a hospital gown and covered with a thin infirmary sheet, there was little else to indicate that anything was wrong.

"Hey," she spoke softly. She nodded at Reverend Bush, who sat on the other side of the bed. "What happened?" she asked Hosea.

"Don't worry, darlin'. It may not look like it, but I'm fine." With his thumb, he gently wiped away a single tear that she didn't even realize had spilled down her cheek. "It could've been serious, but like always, God just did His thing."

Reverend Bush stood. "I'm going to get some coffee. I'll be right back, but take it slow, son," he said, although he looked at Jasmine. "Remember what the doctor said."

Neither looked at the reverend as he strolled from the room. Jasmine laid down her jacket and purse and then eased onto the edge of the bed.

"What happened?"

"I'll shorten this story. Seems I had a blood clot in my leg that traveled to my lungs."

"Oh my God."

"But they caught it. Said I was lucky but I told them luck had nothing to do with it."

"Are they sure you're going to be okay?"

"Yup. I'm doped up right now to stop these chest pains. And I've gotta stay until the clot dissolves, but that's about it."

"How did you get a blood clot?"

He hesitated. "After talking to the doctor, Pops and I figured that it's probably genetic. That's the way my mom died."

"Please don't talk about dying, Hosea," she said as more tears came. "I don't want to do this without you."

He took her hand. "I'm not going anywhere, darlin'. I plan on being here, with you, for a long time."

She blinked back more tears. "I was so scared. So worried."

"Don't worry. Just pray."

"I was afraid that I would lose you," she said.

"I had the same thought as they rolled me in here. All I could think about was I didn't want to go anywhere—not just yet. I don't want to lose you, either."

"Oh, you won't, sweetie."

"Jasmine."

She frowned when he said nothing more. "What is it? Are you in pain?"

He shook his head. "Help me to push this up."

She found the button on the side of the bed.

"I need to talk to you." He took her hand. "When I was on staff at Crystal Lake, one thing that bugged me was that people waited until tragedy hit before they squared their business. Never made any sense to me, until now." He looked down at their hands clasped together. "I've turned into one of those people because when I thought that I might die, and I would never see you on this earth again, I knew I had to get moving."

"Moving?" Jasmine started to shake. Was he talking about going back to Chicago?

"Jasmine, it's time for us to make this permanent. We know what we want and more importantly, we know what God wants. So, what are we waiting for? It's time for us . . ."

She held her breath.

"I love you, Jasmine. And I want us to . . . get hitched." He laughed, then coughed.

"Take it easy," she said, resting her hand on his chest.

"Don't try to change the subject."

Although his eyes sparkled, Jasmine wasn't sure if he meant what he was saying. "Are you serious?"

"Why wouldn't I be?"

"What kind of medication are you on?"

He laughed. "I'm sober enough to know that I want you."

Still she wondered about the drugs. Or was it the stress that came with being rushed to the hospital. "This just doesn't seem like the right time," she said, then asked herself why she was trying to talk him out of it. This was the prize.

"Jasmine, I've known for a while that you were going to be my wife. I suspected it from the moment we met. But I knew it when you ate those hot dogs with me. Anyone who would do that knows how to go with the flow." He laughed, but turned serious. "This has been in my heart for a long time. Now, it's traveled to my head so my lips could move and say the right words."

This was the moment she'd worked for. But she couldn't find joy when she thought about how—on this day—she'd given her body to another man.

That thought brought tears to her heart, and her eyes.

"Ah, darlin', I hope you're not crying because you're about to tell me no."

She shook her head. "No way. I would love to be your wife." She sobbed.

He pulled her into his arms, hugging her. "I can't say this is the reaction I expected, but as long as you're saying yes, I'll take what I can get."

She tried to chuckle. "Yes," she said. "Definitely, I want to marry you."

"Well, now."

Neither had noticed that Reverend Bush was back; Jasmine leaned away from Hosea and wiped her tears.

"Pops, I guess it's you. The first one to know that this incredible woman is making me put a ring on her finger."

Reverend Bush kept his smile, and Jasmine hoped that was all Hosea saw. She hoped he didn't see the reservation that clouded his father's eyes.

The reverend stepped to the bed. Glanced at Jasmine, then said to his son, "Congratulations. If this is what you want."

Hosea frowned. "Come on, Pops, don't hold back all your cheer. I'd thought you'd be a little more excited."

"This just seems sudden."

His frown deepened. "You've known my intentions with Jasmine all along."

Jasmine knew the reverend wasn't concerned with his son's intentions. It was hers that he questioned.

"Yes," the reverend agreed. "But I didn't think you'd do this now." His eyes glanced around the room. "In this place."

"Pops, this is the best place. And the best time." He held out his hand, reaching for Jasmine. "And the best woman." When she clasped her fingers through his, he added, "Sometimes God will put you in a place where you have to make a move. It wasn't until I was lying here that I realized I needed to step up. I'm happy, Pops. Jasmine makes me happy."

She spoke to the reverend but looked into Hosea's eyes. "And Hosea makes me happy."

Reverend Bush stared at Jasmine for a moment. "That's a good thing. Congratulations, then." He shook his son's hand and then hesitated before he wrapped his arms around Jasmine. "I wish you all the best," he said, after pulling away from their quick embrace.

"Looks like I'm interrupting a celebration," a bald man said as he pushed open the room's door.

"Doctor, this is my fiancée, Jasmine Larson," Hosea said. He turned to Jasmine. "I like the sound of that," he whispered.

She shook the doctor's hand and then followed Reverend

Bush from the room when the doctor asked them to step out-side.

Jasmine floated into the waiting room, but she hit the ground when Reverend Bush asked, "Was this your plan?"

She didn't know how to tell him that yes, he was right—she'd had a plan. But it hadn't been about that for a long time.

"I love your son."

"That's hard to believe."

"We've been together for months."

He chuckled. "And that means what?"

"That I've fallen in love with him."

His face squeezed into a sneer. "With him or his money? Or is it his potential?"

"With all of that!" His jaw tightened with her words. "Because all of that," she continued, "makes Hosea who he is. But the best part of him, the part that swept me away, is his heart. I don't expect you to understand, but I want to be a better me because of Hosea."

She thought she'd won him with her words, but when he clapped, her heart ached.

"Great performance, Sister Jasmine."

His insult swelled the hurt in her heart. "What do you want from me?" she whispered.

"I want to know what you're up to."

"Nothing more than to marry Hosea."

"Seems like that's going to happen."

"Because of love, not a plan."

His face was still tight with disbelief.

She said, "You know what, I don't have to convince you. I want you to be happy for us, but really, Reverend Bush, this is between me and Hosea."

"You're right about that. Hosea's grown, so I won't even begin to tell him what to do. But I can tell you." He moved forward, closing the gap between them. "I told you before, I'd be watching. And now my eyes will stay on you." He glared. "I'm not playing with you and you'd better not be playing with my son."

"I'm not."

He peered at her as if he could see something. "I don't trust you, Jasmine. There's something . . ." He stopped.

She stood still, straight, as if she had confidence. But silently, she prayed that Reverend Bush wouldn't see in her the secret that could take Hosea away.

He said, "The stakes are higher now. If you are who you say you are, fine. I wish you and my son a wonderful life. But if there is anything . . ." He left his threat right there.

Her head pulsed with a pain she'd never felt before.

But then, his lips spread into a smile. "Will you please tell my son that I'll be back in a few hours?"

She didn't agree or disagree. She simply watched him put on his jacket and then march down the hall as if it were his sanctuary.

Her head was still pounding when the doctor told her she could return to Hosea.

"Come on over here, darlin'," Hosea said the moment she entered. Then he asked, "What's wrong?"

"I'm just worried."

"I told you, no need. The doctors said I was going to be all right, although God told me that earlier, and that's all I needed to know. In a few days, I'll be outta here." He squeezed her hands.

"Thank God you're going to be fine."

"Yup, with a little medication, a lot of love from you, and all of God's mercy and goodness." He pulled her close and held her longer than he ever had before.

She loved the feel of him and knew this was where she was supposed to be.

This wasn't about lust. This was love.

This wasn't about a plan. This was her purpose.

And she was going to do everything to prove to Reverend Bush that Hosea had chosen the right woman.

Chapter 29

"Hey, darlin'."

Jasmine beamed. It had been a week since Hosea had been admitted and other than the fact that he was still in the hospital, there was no other way to tell that he'd been sick.

"I hope you brought me something good," he said, tossing the magazine he'd been reading aside. "I can't take these hospital cooks no mo'."

Jasmine laughed, as she'd done every day when he complained about the food. "Hosea, I can't sneak anything in here," she said like she always did. "It's against the rules."

"What they're feeding me should be against the rules. In fact, it should be against the law. I need to call somebody and have these people arrested."

Jasmine shook her head as Hosea continued his rampage. He rambled, but Jasmine disregarded his words. She straightened the pillows behind him, smoothed the sheet that covered him, pushed the tray (with the empty plate of the lunch he'd just eaten) aside. She filled his tumbler with water and then held out the glass to him. "Are you drinking enough?"

"Did you hear a word I said about the food?"

"Did you hear what I said about your water?"

He shook his head as he took the glass. "Already pushing me around."

She sat on the edge of the bed. "And you love it, don't you?"

He put the glass down. "I know that I love you." He lifted her hand and kissed her palm. "My hunger hasn't blinded me to that."

Jasmine laughed with him.

"Seriously, though," Hosea began, his chuckles gone. "I want to talk about us."

Jasmine wasn't sure if she wanted to hear this. For the last week, she'd lived in two worlds. In one, she was euphoric, basking in the reality that she would soon be Hosea Bush's wife. But then in the other place, she was nervously waiting for her joy to be snatched away, knowing for sure that somehow her secret would be revealed.

"Darlin', are you listening to me?"

She nodded.

"I don't know how you feel about this, but I don't believe in long engagements. Once God tells you to do something, you just need to do it." He paused. "So . . ." From under his sheet, he took out a black velvet box. Jasmine was frozen for a long moment. "Darlin', aren't you going to say something?"

"How did you get a ring?"

"Well, that's not the first thing I expected you to say, but I've had it for a few weeks. Open the box."

Her hands trembled as she reached for her hope. "This is beautiful," she whispered as she stared at the glimmering marquise.

Hosea twisted the ring from the box and then held it at the tip of her ring finger. "Jasmine Larson," he whispered. "Will you do me the honor of becoming Jasmine Bush?"

"Everytime you ask me, my answer will be the same." She grinned. "Yes. Yes." She tried to hold her hand steady as he slipped the platinum band on her finger. She closed her mind, wanting to center herself in this moment.

Her glance traveled from her ring to her man and emotions flooded her. Feelings she'd never experienced before, couldn't explain now. Before she could think, she closed the gap between them, her lips finding his. She expected him to back away, but when he didn't, she pressed against him. Then parted her lips. Found his tongue. And did a slow dance.

Their first kiss. It wasn't what she expected. It was better.

She didn't know how long they stayed connected, but when she finally pulled away, she was glad he smiled.

"I don't believe in long engagements," he said. "What are you doing tomorrow?"

Jasmine glanced at her ring one more time before she pushed against the hospital room door.

"Son, you can't do this." Reverend Bush's words made Jasmine pause. She'd only stepped out to go to the bathroom. When had his father invaded their space?

"Pops, what's the problem? Why are you hatin' on me and Jasmine?"

That was her cue—to rush in and save herself from whatever the reverend was about to say. But shock sealed her in place.

"This is not about Jasmine. This is about you making this decision now, under duress. You're in the hospital, for God's sake. No one gets engaged in a hospital."

Hosea laughed. "No one? Come on, Pops."

"Okay, but still, you haven't known Jasmine long enough."

"I know you're not coming at me with that. I've known Jasmine since January—almost double the time that you knew mom before you were married. How many times have you told me that when God tells you to find a wife, He won't make you wait long?"

Jasmine heard the reverend sigh.

"Pops," Hosea continued. "Jasmine is the woman God has chosen for me."

"Let's say that's true. Why do you *have* to get married now? What's the rush?"

Hosea paused before he responded, "Pops, I'm trying not to get upset here."

"Then don't. Let's discuss this man to man."

"Jasmine is not pregnant, if that's what you're thinking."

"So, what is this? An emotional decision?"

"Pops, no disrespect, but what kind of nonsense is this? Yes, this is an emotional decision because love is all about emotions."

"I just don't understand. I don't see any exceptional qualities in that woman."

Jasmine held her hands to her face. Felt her ring. Closed her eyes.

"Pops, I cannot believe what you're saying. This is about me and Jasmine. Not you. But let me tell you what I see in my fiancée." He paused. "She's not like anyone I've ever met or dated. Besides the obvious that she's intelligent, fun to be with, and successful in her own right, all of that pales to what she's done for me." His voice became softer. "Pops, it's been a while since you've dated, but today, when you tell a woman how you're trying to live for God, most don't understand. They think you're playing some game because they don't think a man can be celibate. Or if they believe you, they constantly try to change your mind. And then there are some who just walk away. But not Jasmine."

Her pounding heart forced her eyes open.

"I told Jasmine how I was trying to live and though it was hard for her and we had some talks about it, she honored what I wanted to do. She didn't agree, but she honored me. That's what makes me love her, Pops. If she were willing to honor me, like I've honored her while we were just friends, I know she'll honor me as my wife." Through his father's sigh, Hosea continued, "I want your blessing. And I want you to marry us. But honestly, Pops, if you can't do that, it's fine with me. Jasmine and I will be married anyway."

Jasmine held her breath through the silence that followed Hosea's words. When she heard the reverend's footsteps moving toward the door, she rushed around the corner.

This should have felt like a victory, but instead, she felt defeated, beaten down by her fiancé's words. Hosea loved her because she'd honored him. He'd asked her to be his wife based on that lie.

What would happen if he ever found out? She shook her head, not wanting to think about that. There was nothing she could do about the past, but the future, she controlled. And every day she had left in her life, she would make sure that his words were true—she would honor Hosea Bush as his wife.

Chapter 30

So you guys are still doing it in June? What's the rush?" Serena yelled for what seemed like the fiftieth time.

Jasmine jumped into her jeans, slipped into her top, without lifting the telephone from between her shoulder and ear. "I told you, it's better this way."

"This has to be about sex. You just can't wait to get that man into bed, can you?"

Serena didn't know how true her words were. After their kiss last week, being in bed with Hosea was all Jasmine could think about. But this time, it wasn't about a plan. It was only that she was in love and now she wanted to make love.

"Jasmine!"

Her sister's scream powered through her thoughts. "Would you stop yelling?" Jasmine said. "I told you, this is what Hosea wants."

"So this is not about sex?"

"This is not about sex," Jasmine said. And she meant it. "I love Hosea, Serena."

Her sister waited a moment before she said, "I can hear that, Jasmine. And I'm thrilled. But June seventh is four weeks away. I hope I can be there."

"I really want you here, but if you can't, I'll understand."

Serena chuckled. "What has this man done to you? He has my sister all calm and everything."

Jasmine smiled as she dumped the contents from her purse into a backpack. She knew she'd been changed.

"So, how are you going to have that fabulous wedding you wanted?"

"I don't care about that anymore. If I had my way, we would've been married right in that hospital."

Serena laughed. "This is still so unreal to me. My sister is marrying Hosea Bush."

"Get used to it. I'm going to be a minister's wife." They laughed. "But not if I don't get to the hospital and pick up my minister right now."

"Tell him I said hello. And tell him to stay careful. Those blood clots are no joke."

"Don't worry. I don't plan on anything happening to Hosea Bush."

They said their good-byes and then Jasmine dashed downstairs to a waiting cab. As the car sped toward the hospital, Jasmine let the past months drift through her mind. This had happened much faster than she'd expected. It made her pause once again and wonder about all that Hosea had said, that they were together because of God. Was this really God's plan? Was it because His plan was so much better than hers that she would be married months before she imagined? She'd once heard a pastor say that what God had for you was so much better than what you wanted for yourself.

She smiled. She was living proof of that.

Jasmine moaned as soon as she saw the limousine.

This was not the way she wanted to end this day. Only adrenaline kept her awake now. It had been nonstop from the moment she picked up Hosea and then helped him to get settled at his home. Then she'd spent almost an hour in this cab as it crawled from Long Island back to the city. All she wanted was to plunge into her bed and not open her eyes until noon tomorrow. A confrontation with Mae Frances was not on this Saturday night's agenda.

She paid the driver and then slipped from the car, hoping that somehow she could avoid her neighbor. But as she rushed to her building, she heard the footsteps behind her.

"Good evening, Ms. Larson," Henrikas greeted her.

Even though for the last weeks she'd been much more pleasant to the doorman, she didn't pause to speak. Her focus was the elevator. Her hope was that Mae Frances would have the good sense to stop and chat with Henrikas so that their paths wouldn't cross. But when she stepped into the elevator, she discovered that her neighbor had no sense at all.

As if she were alone, Jasmine pressed 8 and kept her eyes on the doors.

The elevator rose to the second floor before Mae Frances said, "Jasmine Larson, do not tell me that you're not going to say a word."

With her stare still on the doors, Jasmine responded, "Based on the last time, I didn't think you wanted to speak to me."

Mae Frances sucked her teeth. "Child, don't be so sensitive. You just made me mad, that's all. It was my anger talking."

Jasmine said nothing.

"Look," Mae Frances continued, "I know you're not . . . exactly like those other Christians. I know you have a bit of a heart."

Jasmine faced her neighbor. "I was just trying to be your friend."

"I know that."

"You make it very hard."

"I know that too." When they stepped off the elevator, Mae Frances followed Jasmine to her door. "Let's make a deal," Mae Frances continued. "Don't talk to me about God and that church thing, and I'll try to never insult you again."

Jasmine couldn't help it, she laughed. "You'll try?"

204 / Victoria Christopher Murray

Mae Frances nodded, serious with her promise. "Do we have a deal?"

Jasmine's lips spread into a smile. How could she not accept this truce? She'd just become engaged, her fiancé was home and healthy. Surely, there was enough happiness to share, even with Mae Frances.

Jasmine shook Mae Frances's hand. "Deal."

"I like you, Jasmine Larson." Without another word, Mae Frances disappeared into her apartment.

Jasmine shook her head. There was no way she would keep that deal. She was about to become a minister's wife. Mae Frances hadn't even begun to hear all that she had to say about God.

Jasmine grappled for the telephone in the dark.

"Hello?" she said with her eyes still closed.

"Darlin', did I wake you?"

Jasmine shot up in her bed. "Hosea, are you all right?"

"I'm better than all right. I'm just calling with some good news about our wedding."

Jasmine clicked on the light and smiled. As they'd rode home from the hospital, Hosea had convinced her that even though their wedding was merely four weeks away, he was still going to make sure she had the day she'd dreamed of.

"The only thing that's going to be missing is the time and stress that comes when people try to go through this for an entire year," he said. "It's not necessary, and I'm going to show you."

"Hosea, all I want is to be married to you. We can go to City Hall for all I care."

"Oh, no," he'd laughed. "We're not going to have some banged-up wedding and then on our fiftieth anniversary, you tell our children that I did that to you. Oh, no."

She'd laughed with him then, and she did now as she thought about his words.

"I contacted Sebastian," he said, pulling her back to the present. "He's going to design your dress."

Jasmine jumped from the bed. "You're kidding, right? Oh my gosh, tell me you're not kidding!"

Hosea laughed. "Which is it? Am I kidding or not?"

Jasmine giggled. Sebastian was a rising designer who had studied for years with Vera Wang and now had his own show-room in Los Angeles. His designs dominated the red carpet at last year's Academy Awards and word was he had already been commissioned to design Oprah's gown for the upcoming Phe-nomenal Women Ball. "I had no idea you knew Sebastian."

"Yeah, we go back a ways. Here's the thing. He's agreed to do your dress, but he needs you in Los Angeles."

Los Angeles, she screamed inside. Brian's image danced through her mind and she closed her eyes, squeezing him away.

Hosea continued, "I'll get your ticket for sometime tomor-row and then I'll have you back here Monday night, Tuesday the latest."

"No," Jasmine said, all joy gone. She would have rather walked down the aisle naked than take a trip to (or a chance in) L.A. "If he can't come here or if we can't do this by phone, I'll just buy a dress."

"But darlin', this is Sebastian. You can get away for a day, can't you? Do you want me to call Malik?"

Tears came to her eyes. This wasn't about work. "I don't want to leave you," she whispered.

He hesitated. "Okay, darlin'. Go back to sleep. I'll figure it out."

"I love you, Hosea," she said, then hung up. As she pulled the blanket to her chin, she wiped her face dry of tears. But fresh ones came, stealing all the joy that should have come with this news. She couldn't even plan this wonderful time of her life without Brian stalking her.

Jasmine reached for the light, but pulled her hand back. She knew she wouldn't be able to sleep in the dark.

Chapter 31

J asmine had doubted Hosea's words.

When he told her they could have the wedding she wanted in four weeks, she knew that wasn't possible. But then, she watched her fiancé work it.

First, two days after he'd called about Sebastian, the famed designer was sitting in Jasmine's apartment, making sketches as she described her dream dress.

Next, Hosea hired Ciara LaReese, a celebrity wedding planner. Before the second week was out, their invitations had been designed and two hundred invites were delivered, the menu had been selected, the musicians had been chosen, and a photographer had been hired.

By the third week, the details of the day were completed: the flowers were ordered, hair and makeup artists were booked, and their photo shoot was scheduled for their picture that would appear in *The New York Times*.

By the fourth week, what had seemed an impossible task was unfolding to be a day beyond imagination. But even with Ciara, the whirlwind planning left Jasmine feeling like an about-to-pop rubber band. It was difficult to eat, hard to sleep, impossible to focus.

"That's normal," Serena had told her when Jasmine complained about not being able to get more than two hours of sleep. "You're suffering from pre-wedding jitters. And it hasn't helped that you've piled into a few weeks what most people do in a year."

"Just take it easy," Malik had said when he noticed the dark circles under Jasmine's eyes at church. "You look exhausted and I know you don't want to look like that on Saturday. Stacy has the club under control; I've got the office. Take this week off."

Jasmine had no intention of following Malik's suggestion, but now, as she tossed through the night, she decided that rest was what she needed.

Sunday's night was just beginning to bow to the light of Monday when her eyes finally closed. But no more than ten minutes later, a knock on her door pulled her back to consciousness. She tried to smother her pillow over her ears when the knock came again. Finally she crawled from her bed.

Mae Frances's smile greeted her. "Jasmine Larson, what are you doing in your bathrobe? I thought you'd be ready for work."

"I'm staying home today," she said, wiping the sleep from her eyes.

"If I'd known that, I wouldn't have come by so early. But since I'm here." She stepped into the apartment. "I got that invitation." She tilted her head as if that would give her a better view of Jasmine. "You're really going to marry the preacher man?"

Even though her bones ached, that couldn't stop her smile. "Yes. On Saturday, I'll be a married woman."

Mae Frances shook her head. "I think that other one was better for you."

There he was again—Brian, invading her happiness. "I'm marrying the man I'm supposed to," Jasmine said, crossing her arms.

Mae Frances shrugged. "Doesn't make me no never mind. I don't have to sleep with either one of them."

The cheer that had come in with Mae Frances was completely gone now. "Is there a reason you stopped by?" Jasmine asked, trying not to sound harsh.

"Yes, I came by to tell you that I won't be able to make the wedding."

Jasmine's mouth opened wide. Mae Frances was the only friend she had. And for a reason she couldn't explain, Jasmine wanted to share her wedding day with her neighbor.

"Now, don't get in a hissy," Mae Frances said as she looked at Jasmine's face. "You know how I feel about churches. But . . ." She paused. "You also know how I feel about you, so I want to take you out to dinner to celebrate."

Jasmine kept her laugh inside. Mae Frances wanted to take her out to dinner? *Please*, Jasmine thought. *I'm the one who'll be paying.*

But then, Jasmine wondered, when was the last time her neighbor had been able to enjoy a meal, or anything outside of her home?

"That's a good idea, Mae Frances," Jasmine said, glad she'd have a way to treat her neighbor. "Where do you want to go?"

"Well, if you can get away for dinner this week, how about we try Jean Georges. I haven't been there in a while."

Jasmine raised her eyebrows. She doubted if her neighbor had ever been to the famed restaurant. She wanted to be annoyed, even angry that Mae Frances would suggest Jean Georges when not a penny would come from her pocket. Still, Jasmine said, "Sounds good. But would you mind if we did lunch instead?" she asked, hoping the lunch menu would be a bit more affordable.

Mae Frances agreed. "Why don't we do lunch today?"

Jasmine had hoped to spend much of the day in bed, but her neighbor's eager eyes made her say, "Sure. Will Gerald drive us?"

Mae Frances raised her shoulders a bit higher. "Of course. Why would I have a driver and not have him take me to lunch?"

Jasmine shrugged. She could ask that and lots of other questions. Like, why did Mae Frances have a driver at all? Or, why didn't she sell the diamonds she wore? Her driver and diamonds could buy her food for quite a bit of time.

But she didn't ask Mae Frances anything. Just waved goodbye after they agreed to meet right at noon.

It was the warmest day of the year, yet Mae Frances wore the fur-trimmed cashmere cape that she favored since she'd shed her mink back in March. Just looking at her wrapped in the wool, over a cream polyester shift, made Jasmine sweat, even though her sleeveless silk tank dress worked well for the almost ninety-degree May day.

Jasmine didn't miss the way the maître d' eyed the two when they strutted into the restaurant. But she kept her head as high as Mae Frances held hers as they were escorted to a table far from the entrance.

"Please bring me a glass of Chardonnay," Mae Frances said the moment they were seated. "Do you want anything to drink?" she asked Jasmine as if she were really going to be paying the bill.

"I'll have hot tea, please," Jasmine said, hoping that would calm her stomach and wake her up at the same time.

Minutes later, the waiter stood, ready to take their orders.

"I'll have the filet mignon," Mae Frances said. "Medium-rare, please."

As Jasmine scanned the menu, her stomach somersaulted. She took a sip of water, and ordered the house salad.

"Is that all you're having?" Mae Frances frowned.

She nodded. "I'm not very hungry."

As soon as the waiter walked away, Mae Frances said, "Since you're always in my business, it's time I got into yours. Why are you marrying that preacher man? Are you pregnant?"

Jasmine opened her mouth wide. Reverend Bush had

thought the same thing. Did the world think Hosea Bush would only marry her if she were pregnant? "No, I'm not."

Mae Frances narrowed her eyes. Studied her. Frowned. "Are you sure?"

"Absolutely."

"Hmph, you've got that glow."

"This is the glow of love."

Mae Frances sucked her teeth. "I ain't never heard of that." She peered at Jasmine. "If it's not a baby, then why are you get‹ting married? It just seems so quick, too soon."

"Hosea and I have been together for five months. It may seem soon to you, but it seems right to us." She wanted to add all the words that Hosea had said to his father—how God brought them together. But that couldn't be part of this con‹versation. "And," Jasmine continued, "I really love him." Even though she repeated this to someone every day, those words were still a wonder to her.

When the waiter settled their meals in front of them, Mae Frances said, "I hope this marriage thing will work out for you."

"It will."

"You probably believe in all of that love is patient, love is kind stuff, don't you?"

Jasmine chuckled. "Oh, so now you're quoting Shake‹speare?"

Mae Frances hesitated for a moment and then laughed. "Jasmine Larson, that ain't Shakespeare. That's from the Bible." She shook her head.

"I knew it was from the Bible," Jasmine lied. "I was just teas‹ing you because you said you didn't want to have anything to do with God."

"I don't. But I've heard a thing or two about that book that He and that carpenter son of His were supposed to have writ‹ten. But anyway, you *really* think you love that preacher man?"

"I don't think it, I know it."

Mae Frances peered at her for a moment. "It's just that I know men. I don't trust them."

"I trust Hosea."

"I hope he doesn't hurt you."

"I'm sure he won't." Jasmine didn't add that he wouldn't hurt her, but she couldn't say the same. She shook away the image of Brian before it came to her mind.

"You're young, Jasmine Larson. A bit too naïve, if you ask me."

Jasmine laughed so loud, she had to put her hand over her mouth. "If there is one thing I'm not, it's young. I'm . . . thirty-five. And I'm certainly not naïve." She paused, seriousness returning. "Mae Frances, the woman you know now is not the person I've always been." In that instant, moments traveled through her memory that made her sad. Situations that she wanted to live over and live right this time. "I've done things I'm not proud of."

Mae Frances waved her hand. "We all have a little trouble in our past."

"My past is not that long ago." She lowered her voice.

"If you're talking about that other man, that's not something to be ashamed of. You were just making up your mind between the two."

Jasmine didn't feel like explaining it all. "Whatever reasons I had, I want to keep my past far away from me. I want to live the rest of my life better and it's all because of Hosea, the preacher man."

Mae Frances chuckled. "I hope you can be happy, but it's hard for me to believe in marriage. Hard for me to believe in men."

Jasmine wanted to tell her that she didn't need to believe in any of that—she only needed to believe in God. But she wanted to have a peaceful lunch.

Jasmine asked, "Your parents weren't happy?"

It was Mae Frances's turn to lean back and laugh. "My

daddy was gone before I could walk. My mom was determined to give me a good life. After college, she made sure I met the right people. And that's when I met and married Elijah Van Dorn."

"I'm sorry life hasn't gone the way you've wanted."

"Well, it's too late for me, but not for you. I love you, Jasmine Larson," Mae Frances said. "Some people may say that I love you like a daughter. So, that's why I wish you every bit of luck with this preacher man."

Jasmine squeezed her neighbor's hand.

For moments, they ate in silence until Mae Frances cut into her steak. "I don't believe this," she growled. Mae Frances waved her hand in the air, signaling for the waiter. "My steak is red," she said with indignation. "I said I wanted it medium."

"I'm sorry, ma'am. I thought you said medium-rare."

"I know what I said, young man. I want a steak—medium, please."

The waiter nodded, reached for Mae Frances's plate, but she slapped his hand away.

Both the waiter's and Jasmine's eyes widened.

"What are you doing?" Mae Frances barked.

The waiter answered, "I thought you said—"

"What kind of restaurant is this? You're actually going to take this steak and nuke it? I want another steak—and I want it medium! Please."

The waiter looked at Jasmine, but she lowered her eyes.

When the waiter scooted away, Mae Frances asked, "So, do you have everything ready for your big day?" as if she hadn't just scolded the server.

It took a moment for Jasmine to respond. "Yes, Hosea planned just about everything."

Mae Frances frowned. "That's not a good thing. You never know how your wedding's going to be now. Men are such—"

Jasmine interrupted. "Mae Frances, would you stop it with your commentary on men and just be happy for me."

"I said I was happy. What do you want me to do? A few cartwheels?"

"I want you to stop talking about Hosea like that."

"I'm not talking about your preacher man. I'm talking about—" She stopped when Jasmine glared at her. "All right, Jasmine Larson. I just hope that one day, I won't have to say, 'I told you so.'"

"You won't."

The waiter rushed back to their table with another steak for Mae France, cooked medium.

Her fingers flittered in the air. "I've lost my appetite," she said. "Wrap that up for me."

The young man nodded.

"Here, take this piece too. Wrap it with that one."

The man frowned.

Mae Frances eyed Jasmine's barely touched salad. "Are you going to finish that?"

Jasmine shook her head.

"Wrap this up too," Mae Frances ordered. "And I only want to see one steak on that bill."

As the waiter marched away, Jasmine stifled her giggle. Now she understood how this woman had survived.

As if she hadn't just scammed the waiter, Mae Frances said, "I hope you enjoyed our little lunch, Jasmine Larson. I know I did."

Mae Frances opened her purse, and Jasmine did the same. She wondered what excuse Mae Frances would use this time—she had forgotten her wallet, or didn't have time to go to the bank. But then Mae Frances slid a fifty-dollar bill onto the table.

With wide eyes, Jasmine said, "Mae Frances, I—this restaurant—it's too much. Let me pay."

Like always, her back became straighter, her face stiffer. "I invited you to lunch, Jasmine Larson. That means I'm paying."

"But, I don't mind—"

Mae Frances held up her hand. "No need to talk about this. I've told you over and over that I'm not a charity case."

When the waiter returned with Mae Frances's food wrapped, she finished the last of her wine, stood, took the package, and handed the waiter the fifty-dollar bill. "Keep the change."

She marched away, not taking notice of the frantic look on the waiter's face.

"Miss," he yelled behind her.

Jasmine tapped his arm, stopping him. "How much is the check?"

The young man's hands shook as he looked down at the check and then the bill that Mae Frances had given him. "It's seventy-eight dollars!"

Jasmine slipped the waiter two twenty-dollar bills. She smiled, and then followed Mae Frances to her waiting limousine.

Jasmine scooted to the edge of the bed and hung her head between her legs.

Almost an hour had passed since she returned from lunch, but still her stomach stirred. She was being held hostage by the nausea.

The telephone rang and Jasmine groaned. She wished the world would vanish—until she could figure out what was making her feel so sick. She took a deep breath before she answered. "Hello." She tried to fill her voice with energy.

"Jasmine," Ciara shouted, her voice frantic. "I just got a call from Reverend Bush and I'm praying. Do you have a copy of your birth certificate?"

Jasmine frowned. "Yeah, why?"

She could hear Ciara's relief. "Thank God. We've been moving so fast, it slipped my mind. We have to get you and Hosea to the City Clerk's office. For your marriage license."

Jasmine sat straight up.

Ciara continued, "Hosea said he would send a car for you so that you can get right there. He has to be back on set in an hour. Can you be ready in ten minutes?"

"No, ah—"

"Jasmine, if we don't get this license, you won't be getting married on Saturday. Hosea's schedule is packed for the rest of the week. We're sending a car now. Be downstairs in ten minutes," Ciara ordered and then hung up before Jasmine could protest further.

Slowly, Jasmine lowered the telephone.

The quickness of this wedding, the sickness that had overwhelmed her, had taken away her skills. She'd forgotten about a marriage license. Forgotten about how she'd have to walk into the clerk's office and produce a birth certificate that would show her real age. And a driver's license that would confirm what her birth certificate said—that she was a liar.

She rose from the bed and rushed into her closet. Inside, she lifted the plastic box that held her important papers and she gasped as she opened the top. Along with her birth certificate was her marriage certificate, as well as her divorce decree. All of these papers were in full view for the man who would be moving in with her next week.

Maybe I should burn these. But whatever she decided to do with the papers that held her ex-husband's name, she couldn't think about that now.

Jasmine stuffed her birth certificate deep inside her purse. She wasn't sure how she would handle the situation, but she knew that Hosea would never see her papers. He couldn't—even if it meant not being able to get a marriage license.

"It won't come to that," she said as she locked her front door. But as she rode the elevator down, she wasn't so sure of her words.

◆ ◆ ◆

She saw Hosea the moment the Town Car slowed in front of the City Clerk's office. And her nausea returned. When the car stopped, he rushed over and helped her step out.

"Hey, darlin'," he said, and kissed her cheek. "Can you believe everyone forgot about this?" He took her hand and led her up the steps into the City Clerk's office. A guard directed them to Room 203. "We wouldn't be getting married on Saturday if Pops hadn't reminded me."

As he rushed toward the room, Jasmine was glad that Hosea didn't notice that she had not spoken. She couldn't use her energy to speak. Had to use every bit of strength to concentrate only on the task in front of her.

Although two couples were talking to clerks, there was no one in line and a slim, fifty-something woman motioned for them to step to her station.

"We're getting married on Saturday," Hosea said. "And we forgot to get the license. I hope it's not too late because I want to marry this woman."

The woman laughed. "You have plenty of time. You actually have up until twenty-four hours before the wedding."

Jasmine thought, *Good to know.*

The woman peered at the two. "So, are you the couple?"

Hosea nodded. "Doesn't she look like my wife already?"

The woman laughed again. "Yes, she does. So lovely, both of you. Now, there are two ways to do this." She paused. "I can give you forms to fill out, or I can input this information right into the computer. Which would you prefer?"

"The forms," Jasmine said.

"The computer," Hosea said.

They looked at each other and the woman chuckled. "Oh, no, your first fight," the woman kidded.

"It's just that I'm in a hurry," Hosea said, "and I thought the computer would be faster."

"It would be." The lady tapped on the keyboard in front of

her. "This won't take long. I just need your driver's licenses and your birth certificates."

Jasmine watched as Hosea placed an envelope on the counter. Slowly, she pulled her certificate from her purse and then shifted through her wallet for her license. She waited until the woman looked up before she handed the papers directly to her.

The woman scanned Jasmine's driver's license and birth certificate. "Is this information correct?"

Jasmine swallowed, nodded.

"You live in Florida?"

"Oh, no, I'm a New York resident now. Is this a problem?"

"No, as long as you're getting married in New York." The woman rested Jasmine's documents on the counter and tapped the computer keys. "Give me your current address."

As Jasmine responded, she could see Hosea twisting his neck, glancing at her papers.

"So, sweetie, you're in a hurry?" she asked, forcing him to face her. "What do you have going on today?"

"Just meetings, and then more meetings."

"I'm sorry that you're so rushed," she purred straightening his tie.

The way he grinned, Jasmine knew his thoughts about her papers were forgotten.

He said, "I don't mind being rushed this week because I don't want anything on the calendar while we're on our honeymoon."

She hugged him. Over his shoulder, she watched the woman's fingers glide across the keys.

"Okay," the woman said and pushed Jasmine's papers aside. "Now, Mister . . . ," she paused as she looked at his driver's license. "Mr. Bush. Hosea Bush." She paused again and then glanced up. "You're Hosea Bush?" She beamed. "I didn't recognize you."

Hosea grinned. As he gave the woman his New York address, Jasmine slid her papers off the counter and stuffed them back inside her purse. She didn't breathe until her bag was zipped and snug against her side.

"Darlin', did you hear that?"

"No, I'm sorry, what did you say?"

"Ms. Lewis wants me to speak at her church. To their teen ministry," he said as he handed the woman a business card.

"That would be terrific," Jasmine said, taking Hosea's arm. "My husband is a wonderful speaker."

"Oh, I'm your husband already, huh?" He grinned.

"My first and last," she said.

"Well, that answers my next question," Ms. Lewis said, "but I have to ask anyway. Have either of you been married before?"

"No," Hosea said.

"Why do you need to know that?" Jasmine's voice quivered.

Ms. Lewis waved her hand in the air. "You would not believe the number of people who come in here trying to marry someone, when they are already married. If someone were married before, we'd need the divorce certificate."

"Neither of us were married," Hosea said.

Ms. Lewis turned back to the computer and tapped more keys. Jasmine's heart pounded and she wondered why she'd ever told that lie.

"Well, that just about does it," Ms. Lewis said, minutes later. "It'll take just a few minutes for the license to print."

Hosea glanced at his watch. "Do I have to be here for that?"

"No, not if your fiancée can wait."

"Great. I'll see you later, darlin'." He kissed Jasmine's cheek. "And don't lose that license. We have a date on Saturday." He waved to the clerk and then disappeared into the hallway.

"He's a wonderful young man."

Ten minutes later, she handed Jasmine the form that gave the state's permission for the two to wed. "I wish you a long, wonderful, and prosperous marriage," Ms. Lewis gushed. "May God bless you."

"He already has," Jasmine said speaking the truth. It was clearer than it had ever been before that God wanted her united with Hosea. Because in spite of all that she'd done wrong, he was blessing her.

"Thank you, God," she whispered the moment she was in the hallway. "I promise, no more lies."

Chapter 32

Jasmine's head was as heavy as a boulder.

She'd hoped just laying her head on her desk for a moment would help, but minutes later, she still hadn't raised her head.

She'd felt this way all week, even though she'd taken three days off. After getting the marriage license on Monday, she'd expected to spend the rest of the week lounging, but wedding plans would not let her rest.

On Tuesday, Sebastian called to announce that her dress was ready. But at the fitting, he had fussed like a disapproving parent.

"Cherie, this is not good. We are not happy." He'd flitted around, adjusting, tugging, marking as she stood in the middle of the living room in her dress. "We are eating too much and we cannot do that. This material is temperamental and we must do everything we can to look fabulous."

Jasmine had wanted to tell Sebastian that she hadn't felt well enough to eat at all. But she didn't have the energy to defend herself.

Then yesterday, after meeting with Ciara for a final run-through, she'd accompanied Hosea to his doctor's appointment. At least her fiancé was doing fine.

This morning, when she'd awakened, she decided to dash into the office to clear her desk.

But from the moment she'd arrived, she'd felt dizzy, on the verge of collapsing.

A quick knock on her door startled her, but Jasmine wasn't able to lift her head before Tina walked in.

"Why are you here?" her assistant asked. "You're getting married in two days."

As if she needed that reminder. Every fiber of her being had been consumed with thoughts, plans, meetings about her wedding. She'd anticipated this day for her entire life, but now she couldn't wait for Saturday to come—and then to go.

Her eyelids were heavy when she focused on Tina.

Tina said, "There's nothing for you to do. Malik and I have all of your projects under control." She paused and tilted her head. "You really don't look well." Tina parted her lips as if she had more to add.

Jasmine held up her hand, stopping her assistant. She knew how she looked. "I'm just tired."

"Then go home," Tina stated the simple solution. "You've got to be fresh for the rehearsal tomorrow and even better for Saturday."

Jasmine glanced at her watch. It was just before noon. That would give her well over twenty-four hours to get it together for the rehearsal dinner.

"Okay" was all she could say.

When Tina rushed out of the office after her phone rang, Jasmine slipped the strap of her purse onto her shoulder. She stood, but less than a second later, she fell back into her seat. She waited, stood, and this time, moved toward the door. Her steps were cautious as she approached Tina's desk.

"I'll see you Saturday," her assistant gushed with excitement.

Then Jasmine passed Gabriella. "Let me know if you need anything for the rehearsal tomorrow," she said.

Jasmine forced a smile. She didn't know why Gabriella had

to be at her rehearsal dinner, but she didn't have the power to think or talk to Malik about it.

As she waited for the elevator, she told herself that all would be well. She'd go home, rest, and then be ready to blush like the virgin bride that everyone expected her to be.

Chapter 33

JUNE 5, 2004

J *asmine wanted to throw up.*
But Ciara had just given the signal for the doors of the City of Lights at Riverside Church to open wide.

She took a deep breath, squeezed her bouquet tighter, and began her jaunt down the aisle as the organ's chords sang Mendelssohn's "Wedding March."

What was I thinking? Jasmine wondered as she focused on keeping her stomach still. How she wished she'd asked Malik to walk beside her. But she'd wanted every eye on her—only her. Now the guests' smiling stares unnerved her. Could she complete this fifty-foot walk without collapsing?

Three steps from the altar, she noticed her husband to be. And then she saw his father, standing near. And again she prayed that her body wouldn't betray her.

The music stopped. And in the silence Jasmine wondered if anyone heard her stomach grumble.

"Dearly Beloved," Reverend Bush began.

Hold on, girl. She just had to make it through the nuptials.

"The marriage into which the two of you are about to enter is one which you promise to fulfill, not for a limited time, but for the rest of your lives. It's a union ordained by God."

She closed her eyes at Reverend Bush's mention of God and wondered what kind of divine punishment awaited her as she stood at this altar professing to love one man, yet carrying another's child.

She swayed, and Hosea squeezed her hand. She looked at him, his face creased with a frown. She held his hand tighter, and then they turned back to Reverend Bush.

"The success of your marriage depends on the love, consideration, and trust that you have now, but that you will foster in the coming years."

Trust. She swayed again. She needed to focus and her eyes wandered to the gold cross that covered the wall behind the altar. *Please, God,* she kept saying inside.

She knew God had heard her when she was able to repeat her vows and exchange rings without falling. She knew God was on her side when Reverend Bush said, "I now pronounce you man and wife."

She knew God loved her when Hosea lifted her veil and his lips met hers with a gentleness, a fullness of love that she had never before felt. She'd made it. She was Hosea Bush's wife.

What began as a daunting day had morphed into the beauty of all she'd expected.

The reverend's pronouncement, "Ladies and gentleman, let me be the first to introduce my son and daughter-in-law, Minister and Mrs. Hosea Samuel Bush," swept away her nausea.

At their reception, Jasmine basked in the glow. With her arm wrapped inside her husband's, they greeted almost every one of the two hundred guests who partied to the five-piece band and consumed the delicacies that had been prepared by one of New York's premiere chefs.

In between their greetings, Reverend Bush pulled the two aside. "I wish you both all of God's blessings," he said.

"Thank you" was her only response, as she hugged him, hoping his words were a peace offering.

During their first dance, Jasmine leaned into Hosea and together they'd swayed to the beat of Luther's promises.

Here and now, I promise to love faithfully . . .

This was a promise that love would help her keep. She
would be faithful always, and now, she could make that vow
with surety.

After the dance, Ciara rushed them to the cake, anxious to
get the planned pictures of the reception. But the moment
Hosea playfully covered her lips with the pistachio cream, the
queasiness rushed her like flood waters. She'd excused herself
and dashed to the bathroom. Inside, she hiked her dress above
her knees, flushed the toilet so no one could hear, and then
gagged until she was empty.

Minutes later when Jasmine returned to the reception, she
knew God's mercy was still with her.

"It's time for us to go," Hosea whispered with love-lust in
his eyes. He announced to their guests, "We didn't plan to stay
here all night!"

Jasmine smiled as guests laughed, applauded, and wished
them well, but inside her stomach swirled and twirled as if it
were preparing to take flight.

Serena stopped them as they rushed to the door. She
wrapped her arms around her sister.

"I love you," she whispered.

"I know."

Hosea hugged Serena. "I just want you to know that I will
love your sister forever. She's in good hands."

Serena's cheeks were covered with her tears—but she
smiled. "I know she is."

A Town Car whisked them to the Ritz-Carlton on the
other side of Central Park. It took only minutes before they
were left alone in front of the double doors of the twenty-fifth-
floor suite.

"Darlin' . . . you're choking me," Hosea stuttered. He stumbled, but regained his balance as Jasmine eased her grip

around his neck. Still, she kept her head resting on his shoulder as he carried her over the threshold.

With a grunt and a chuckle, Hosea eased Jasmine onto the
floral couch in the living room, and the jeweled tiara she wore
slipped through her curls onto the floor.

Hosea smiled as he leaned over his bride. "My queen has
lost her crown."

It wasn't his words that made her lips twist into what
looked like a smile. It was the way her stomach curled that
contorted her face.

He frowned. "Darlin', are you okay?"

She nodded, afraid to open her mouth.

"You don't look so good." His eyes searched hers.

She inhaled, prayed, then said, "I'm just tired. And my
stomach is a bit upset."

He placed the back of his hand against her forehead. "You
feel a little hot. Maybe you're coming down with something."

She shrugged, and moved her glance away from his.

Hosea's sigh was deep. "There should be some champagne
in the refrigerator. Maybe the carbonation will help."

As Hosea moved toward the bar, Jasmine slipped off her
jewel-studded sandals, and then glanced around the capacious
space. This suite could rival in size and luxury most Manhattan apartments. It would have been beyond a pleasure to
spend the first night of her marriage there before they left the
next evening for Bermuda.

But as she watched her husband fill a crystal flute, she
dreaded the coming hours. How were they supposed to con-
summate their marriage when her stomach was on the verge of
erupting?

"Darlin', I hate to say this, but you look worse."

Heat swept over her, forcing beads of perspiration to pop
through her skin. Without a word, Jasmine took the flute; the
chill of the glass and the sparkling bubbles cooled and calmed
her when she took a small sip.

Hosea sat beside her, pulled her back into his arms. "You're really not feeling well."

"No," she whispered. She couldn't look at him. Didn't want to see the disappointment in his eyes that she heard in his voice.

Hosea stood. "You need a good night's rest."

He took her hand and eased her from the couch.

"What did I do to deserve you?" she asked.

"We have the rest of our lives to figure that out."

When she stepped inside the bedroom, Jasmine stopped. "How—" The all-white room was illuminated with a golden glow from dozens of flickering flames, the vanilla candles releasing their scent.

"I wanted this to be perfect for you," he said.

"It is."

Hosea stood behind his wife and unzipped her gown. Then, she slipped the straps from her shoulders. The satin dress spilled to a soft pile around her ankles. She was left covered only in the La Perla set that she'd purchased for this night. Even in the candlelight, the look of want in his eyes was clear, and it melted her. She wanted to give herself to him.

Hosea folded back the satin duvet on the bed and helped her slip between the sheets. She snuggled into the softness of the luxury linen, and he sat on the bed's edge.

"I love you, Mrs. Bush."

She'd heard the words "Mrs. Bush" from others throughout the day, but this was the first time she heard them spoken with such love.

She wrapped her arms around Hosea, held him tight, apologizing wordlessly. Then, he gently laid her back on the bed.

He kissed her forehead. "I'm going to take a shower. Will you be all right?"

She nodded.

He kissed her again, before he disappeared into the bathroom.

Jasmine snuggled into the softness of the down feather pillows. Never had she imagined a sexless wedding night. In her mind, she replaced this truth with the way she wished life was—without Brian, without a baby. Just a night filled with expectations and no regrets.

She closed her eyes. She'd take care of this. In two weeks, she'd be the happy wife, ready to truly start her life as Mrs. Hosea Bush.

She sunk deeper into the sheets. All she had to do was get through the next fourteen days, and then she'd be completely at peace.

Chapter 34

J asmine *raised her head* slightly and glanced at the clock. The digital numbers displayed 9:47. Forty-five minutes had passed since she'd first awakened.

With a deep breath, she rose slowly, waiting for that feeling. Nothing.

She glanced at Hosea, still asleep, then carefully slipped from the bed. With slow steps she crept toward the bathroom. Inside, she moved with caution, across the cool tile until she faced the mirror. A smile filled her face. No quesiness, no rumbling, no nothing.

She waited for more minutes until she was sure and then she scurried back to the bedroom. Sliding under the covers, she nestled against Hosea's chest. It didn't take a minute for him to stir.

"Good morning," she whispered.

His eyelids fluttered, and then opened.

"Do you remember?" she asked.

His eyebrows furrowed together.

She said, "We were married yesterday."

He smiled. "I remember."

"And then last night, I didn't feel well."

"I remember."

"But," she snuggled closer to him, "I'm feeling wonderful now."

He looked at her. "Are you sure?"

She nodded. "But, first . . ." She wiggled from his arms. "I want to take a shower."

He pulled her back. "You don't have to do that."

"Yes, I do." She giggled as she tugged from his grasp. As she stepped away, she could feel his eyes on every part of her body. She slowed, added more swerve to her curves. When she glanced over her shoulder and winked, he moaned.

With joy, she turned the shower's hot water on full blast. She tossed her bra and thong aside, and then glanced at her nakedness. If she were pregnant, she couldn't be more than a few weeks. But she could see the subtle shift in her body, the fullness that came to a woman with child.

"I'll take care of this," she whispered.

The door swung open, and she jumped.

Hosea stood at the threshold, his eyes plastered on her.

She faced him, wanted him to see all of her. Finally, she stepped forward. All she wanted was to devour him, but he gently grasped her wrists.

With whispery kisses, his lips met her nose, her eyelids, and with the tip of his tongue, he traced the line of her eyebrows.

Her breathing quickened and she pulled him closer.

He backed away, just a bit. "Slow down." His voice was thick with desire. He buried his face in her neck, nibbling softly until she moaned.

His hands began their own exploration, tenderly touching, curiously discovering.

"Please," she begged.

His tongue traveled the trail his hands had set and Jasmine felt as if she might soon stop breathing.

"Please," she panted.

With swiftness, he lifted then carried her to their bed. The comforter was cool, but only for a moment. He ignited the flames within her once again when his hands, mouth, fingers, lips continued their journey. She tried to begin her own search, but he held her hands at her side.

"Please," she moaned, knowing she soon would explode.

She squeezed her eyes and he continued his passage, making her fire-hot body tremble.

She'd never made love like this before.

Finally, he stretched on top of her. "I love you, Mrs. Bush," he said the moment he joined her and she groaned with pleasure as she lifted herself to meet him. Their moans played a symphony and they waltzed to their music, in rhythm, step-by-step.

When there was nothing left, they lay holding each other, their breathing in sync.

Finally, Hosea said, "Mrs. Bush."

"Yes." She smiled.

"I think you forgot something."

She frowned.

He said, "Did you leave the shower running?"

Chapter 35

Bliss was all she knew.

Jasmine didn't want this time to end. Even now, as she listened to the sound of the shower's rain coming from her bathroom, she wanted to join her husband, but he'd already warned her.

"Stay away from me, woman," Hosea had teased when he rolled from the bed just minutes before. "I've got to get to work!"

"Don't you want to stay home with me?" she'd whined.

"I do, but we've played for two weeks, I've got to get to the studio." He laughed as he trudged to the bathroom.

Indeed, they had spent fourteen days romping through paradise. Although their private villa at Cambridge Shores in Bermuda gave them access to two private beaches, they'd rarely ventured from their honeymoon home. Instead of playing golf and tennis and snorkeling in the blue seas, they'd done little more than make love, order exotic dishes from room service, and then make love again.

Yesterday, they'd begrudgingly returned to New York, but they'd continued their celebration by consummating their union in each room until they finally collapsed into bed well after midnight.

It had been two weeks filled with joy—except for her intermittent bouts of nausea that blessedly, she'd been able to hide from Hosea. Still, the queasiness was so infrequent that it made her wonder—maybe her pregnancy scare had been nothing more than jitters. Or maybe God had answered her prayers. Still, she needed to be sure, and that thought took her cheer away.

Her heaven returned when Hosea sauntered from the bathroom with a towel tucked at his waist. Her husband was unlike any man she'd been with. All of her conquests had been fit enough to be models for Gold's Gym. But not Hosea. A slight roll of skin hung over the towel around his middle. And there were other parts of him that were cushier rather than muscular. Yet, she loved every extra inch of him. All of the plans she once had to change him were gone. She loved the man he was.

"I cannot believe you're going to leave without making love to me." She wrapped the silk sheet around her, then sauntered to where he stood. "How can you do this?" she whined before she dropped the sheet to the floor.

Hosea swallowed, his eyes ingesting her. She reached for his towel.

"Stay away from me," he groaned. "Please, I'm trying to get to work."

"All I want is a kiss."

He looked at her as if he didn't believe her, but then brought his lips to hers. Quickly, he backed away. "That's enough," he breathed. "Or I'll never leave."

She pouted playfully, as she watched him dress.

"So, what are you going to do today?" he asked.

She turned away, afraid that her eyes might not lie as well as her lips. "Nothing much." She strutted back to the bed. "I told Malik I'd be in on Wednesday; I just want to take these two days to rest."

He leaned over her. "Well, as you're resting, just make sure that you're thinking about me." He kissed her. "Just like I'll be thinking of you." Before he walked out the bedroom, he added, "I'll be home as early as I can."

"I'll be waiting for you."

She waited until the front door closed and then she jumped from the bed.

Jasmine dashed back into her building, past a grinning Henrikas.

"That was quick, Mrs. Bush," he said with extra emphasis on her new name.

She greeted him with a nod, then rushed to the elevator. When the doors opened, she hurried forward and bumped into Mae Frances.

"What the—" Mae Frances stopped. Glared at Jasmine. "What has you in such a hurry and when did you get back?" she asked as if she were owed an explanation to both questions.

Jasmine pushed past her neighbor and held the Open Door button. "We got home yesterday."

Mae Frances smirked. "Did you have a good honeymoon?"

Jasmine nodded. "Mae Frances, can we chat later?"

The woman peered at her through narrow eyes. "Yes," she said slowly. "I'll stop by later and—" the elevator door closed on the rest of her words.

Inside her apartment, Jasmine didn't stop moving until each of the nine boxes she'd purchased were lined on the bathroom counter. Then, she sat on the commode and stared at the pregnancy tests.

"Okay, Lord," she said. "I need you like I've never needed you before."

Jasmine picked up the first box, read the instructions. Did the same with the rest. Then she paced and wished there was someone she could call to hold her hand. But her friends list was short; she was on her own.

She began with the test she'd seen most often on television, then took each one until nine strips lined the bathroom counter. She paced. Thought. Prayed.

The waiting sobered her, made her forget the beauty of the past weeks. Made her think only of the horror of what these results could bring.

She sat again on the commode. Listened to time passing. Finally, she moved in front of each box. Slowly. Studied each strip. Carefully.

Nine times—she was pregnant.

She didn't know why she trembled as she staggered back to the toilet. Her heart, her body had already told her. But the absolute truth sickened her. And now, she was scared.

The knock on her front door made Jasmine leap from the toilet.

She had no idea how long she'd been in the bathroom, holding a death-grip stare on the strips. Hoping that her glare could turn fact to fiction. But now, with a quickness, she stuffed all the evidence into the shopping bag.

The knock came again and she had a vision of Hosea standing on the other side of the door, wondering where were his keys and why did he have to wait so long for his wife to answer.

She kicked the shopping bag underneath the bed, then straightened the bedskirt. When she opened the door with a smile, the ends of her lips dipped a bit.

"Are you okay in here?" Mae Frances brushed past Jasmine. "You asked me to come over and then you take all day to answer the door."

She didn't remember inviting Mae Frances anywhere, but all she said was, "I'm sorry. I was unpacking."

Mae Frances sat on the couch. Crossed her ankles. Rested her hands in her lap. Patted a spot next to her and said, "Sit down. Let's talk."

Not now, she thought. How could she chat when she was consumed with misery?

"Jasmine Larson, what is wrong with you?"

In her mind, she saw the truth again, wrapped in the preg-nancy strips—all blue. She squeezed her eyes shut, but the tears flowed anyway.

"Jasmine Larson?" Mae Frances's voice was softer this time. She tried to keep the sobs inside, but now she cried. And when Mae Frances wrapped her arms around her, she cried more.

"Child, don't tell me that man has done something to you al-ready?" She led Jasmine to the couch. "I tried to tell you. Men—"

"I'm pregnant." Her words shocked them both.

It took a moment for Mae Frances to say, "Child, please. You've been married for three minutes. You can't possibly be pregnant. And even if you were—"

"I'm pregnant, Mae Frances," Jasmine interrupted. "But it's not Hosea's baby." She left the truth right there.

Mae Frances frowned. Then her eyes became quarter-size wide. "That other guy?" she whispered. "The one who I thought was better for you?"

Jasmine nodded.

"Oh, Jasmine Larson, you stepped into some serious stuff, didn't you?"

Jasmine said nothing.

"Child, how did you end up pregnant? Didn't you use a condom?"

It made her crazy, the way Mae Frances spoke like an in-formed, responsible forty-year-old. If only she had acted like one.

"I wasn't thinking. . . ."

"Obviously," Mae Frances stood. Walked back and forth in front of her friend. "Well, I don't understand why you're cry-ing. You know what you have to do."

"I know," Jasmine said, wiping her face clear of the tears. "It's just that it's been so much pressure not knowing, and now knowing—"

Mae Frances waved her hand, as if she were erasing Jasmine's words. "You don't have the time for emotions. Just do what you have to do." Mae Frances paused her words, stopped her pacing. "You *are* going to take care of it, right?"

"Definitely."

"Good, because this is not the time to go Christian on me."

Her neighbor's words carried an extra sting. God's thoughts hadn't been any part of hers. But surely God wouldn't mind an abortion in this case. He was the one who wanted her to be with Hosea. Certainly He knew what would happen if Hosea learned of this.

"We need to get moving." Mae Frances was in command mode. "A doctor who takes care of these things had an office in this building a few years ago. He's moved, but I'm sure I have the number. So, you make an appointment, have the abortion, and your husband will never know."

Jasmine's glance rested on the picture on the mantel. The photo of her and Hosea that had appeared in *The New York Times.* It made her shudder, the way he'd held her, like he'd always love her, always trust her.

She turned away, looked instead at Mae Frances. "Can you get me that number?"

Mae Frances beamed as if she'd just won a prize. "I'll be right back."

When Mae Frances closed the door, Jasmine sank into the couch. *This has to be from God,* she thought. Or it wouldn't have been so easy. He understood.

Everything will be fine. Hosea will never know.

When the door opened, she spun around. "Mae Frances—"

"I can't believe you've forgotten your husband already," Hosea joked.

"Sweetie!" Jasmine breathed to keep her voice steady. "What are you doing home?"

"I got that thing."

She frowned.

"That thing where I'm missing you, wanting you, can't get enough of you."

She tried to chuckle, moaned instead.

"What's wrong?" he asked as he put his arm around her.

"Nothing. I'm just surprised to see you."

He kissed her. "I thought I'd come home . . . for lunch," he said huskily.

"It's barely ten," she said.

The adoration in his eyes as he pulled her into his arms said that he would love her always. That made her hold him tighter.

"So," he began. "Can I get some . . ." He nuzzled her neck.

The knock on the door stopped her response. "Sweetie," she started with as much calm as she could gather. "That's Mae Frances."

He leaned back. "I know you're not going to open the door."

Her neighbor knocked again. Again. Again.

He said, "I'll get it."

"No," and then she lowered her voice. Placed her lips against his ear. "Go into the bedroom. Get ready for me."

He grinned. "That's what I'm talking about." As he strolled away, he added, "Don't be too long. I only got an hour . . . or two . . . or three."

"Close the door," she said with a smile in her voice. "If Mae Frances gets a peek, she might try to steal you away."

He laughed; she didn't. At the door, she blocked her neighbor's entrance. "Do you have the number?"

Mae Frances frowned. "Why are you whispering?"

"Hosea's home."

"In the middle of the day?" Mae Frances shook her head as if she didn't approve. "Don't get used to this. It won't last," she said like the expert she was on bad marriages. She handed Jasmine a torn piece of paper. "Call right away."

Jasmine thanked her before she closed the door.

"Darlin', what's that?"

Before she faced him, she stuffed the telephone number into her jeans. Then, turned, smiled, said, "A recipe."

"Oh, yeah?" He grinned and stepped toward her wearing nothing under his open bathrobe. "Let me see."

She shook her head. "No, let *me* see," she said as she rolled the robe over his shoulders.

She squealed as he lifted her. When he laid her down and rested on top of her, she thought about the shopping bag hidden beneath their bed.

But when her husband kissed her, he took away all thoughts of the tests, the baby. Erased everything that wasn't centered completely on him.

Chapter 36

J asmine stood at the door until Hosea stepped into the elevator. She waved, but before she could close her door, Mae Frances opened hers.

"Jasmine Larson, what's going on?" Mae Frances asked. "I waited all day yesterday, and I almost came by last night, but I knew the preacher man was probably home," she said, as if that irritated her.

Jasmine tightened her bathrobe and stepped into the hall. "I'm sorry," she whispered. "Hosea stayed home for the rest of the day and I couldn't call. But I'm going to right now."

"Well, let me know how it goes," Mae Frances snapped.

Inside her apartment, Jasmine leaned against the closed door. Thought about what she had to do. Held her hand over her stomach. Let it rest there for long moments. Imagined the baby inside. Then shook her head, wiping that image away. She couldn't allow herself to think of this as a baby. She had to remember that this was a problem.

She took determined steps into the bedroom. Inhaled a cleansing breath, and dialed the number. Minutes passed after a receptionist asked her to hold for a scheduling nurse. Jasmine paced with anxiety.

A woman came onto the line, identified herself and asked, "Ms. Bush, were you referred by a doctor?"

"It's Mrs. Bush," Jasmine said, and then wondered why she'd carelessly given her real name.

"I apologize, Mrs. Bush. Were you—"

"No," Jasmine said quickly. "A friend referred me."

"Okay. I hope you're aware that our doctors only do first trimester abortions. How many weeks are you?"

Her pacing began again. "I'm not sure exactly."

"You're calling to schedule an abortion and you don't know how far along you are?" the nurse asked with a frown in her voice. "Have you taken a pregnancy test?"

"I've taken those home tests." Jasmine stopped. She'd forgotten about the shopping bag under the bed and she pulled it from its hiding place. "I took nine tests and they were all positive. So, I'm absolutely sure that I'm pregnant."

"Jasmine."

The sound of him made her lose her grip on the phone. She whipped around. Hosea stood in the doorway, stiff, his eyes wide with shock.

Slowly, she lifted the phone from the floor, her eyes not parting from her husband. She hung up, without speaking another word to the nurse.

"Jasmine," he repeated her name.

"Hosea." She stood frozen with fear. "Hosea, I'm so sorry."

He frowned. "Sorry?" He moved toward her. "Darlin', why would you be sorry?"

He pulled her into his arms. She could feel the tears building, but she couldn't lose it now. Somehow she had to explain, make him understand.

He leaned back. Looked into her eyes. "My baby is going to have our baby. But are you sure? Isn't it too soon to know?"

She shook her head, mystified by his words. And then she realized, no matter what he'd heard, she'd said nothing to implicate herself. Nothing that would make Hosea know that she was a liar. And a cheat. And carrying another man's seed.

"Darlin', sit down," he said softly as if volume could hurt

her. He held her as he led her the few steps to the bed. "Are you sure you're all right?"

She nodded, feeling safer in the silence.

"I don't understand," he said. "When did you take these pregnancy tests?"

"Just a little while ago," she squeaked.

He shook his head. "I'm going to be a father, a daddy. Already. Wow."

"Are you upset?"

"Upset? I'm thrilled." He pulled her close. "Just a little stunned because it's so soon. What made you decide to take those tests? I mean, it's only been two weeks."

She shrugged. "I just had a feeling?" Her words sounded more like a question. Sounded like she wanted to test her comment first to see if he believed it before she committed to the statement. When he nodded, she continued, "I've heard about women who got pregnant on their honeymoon. I wasn't feeling well, so I thought I'd check." She paused. "I . . . I was surprised."

"Okay," he said, taking hold of her hand. "Give me the details. What did the doctor tell you?"

She shook her head. "I was just about to make the appointment." She looked at the telephone. "I wanted to find out for sure."

He chuckled. "Nine tests aren't enough for you?"

"I . . . I just wanted to be sure?" Again, a question wrapped inside her statement. Her voice quivered.

"Don't be upset." He kissed the palm of her hand. "Let me call the doctor back; I'll make the appointment."

"No, I—" she stopped, needing time. "I want to talk to the doctor myself."

"Okay, but let's get in to see him right away. This afternoon." He reached for the phone. "First, let me call the studio. Tell them I won't be back today."

Think, Jasmine. Think.

"Okay," she agreed.

Think, Jasmine. Think.

"Hosea, what are you doing home?"

It seemed to take a moment for his brain to catch up with the question. "Oh, I left some papers here. Thought I was going to do a quick pick-up, but this . . ." He paused. "I'm so glad I came home," he said wrapping his arms around her once more.

For a moment, she allowed herself to take pleasure inside his embrace. Imagined for a second that this was really his child. Dreamed that his joy was hers too.

"I'll call the doctor," she said finally, "but I don't want to go in today. I'm not feeling well and one day won't make a difference."

Hosea frowned. "If you're not feeling well, we need to get to the doctor."

"It's not serious," she said, pretending this was all about nothing. "I'm just tired. And I want a chance to get used to this."

He frowned, still unsure.

She said, "I would not do anything to hurt . . . our baby. Don't worry."

"If you say so. But don't tell me not to worry. That's my job. To worry about you," he put his hand on her stomach, "and our little one." He shook his head again. "Well, rest today, but make that appointment for tomorrow. No matter what time, I'll be there with you."

She nodded, leaned against the headboard, yawned, played this lie to the end.

"I hate to leave you." He kissed her forehead. "Are you sure you don't want me to stay?"

"No," she said quickly. "I'm not sick. What are you going to do if I'm really pregnant? Stay home every day?"

He laughed, kissed her again. "I'll call you as soon as I get to the studio."

She followed him with her eyes as he walked out their bedroom. She could hear him in the loft, shuffling through a box that remained unpacked. She heard every paper he lifted, every book he opened. Why hadn't she heard him when he came into the apartment?

"Darlin', you know what I was thinking?" Hosea asked, interrupting her whirlpool of thoughts. "Maybe this is why you were so sick on our wedding night." But before the words were out of his mouth fully, he said, "Duh, how could you have been pregnant before we were married?" He laughed, unaware that his words had stopped her heart. "Don't mind me," he said before he kissed her again. "I'm so excited, I'm not even thinking."

"Hosea, please don't start acting crazy about this," she said, glad he couldn't see the way her hands shook under the blanket. "First, we need the test; I may not be pregnant."

"Oh, you're pregnant, darlin', I can feel it." He chuckled. "And if you're not, I'm going to sue all those pregnancy-test companies for getting my hopes so high."

She faked a laugh with him. "Still, sweetie, it's really, really early. Anything can happen."

"Don't claim that, Jasmine," he said, serious now. "Nothing's going to happen. Not to you. Not to our baby." He hugged her. "Call me if you need me, okay?" He walked to the bedroom door, but then turned back. "Jasmine, I didn't think it was possible, but, I love you more right now . . ." He stopped. "Thank you for giving me this gift."

She nodded without words. Didn't even breathe again until the front door closed.

How could you have been pregnant before we were married?
She still trembled at the truth of his words.
I love you more right now.
She tried to think, but her mind was absent of solutions. Finally, she slipped into a sweatsuit, picked up her keys, and walked across the hall. She didn't have any answers, but she had a feeling that Mae Frances would know exactly what to do.

◆ ◆ ◆

Mae Frances didn't utter a word when she opened her door. Just invited Jasmine in, motioned for her to sit on the couch.

"What happened?"

Jasmine recounted the massacre that her heart had just
taken. "I don't know what to do," she said finally. She stood,
paced. "But I can't go to a doctor with Hosea."

Mae Frances sat, thoughtful. "You can still have the abortion. Then tell him it was a miscarriage."

"Unless I have an abortion today, that won't work. Hosea is
not going to let another day go by without my seeing a doctor.
And believe me, he'll be right there with me."

"So, are you saying you're going to have this baby?"

It wasn't until Mae Frances asked the question that Jasmine
realized that was exactly what she was saying. She staggered
back to the couch; the thought took her breath away. In the
weeks that she'd suspected this pregnancy, never once had she
considered having this child. That was an impossibility.

But now, as she thought about it, it was an abortion that
was impossible. If she aborted this baby and then told Hosea
she'd had a miscarriage, he would insist on speaking to the doctor. And, if she told him that she'd had a miscarriage at home,
he would insist on taking her to the doctor. And if she didn't
oblige, he would be suspicious. And suspicion triggered questions. And questions demanded answers. And every answer
would have her appearing in front of a judge in divorce court.

"I can't have this baby," Jasmine said, placing her hands on
her stomach. "There has to be another way."

Mae Frances's eyes were sad as she glanced at where her
friend's hands rested. "There are doctors who could give you
something . . . some kind of poison . . . make it look like a miscarriage."

Jasmine jumped up.

Mae Frances said, "But I wouldn't recommend that. Could
kill more than the baby. Could kill you."

Jasmine leaned against the mantel that held the empty picture frames. "Oh, God," she moaned, feeling the nausea rising. She couldn't ingest poison, but on the other hand, giving birth to this baby would be just as toxic. How could she live the rest of her life with this lie?

"Do you think you can pull off having this baby?"

"I don't know," Jasmine whispered. "What do you think?"

Mae Frances shrugged. "I think you should pretend the miscarriage. Have that baby sucked right out of you."

Jasmine rushed back to the couch. Held her head in her hands.

"If you can't do that . . ." Mae Frances strolled to the wooden desk that stood on three legs and a stack of old tele- phone books. From a pile of papers, she lifted a card and handed it to Jasmine. "Call him," she said. "He'll help you."

Jasmine took the card. *Dr. Jeremy Edmonds.*

Mae Frances walked out of the room, returning a momemt later with a cordless phone. "Call Jeremy. Tell him you need him to convince your husband that you are only two weeks pregnant."

"Who is he?"

"Don't worry; Jeremy is a good doctor."

Jeremy. "Can he be trusted?"

Mae Frances crossed her arms, twisted her lips, and re- leased enough of a breath to make her annoyance apparent. "Would I put you in touch with someone you can't trust? Je- remy is a reputable doctor who's caught in this web of ridicu- lous malpractice insurance premiums. So, he's been forced to make some . . . unscrupulous moves. Believe me, you can ask any number of people and they'd be able to refer you to some- one like him. It'll cost you, but it'll be worth it."

Jasmine nodded. Dr. Jeremy Edmonds could help her weave this web of deception. Could she do this? Did she want to?

"It's not like you have a lot of choices," Mae Frances said, reading Jasmine's thoughts. "And you don't have much time."

Mae Frances looked at her watch. "Your husband is going to take you to somebody's doctor tomorrow."

With the tips of her fingers, Jasmine massaged her temples, hoping to ease the confusion that had latched onto her.

"This is your only hope," Mae Frances said. "Because if your husband finds out—"

That is not an option. "It will work out," Jasmine said, as if just speaking it would make it so. "This bed's been made—"

"And now you're going to have a baby in it," Mae Frances finished. "Look at it this way, that baby is going to be your insurance policy. If anything ever happens between you and the preacherman, he'll have to pay, because of the baby. Here," she said. "Make the call now."

Jasmine shook her head. "I'll do it from home."

Mae Frances laughed. "Jasmine Larson, please don't tell me you're that dumb. Your husband just heard one conversation; do you want him hearing this one too?"

Jasmine hesitated then grabbed the phone, dialed the number, and after she told the nurse she was referred by Mae Frances Van Dorn, was asked to hold for the doctor.

Even as she talked to Dr. Edmonds, it amazed Jasmine the way her life had changed. She'd never thought about being a mother, but this might not be so bad. The way Hosea looked at her earlier—Mae Frances was right. This baby could be insurance. But not in the way Mae Frances thought. This baby could insure that Hosea would always love her. She would, after all, always be the mother of his child.

Chapter 37

J asmine *hadn't known what* to expect.

But as her eyes roamed, there was nothing in the doctor's office that would spill her secret. Degrees that had been received in the sixties from Ivy League schools and other framed notations of accomplishments peppered the walls. The furniture—heavy, expensive—befitted any Upper East Side workplace.

Hosea paced behind her, but she sat, sure that her anxiety was greater than his. On the telephone, Dr. Edmonds was professional enough, but now Jasmine quivered with liar's remorse.

Before she had time to wade in regret, Dr. Edmonds sauntered in.

"Good morning," he greeted them as Hosea sat next to her. "So," Dr. Edmonds began, "you two think you're pregnant."

It took a moment for Jasmine to close her mouth. She recognized this man—the only person she'd ever seen come out of Mae Frances's apartment.

Hosea spoke as she stared. "We've only been married for two weeks," he said, "but my wife took those home pregnancy tests and they were all positive."

Dr. Edmonds smiled as if he didn't know their story. "Congratulations."

"But don't you need to test her?" Hosea asked.

"Definitely, but those tests are pretty reliable."

"Doctor, as I said," Hosea continued, "we've just gotten married; will you really be able to determine if my wife is pregnant this soon?"

The doctor chuckled. "Modern medicine has come a long way. We can revive a dead man. Certainly, we can tell when a woman is pregnant, almost at the point of conception. I'll perform a blood test which can detect pregnancy just four days after a missed period."

Hosea nodded, squeezed Jasmine's hand.

"Well, Mrs. Bush, I have all of your information. Let's get started."

When they both stood, the doctor said, "Mr. Bush, would you wait here? This won't be long."

His stance said he didn't like that idea, but Jasmine knew the doctor's plan. He'd examine her alone, get the results, and then they'd talk before they faced Hosea.

Jasmine kissed Hosea and then followed the doctor—to begin to lay the lies that would become the foundation of the rest of her life.

Even swanky Upper East Side doctors used the thin blue paper robes.

Jasmine's arms were covered in goose bumps as she held the clipboard in her hand. She'd answered the three pages of questions that had only served to raise her anxiety. And now waiting didn't make it any better. The quick knock on the door gave her relief.

"Mrs. Bush?"

After she said "Yes," he entered with a smile. She tried not to stare, as he took the clipboard from her, but she was tempted to ask if he were Robert Redford's brother. His looks seemed wasted here, where he was forced to deliver babies and cover up indiscretions for extra money. Surely he could play a fifty- or sixty-year-old leading man in somebody's movie.

"You can relax, Mrs. Bush. It's just the two of us now."

She half-grinned.

"So," he said, beginning his examination. "How have you been feeling?"

"Fine, if you don't count the nausea."

"That's normal, especially for being eight weeks pregnant. That's what you said, right?"

"That's what I think. Will I know for sure from the blood test?"

"No, we'll just know that you're pregnant," he said as he listened to her heart beat. "We'll need the ultrasound to determine dates." He jotted notes onto a chart. "Have you ever been pregnant before?"

She shook her head.

"Okay, Mrs. Bush. The nurse is going to take your blood."

"Doctor, my husband—"

He held up his hand. "We'll make this work for you," he said as if he'd done this a million times.

"But if I'm right, and I'm eight weeks pregnant, how will we explain the baby's early arrival?"

The doctor chuckled. "That'll be easy enough. I'll know more as your pregnancy progresses. But, there are a number of ways to explain a premature birth." He flashed his actor's smile again. "Relax, your husband won't suspect a thing." Now she was sure—he had done this a million times.

"And your . . . fees?"

"We'll discuss that. You're a friend of Mae Frances Van Dorn, right?"

His question took her away from the seriousness of her situation. Allowed her curiosity to return. "Yes."

"Then I'll take care of you."

"How long have you known Mae Frances?"

"For many years."

She wanted more. But before she could ask another question, he left the room.

◆ ◆ ◆

"You are pregnant."

Hosea cheered, the words sending him into a joy-ridden tail-spin. But Jasmine didn't share his zeal. To her, the doctor's words made certain that she would spend the rest of her life as a liar.

Hosea took his wife's hand and kissed her, and Jasmine smiled as if she were pleased too. She pretended to listen as Hosea queried the doctor.

"Is it okay for her to work?"

The doctor tried, but couldn't hide his chuckles. "Of course; your wife is healthy and from what we can tell at this point, this should be a normal pregnancy. We'll want to watch things a bit, since your wife is—" the doctor paused, glanced down at the chart.

Hosea said, "She's thirty-five."

"Yes." The doctor glanced at Jasmine. She stared straight at him, unblinking as if she really was five years younger.

She'd told the doctor the truth. After the nurse had taken her blood, she'd asked Dr. Edmonds if being forty would affect her or the baby.

"The chance of complications increases each year after a woman leaves her twenties," the doctor explained. "But in today's times, women are having babies well into their forties, even their fifties. Prenatal care is the key."

"Mr. Bush," the doctor said, grabbing Jasmine back from their earlier conversation, "there's no need to worry. Women have been doing this since the beginning of time."

"I understand, but no woman has ever done this for me."

His voice was so soft, his words so sincere, it tugged at her heart. Made Jasmine almost want to tell him the truth. Almost.

Dr. Edmonds nodded. "Mrs. Bush can do everything she would normally do. Of course we want you to eat right and only do the exercise that you're used to doing."

Jasmine nodded, and smiled when Hosea squeezed her hand again.

"So, that's it for today. Again, congratulations." The doctor stood, dismissing them. His lies complete.

Jasmine had no idea how long Hosea held her once they were outside of the office. "I love you," he said so many times she almost tired of hearing it. Almost.

She held him too, saying nothing. Just tried to believe that life would still be normal. When they got into the car, Hosea said, "We've got to do something to remember this day."

"Let's go home."

He grinned. "I'm with you. We can begin practicing for baby number two."

But a celebration was not in her thoughts. She hadn't been able to wrap her mind around the verity of the fact that she was going to be the mother of Brian Lewis's baby. For the next ten, twenty, thirty, forty years, maybe even fifty years, she'd keep that secret. The thought overwhelmed her, made her want to stay in bed for all that time.

She said nothing for the ten-minute drive home, and once there, she headed straight to the bedroom.

"Darlin', what's wrong?" Hosea asked as he turned back the comforter, making room for her to crawl in.

She nodded. "I just need a nap. Need to push this aside for a moment."

He sat on the edge of the bed. "I guess we never talked seriously about having children, but Jasmine, I couldn't be happier." She let seconds tick by, said nothing. He asked, "What about you?"

"I'm . . . surprised. I'm overwhelmed." When he frowned she added, "But, I'm happy," she said, making his smile return.

He reached for the pillows and made her comfortable.

"Aren't you going back to work?" she asked, trying to keep the hope out of her tone.

"No, I told them I wouldn't be in today."

She wanted to tell him to go because it was hard to look at

him now. Yet she said nothing more. Just closed her eyes, laid her head and her burdens down.

But minutes later she was shaken awake; thoughts of her troubles dragged her back to consciousness. She couldn't rest with the mantra blasting in her mind.

How am I going to do this?

It had been her plan to never have a plan again. But now, life would be nothing but a plan. A well-thought-out plot to keep her child's paternity an everlasting secret.

She sighed, knowing that she had to accept this fate. Because now, short of throwing herself down a set of stairs, she would have this baby, call it a Bush, and tell tales for the rest of her days of how Hosea knocked her up on their honeymoon.

But as she thought about it, there was really no reason why she couldn't pull this off. As mammoth as this seemed, she was Jasmine Larson Bush, the master planner. The rock on her left hand proved how good she was.

"Darlin', are you awake?"

"Yes, sweetie," she said when Hosea walked into the room.

"Good, because I have a surprise for you."

Jasmine waited; surprise had become synonymous with gifts from the best shops, dinner at first-class restaurants, and attending special events with some of the city's most elite. Now that she was carrying *his* child, she couldn't wait to hear what this surprise might be.

Hosea said, "I've ordered all your favorite dishes from 'Twenty-one.' They'll be delivered within an hour."

Jasmine clapped. That restaurant didn't do take-out or delivery. But she'd come to understand that celebrity had its privileges. She wrapped her arms around Hosea's neck. "That's great. We can have a romantic lunch and then—"

He moaned as he kissed her. "We may not be able to do that for a couple of hours because Pops is on his way over."

"Pops?" she asked, hoping that he'd given that name to someone besides his father.

"Yeah." He chuckled. "It's kinda funny to hear you call him Pops. What do you plan on calling him anyway?"

She wanted to tell Hosea that she didn't plan on calling his father anything. Didn't want to say his name—or see him—at all. She asked, "Why is your father coming over here?"

"Well, we haven't seen him since our wedding."

"And?"

"And I can't wait to tell him that he's going to be a grandfather."

No way, she thought. She'd never be able to convince the reverend the way she'd convinced his son. The son loved her. The father didn't; he would take a single look at her and know. "Hosea, it's too early to tell anyone."

"I think we should tell the world."

"The doctor recommends that we tell no one until we get through the first trimester."

Hosea frowned. "I didn't hear him say that."

"He said that in the examination room," she lied.

"So, you want me to wait three months before I tell anyone about the second happiest event of my life?"

"Well, maybe we won't have to wait the entire three months, but I certainly don't want to mention it now."

Hosea sighed. "Okay, I don't understand, but if you don't want to tell people for a while, I'll go along."

Jasmine exhaled.

"So, we'll only tell Pops, and Serena too, if you want."

Jasmine answered him with a moan.

He said, "What's wrong with telling just the two of them?"

"Hosea, please, sweetie," she begged. "I don't want to tell anyone."

"My pops and your sister are not just anyone. My father has waited a lot of years to be a grandfather."

"That's my point. He's waited and it would be hard to go back to him if something were to happen to this baby."

Hosea frowned. "Jasmine, 'this' baby is 'our' baby."

"I know, it's just that—"

He interrupted. "I don't know why you're talking like you expect to lose our baby." He lowered his voice. "We're not claiming that, and it would help to have Pops and Serena praying for us anyway."

She held out her hand and when he took it, she pulled him onto the bed. "Sweetie, you and I are a family now. It's not that we don't need other people's prayers, but we have to stand for ourselves, together. And this is a wonderful time to begin doing that."

He sighed.

"I know nothing is going to happen to . . . our baby." She rested his hand on her stomach. "But I also know how hard it would be if something were to happen. And it would be so much harder on me if I started telling people." When he said nothing, she added, "Did you know that Tina just had a miscarriage?"

His eyes widened. "No, I didn't know that."

Jasmine nodded. "And she spent an hour in my office crying about it. She's been so stressed. And then there's my cousin . . . ," she paused, trying to think of a name, "Faith. She had three miscarriages before she carried her son to term." She stopped again. "And Dr. Edmonds told me fifty percent of all pregnancies end in a miscarriage." She paused and checked those words into her memory to give to the doctor later. Just in case. "All I'm saying," she continued, "is that I want to share this beginning with just you and me, and our baby." Then, she added, "And God."

A moment passed before he nodded. "I can't say I agree, but I don't want you under any stress. So we'll do this your way, but I was sure excited about giving Pops this news."

"We will. Soon."

"So, what are we going to tell Pops now?"

"Tell him to stay home." She spoke the words before she could stop herself. "So we can be alone." She kissed him.

"I wish," he moaned. "We'll just say we wanted him to be the first to visit us as husband and wife."

She stood, "Okay, I'm going to freshen up a bit." She took a few steps, stopped. "By the way, don't say anything to Tina about her . . . miscarriage. It's still really hard, you know?"

He nodded, but then the ringing phone brought his smile back. "That's either Pops or the food."

Inside the bathroom, Jasmine leaned against the closed door and wished there was a window she could escape through.

She turned on the faucet and splashed water on her face. She'd handled the reverend before and certainly she would handle him now.

"So," *Reverend Bush began* as he leaned back in his chair. "Do you two plan on staying here or will you be looking for another place?"

Jasmine's eyes narrowed, trying to decipher his words the way she'd been doing all afternoon. Every word he spoke, every gesture he made, every time he laughed, or didn't, Jasmine became the explorer, searching for the true meaning.

The reverend was pleasant enough. He'd smiled and played nice from the moment he arrived. But although he'd asked about Serena and her daughters, shared in their memories of the wedding, and now wanted to know more about their future, Jasmine wasn't fooled. She knew behind that gleaming smile, the reverend was just waiting for her to fall, drop to the mat so that he could give her a ten-count.

"We were thinking about looking for something right away," Hosea said. "But now . . ." He stopped, looked at his wife, eyes pleading, for permission to say more.

Jasmine jumped from her chair. "Are you finished, Reverend Bush?" Before he could respond, she lifted his plate. Made a pile with that one, hers, and Hosea's. She rushed into the kitchen, knowing Hosea would never say a word about the baby without her.

Still, she listened, as she placed the remnants of their dinner on the counter.

"So, are you going to be moving?" the reverend asked again.

"Yeah, we're going to be looking for something larger."

"I know a good realtor on Long Island."

"Actually, Pops, we've looked at some of those condos on Park Avenue, although I think they're a bit pricey. But either way, we plan to stay in the city."

"Really?" His tone carried a frown. "I would have thought you'd want to stay on the Island. It's a much better place to raise children."

Jasmine rushed back into the dining room. "Reverend Bush, can I get you anything else?" Her question sounded like the benediction—be blessed and may peace be with you as you get out of my house.

This time, it was the reverend's eyes that narrowed. Like he was doing his own exploration of her words. "Pops," Hosea began before the reverend could respond to Jasmine, "I told Jasmine she can't keep calling you Reverend Bush."

Hosea chuckled. His father chuckled.

Jasmine did not.

"Yes, Reverend Bush does seem a bit formal, Jasmine," he said. "What would you like to call me?"

In that instant, she knew this was what God's grace was about—the Lord providing you with a muzzle when you needed it most. Instead of the litany of names she had for him, she only said, "Reverend Bush is most comfortable to me . . . right now."

Hosea stood, strolled to where his wife stood, and held her from behind. "Come on, happy families don't call each other by their last names." He chuckled as if he'd told a joke.

"Son, it doesn't matter what Jasmine calls me. All that matters is how she feels about me, and how I feel about her."

Their eyes met, a staring duel.

He said, "It's taking me some getting used to, having a daughter-in-law."

Jasmine's arms crossed.

"But today was enjoyable. I'm glad you invited me into your home, Jasmine."

"This is Hosea's home too."

"Indeed." He nodded. "Jasmine, I'm fine with whatever you call me." He passed her the smile again, the one that she knew was meant to disarm, make her believe that all was well up until the moment the gauntlet chopped her body in two. "I had a good time," he said as he stood. "We'll do this again. Next time at my house."

Jasmine took slow steps toward the reverend as he reached for her, then held her as if he really were a loving father-in-law.

While the reverend embraced his son, Jasmine wondered what the reverend's game was. And then she wondered if he had a game at all. Maybe the grudge was over. Maybe the truce had begun.

Once alone, Hosea said, "I only have to repeat that performance for eighty-nine more days." He sighed. "I don't know how I'm going to do it."

"You'll do fine."

Suddenly, Hosea lifted Jasmine's tank top. "This is your daddy, little one. We're getting the world ready for you." He kissed her stomach. "I love you already."

Her eyes watered as she held her husband. But an instant later, she squeezed her eyes shut, trying to force away the image of Brian Lewis charging into their lives, demanding that Hosea never call himself Daddy again.

Chapter 38

ood morning, Mrs. Bush," Mae Frances's driver said the moment she stepped out of the building. "I haven't had a chance to congratulate you."

"Thanks, Gerald. You're waiting for Mae Frances?"

He nodded, looked at his watch. "Yeah, but I'm a few minutes early."

"Doing anything special with Mae Frances today?"

He shrugged. "Unless she has a special errand, we'll be doing what we do every Monday and Thursday, drive around Central Park. Just enough to get Mrs. Van Dorn out of the house."

Jasmine still couldn't figure out how a woman whose cabinets were bare could afford a driver. "So, what do you guys do on the other days?" she probed.

He frowned. "I'm only here on my days off, Mondays and Thursdays. Sometimes, I get by on a Sunday, but that's not often."

It was her turn to frown. "I didn't realize you only worked two days a week."

"I work five days, I just come here on my days off for a couple of hours." He leaned forward, lowered his voice. "It's been tough sometimes, but I felt sorry for Mrs. Van Dorn after the divorce. So, I asked Dr. Van Dorn if it was okay if I took her around the city a couple of days a week. He said it was fine as long as he didn't have to pay for it." He shrugged. "I didn't ex-

pect it to turn into so many years, but I just call this my volunteer time."

Volunteer time? Jasmine's frown deepened.

He said, "I'm sure glad you and Mrs. Van Dorn are friends,
Mrs. Bush. She's been a lot happier since you came into her
life. Before you, no one came to see her, except for Dr. Edmonds."

The mention of her doctor's name tickled her curiosity
again. But before she could ask a question, Mae Frances's voice
floated over her shoulder.

"Jasmine Larson, seems you're running late this morning."

"Yeah," she said wanting to push her friend back into the
building. "I have some errands to run before I go into the office."

"Do you want a ride?"

"No, thanks."

The woman peered at Jasmine. "Are you all right?"

"I'm fine. I'll see you later."

Mae Frances slipped into the backseat and Jasmine
watched the car weave into traffic.

So Gerald brought his car by twice a week to drive Mae
Frances around for free. Jasmine shook her head. Mae Frances
had a boatload of tricks.

"She's just doing what she has to do," Jasmine whispered as
she raised her hand to hail a cab, but those words made her
shiver and she lowered her hand. Rested it on her belly. She
was no different than Mae Frances. They were both just
women who were doing what women sometimes had to do.

Chapter 39

Jasmine rushed into her office, slammed the door, unzipped her
skirt halfway, then exhaled.

She waited a moment before she flopped into her chair.
That was the most embarrassing thing that had ever happened.

She looked down at her suit where the button had been—
the button that had just popped off her jacket while she was
standing in front of the room presenting Rio's financial report.
She didn't care that the button had come off her designer suit.
She only cared that the button had burst off her suit in front
of thirty people.

It wasn't that she'd gained a lot of weight. In twelve weeks,
barely eight pounds. But still, every pound had congregated at
her middle—and it thrilled Hosea.

"How much weight have you gained?" he asked almost
every morning.

She'd stand on the scale and then moan the results.

"Don't be upset, darlin'," he comforted her. "According to
Dr. Edmonds, you're right on track."

It wasn't the weight gain that bothered her; it was that the
weight gain could spill her secret. She still had a month to go
before she came to the end of the first trimester—that was the
lie. She was already twelve weeks and starting to show.

But the cover-up continued. Only Dr. Edmonds and Mae

Frances knew her truth. And although there were times when she wished she had someone she could really talk to, there was too much danger in sharing this beyond those two.

She sank deeper into her chair when she heard the knock on her door.

"You okay?" Malik asked, when he stepped inside.

She nodded. "I needed to review some numbers for this afternoon's meeting."

"I was just checking because you seemed . . . different."

She tilted her head. "What do you mean?"

He shrugged. Sat down. "I don't know. Different. You're glowing. Guess married life agrees with you."

She smiled. "Definitely."

"Did I ever apologize for thinking that you and Hosea were just . . . business as usual?"

"No, you didn't," she said sternly, but then added a grin. "But I accept your apology."

"I'm glad you're happy, Jasmine." He stood. "And I'm even happier that you're working here." He shook his head. "Our numbers are outstanding. I'm surprised you haven't hit me for a raise."

"That's coming." She laughed.

"Oh, I almost forgot. I need a big favor."

"Anything for you, Godbrother."

"You know that workshop I planned to do in L.A. for J.T. and Lamont?"

She blinked, swallowed, nodded.

"Well, I'm in the middle of a major contract negotiation and I can't leave New York. I need you to cover for me. Gabriella's working on your reservations. You'll be going to L.A. next Wednesday."

She shook her head.

"Don't worry," he continued. "I know your plate is full, but you won't have much to do."

She needed to tell him this trip would never happen. But her mouth was as dry as Death Valley.

He continued, "I've prepared the entire presentation."

"Malik," she said finding her voice. "Just postpone the workshop until you're able to go."

He shook his head. "I don't know how long I'll be stuck here and J.T. and Lamont need some direction. This club may have been their idea, but our numbers are better."

"I can't go to Los Angeles."

He looked at her as if he didn't understand her words. Sat down slowly. Stared. "Why not?"

She shrugged, wishing she had more time to come up with an excuse. "I have a lot to do."

"Not good enough, Jas. You'll only be gone a day or so."

"I *can't* go."

"Why not?"

"I just got married."

"I'm asking for one night." He paused, leaned across the desk. "Come on, Jas, I need you."

He stood, but before he could take a step, Jasmine said, "I'm pregnant."

Slowly, he returned to the chair. "Wow, you and Hosea didn't waste any time."

She lowered her eyes.

He said, "I guess I should say congratulations."

"Yes," Jasmine said, her eyes darting from the desk to the window, to the wall, to the door. "We're very happy."

When she looked at Malik, his eyes were narrow. "What's up, Jasmine?"

"What do you mean?"

"This doesn't make sense."

"What? My being pregnant?"

"Being pregnant so soon surprises me, but it's the way you're talking about it. You sound . . . like you've practiced these words."

"I don't know what you're talking about. Like I said, we're very happy."

"There you go again." He leaned forward. "So, are you really pregnant or did you just tell Hosea that?"

The question surprised her. "Yes, I'm pregnant. Why would I make that up?"

He shrugged, but the way he peered at her made her move to one side of her chair, then the other. "How far along are you?"

"About six weeks," she said, being very aware of where she was supposed to be.

"Wow, you've only been married six weeks."

"I said 'about' six weeks. We haven't had an ultrasound yet, but we know it happened in Bermuda."

His eyes pierced her, making her shift more.

The two closest men in her life were so different. Hosea trusted her, suspected nothing. Malik never trusted her, suspected everything.

He whispered, "It's not Hosea's baby."

Her first thought through the blasting beat of her heart was, men don't have intuition.

"Whose baby is it?" he asked.

"I cannot believe you're asking me that." She put as much indignation as she could into her tone.

"Whose baby is it?" he asked, as if he refused to be denied.

She stood, planned to stomp across the room and out the door. But her skirt fell a bit; she'd forgotten the zipper. So she returned to her chair. But still, she spat with fury, "This is ridiculous."

He backed away, but his eyes stayed settled on his godsister.

Jasmine crossed her arms, lowered her eyes.

"You just gave yourself away, Jas."

She said nothing.

"You never said this is your husband's baby."

She raised her eyes, looked at him.

He said, "Brian Lewis."

His name took her breath away.

His intuition continued, "You're carrying Brian's baby."

Jasmine leaned back in her chair. This was a secret that she'd vowed to carry for the next, ten, twenty, thirty, forty, even fifty years. It couldn't be this easy.

"No," she denied.

He leaned forward, looked through her. "Jasmine, I know you."

Her hands rose to her face, covered her shame.

"Jasmine, this is crazy. You're still sleeping with Brian?"

"No," she said. "I swear I haven't been with Brian since before my wedding. Way before my wedding."

"Couldn't have been too 'way before'."

"I haven't been with Brian since Hosea asked me to marry him."

"That can't be true if you're six weeks pregnant."

"I'm not, I'm twelve weeks . . . or so."

"Oh, God—"

"But I tried to get rid of it." Then, she explained, how the truth became a lie. And how now, she was going to make this lie the truth. "I did everything I was supposed to do, but now Hosea thinks this baby is his."

"What about Brian?"

"I never cared about Brian. I don't even like him."

"You like him enough to have his baby."

"It's not his baby. It's mine and Hosea's."

"Saying that won't change the baby's DNA. It's not Hosea's and you need to tell him."

Jasmine wondered why she never noticed before that her godbrother didn't have much sense. "You're kidding, right? What do you think Hosea will do if I told him that?"

"He'll leave you."

Her eyes widened. "That's what you want?"

"He'll leave you. And then, he'll come back." He paused. "He won't be happy, but trust me, if you tell Hosea now, he'll be upset, but at least you would have told him early. The two of you can face the truth together."

She shook her head.

"But if you don't tell him, you'll be building lies. And trust me, one day, he'll find out. And it won't be the baby that will bother him then." He paused. "This won't stay a secret."

"Yes, it will."

"It took me," he paused and looked at his watch, "three minutes?"

"I just got a little rattled. And maybe subconsciously I wanted you to know because this has been so hard. But this stops with you. I'll do anything to make sure Hosea never finds out."

Malik shook his head.

She said, "I pray I can trust you."

He held up his hands. "I won't say a word. Not my place." He stood and walked out of her office.

Jasmine had no fear—this would never travel beyond Malik. And perhaps this happened for a reason. He was her practice test. She'd failed, but it was only Malik. Next time, Reverend Bush would be the one she'd have to convince. When she faced her father-in-law her performance had to be Oscar worthy.

Chapter 40

J asmine squirmed as the sonographer rubbed the gel across her belly.

"You okay?" Hosea asked as he held her hand.

"Yes, it's just cold."

"Sorry," the woman said before she pressed the transducer onto Jasmine. "I should have warned you. Now, let's get a look at your baby." Hosea and Jasmine stared at the black, white, and gray sketch on the monitor. The sonographer said, "We're getting some good pictures here."

Jasmine frowned. The scratchy image on the computer didn't look like much of anything to her.

"The white and gray spots are your baby. See, here's the head . . ." The woman continued, clarifying.

"Wow," Hosea whispered.

The sonographer's explanations brought their baby to life, and Jasmine's heart fluttered.

"By the way," the woman began, "how far along are you?"

"Twelve weeks," Hosea said as if he'd been counting every day.

"Really?" She frowned.

Jasmine's heart pounded. "Ah, what's all the black space?" she asked.

"Darlin', remember she explained. That's the fluid and . . . other stuff, right?"

The woman laughed. "Close enough."

"I'm sorry, I just forgot," Jasmine said. She blew a breath of relief when a moment later, the sonographer turned off the monitor. "We're done."

"That was something," Hosea said as the woman wiped the gel off Jasmine.

It certainly was, she said inside as she thought about how close the sonographer had come to revealing her secret. Dr. Edmonds was supposed to take care of this; she couldn't afford this kind of mistake.

"This is for you." The woman handed Jasmine a printout before she left the room.

The two stared at the image.

"This is our baby's first picture," she said.

Hosea peered at the photo. "Can you tell if it's a boy or a girl?"

Jasmine scooted up. "Does it matter?"

He shrugged. "The politically correct answer is that I want a healthy baby, right? But, I gotta admit, I wouldn't mind a son. Just one thing, though," Hosea added. "He won't be a junior."

"Why not? I love your name."

"No, you love me. I gotta tell you, it hasn't been easy."

She tilted her head.

He said, "I guess you haven't read about Hosea in the Bible. How God told him to take a whore for a wife." He shook his head. "You wouldn't believe the jokes I had to hear in Sunday school."

Jasmine tried to swallow the expanding lump in her throat. "Is that true?" she squeaked. "Does it really say that in the Bible?"

"Yup." He chuckled and lifted her face with his fingers. "Why're you looking like that? God's not talking about you."

He held her, but this was one time when his arms couldn't bring Jasmine comfort.

◆ ◆ ◆

Hosea put his man-of-the-house foot down.

"No matter what you say, Jasmine, we're gonna tell the world tomorrow," he exclaimed once they were alone after Dr. Edmonds reviewed the ultrasound results.

"Everything is moving along fine," Dr. Edmonds had said moments before.

Now, Hosea pulled Jasmine from the examination table and lifted her into the air. "I can't wait to tell everyone. We're gonna have a baby." He bowed, and as had become his manner, he kissed her stomach.

Jasmine smiled as if she was pleased. But her thoughts were beyond this moment. Now the real theatrics would begin.

She was ready for her husband's next words.

"Let's go tell Pops."

She knew that's what he would say. That's why she'd worn a tunic with her jeans today; there was no need for Reverend Bush to see the bit of extra weight she carried.

"Pops had a trustees meeting this morning, so he should still be at church."

The confidence she had dipped just a bit. She was ready to face Reverend Bush, but not Brother Hill and the rest of the reverend's rabble.

But then she remembered—she was the master planner, the great pretender. It didn't matter who was there.

As Hosea helped her into the SUV, she thought about the three months that had passed. Her husband suspected nothing. All that had changed was his growing love for her. And his love for his baby. It was evident in the words he spoke.

"Our baby will have the best of everything," he'd said one night as he held her in bed.

"Definitely."

"I'm not just talking about having good parents, and living in a nice home, and going to the best schools. I want our baby to be truly happy. From the moment he's born, I want him to know the love of God and to just be happy every day he walks this earth."

"Hosea, that's so sweet."

"I mean it, darlin'. If I could buy that for our baby, I'd pay any price."

That had been the wonderful proof she needed—he loved their child.

Their SUV swerved into the City of Lights parking lot and Jasmine took a deep breath.

"Hosea," Mrs. Whittingham exclaimed the moment they stepped inside the church. And then she noticed Jasmine. Her smile stayed, sans the warmth. "Jasmine."

Jasmine moved to the side as Hosea hugged her. Since their wedding, Mrs. Whittingham had been pleasant enough, but Jasmine knew the woman didn't like her. *Not that it matters,* she thought as she twirled her ring on her finger.

Still fondling her ring, she followed her husband into Reverend Bush's office.

Months of dress rehearsal; now, she was stepping onto the stage.

"Son!"

The reverend's smile stayed in place while he hugged Hosea, then dimmed just a bit when he embraced Jasmine.

"This is a pleasure," the reverend said as he motioned for the two to sit. "Were you hanging out in the neighborhood?"

"No, Pops, we made a special trip to see you."

The reverend leaned back in his chair. "Is that right?" Then, with a smile, he said, "Don't tell me you're here to ask for money?"

The two men laughed.

Hosea said, "Pops, it's been years since I've hit you like that." Turning to Jasmine, he explained, "When I was a teenager, I'd take the Long Island Rail Road, then hop on the train to talk to Pops here because I couldn't talk to him at home."

The reverend nodded. "That was my son's trick," he said to Jasmine. "He couldn't get a thing out of his mother."

"But I could get everything out of Pops!"

The men laughed again.

"You know what they say about payback," the reverend chuckled. "I can't wait to see how you'll handle your children."

Hosea looked at Jasmine, grinned.

"Well, Pops, you might get to see that sooner than you think." He reached across the space and took Jasmine's hand. "We have some news."

The reverend's chuckles went away.

"We're having a baby."

The reverend blinked, trying to make room in his mind for his son's words. "A baby?" he said as if that were a foreign concept.

Hosea nodded.

While Hosea grinned, Jasmine sat, adrenaline pumping, preparing.

"A baby?" the reverend repeated.

"Yeah, Pops. You're going to be a grandfather."

"A grandfather?"

Hosea chuckled. "I know this is a surprise, but I didn't think you'd be at a loss for words."

In slow motion he stood, walked around the desk. "Well . . ."

Hosea stood with his father, hugged him. "Pops, I'm gonna be a pops."

Hosea laughed; the reverend tried to chuckle.

Then, the reverend turned toward Jasmine. He edged closer. Her hands contracted into fists. He embraced her.

"This is a surprise," the reverend said.

"Yup," Hosea said, sitting back down. Jasmine did the same. "It was a surprise to us too, but we're ready." He winked at Jasmine.

"Well, it's good to be ready, but . . . this is so soon."

A shadow of doubt veiled his eyes and launched Jasmine into action. "It seems soon," Jasmine agreed. "But I was think, ing that this is just part of God's plan."

As if he hadn't heard her explanation of divine involve, ment, the reverend asked, "Who's your doctor?"

She hesitated. "Dr. Edmonds." She stared at the reverend for signs of what that question meant.

The oddity of that inquiry only seemed to affect her.

Hosea said, "He's great, Pops. Dr. Edmonds is taking good care of us."

The reverend seemed surprised. "So, *you've* met the doctor."

"Yup. And everything's fine. Jasmine's healthy. The baby's healthy. In six months, you'll be able to add a new name to the City of Lights membership roster."

"Six months," the reverend said as if he were calculating in his head. Reservations still darkened his eyes. "Well," the rev, erend said again. "I'm going to be a grandfather. And you two," he crossed his arms, "are going to be parents. Well. Congratu, lations."

Jasmine didn't think it was possible, but Hosea's grin widened as if he didn't notice his father's doubts. "Pops, I'd like to announce this in church tomorrow."

"Really?"

It was the first time Hosea frowned. "Yeah, like we've done everything else. Thought it would be good to keep the saints praying."

"That's always a good thing. But I'm wondering if we should wait a minute. It's still pretty early . . ."

Hosea looked between Jasmine and his father. "Have you two been talking? Jasmine wanted to wait too."

"You don't want to announce this tomorrow?" the reverend asked her.

Before she could answer, Hosea said, "No, she's fine now, but she's wanted to keep this a secret for months. Made me wait this entire first trimester."

"Really?" the reverend frowned. "When did you find out that you were pregnant?"

"Reverend Bush," she began before her husband could answer. There was no way she wanted him to know that they'd known almost from the moment they'd returned from their honeymoon. Hosea believed that, but she didn't think Reverend Bush would. "We've known for a while," she said taking charge. "But we didn't want to tell anyone until Dr. Edmonds gave the go-ahead." She moved to the edge of her seat. "Once we got the word, we wanted you—our baby's grandfather—to know first." She placed her hand on her stomach.

Hosea beamed, but the reverend just stared.

"Well," Reverend Bush said after a moment, "we'll make this announcement tomorrow."

"Great," Hosea said, standing. He took Jasmine's hand and lifted her from her seat.

In the few minutes that Hosea and his father chatted, Jasmine watched the reverend. Looked for his thoughts. But he kept his eyes from her. Acted as if she hadn't just told him that she was carrying his grandchild.

At the door, Reverend Bush hugged her, but his good-bye embrace lacked even the lukewarmness that his greeting held.

It was then that she knew she was in trouble.

Chapter 41

Malik, I'm in trouble."

Her godbrother stepped into her apartment. He paused at the door and looked around. "I guess Hosea's not here."

Jasmine shook her head. "He's assisting with the second service and then he'll be going over final plans for the church picnic next Sunday."

Malik nodded, then sank onto the couch. Clasped his hands together. "So, what's up?"

"Look, I know you don't approve, but I need your help."

He shook his head. "I'm not getting involved."

"I wanted to ask," she began, ignoring his words, "did Reverend Bush seem strange to you this morning when Hosea and I made the announcement about the baby?"

Malik frowned, shrugged. "No."

"I don't think he believes me."

Her godbrother's eyebrows rose. "He doesn't believe that you're pregnant or that the baby's Hosea's?"

"I don't know. But when we told him yesterday—" She stopped.

"I'm not surprised. The reverend's no fool."

"And Hosea is?"

"Not a fool. Just in love. Because if he wasn't, he'd be doing his own calculating."

Jasmine discarded Malik's words. She didn't care why Hosea believed her. Just that he did.

"So, you think there's a chance that Reverend Bush doesn't believe me?"

"I think there's a very good chance that he believes something's up."

"Why?" she whined.

"Well, maybe it's because it happened so soon and he knows it wouldn't be so easy for a forty-year-old woman to get pregnant that quickly."

"I'm not forty. I'm thirty-five."

"What?" He shook his head as if he were confused.

"I told Hosea I was thirty-five."

"Jasmine," Malik moaned. "How do you expect to get away with all of these lies?"

That was a question she was beginning to ask herself.

He said, "Hosea's going to know once he talks to the doctor."

"No. He's not," Jasmine said strongly.

Her godbrother stared at her for just a moment before he said, "I don't even want to know."

"You have to talk to Reverend Bush for me."

"No."

"Find out what he knows."

"Did you hear what I said? No."

"I don't need you to lie or anything. Just find out if Reverend Bush suspects anything."

"Even if I were to talk to him, Reverend Bush isn't going to tell me anything about my godsister." He sighed. "Instead of playing this game that you're bound to lose, tell Hosea the truth."

"Not an option."

"Let me ask you this. You suspect that Reverend Bush knows something."

She nodded.

"If he's suspicious, he's going to keep looking. And if he looks too deeply, he's going to find what he's looking for."

Jasmine remembered the reverend's words:

I don't trust you, Jasmine.

"And when he finds something," Malik continued, "he's going to tell Hosea. What do you think will happen then?"

Jasmine closed her eyes. What happened to the simplicity of this plan? She should have faked a miscarriage.

Malik stood, moved to where Jasmine stood. "Tell him, Jasmine, before someone else does," he whispered, trying to put warmth into his warning. "If you tell him, I think you'll have a chance of saving your marriage. But if this news comes from someone or somewhere else, you'll lose him for sure."

Malik hugged her, then left without another word.

Chapter 42

J ust the aroma of the barbecued ribs added inches to her hips,
but Jasmine didn't care.

She inhaled again before she picked up a bone, sucked
the meat into her mouth, and then moaned with pleasure.

Hosea said, "It's good to see you eating, darlin'."

Jasmine didn't respond. Didn't take another breath or a
break. Didn't notice the children running through the park,
nor the men slamming dominoes at the adjacent table. All she
could do was eat.

For weeks, crackers had been the main staple of her diet.
But the nausea had passed, and was replaced by the desire to
consume anything.

"Hey, you guys." Malik swung his legs over the wooden bench.

"Hey, yourself," Hosea said.

Jasmine waved.

"You have to excuse my wife." Hosea chuckled. "She's a little bit hungry."

"I can tell," Malik said as Jasmine traded her rib for a
spoonful of potato salad.

"So, you came alone, bro?" Hosea asked.

"No doubt. There're two places a man shalt not invite a
woman: to a wedding and to church."

Jasmine frowned. "This isn't church."

"It's a church picnic. And any time you ask a woman to join you for church or a wedding, it's beyond a date. That's darn near a commitment."

Hosea laughed, and Jasmine rolled her eyes.

"Darlin', didn't I invite you to church?" Hosea kissed her cheek, then glanced at his watch. "I'm one of the umps for softball. You gonna play, Malik?"

"Nah, I'm going to hit the courts."

"Okay, catch up with you later." Hosea stood and folded his empty paper plate. "You want me to take yours, darlin'?"

Jasmine slapped his hand as he reached for her plate; Hosea laughed before he stepped away.

Malik asked, "Did you guys just get here?"

Jasmine shook her head. "Been here a while, but we drove up ourselves. I didn't want to be stuck on the bus for an hour with these church folks," she whispered as she glanced at the crowd who had gathered at Bear Mountain State Park. Some five hundred City of Lights members had joined Reverend Bush for the annual anniversary celebration.

Malik said, "These are your people now."

They laughed, but then Jasmine leaned toward Malik. "Did you talk to Reverend Bush?"

"Didn't I tell you that I wasn't going to do that?"

"Yes, but I was hoping your love for me would override that," she said before she shoveled a spoonful of baked beans into her mouth.

Malik hesitated. "I talked to him."

She stopped chewing and pushed her plate aside.

"He didn't tell me anything."

"What did he say?"

"Nothing. We just chatted about you. I told him I thought you and Hosea were really happy."

"What did he say?" she repeated.

He shrugged. "He said he thought you and Hosea were happy too."

"So, you don't think he suspects anything?"

"He didn't give me any signs. There was one point when he seemed a bit surprised by something I said. I can't remember what it was, but really all he said was that he knew Hosea loved you and that you loved Hosea."

Jasmine exhaled.

"But, don't get it twisted. I still think you need to talk to your husband," Malik said. "Because I know the reverend. If there's a secret to be found, he'll find it."

Jasmine shook her head. "I just have to be careful."

"You'll never be able to be that careful."

"How many women do you think are out there who have passed their children off to a man who is not the father?"

"None of them are the daughter-in-law of Reverend H. Samuel Bush."

Jasmine pushed away from the picnic table. "He's just a man," Jasmine said with more confidence than she'd had in weeks. "And I can handle any man."

Malik took a sip of his soda. "Whatever."

"I'm going to get some dessert. Do you want anything?"

"Nah, I'm gonna head over to the basketball courts."

As Jasmine passed the spread of apple and peach pies, red velvet cakes, and brownies, she decided to get a little of everything, to celebrate. Seemed Reverend Bush didn't know a thing.

After she packed a plate with sweets, she reached for a soda.

"Let me help you," a voice behind her said.

She faced Reverend Bush and he eyed her plate. "I guess you're not suffering from morning sickness."

She waved her hand. "That stopped a while ago."

"A while ago?"

She hesitated. "Yes, right before the end of my first trimester."

He tilted his head. "My wife had morning sickness well into her fourth month."

"I guess every woman is different."

"No doubt." As Jasmine reached for the soda, Reverend Bush, said, "I'll walk you back to your table."

Jasmine wanted to tell him to go away, but she moved with quick steps, hoping he'd disappear once she sat down. But then he took a seat next to her.

"You know, Jasmine, it's a shame that you and I haven't spent more time together. Here you are, married to my son, and I feel like I hardly know you."

"Well, that isn't totally my fault, Reverend Bush. You've made it clear how you feel about me."

"But now, we're family. And you're carrying . . . my grandchild, right?"

It was the way he spoke those last words that made her only nod.

He said, "I think it's time we talked."

"What do you want to talk about?"

The reverend shrugged. "Well," he paused. "Tell me about your first marriage."

Jasmine could barely breathe. *My first marriage?* She took a long sip of soda, kept her eyes away from him, until she said, "I'm sorry, what did you say, Reverend?"

He smirked, and repeated his question.

"Reverend Bush, I've never been married."

His eyebrows rose. "Really? Malik told me you were divorced."

Inhale. Exhale.

"I asked Hosea," he began, "but he said you'd never been married."

Exhale. Inhale.

She said, "My sister is married, but her husband passed away. Is that what you're talking about?"

"No. Malik said *you* were married. And that *you* were divorced."

"I . . . I don't know . . . I've never been married."

"Why would Malik say otherwise?"

"I . . . I don't know . . . maybe he was confused?"

Reverend Bush bobbed his head. "Maybe." He pushed away from the table. "Well, I need to mingle. I can't spend all my time with my daughter-in-law, can I?"

Jasmine gasped for air as he strutted away. When she could no longer see him, she stood and rushed through the park, past the rows of picnic tables crowded with parishioners eating, chatting, totally oblivious to the fact that her world was about to end. Her eyes scanned the grounds until she found the basketball courts. Malik stood on the sidelines watching a half-court game. She grabbed his arm.

"Why did you tell Reverend Bush that I was married before?" she hissed.

"What?"

"You told Reverend Bush that I was divorced and Hosea doesn't know that. He thinks that I was never married."

Malik took her hand, moving her farther away from the crowd. "Jasmine, everyone knows that you were married. Why would you tell Hosea that you weren't?"

Tears stung her eyes. "He's a minister and I didn't think being divorced was good."

Malik moaned. "This is what I'm talking about, Jasmine. Lies are like boomerangs. They always come back."

She felt like crying a river, but she just stood, listening, trembling.

"I'm trying to help, Jasmine. This is out of control and it's only going to get worse. Look," he said softening his voice, "if you want, I'll do it with you. I'll be there. But please. Before this really blows up, tell Hosea the truth . . . about everything."

She sniffed back her tears. "I'm going to the restroom."

"Are you okay?"

She nodded and turned away. But as she moved toward the restroom, her steps slowed. Reverend Bush stood leaning against the brick building that housed the ladies' room.

She stopped.

They stared.

Then he walked away.

Jasmine stood still for only a moment before she scurried through the park in search of her husband.

"*Sweetie, we have to go,*" Jasmine called to Hosea as he stood be‹ hind home plate.

Hosea signaled to one of the men sitting on the bleachers. Then he took Jasmine's hand. "What's wrong?" he asked. Con‹ cern added lines to his forehead.

"I feel sick. It's too hot out here."

"I should have thought of that. We should have stayed home."

"Oh, no, sweetie, I'm fine. I just want to go."

"Okay, let me find Pops."

"No!" She paused. "With all these people it will take for‹ ever to find him, and then he'll try to talk me into staying, and then I won't want to disappoint him, and then—"

"Okay, let's go." He held her as they wandered toward the parking lot.

But even when their car exited the park grounds, and Jas‹ mine closed her eyes, rest would not come. Reverend Bush marched through her mind, taunting and teasing, telling her that she was not safe.

By the time they entered their apartment, Jasmine was ex‹ hausted.

"I'm sorry," she said to Hosea before she climbed into bed. "I know you wanted to stay at the picnic."

"The only place I want to be is with you and our baby. Get some rest. I'm going to hang out in the living room."

Still, Jasmine could find no peace. For hours she tossed, warring with the images that bombarded her mind, until they finally overtook her.

First, Reverend Bush came to her, "I know what you did this summer."

"No."

"I know about you and Brian."

"No."

"I know about the baby."

"No."

He laughed so loud, she had to cover her ears. Then the reverend faded. In his place, Hosea stood, holding two suit-cases. "You're a liar."

"No."

"And a cheat."

"No."

"You should have told me. If you'd told me, I would've stayed."

"No," she screamed.

Then her husband marched toward the door. In the back-ground, the baby cried. But it hadn't been born. Yet, the infant's screeches blended with her screams, creating a mournful melody that played as Hosea walked farther, farther, until he was gone.

"Please come back, Hosea. I love you. Please come back. Don't leave me, Hosea."

"Jasmine," Hosea called.

In her sleep, Jasmine's screams continued.

"Hosea, please don't leave me," she cried.

"Darlin', I'm not going anywhere. I'm here," he said, shak-ing her awake.

But her cries persisted, "I'm sorry. I'm sorry. I'm sorry."

"Jasmine, wake up."

Her eyes focused—on her husband, holding her, trying to calm her.

"You don't have anything to be sorry about, darlin'. It was just a dream."

"A dream?" she whispered, her eyes focused on Hosea.

"It was just a dream," he repeated over and over.

But Jasmine knew the truth. This was not a dream at all.

Chapter 43

Pregnancy privileges had given Jasmine a free pass.

She knew Hosea wasn't surprised when she told him she wasn't up to going to church. After her nightmare, neither had closed their eyes until the morning's first light peeked through their windows. It was exhaustion, coupled with the thought of looking Reverend Bush in his eyes—and him looking into hers—that made Jasmine beg for more rest.

But now, an hour after Hosea left for church, Jasmine was still awake. Sleep avoided her like an elusive lover, promising but never delivering. Every time she closed her eyes, visions shook her awake. Reverend Bush taunted her. Hosea stomped away from her.

Although her eyelids felt like fifty-pound weights, she slipped into her bathrobe and grabbed her keys. She scurried across the hall and shivered as she knocked on Mae Frances's door, even though the summer's heat clogged the hallway.

"Well, Jasmine Larson," Mae Frances said when she opened the door. She clutched the collar of her well-worn robe. "I thought you'd be in church."

"I wasn't feeling well."

Her smirk disappeared. "Come on in, child. I'll make you some tea."

Minutes later, Jasmine sat next to Mae Frances, their silver teacups filled.

Jasmine said, "I'm thinking about telling Hosea the truth."

As if Jasmine had said "the sun is shining," Mae Frances took several sips before she gingerly placed her cup down. Then, with the same casualness, she said, "Why would you do something that stupid?"

The gruffness of her neighbor's tone didn't bother Jasmine; she just needed someone to listen to her thoughts. She carried Mae Frances through the past days—her encounter with her father-in-law, her discussions with Malik, her nightmare. "I'm afraid Malik is right. This will never stay a secret."

"You're listening to men, now listen to me. What do you think your husband will do when you tell him?"

"He'll be upset—"

"He'll be more than upset."

"I know, but I'm trusting that he knows I love him."

"Please, you can't trust a man."

Jasmine sighed. "Mae Frances, that's your experience—"

"Jasmine Larson, you don't know anything about my experience. Let me tell you." She stood, with her head high. "Men don't know how to love." She held up her hand before Jasmine could protest. "I thought my husband loved me. But when I made a mistake, all he did was run out that door." She pushed her shoulders back before she faced Jasmine. "I made the same mistake. I had an affair, and Elijah Van Dorn left me."

Jasmine's mouth opened wide. "I thought you said your husband left you because you were black."

"He did. I have no doubt he would have stayed if I were white."

That made no sense to Jasmine. "Mae Frances, I don't think color has anything to do with this."

"Then you're naïve, because the affair was just an excuse for him to get out of this marriage. But if you don't believe that, remember this. Elijah Van Dorn is a Christian, just like your husband. And Christians preach forgiveness, but they don't live it. Christians will judge you and run out when the situation gets tough." She held her head as if the memories made her ache. "In fact, it was my husband's father—the minister— who found out about my affair and told his son to leave me."

Jasmine pressed her hand against her chest. Mae Frances's life was her nightmare. "But this just proves what Malik told me," she said, though her heart thumped hard against her chest. "These things never stay a secret. If Hosea is going to find out, it's better if he hears it from me. And it's better if he hears it now, rather than later."

"What kind of logic is that?" Mae Frances asked as if she thought Jasmine wasn't very bright. "Even if you accept that the preacher man will eventually find out, later is always better. Later translates into more money that he'll have to pay you."

"I'm trying to save my marriage. I'm not thinking about money."

Mae Frances laughed. "Who are you kidding, Jasmine Larson? It's all about money. Isn't that why you went after the preacher man?"

Jasmine's eyes widened.

Mae Frances sucked her teeth. "You think I don't know. Jasmine Larson, you are who I used to be."

Those words made Jasmine shudder. She stared at her neighbor, starting at her feet, covered by terry cloth slippers with holes the size of nickels, up to the same dingy white bathrobe that she'd worn for months. She ended at her face that was dressed with the thickest coat of two shades too light makeup, even in the earliest hours of the morning. But what was startling was the way Mae Frances's lips twisted against the hardness of her jaw. And the way her eyes glared under the frames of her penciled eyebrows. The stench of bitterness was her perfume.

"Your husband will leave you," Mae Frances said as if her fate would become Jasmine's. "You tell the preacher man tonight, and you'll wake up alone tomorrow."

Jasmine said nothing more.

"Look," Mae Frances continued, "I think you're just worried about how you're going to pull this off. Calm down, and know that I'm on your side. I'll help you get through this. But remember, what happened to me will happen to you if you don't listen."

Sipping the last of her tea, Jasmine let her eyes wander around her neighbor's living room. The tattered furniture, the empty picture frames, even Mae Frances herself, an aged relic.

"You are who I used to be." She heard Mae Frances's words in her head.

Jasmine put down her cup. Smiled at Mae Frances. "You've really helped me. Thank you."

Mae Frances smiled. "Well, I'm glad you were listening."

"Yes, I was."

"Good, then you know what to do."

"Yes, I do." Jasmine stood and walked out the door. She knew exactly what to do because she would do anything not to become Mae Frances.

Chapter 44

Nepotism was hard at work.

Jasmine hadn't spent a full day at Kincaid Enterprises in a week, but Malik hadn't seemed to notice.

"Take all the time you need," Malik had said at the beginning of the week when she told him what she was thinking. "I just want you to do the right thing." He'd squeezed her hand and told her he'd be there for her.

Since Sunday, thoughts had ping-ponged through her mind; she didn't know which way to go. The ringing telephone grabbed her from her thoughts.

"Jasmine, this is Reverend Bush," he said after she'd said hello.

The shock of his voice made her drop the budget she was reviewing. He'd never called her at work; he'd never called her at all. Her heart pounded with the knowledge that this was the moment. Her father-in-law was about to do what Mae Frances's father-in-law had done—announce that the gig was up.

"How are you feeling?" he asked.

"Fine."

"We missed you in church on Sunday. Hosea said you weren't well."

"I'm better now."

"Good. You know that's . . . " he paused, letting silence sit before he spoke, "my grandchild you're carrying."

Jasmine pressed the phone closer to her ear. Tried to hear the words the reverend didn't say.

"I'm glad you're doing better. Take care and I'll see you on Sunday. And Jasmine," he stopped again. "I was telling a young woman the other day that sometimes we get ourselves into sit/uations where we don't see a way out. But God always gives us a way. You just have to listen and be obedient."

"Good/bye," she said, because she didn't have the strength to hold on to the phone any longer. Her heart slammed against her chest. A matter of time was all that separated her lie and the truth.

Tears burned her eyes again, and she wondered how many of those she had left. Every time she tried to imagine the talk—what she would say, what Hosea would say, what she would do, what Hosea would do—she couldn't fathom it. It seemed impossible that she was even thinking about telling her husband. But Mae Frances's story and now Reverend Bush were leaving her no choice.

Tina was already at lunch when Jasmine grabbed her purse and left. Inside the cab, it took minutes before she conjured up the nerve to dial the number.

"Talk to me."

"Hey, sweetie. I was calling to find out what time you'll be home."

"It's like that, huh?" Hosea chuckled. "You can't wait to have your hands all over me. So, what do you have in mind for tonight?"

"I want to talk."

She could hear his frown. "Talk? That's not what I had in mind."

"I know. But I really need to talk to you."

"Are you all right? Is it about the baby?"

She swallowed. "I'm fine and the baby's fine."

"Okay, I should be home by six."

"Good, and Hosea——," she swallowed again, "I love you. I really do."

"I know that, darlin'. And I love you."

Her lips trembled as she clicked End. That's what she was counting on——love that would keep them together.

As the cab edged up Avenue of the Americas, Jasmine clicked her phone again.

"Hey," Serena answered. "What's up, Big Sis?"

"I need a favor," Jasmine said. "And I need you to do it without asking questions."

"Uh-oh."

"I need you to pray for me."

"What's going on?"

"I said no questions."

"I don't care. What's going on?"

"Nothing."

"I haven't spoken to you in weeks and now you're calling for prayer? What's going on?"

"Just trust me. Just pray."

"Is it the baby? Hosea?"

Jasmine sighed. "No."

After a pause, Serena said, "Okay, just tell me that neither you nor the baby are in physical danger."

"We're not."

"Okay, but let's pray right now." She didn't wait for Jasmine to respond. "Father, we come to you with praise and thanksgiving, even though our hearts are heavy. Father, we pray that you will reach down and give us wisdom and guidance. You said, Lord, that all we had to do was call to you and you would answer and tell us the things we do not know. So please, order our steps, Lord, so that we can make the right decisions. And Lord, we pray for your peace that surpasses all of our understanding. We ask these blessings in your son Jesus' name. Amen and amen."

"Thank you," she whispered and then she clicked off the phone before Serena could ask another question. "Amen and amen," she repeated as the cab driver slowed in front of her building. The only sermon Jasmine ever remembered was one she heard when she attended church with her best friend in Los Angeles. The pastor had preached for an hour about the meaning of "Amen."

"Amen means 'so be it,'" Pastor Ford had said. "Amen is the seal to your prayers."

Jasmine handed a ten-dollar bill to the driver and didn't wait for change. *So be it,* she repeated as she stepped into the building and then rode the elevator up. As she imagined the talk with her husband, she placed her hand on her stomach. "So be it," she whispered right before she stepped into the apartment. "So be it" were her last words as she made her decision to do it.

The living room was still bright with the day's light, but lavender-scented candles—Hosea's favorite—flickered throughout. Inside the kitchen, the aroma of curried chicken—Hosea's favorite—wafted from the stove top into the dining room. Lastly, the CD *I Prayed for You*—Hosea's favorite—whispered in the background.

From the center of the room, Jasmine surveyed her creation. It was the perfect place to deliver this devastating news.

She glanced at the clock—a bit after six. She paced, and her eyes focused on the Bible resting on the end table. Lowering herself onto the couch, she lifted the book, but when she opened the pages, she didn't know where to turn.

Her arms folded around the Bible. "Okay, God. I guess this proves I'm not a good Christian. But I've tried; I go to church, I gave up . . ." She paused and thought about the other promises she made to God. "Okay, I know I gave up lying and not sleeping with married men, but I didn't mean for any of this to happen. I didn't go after Brian, and I hate that I lied about this baby, but I didn't know what else to do." She sighed. "You know I've tried because you gave me Hosea. He is everything I've searched for in a man, God, and I thank you for him. I probably haven't thanked you before, but I always hear Christians say that you know our hearts. So, you know mine, don't you?" She took a breath. "God, I messed up. But I never meant to hurt Hosea and I don't want to hurt him now. So please, give me the words to say. And God, give Hosea the heart to hear. Let him know that what happened has nothing to do with our marriage. Please, God, make this situation build us up, not break us down." She paused again. "If you do this for me, God, I promise to go back to all the promises I made to you before. I won't miss church, and I will stay away from all men. And I will never lie again." She hesitated. "Except for this one last time because Hosea has to believe that I was with Brian only once. So please forgive me and just be with me as I tell—" The sound of the key in the lock stopped her words. She returned the Bible to the table and stood up.

"Hey, sweetie." Even though she wanted to greet him with a hug, her trembling legs held her in place.

"Hey," he said, sounding weary.

Jasmine frowned as Hosea slipped off his jacket and tossed it over the couch, before he kissed her. Then he plopped onto the sofa.

"What's wrong?" she said, lowering herself next to him.

He shook his head. "It's been a tough day." He leaned back against the couch, closed his eyes, and then pulled Jasmine close to him. "I spent the afternoon talking about cheaters."

"What?"

"Triage wants to do a show about men and women who cheat. He says it's a popular topic and one that needs to be talked about in church. But I'm telling you, I don't want to do it."

It took a moment for Jasmine to speak. "So . . . so, why are you doing it? You're the executive producer."

"And so is Triage; he thinks it will be a ratings bonanza. He says everybody wants to hear about someone cheating." Hosea shook his head. "Talking about it all afternoon took everything out of me. You should have heard—"

Jasmine couldn't hear another word. A show about cheaters? Why did that happen today?

Then it hit her. This was God's intervention.

"Anyway," Hosea said pulling her into his arms. "How was your day?"

"Fine," was all she could say.

He sat up straight. "Darlin', I'm sorry. You wanted to talk, and I've been going on and on about that crazy show. I should have walked in here, kept my mouth shut, and listened to you."

That thought made Jasmine feel faint. If that had happened, it would have been an all-for-nothing confession.

"Hey," Hosea said, taking notice of the room. "Candles, music." He grinned. "This must really be big. Talk to me."

"I . . . I think it's time for us to make some decisions." She paused. "We need to decide . . . when we're going to move. We have to start looking for something."

He sighed. "I know. It's just that I've been so busy with the show; now, I'm thinking maybe we should wait until the baby's born. I don't want you under any pressure or stress. Would you mind if we waited?"

"Not at all. We can set up the guest room for the baby."

"Sounds like a plan." He kissed her stomach and then placed his hand there. "You know, today I discovered how blessed we are. You too, little one," he spoke to where his hand rested. "It seems that it's difficult to be happy in relationships these days. But you know what people say, what God has for you, He has for you. And I'm so glad that He had the two of you for me."

Jasmine held him tighter. "Me too, sweetie."

"Something sure smells good."

"Well, dinner's ready." She tried to push herself up from the couch, but he pulled her back down and kissed her as if he would love her forever.

Inside his embrace, she knew that this was a sign from God. She wasn't supposed to say a word to Hosea. Her lie would have to be the truth forever.

Chapter 45

The weeks crawled forward and Jasmine basked in the bliss of living in the center of Hosea Bush's world. She came to see herself through her husband's eyes and she loved that she was going to be the mother of his child.

Thoughts of Brian returning to claim what was his passed. She was sure he'd never suspect, and even if he did, he'd never want this baby. So her heart and mind came to believe that the child in her womb belonged to the man she loved. And she adored Hosea's baby.

Still her primary focus was her husband. During the week, she spent her days making sure that Rio continued to thrive. But nighttime belonged to her husband. Every night, Hosea came home to the aromas of his favorite dishes and many new ones that soon became favored. Jasmine focused on making her condo his castle, from the china they ate on each night, to the sateen sheets that covered their bed, to the fresh Egyptian towels that waited for him each morning—her husband was her king.

"I don't know how you do this, darlin'," he said one night after he sat on the couch, sated from the barbecued salmon she'd prepared. "You work all day and then take care of me all night."

"And nighttime is the only time that really matters to me," she told him.

The love she gave was reciprocated. Not a moment passed when she didn't feel the depth of Hosea's adoration. From his late-night jaunts to satisfy her midnight cravings for pickles, peanut butter, and butter pecan ice cream, to the way he massaged her feet nightly, and all the in-between affection that he showered on her—she never doubted his love.

Life at home was a wonder, but Jasmine also enjoyed the celebrity of Hosea's world. At least once a week, they attended a museum benefit, or a charity fund-raiser, or some celebrity bash, mingling sometimes with the rich, most times with the famous of New York City. And at all times, Hosea proudly held her arm, introduced her as his inspiration, his wife, never told, only showed the world that he loved her.

But there were still times when her secret stalked her and snatched away the magical moments that had become her life. Mostly, the stalker crept through her mind on Sundays as she sat in the front pew of City of Lights. As Reverend Bush preached, and the congregation "Hallelujahed" and "Amened" themselves into a frenzy, she'd watch her charismatic father-in-law and know that he was the only one who could crash her world.

Somehow, she had to find the key that would forever lock away the reverend's doubts. But how could she persuade him that she was no longer the woman who had strutted down the church aisle in a yellow suede mini skirt?

Two days before Thanksgiving, the answer came to her. In her, Reverend Bush saw nothing but duplicity, the opposite of what he valued most: honesty and integrity. She had to become what he respected.

The moment she realized this, she picked up the telephone. Reverend Bush answered his cell, and they exchanged greetings before Jasmine shot straight to her purpose. "Reverend Bush, I'm sure you're very busy," she said. "But I'm hoping you'll be able to squeeze me into your schedule today, for just fifteen minutes or so."

She wasn't surprised at how quickly he said, "I'm on my way to the church now, Jasmine. Is this a good time?"

They agreed to meet in thirty minutes. Twenty-five minutes later, Jasmine stepped into his office.

He stood behind his desk as if she were one of his parishioners stopping by for his counsel. "Good to see you, Jasmine."

She laid her coat across her lap, and with a deep breath said, "Reverend, I've said this so many times I'm sure you're tired of hearing it. But I love your son."

He looked at her as if he wanted to ask why she was wasting his time with this nonsense, but he motioned for her to continue.

"It's because I love him that I've decided there's something I have to do." She paused. "I haven't been completely honest with Hosea and I want to be."

He smirked, as if he always knew she had secrets. "Well, Jasmine, if there is something you need to talk to Hosea about, I don't know why you're here."

"Because what I have to tell my husband concerns you."

His smirk twisted into a frown.

"Reverend Bush, I'm going to tell Hosea about what happened when I first came to City of Lights."

His eyes thinned to slits. "Jasmine, if this is a threat—"

She held up her hand. "No, Reverend Bush. It's not. I know what I said to you a few months ago and I so regret that." She took a dramatic breath. "I'm going to tell Hosea the complete truth. How I pursued you. How you tried to dissuade me. And I'm going to tell him that I threatened you."

The reverend peered at his daughter-in-law for a long moment. "Why now, Jasmine?"

She sighed. "I've never loved anyone the way I love Hosea," she said meaning every syllable. "But I don't think we can build a solid marriage if I'm holding this secret."

"That's true. Secrets will always haunt and destroy."

Jasmine nodded. Thought about the real secret. Pushed

that thought aside. "I'm only here because I wanted you to know. I didn't want you to be surprised, in case Hosea says any‹ thing. Didn't want you to think I was up to something, like you always seem to think."

A few beats and then, "To be honest, Jasmine, I've never trusted you."

"I know."

"But I pushed my doubts aside when I realized Hosea loved you."

"Thank you for that."

"But it all came back when Malik told me you'd been mar‹ ried before."

Jasmine didn't move a muscle.

"But," he continued, "when I asked Malik again, he ex‹ plained that he'd left Los Angeles and lost touch with your family. He said he'd heard you were serious about someone and thought you'd married, but that you two had never dis‹ cussed it. He apologized for getting it wrong and causing con‹ fusion."

The first thing she was going to do when she left the church was find Malik and promise to name this baby after him.

The reverend continued, "So, I have to admit. My doubts have faded."

Her lips slipped into a slight smile. "I'm glad because what Hosea and I have is real."

He peered at her so long that she began to shift in her seat. "I'm beginning to see that."

"And I would do anything for your son."

"Something inside of me has known that, Jasmine." But there were still shadows of doubt in his tone. He said, "I guess this could be a new beginning for us."

"That is all I've wanted since I started seeing Hosea," she said honestly. She lowered her eyes. "There is one last thing I hope you'll do for me." She looked directly at him. "I hope you'll forgive me, Reverend Bush. What I did—"

He held up his hand. "Enough said." He studied her a bit more. "I'm glad you came here, Jasmine."

She stood and before she could move, Reverend Bush came from around his desk and helped her into her coat. When she faced him, they hesitated before they embraced.

"This little one is beginning to get in the way, isn't he?" Reverend Bush said.

She laughed. "You sound like your son, claiming a boy. I hope neither of you will be disappointed if we have a girl."

"I just want a healthy grandchild that will grow up to be happy and love God with all of his—or her—heart."

She smiled. "Thank you, Reverend Bush."

Before she stepped outside, he said, "My son is right. We're going to have to work on that name thing. I don't want my grandson asking me why his mother calls me Reverend Bush."

"I'll work on it."

Minutes later, Jasmine was leaning back in a cab, coasting downtown, and savoring this sweet victory. She never thought it would be this easy.

This would end here—she had no intention of saying anything to Hosea and she was sure Reverend Bush would never mention a word to his son. There was no need to blur the future with past mistakes.

Now both Bush men were on her side. She rubbed her stomach as the car sped down Central Park West. In a way, she too hoped for a boy. That could be the ultimate key to the Bush men's hearts.

From the cab, Jasmine peered into the building.

"Do you need any help, lady?" the driver asked.

"No." Jasmine balanced the basket and motioned toward Henrikas. When he rushed to her, she said, "Is Mae Frances in her apartment?"

"Yes, Mrs. Bush, I think so."

"Good," she said handing him the basket. Give me enough time to get to my apartment and then do exactly what I told you."

Jasmine wasn't sure how long she'd have to wait, but fifteen minutes after she'd entered her apartment, the banging began.

She waited a moment before she swung open the door. "Mae Frances," Jasmine said as if she were surprised.

Her neighbor stood, stiff and stern, holding an oversized basket with a turkey so large, it hid most of Mae Frances's face.

Jasmine said, "Oh, my goodness. Did you bring that for me?"

Even behind the turkey's legs, Jasmine could see Mae Frances's scowl. "Jasmine Larson, did you send this?"

Jasmine frowned. "What are you talking about?"

"This basket. Henrikas Babrauckas called and said that a friend left it for me."

"Well, I'm certainly your friend, but you can't blame this one on me." Jasmine tilted her head. "You have other friends, don't you? What about . . . Dr. Edmonds?"

Her scowl softened; she almost smiled. Took a step back. "Well, I just wanted to make sure you weren't doing your charity thing again."

"Nope, I know you don't need my help." When her neighbor turned away, Jasmine sang, "If I don't see you, have a great Thanksgiving."

Mae Frances grunted her thank you and then closed her door.

Jasmine grinned. Her neighbor thought she was the only one with tricks, but she didn't know anyone who could out trick her.

Chapter 46

Their first Christmas was meant to be together . . . alone.

But that is not the way Reverend Bush wanted it. When he called and asked Hosea and Jasmine to join him at his house for dinner, there was no way Jasmine was going to deny him. Their truce had blanketed their family with peace, and she planned to keep her life wrapped in that tranquility.

As Hosea navigated their car through Manhattan, Jasmine leaned back and enjoyed the sights—the passing cars, some wearing holiday wreaths, speeding to their dinner destinations. The pedestrians braving the December winds, their arms heavy with gifts. Snow piled five inches high, the night having fulfilled the promise of a White Christmas.

Jasmine glanced at Hosea. As if he felt her, he turned and took her hand. And like she always did at his touch, every part of her warmed. She never expected to be this happy. "Amen and amen. So be it," she whispered as she did whenever that thought came to her.

"You say something, darlin'?"

"I said you're the best Christmas gift I've ever received."

He grinned.

He hadn't come wrapped in the package she expected, but he was sure 'nuff a gift from God.

Forty minutes after they'd left the city, Hosea eased his SUV in front of a red brick split-level home.

"Now before we get out," Hosea began, "you have to promise me that no matter what you see or hear, you'll still be my wife when we leave tonight."

She laughed. "What's behind those doors?"

"I don't know who Pops is having over. But there are people alive who knew me before I wore braces. And you never know what an old person might say."

She leaned across the console and kissed him. "Don't worry, sweetie. I'll love you always."

"That's what I'm talking about."

He held her hand as she waddled across the freshly shoveled driveway. Opening the front door, he yelled, "Anybody home?"

Chatter, laughter, the clanging of glasses fused with Nat "King" Cole crooning about chestnuts—the home was merry with Christmas.

Standing at the edge of the living room, Jasmine forced herself to stay in place when all she wanted to do was cut and run. She hadn't asked about Reverend Bush's guest list, but she should have known his home would be filled with those he considered family—his church family. Among the dozen or so familiar faces from City of Lights, there was Brother Hill and Mrs. Whittingham moving around the ten-foot Christmas tree as if they were at home.

"Son!" Reverend Bush exclaimed when he finally noticed the two. He hugged Hosea and then kissed Jasmine.

"Welcome to my home, Jasmine. I can't believe this is your first time here."

"Well, Pops, you have to admit, this is kinda far and we see you every week in the city."

"Still," Reverend Bush said to Jasmine, "I'm glad you're here." He helped her with her coat and then grinned. "My, my," he said as Jasmine straightened her sweater over her swollen stomach.

"I know," Jasmine breathed. It seemed as if her waist had expanded ten inches since last Sunday. Although she no longer searched for his suspicion inside his words, Jasmine still had to be careful. These last weeks were going to be the hardest. The lie was that she was almost twelve weeks away from giving birth. But the truth was she was six weeks away.

Reverend Bush said, "Looks like you're almost ready."

"That's what I said, Pops. But Dr. Edmonds said that the baby is just healthy."

Reverend Bush said, "Maybe you're having twins."

"Wouldn't that be great?" Hosea beamed.

"No!" Jasmine said to both laughing men. "It wouldn't be great."

"Come on in," Reverend Bush said, leading them into the sunken living room. "I'll get you some eggnog."

Brother Hill was the first to greet them. "Hosea." He hugged him and then said, "Jasmine."

With a nod, she said hello. Did the same with Mrs. Whittingham. She tried to keep her festive smile as others came over to spread their Christmas cheer. Everyone had something to say about the baby—boy, girl, twins, carrying high, hanging low, coming early, never early, long labor, the commentaries continued. And then there was the laying on of hands—everyone touched her stomach as if her body belonged to them.

Not forty-five minutes passed before Hosea grabbed her and the two slipped from the room. Following her husband, she climbed the short steps that led to the second floor.

"Where are we sneaking to?" Jasmine giggled.

"My old bedroom," he whispered. "I could tell those people were getting on your nerves."

"No, they weren't."

"Stop lying. They were getting on my nerves too."

They held their laughs until Hosea opened the door to the room farthest down the hall. When Jasmine stepped inside, her giggles stopped. She had stepped into the middle of the 1980s.

One wall was covered with faded pictures of Magic Johnson and Kareem Abdul-Jabbar. On the other, the dulling posters were of Michael Jackson in his Billie Jean pose and a picture of the ensemble from "We Are the World."

Slowly, she walked through the room past the long twin-sized bed and the dresser covered with dusty trophies.

"I received these for track and field," Hosea said, holding up one of the awards.

"You ran track?"

He nodded. "What did you think? I was a bowler?"

"Well, a runner—"

"You'd better take that look back. I was slender in my early years."

"I love you the way you are now."

Her journey continued, touching, exploring, connecting with her husband's past. In front of the dresser, she paused. Picked up a picture. Laughed out loud.

"I know you ain't clownin' a brother," he said.

"I don't have to." She held up the senior class picture for him to see. "You did a pretty good job clownin' yourself. I'm glad you got rid of that curl."

"Shoot. That was nineteen eighty-eight. I'd like to see what you looked like then."

She shook her head. "I ain't crazy. You're never going to see any old pictures of me."

"Hmph. I bet Serena's got a couple of photos."

She laughed, but made a note to speak to her sister. Hosea couldn't see or be told anything without her approval.

Inside, she sighed. It was moments like this when she longed to tell Hosea the truth. She wanted to share all of herself.

Hosea pulled her into his chest, wrapped his arms around her. But it was moments like this, when his arms were warmer than her mink coat, that she knew her lie was stronger than the truth could ever be. Hosea loved her more because she was carrying his baby.

"Next year at this time, we'll be celebrating our second Christmas with our first child." He paused. She couldn't see his eyes, but she could feel his thoughts.

"You're thinking about your mom," she whispered.

"How'd you know?"

"Because I'm thinking about my mom . . . and my dad."

With the tips of his fingers, he lifted her chin. "You okay?"

She nodded. "I have a little bit of sad, but I'm mostly happy."

"I have some sad too. But I have a lot more happy because of you."

A knock startled them, and Reverend Bush opened the door.

"Son, didn't I tell you not to bring girls up here?" Reverend Bush laughed.

"Oh, my bad."

"Well, whatever you two are doing, it has to stop. We're about to chow down."

"Gotcha, Pops."

When the reverend closed the door leaving them alone, Hosea said, "I wish we didn't have to go down there."

"Are you kidding? That's where the food is and our baby is hungry."

"Is she now?" Hosea said, before he bowed and kissed her stomach.

"Oh, she's a she today, huh?"

He grinned. "Just want you to know that I'm an equal opportunity dad." He paused. "Dad, dad. I love that word."

"Let's go eat," she said.

"Well, you're in for a treat. Mrs. Bower has been Pops' cook since Mom passed. And I'm telling you, she can whip up some things that will have you slapping somebody else's mama."

She grabbed his hand. "Now that sounds like fun." She laughed as she imagined giving Brother Hill or Mrs. Whittingham a slap or two. But she got rid of that un-Christian thought. It was, after all, Christmas.

Only remnants of the dinner remained.

Still, the aroma of the Cornish hens, ham, macaroni and cheese, yams, collard greens, rice with gravy, and biscuits spilled into the living room. Jasmine staggered in first, and flopped onto the couch.

"You were right," she said, when Hosea lowered himself next to her. "Mrs. Bower sure can cook."

Hosea laughed.

"Okay." Reverend Bush clapped his hands twice. "Our stomachs need a little time to make room for the dessert. So, I say, let's get to the gifts."

Jasmine closed her eyes and moaned. She'd indulged well past the point of satisfaction and was sure she'd be wedged to this couch for the next month. But still, she wished she and Hosea could make a graceful exit since they'd agreed not to exchange gifts until after the Christmas rush.

"Darlin'."

"Hmmm." She didn't open her eyes.

"Look at this."

First, she peeked through one eye and then the other. Then both stretched wide with surprise. "I thought—"

"We weren't exchanging gifts?" He chuckled. "You didn't think I'd really stick to that on our first Christmas."

She grabbed the light blue box and when she lifted the lid, she gasped at the diamond key-shaped pendant. "This is beautiful."

"I just wanted you to know," he said, tapping his chest, "that you will always have the key to my heart."

It had to be the corniest line she'd ever heard, and the most wonderful. She hugged him, held him as close as her swollen belly would allow.

She twisted around and held up her ponytail as he clasped the chain. The key rested just inches above her heart. "I'm never taking this off."

She leaned back into his arms and watched the others across the room.

"Now this is nice," Reverend Bush said as he pulled a purple silk monogrammed smoking jacket from a box.

"That's very nice," Mrs. Whittingham gushed.

"This is from my son and daughter-in-law." The reverend grinned. "But if I had to guess, Jasmine picked this out because my son, although I love him, his taste isn't this good."

They laughed.

"First of all, Pops, I've got great taste. Look at the woman I married."

Jasmine didn't miss the glance that traveled between Brother Hill and Mrs. Whittingham.

"And second," Hosea continued, "I'll have you know I selected that for you. So, now what do you have to say?"

"Only thank you, son." He hugged him and then kissed Jasmine. "Now, I have something for you two." He handed them a Ralph Lauren box.

They scooted to the edge of the couch and Jasmine took out a pink-and-blue coverall. Underneath, there was a pink-and-blue hat and matching booties. And finally, Jasmine pulled out a cashmere baby blanket.

"I know we still have a few months, but I want to make sure that my grandchild comes home in style."

"This is perfect." Jasmine grinned. "It'll work for a grandson or a granddaughter."

The reverend laughed. "I was trying to be right, but then I couldn't help myself." He handed a second box to Hosea.

Laughter lifted through the room when Hosea held up the catcher's mitt.

Reverend Bush shrugged. "Sue me. But first, I'd like to make a toast. Does everyone have eggnog?" The reverend waited until all held glasses were raised in the air. "To my friends and family. As we celebrate the birth of our Lord and Savior this is the perfect time to note new beginnings. While I'm fortunate to be surrounded by old friends, this Christmas holds new blessings. First, my son is home for good." He smiled at Hosea. "And then, he blessed me this year with a daughter-in-law. And now on this day when we celebrate one birth, we are looking forward to another—my first grand-child." He paused as everyone's eyes turned to Hosea and Jasmine. Even Brother Hill and Mrs. Whittingham wore smiles. "Welcome to this family, Jasmine. And I look forward to a life-time of Christmases with you, Hosea, and . . . my grand . . . children."

With nods and "Cheers," they clicked their glasses.

Jasmine smiled. "Thank you." She paused before she added, "Dad." She spoke softly, as if she didn't want him—or anyone else—to hear.

But his smile revealed that he'd heard and was pleased. "Okay, let's continue this gorge feast. Our desserts are waiting."

While the others followed Reverend Bush, Hosea pulled Jasmine back down on the couch with him. "This is the happi-est I've seen my pops in years."

"Really? I can't imagine him any other way," Jasmine said, thinking that even when he was beating her down with his words, he always did so with a smile.

"Pops hides it, but I know it's been hard since Mom passed. But now, that look in his eyes." Hosea stopped and pulled her closer. "The Bush men are happy and it's all because of you."

Jasmine snuggled deeper into her husband's embrace and fondled the key on her neck. "Amen and amen," she whispered to herself.

Chapter 47

J asmine wore nothing but a T-shirt.

It was the same T-shirt—her husband's—that she wore last night as she and Hosea had snuggled on the couch and sipped sparkling cider, munched Oreo cookies, and watched *New Year's Rockin' Eve* without Dick Clark counting down to 2005.

By twelve-ten, they were in bed and it was the best New Year's she could remember.

Even this morning, as they lay holding each other and doing nothing more than staring at the ceiling, Jasmine did not want to get out of bed.

"Darlin', what time are we supposed to be at Rio?"

"Noon," she moaned. "I wish I'd never agreed to go."

Although the club had been open until four that morning with partiers bringing in the New Year, Rio was opening again at noon for what Malik called a New Year's fête. The club's standard Mexican fare was being traded for African American New Year's Day staples: gumbo, black-eyed peas, red beans and rice, country ham, fried chicken, and cornbread. The only thing missing were the chitterlings that Jasmine had refused to allow within a mile of the club.

"If we're supposed to be there at noon then get up now." Hosea nudged his wife. "You first."

"Why?"

"Because you take much longer than I do."

"Well," she began, "we could shower together."

"And we'll never get out of here. Now, go."

With a sigh, she rolled from the bed. She really wanted today alone with her husband. It was more than just a newly-wed thing. Jasmine wanted to savor these moments of togeth-erness, knowing that in a few weeks, the times when they could say "just the two of us" would be forever gone.

Her legs were heavy as she shifted toward the bathroom. A month ago, with Hosea watching her, she would have added a bit of sway to her step. But now all she could do—four weeks before she was due to become a mother—was place one foot in front of the other.

Still, with the appreciation that only a man in love could give, Hosea whistled.

Two hours later, they were standing in the middle of Rio, only fifteen minutes after noon.

"Hey," Malik greeted them over the blasting music. Today, Usher and Alicia Keys replaced the regular beats of Shakira and Cabas.

Malik kissed her cheek and then shook Hosea's hand. "I wasn't sure if you'd make it."

"If I'd known I had a choice, my husband and I would be at home, in bed, right now."

"Oh." Malik held up his hand. "Too much information, Godsister," he joked. "But, don't stretch yourself. I know you get tired quickly these days, so head out whenever you want."

"Don't worry. I'm not going to let her overdo it," Hosea said.

They zigzagged through the maze of rented-for-the-day ta-bles that covered the dance floor. Invited guests were sprin-kled through the space, but Jasmine knew the club would be filled once the late-morning risers started arriving. They set-tled at a table away from the center of the festivities.

"In the back, in the corner, in the dark," Jasmine said. "If I didn't know better, I'd think you had a few illicit thoughts, Mr. Bush."

He chuckled. "I always have illicit thoughts when I look at you, darlin'."

"I doubt that," she said, easing her swollen middle between the chair and the table. She'd done the best she could with her weight but still, she'd gained twenty-three pounds, normal for a thirty-six-week pregnancy. But it was enough to raise eyebrows whenever Hosea proudly announced that their baby was due in March.

"Wow, are you having twins?" was what she heard constantly.

Blessedly, Hosea still had no suspicions. Blinding love and Dr. Edmonds made sure of that.

"Darlin', do you want something to drink?"

She nodded. "Orange juice." Jasmine pulled her compact from her purse as Hosea walked away. And, she freshened her lip gloss.

"Hey, darlin'."

She smiled. Looked up. He snatched her smile away.

"Brian," she sputtered his name.

"You're looking good." He sat down before she could stop him.

"What—what are you doing here?" she asked, trying to catch her breath and a glimpse of Hosea at the same time.

"I came to see you."

"I'm . . ." she paused, trying to remember what she needed to say, "here with my husband."

"I heard you got married." He poked out one of his lover's lips. "Gotta tell you, Jasmine, my feelings were hurt again. I don't know how you keep losing my address. Another party, and I didn't get an invitation."

"Brian, please, I can't—" She edged closer to the table to conceal her added weight.

He leaned across the table, taking away what little comfort she had left. "I know you can't right now, but we can still work this out." He grinned. "It's actually better when both cheaters are married."

She wanted to tell him "Never again." But her brain had stopped telling her lips what to do. Her mind was only sending signals to her lungs commanding her to breath.

"So, whaddaya say? When can we get together again?"

"Hey," Hosea said, placing a glass on the table. "Here's your juice, darlin'." Then, he turned to Brian. "We've met, haven't we?"

Brian stood. Shook Hosea's hand. "Yes, at the restaurant. I was with my wife and—"

"Yeah, I remember," Hosea said as he sat and motioned for Brian to do the same. "Brian, right? So, what brings you to New York?"

"Your wife." He paused just long enough for Jasmine to believe these were the last moments of her life. Then Brian chuckled. "I always like to come to New York to support Malik and Jasmine." His eyes roved through the club. "They've done a fantastic job with Rio."

Hosea peered at him. "You came all the way to New York for this?" he asked, his voice stiff.

"That and other things." Brian grinned. Looked at Jasmine. "So, I hear congratulations are in order. You two hooked up, huh?"

"Yeah." Hosea's smile was back. "She holds the key to my heart." He took her hand and squeezed it.

"That's great. I guess I don't have to ask what you've been up to." Brian laughed.

Hosea said, "No, I guess you don't. Our baby's due in a couple of months."

Brian's grin went away. He looked at Jasmine. "You're pregnant?"

She slipped her hand away from Hosea. "No," she said, protecting her bulging middle.

Hosea frowned. "Darlin', are you all right?"

Heat rose inside of her and then pushed its way to her skin.

"Darlin'?"

Jasmine blinked. Stood. Reached for Hosea, but her eyes met Brian's.

She watched as his glance lowered to her belly. He stared and then his eyes reached back for hers. They connected.

"Darlin'?"

She could hear Hosea, but couldn't see him. Could only see Brian.

"You're pregnant," Brian repeated.

And then her world faded to black.

Chapter 48

H osea!"
"I'm right here, darlin'."
She felt his hand on her arm, but when she tried to lift up, he gently guided her back down.

"Where?"

"You're at Mount Sinai. You fainted."

Her eyes searched the space. Besides the twin-size cot on wheels, only a stool and a counter filled this small room.

"What—" And then the memory rushed back. Brian. "Hosea!"

"I'm right here," he squeezed her hand, "you're going to be all right."

"The baby?"

"The doctor said you're fine, the baby's fine. He'll be right back."

Jasmine nodded, but still her heart pounded as the memory of Brian stayed. What happened after she fainted? Had Brian said anything?

She glanced again at Hosea. Only concern covered his face.

"It's all right." Hosea stroked her arm.

She repeated those same words silently.

"It's actually better when both cheaters are married."

She remembered Brian's words and hated that he'd called her that. Hated who she used to be. Hated that she had to live with this.

"Mrs. Bush, you're awake."

Jasmine turned to face the young black doctor entering the room with a chart in his hand.

"Darlin', this is Dr. Austin."

"How are you feeling?" the doctor asked.

"Fine, but how's my baby?"

"Your baby is fine, but there is a slight problem. Your blood pressure is elevated, and we're going to do an ultrasound to check on the baby."

Hosea said, "We had an ultrasound a few months ago."

"That's fine. It doesn't hurt the baby," the doctor said as attendants came into the room.

"I'm going with her," Hosea demanded.

"No problem."

As the doctor gave directions to the attendants, Jasmine reached for Hosea.

"It's going to be all right, darlin'."

She nodded, squeezed his hand, and with the other she rubbed her stomach.

The doctor turned off the machine and with little more than a thin smile, he left the room.

"I'm scared," Jasmine said to Hosea.

"No need, darlin'."

"But did you notice how he didn't say a word as he did the ultrasound?"

Hosea shrugged. "That's just his style." He tried to chuckle, but Jasmine didn't join him.

When Dr. Austin entered the room, Jasmine pushed herself up. "How's my baby?" she asked before he could speak.

"The baby's fine, but we're still concerned. Your blood pressure is still elevated, in fact, it appears to be rising."

"Why is that, Doctor?" Hosea asked.

"We're not sure, but we don't want to take chances, so we're going to take the baby."

"Take the baby?" Hosea and Jasmine said together.

Dr. Austin held up his hands. "We're going to do a Cesarean. Now don't worry," he said when he looked at their expressions. "Almost a third of all babies are born this way. We just want to be on the safe side."

"But, Doctor," Hosea said. "Isn't this too soon?"

"It's a few weeks early, but—"

"A few weeks? We're talking almost ten—"

Jasmine squeezed her eyes shut, moaned as loud as she could.

"Darlin', what's wrong?"

"My—my back," she said, hoping that would be enough to keep Dr. Austin's focus away from how far she was in her pregnancy.

"You're having back pains?" the doctor asked, his forehead filled with lines. "Where exactly?"

"All over. Hosea, please call Dr. Edmonds. I want Dr. Edmonds."

"Okay, darlin', calm down." He turned to Dr. Austin. "I've paged our doctor. Do you think we have time to wait for him?"

"Yes, there's no immediate danger." He glanced over Jasmine's chart. "But in the meantime, we need something from you, Mr. Bush. If you can go to the lab, we'd like to draw some blood." Before Hosea could ask, the doctor added, "It's just a precaution. Did Dr. Edmonds talk to you about your baby's condition?"

"What's wrong with my baby?" Jasmine cried.

"Mrs. Bush, please calm down. If you prefer, I can talk to your husband outside."

"No!" Jasmine couldn't let that happen. She had to know what was being said.

"Darlin', stay calm, okay?"

She nodded.

"Go ahead, Doctor."

"All right. To put this simply, your baby has a rare condition called PKL. In layman's terms that means that under certain conditions, at birth, your baby could have a problem with bleeding."

"Like a hemophiliac?"

"It's the same concept, but this is a condition that is only triggered during birth."

"That sounds serious, Doctor."

"It can be. I'm a bit surprised that Dr. Edmonds didn't discuss this with you, but it's probably because it can be controlled. I'd just like to have the blood available, just in case."

Jasmine felt as if she couldn't breathe. "Doctor, I want you to use my blood for our baby."

"Mrs. Bush, we need to get you prepped. Mr. Bush will work just fine."

She pushed herself up straight, needing air to breathe—to think.

"Don't worry, darlin', I'll be right back." Hosea kissed her, then turned to the doctor. "Let's roll."

She had to do something. Do something. Something. But by the time her lips moved, Dr. Austin and Hosea were out of her sight.

She couldn't believe this was going to end like a bad romance novel. In the middle of surgery, the doctor would pronounce that Hosea Bush was not the father of this baby. And in front of all the staff, she would be exposed as an adulterer.

"It's over," she whispered.

"I'm sorry, Mrs. Bush, did you say something?" a nurse asked.

Jasmine shook her head.

"Okay, let's take off your jewelry," she said, handing a packet to Jasmine. "We'll give this to your husband."

Jasmine felt as if she were moving in slow motion. *It's over,* she thought again and again as she took the diamond key from around her neck.

"Now, let's get you ready to be a mommy!"

The nurse's cheer was not contagious.

As she was rolled toward the operating room, Jasmine tried to remember the touch of Hosea's lips as he kissed her. Tried not to think that would be the last kiss they'd ever share.

Jasmine waited for Hosea to hate her.

He rushed into the surgical room and took her hand. "Are you ready, darlin'?" he asked.

She nodded, not understanding. *Maybe he just doesn't know yet.*

"Hello, Mr. and Mrs. Bush."

She sighed with relief. "Dr. Edmonds."

"I'm ready, Mrs. Bush, are you?"

She nodded.

With Hosea holding her hands, Jasmine squeezed her eyes shut. When the doctor announced that he'd made the first incision, she opened her eyes. Felt nothing.

Five minutes later, she heard the first cry.

"We have a baby," Dr. Edmonds announced. "At seven-oh-three, on New Year's Day, we have a baby girl."

"Darlin', it's a girl," Hosea said as the doctor held up the squirming infant with almost more hair than size. Dr. Edmonds handed their baby to the nurse, then said to Jasmine, "Now, let's fix you up."

"Darlin', we have a little girl," Hosea repeated.

"I know," she said.

Minutes later, while the doctor still worked, the nurse handed the baby to Jasmine.

"Is it safe for me to hold her?" Jasmine asked.

"Definitely. You have a healthy six-pound, two-ounce baby girl."

"Six pounds, two ounces?" Hosea said. "Are you sure? She's so early, I would've thought she would've been smaller."

Before Jasmine could think, Dr. Edmonds said, "Those prenatal vitamins and Mrs. Bush's good diet certainly helped," he explained without lifting his eyes from Jasmine's abdomen. "It's actually good that the baby came early. No telling how much she would have weighed if she'd gone full term." Dr. Edmonds chuckled.

"So, what about the PKU?" Hosea asked.

Jasmine wondered if his questions would ever stop. Wasn't it enough that they had a healthy baby?

Continuing, Hosea said, "Will she need a blood transfusion?"

"Not at all," Dr. Edmonds said. "She made it through just fine." Dr. Edmonds looked at Jasmine and winked.

She smiled her thank you, then raised her eyes and said, "Thank you," to God inside. She looked down at her baby and then at her beaming husband. It was official now. She had a baby. Her baby. Hers and Hosea's.

Jasmine didn't know where she was when her eyes fluttered open.

But then she saw Hosea, sitting in the chair across the room, his head back, mouth open, performing a snoring symphony just like when they first met.

She pushed herself up, but when she edged her legs over the side of the bed, she moaned, awakening her husband.

"Darlin', are you all right?" Hosea jumped from the chair.

She leaned back on the bed. "Yeah, I'm just a bit sore."

"Dr. Edmonds said you would be. You need to take it easy."

"I don't know how I'm going to do that," she said. "We have a baby."

He grinned, sat on the edge of the bed. "Well, I'm going to take care of both of you."

"I want to see her. What time is it?"

He glanced at his watch. "It's late, almost ten, but the nurse said we could feed her when you woke up."

"Hosea, I can't wait. Do we have to go to the nursery?"

"Nah, since she's a normal weight, they'll bring her to us. The only thing is that she can't sleep in here."

Jasmine nodded. "That's okay, as long as I can see her now."

Hosea stepped outside, and minutes later the nurse rolled their baby inside the room. She parked the crib next to the bed, then handed the baby to Hosea.

"Wow," he said as the baby rested in the crook of his arms. "She's so tiny."

Jasmine's cheek almost ached with her wide smile as she watched her husband holding their child. But right after the nurse stepped away, he passed their baby to Jasmine.

"Here, you take this little one. I don't want to hurt her," he said.

"You won't." Jasmine chuckled. "You'll be fine." Then, she looked down, and said, "Our little one."

After a moment, Hosea said, "Darlin', we can't keep calling her 'little one.'"

For weeks, she'd considered this, but had kept the thoughts to herself. She needed one final way to bond Hosea to their daughter. "I really want you to name her."

He smiled. "Well, there was one name that we both liked." He paused. "Little one," he said to their baby, "the perfect name for you is Jacqueline. Jacqueline Elizabeth. Jacqueline Elizabeth Bush."

Jasmine repeated the name. "I love her initials. We can call her Jeb. Jeb Bush."

"I don't think so," he said with a lot of bass in his voice.

Jasmine laughed.

"Hey, I have something for you." From his pocket, he removed the necklace and hooked it onto her neck. "I need to buy one of these for Jacqueline too. Because now there are two women who have the key to my heart."

Cuddling their baby, Jasmine gently kissed her husband.

Chapter 49

Jasmine never imagined feeling this way.

She expected to be a wife. Expected to have a career. Never considered being a mother.

She stood over the crib in the nursery and peered at her sixteen-hour-old daughter, the little one who had planted herself in the center of her heart. Jacqueline wiggled, stretched, and still she slept. Jasmine kissed the tips of her fingers and placed them on her daughter's forehead, then, she whispered to the nurse, "I'll be back."

As she inched toward her room, Dr. Edmonds came behind her.

"Let me help you," he said, taking her arm. Once she was in the bed, he asked, "How are you feeling?"

"Good. I'm still sore, though."

"That's normal; give it three to four weeks. Take it easy for now. We don't want anything to agitate the stitches."

She nodded. "Have you seen Jacqueline?"

He smiled. "Yes, beautiful name."

"Is she all right."

"Yes, again," he said and eased onto the stool. "She was only a few weeks premature. Actually, she was within the normal range. She's fine."

"What about that . . . PKL thing Dr. Austin mentioned?"

"That's only a risk at birth."

"So," she looked down at her hands, "there won't be any need for Hosea's blood again?"

"No, in fact, there was no need for his blood yesterday. Once I found out what was going on, I had a nurse . . . take care of it."

She nodded. "I'll never be able to thank you enough." She felt the need to add, "I do love my husband," and glanced at her ring.

"Not that it's any of my business, but Mae Frances told me that."

She smiled at the thought that her neighbor would have spoken those words.

"I'll check on you in the morning around ten. If all goes well, you'll be going home if not tomorrow, the next day."

As the doctor walked away, Jasmine marveled at her miracle. She had made it—Hosea would never find out.

The door creaked open.

"Hey," Malik grinned. He kissed her cheek and handed her a basket of flowers. "How're you feeling?"

"Wonderful. Ready to get out of here, though. I want to take Jacqueline home."

He smiled as he sat in the chair. "I got a peek of her in the nursery."

"Isn't she beautiful?" Jasmine gushed.

"Spoken like a new mother." Malik chuckled. "Who would have imagined this? Jasmine Larson, a mother and liking it."

"Jasmine Larson Bush," she corrected, "a mother and loving it. And you should see Hosea," she said. "This morning he came here with cigars. I didn't even know men still did that." She chuckled.

Malik let go of his smile. "I still wish—"

Jasmine held up her hand. "Malik, please don't go there."

"Where's Hosea now?"

"He had to go to the studio. He'll be back this evening."

The look on Malik's face made Jasmine say, "You are just not going to let this alone, are you?"

"Jas, I'm never going to say anything, but I just can't—as I was looking at Jacqueline, it was hard not to think about what I know."

"What you know is that she is my baby. Mine and Hosea's." Malik shook his head.

She said, "Would it make you feel better if you knew that God wanted it this way?"

He frowned.

"God's been all up in this, Malik. Yesterday they took blood from Hosea for Jacqueline. But by God's grace, we didn't need it."

"That wasn't God's grace, that was just luck."

"I thought Christians didn't believe in luck."

"We don't, not when we're walking in God's word."

Jasmine folded her arms. "Like I'm not?"

He shrugged. "Look, the only reason I keep harping on this is that I know the longer this secret goes on, the worse it will be when he does find out."

Jasmine sighed deeply. "Why do you keep insisting that Hosea will find out?"

"Because secrets never stay silent."

"Stop it," she hissed. "I've done everything I can and I'll do everything I have to. Hosea will never find out that he is not Jacqueline's father."

The hospital door creaked open. A second ticked by. Then another. And another.

Reverend Bush walked in.

Seconds ticked to a minute.

All that could be heard was the thumping beat of Jasmine's heart.

Finally, "Malik, I need to speak to Jasmine, alone."

For the first time Malik moved. Turned his head, glanced at Jasmine.

Although she sat rigid with terror, she nodded. Tried to put an "I got this" smirk on her face, but she fooled no one.

Her heart continued its assault as Malik picked up his coat, glanced at Jasmine again, and then stepped slowly from the room.

More silence.

More fear.

Maybe he didn't hear, Jasmine prayed. She repeated that hope in her head.

"I came to see my granddaughter." Only his lips moved. He stood as stiff as she sat. "But first, I wanted to see how you were doing."

She wanted to tell him that she was fine. Start a normal conversation. Make him forget what he may have heard. But she couldn't find her voice.

"You said . . ." He paused as if he didn't want to speak the next words. "Hosea is not Jacqueline's father."

It's over. "Reverend Bush—"

He held up his hand. "Jasmine, don't say a word unless you're going to tell the truth."

"It's not that simple."

"I just want to know, yes or no."

She said nothing.

"That's my answer."

"Reverend Bush, please—"

He held up his hand. It surprised her, the way he looked at her. With more disappointment than scorn.

Maybe it's not over.

"I'll give you twenty-four hours to tell Hosea."

Her eyes widened. "No!"

He stared her down. Still, his glance held more regret than contempt.

"Reverend Bush, please. I can't tell Hosea. I love your son."

"Either you tell Hosea or I will."

Think, Jasmine, think.

She needed time. Just a week, a day even—time to make a plan.

"All right, but please, Reverend Bush, let us take Jacqueline home. Then, I'll tell him. At home. Not here." She paused, and her eyes roamed around the hospital room.

His silence made her think she'd won her appeal.

"Twenty-four hours." He glanced at his watch, said, "Tomorrow morning at eleven, I will call my son."

Her heart stopped pounding. Stopped beating altogether. "No," she whispered, as she fondled the diamond key around her neck.

With sad eyes he turned away and almost staggered out the door.

All afternoon, the nurse rolled Jacqueline into Jasmine's room. All afternoon, Jasmine fed her baby, changed her, held her. And as she embraced her daughter, she prayed. And prayed. And prayed that God would pour out a miracle from heaven.

In between, Jasmine tried to sleep, but images accosted her, beating her down until she begged God for mercy.

But mercy never came. All she could see was the vision of Hosea, walking farther, farther away, until he was gone.

"No," she whispered. She wouldn't let him leave her.

"I need time," she spoke to herself. At least she'd have all night. To sit, think. Devise the plan that would keep the promise that not until death would they part.

"Hey, darlin'." His greeting came into the room almost before he did. "Did you get some rest?"

She sat up. Gripped the blanket as he kissed her.

"Sorry it took me so long to get back. Hey, I just saw Jacqueline," he said. "She gets more gorgeous by the hour. And you know what? She grinned when she heard my voice."

Her face smiled; her heart cried.

"I'm telling you, darlin'," he paused, leaned forward. "We

did good." He added, "I was trying to figure out who she looks like."

Oh, God.

"She has your eyes, but she definitely has my mouth." He beamed. "So, did Dr. Edmonds say when we can break out? I want to take my girls home."

"He said he'd see me in the morning."

Hosea frowned. "I wanted to be here when you talked to him, but I have to be at the studio. I can be here by noon, though."

By noon, Reverend Bush would have made the call that would send their marriage to death row. If Hosea had to know, she had to tell him. Only she could make him understand.

He said, "I can't get out of the meeting."

"That's all right, I can talk to him," Jasmine said, although her thoughts were nowhere near Dr. Edmonds.

"Okay. Well, you tell him that I want my girls home." He glanced at his watch. "You know, they're gonna be kicking me out of here any minute. I didn't realize I'd spent so much time with Jacqueline, but I couldn't help it." He chuckled and kissed Jasmine's forehead. "I can't wait to be home with you and our baby."

He didn't seem to notice that she couldn't speak.

"I hate leaving you here," he said wrapping his arms around her. "Hate that I'm going to be in bed alone tonight." He kissed her again. "I'll call as soon as I get home."

He was already moving to the door when she called his name.

He turned and her heart squeezed all hope from her. In his eyes, she saw all the love he held—for her, for Jacqueline. "Yes, darlin'."

There was no way she could do this.

"I'll give you twenty-four hours."

She had to do this now.

"Jasmine, what's wrong?" he asked stepping back reaching for her.

"There's something—" She stopped. Looked down at her hands. Clasped them together and still they trembled.

Please, God. Give me the right words.

He sat on the edge of the bed again. "Jasmine?"

There were tears in her eyes when she said, "Hosea, I love you so much."

He grinned. "Is that what you wanted to tell me? I know that. And, darlin', you don't have to cry about it. It's just the hormones—you just had our baby."

"Hosea," she sobbed, "I love you and I would never do anything to hurt you—"

He took her hands, kissed her palms.

"—on purpose."

He frowned.

"Hosea, when I met you my world changed."

"For me too, darlin'."

"But for me, you were so different. You talked about a celibate relationship. I'd never heard a man say that. I didn't know men like you existed."

"And aren't you glad we waited?" he said.

"Yes, but still, what you wanted was so different for me. I thought sex had to be part of a relationship. I thought I needed sex to live, and I thought I definitely needed sex to love."

He grinned. "Well then, you and I have quite a testimony." He paused, turning serious. "I should do a show about this. How relationships really are better without sex before marriage."

"Hosea." But she could say no more. She couldn't do this. She'd have to think of another way.

He pushed himself from the bed. "I want to sneak by the nursery and kiss Jacqueline good night." He blew her a kiss. "See you tomorrow, darlin'."

He walked toward the door.

"I'll give you twenty-four hours . . ."

His hand grabbed the door handle.

"And then I'm calling my son . . ."

The door swung open.

"Hosea, I had an affair," she blurted, as if it were one word.

He stopped, his back still to her. Nothing but silence, as the door swung closed.

Then, he faced her.

"What did you say?" His voice had changed. Was deeper now.

Her tonsils were swollen, stopping her words. But the way he glared at her, she knew she had to speak. "I had an affair. And the baby, our baby is not—" She stopped, choking on the next words.

"What about . . . Jacqueline?" His voice, another octave lower.

Her eyes searched his. Love was still there, though not as clear.

She pushed the words through her throat. "She's not— you're not—."

She watched his Adam's apple inch up, then back down. "What are you saying?"

She searched for just a few words that would capture it all. But when his eyes thinned to slits, she didn't have to say any more.

"Are you saying that Jacqueline is not my daughter?"

She pressed her lips together, nodded.

"You cheated on me?"

"No," she cried. "It was before. It was—" She stopped; she'd never reveal that it happened on the day he'd asked her to marry him. "It was before we were married, before we were engaged." She reached for him, but he left her hands hanging in the air.

"I'm sorry." She sobbed.

She watched the transformation. The way his face changed, from confusion to understanding. From bewilderment to despair.

"Hosea, I love you."

Those words made the transformation complete; his face was painted with disgust.

"Please, give me a chance to explain."

He shook his head. Didn't say a word. Backed away. His eyes stayed on her, locking their glance. He continued his journey back toward the door. Farther, farther away from her. Until he was gone.

Just like in her dream.

Chapter 50

J asmine *followed Malik into* the apartment and the moment she stepped over the threshold, she held Jacqueline tighter.

"Where do you want me to put this?" Malik motioned to the baby carrier he held.

Jasmine nodded toward the couch.

She stood in the middle of the room, stiff, straight, feeling like she was in Oz. Wishing that a click of her heels could take her back to before.

Malik took Jacqueline from her arms and sat on the couch. Still Jasmine stood, until her brain demanded that her feet move.

She inched toward the bedroom, although she was sure what she would find. Her suspicions were confirmed: missing suitcases, clothes, toiletries. He'd left remnants, enough to prove he'd once been there. Not enough to confirm that he'd ever be back.

She returned to the living room and watched Malik cuddle Jacqueline—the way Hosea was supposed to.

She wept.

Malik rested Jacqueline in her carrier and then embraced Jasmine.

"Go ahead and say it," she sobbed.

"This is not what I wanted."

"I never wanted to tell him because I knew he would leave me." She wiped her tears and fell onto the couch. "I have no idea where he is. I called his cell a million times yesterday, and called the studio so much, his assistant stopped answering."

"This is tough, Jas. Give him time."

"Time's not going to fix this."

"I think it will. But it's not like he can say right now, 'Oh, okay. She isn't my baby. No problem.' This is a lot for him to handle, but he'll work it out."

She fingered the diamond key still resting on her neck. "He's never coming back."

"You don't know that."

"The most important thing to Hosea is loyalty. And honesty. I betrayed him on both counts."

Malik stayed quiet as if he'd run out of comforting words.

Jacqueline's whimpers invaded her grief and Jasmine lifted her baby into her arms.

Malik sat next to Jasmine. "So, what's next?"

Jasmine sighed. It had only been thirty-six hours since she'd been forced to tell the truth. She hadn't given thought to anything beyond the hole her heart held. "I don't know. We were going to start looking for a nanny this week. There were a lot of things . . ." Her voice trailed off. "Malik, what am I going to do?" she whispered as she rocked Jacqueline in her arms.

"You're going to hang in there and we're going to pray."

"God doesn't have a whole lot of reasons to help me right about now."

"Just remember, Jas, Christ is all up in this forgiveness thing. If God can forgive you, Hosea can too."

She kept his hope away from her heart and just rested in the comfort of his arms.

"I called Brian," he said suddenly.

As she looked into her daughter's face, she whispered, "Please don't tell me you told him."

"Didn't have to. I called because I wanted to make sure he wasn't going to be a problem for you, but before I could say

332 / Victoria Christopher Murray

that, he told me that he didn't want any trouble." He paused. "He didn't come out and say it, but I think he suspects."

She smirked. "I guess he doesn't want to mess up his happy home."

"I'm sure."

Jasmine allowed her thoughts to linger. She'd lost Hosea. Brian deserved to lose too. She could make him pay big-time and at the same time hand Alexis the ultimate "got-you-back."

Jacqueline wiggled in her arms and when she settled, Jasmine kissed her forehead. In her daughter, she didn't see revenge—only love. She didn't see Brian—only Hosea.

"Malik, do you really think I can get Hosea back?"

She could feel him nod.

She snuggled deeper into his arms. Closer to his heart. She wanted to feel his hope.

Chapter 51

In her dreams, Jasmine heard the knock first.

Then, the baby's cries, and her eyes popped open. "I'm right here," she cooed over the bassinet, just as she'd been doing every hour or so all night.

She lifted her baby, and once again, heard the knock. Waited a moment, then the knock again. "Hosea," she whispered. Holding Jacqueline close, she rushed to the door.

"Good morning, Jasmine Larson," Mae Frances beamed. She stepped into the apartment. "Henrikas Babrauckas told me you had the baby. I'd wondered where you were for the past couple of days."

Mae Frances peeked at the bundle Jasmine held and smiled. "I'm glad you had a girl. Isn't she the cutest thing."

Exhaustion had her eyes heavy, but still Jasmine found her smile. "Thanks, but I've got to clean up this cute little one."

She hadn't changed many baby's diapers in her life, but the night's practice almost had her perfect. As she held Jacqueline with one arm, she laid the changing pad on the couch, then rested her daughter down. Jasmine cleaned, changed, and had Jacqueline content with a bottle within minutes. All the time, Mae Frances stood, her hands folded, as if she were proud.

Jasmine tossed the blanket she used onto the floor and then settled on the couch. Mae Frances sat next to her.

"So," Mae Frances began, "you slept out here all night?"

Jasmine sighed, wishing she'd never answered the door. She didn't feel like sharing the state of her marriage. Didn't feel like hearing any more of Mae Frances's thoughts on men. "Yes." Then, she added the lie, "It worked better for Hosea—"

"Hosea?" Mae Frances interrupted. "The preacher man didn't sleep here last night," she said as if the entire city knew this fact. "I saw him stomp out with a couple of bags and a glare on his face that said he was never coming back."

Inside, Jasmine moaned. *Never coming back.* She lowered Jacqueline into the bassinet.

"Guess he found out about the baby," Mae Frances probed.

Jasmine faced her neighbor. "Yes. I told him."

Mae Frances raised her eyebrows. "Why did you do that?"

"His father found out," Jasmine said simply, "just like your father-in-law did. So, I didn't have a choice."

Mae Frances shrugged. "There are always choices. You could have denied it. That's what I did."

Jasmine didn't feel like reminding Mae Frances that obviously her lie hadn't worked.

"Well, if that's the way he wants it, let him be," Mae Frances said. "You can't force a bad man to do good."

"Mae Frances," Jasmine raised her voice, then softened, after she glanced at Jacqueline. "I'm not going to let you talk about my husband."

"He's still your husband?" And her look added what she didn't say, "I don't think so."

Jasmine stood, folded her arms. "He's my husband until a judge says differently. So, either you accept that or—" She paused and looked at the door.

Mae Frances stayed settled on the sofa, as if she never had any plans to move. "Jasmine Larson, why do you do that? Work yourself into a tizzy over nothing. If you don't want me to say anything about the preacher man, I won't. Don't matter much anyway, since I doubt—" She stopped, pressed her lips together. "Anyway," she began again, "my point is that I've been through this and I can help you. I'll take care of you." Inside, Jasmine laughed. How was Mae Frances going to take care of anyone? But she said, "Thank you."

"And while you're at work, I'll take care of the baby."

That will never happen, she thought. Jasmine couldn't imagine the types of things Jacqueline would be saying by the time she was two if she spent any time with Mae Frances. But she smiled like she agreed. "Mae Frances, can I ask a favor? I'm really tired."

"Of course you are. Go on, get into bed. I'll watch the baby."

"No," Jasmine said a bit quickly. "That's not necessary; I'm fine." She added, "But if we need you, I'll call."

Mae Frances stood. Before she stepped out the door, she added, "I'm really sorry this happened with you and the preacher man," she said, although the gleam in her eyes belied her words. "But don't worry. Women like us stick together, don't we?"

Jasmine's mouth was still opened wide after Mae Frances closed the door behind her. *Women like us?*

"I don't think so," Jasmine whispered as she peeked at her daughter. No, she was nothing like her neighbor. And now after listening to Mae Frances, her determination was back. Thanks to her neighbor, Jasmine was going to find a way to get Hosea home.

It *didn't feel as if* her eyes had been closed for longer than a moment.

But a knock awakened her and Jasmine groaned. She was tired of Mae Frances and she was going to tell her neighbor so.

"Mae Frances," she said, opening the door. She stopped. And her eyes watered.

"Do I look like Mae Frances to you?" Serena rolled her suitcase into the apartment.

Before the first tear fell, Jasmine collapsed into her sister's arms.

"It's okay," Serena whispered as Jasmine's tears fell onto her shoulder. "I'm going to make sure that everything is okay now."

The sisters were sipping tea.

"I cannot believe you kept this from me," Serena said after they'd talked for more than an hour.

Jasmine checked the bassinet before she said, "I didn't want you to know. Didn't want you to have to lie to Hosea."

"I wouldn't have lied."

"That's why I didn't tell you." Jasmine sighed. "I should have listened to Malik, though. Because now——" She shook her head. As she'd relived the past days with her sister, the confidence she'd been building about Hosea's return waned.

Serena took a sip of tea before she said, "I think you still have a chance with Hosea. I will never forget the way that man looked at you at your wedding. He was so in love."

"Key word—was."

"That kind of love doesn't go away."

"It does when there's another man involved."

"You're not involved with another man."

"Maybe not another man. Just another man's baby."

This time, they both looked into the bassinet.

Serena sighed. "That's the tough part, but Jas, I think you can get to Hosea. Talk to him. From the heart. And this time, tell the truth."

"From the moment he walked out of that hospital room, I've been trying to reach him. But I can't get him on his cell. Can't get him in the studio." There was sadness in her sigh. "I was sure by now he'd have come to see Jacqueline." She remembered the way Hosea kissed her belly every day. "I know he loves her."

"I believe that too. I heard it in his voice every time I talked to you guys. Hosea loves both of you."

"Even if that's true, I think there are other people influencing him." When Serena frowned, Jasmine continued, "His father. I'm sure he's shouting hallelujah right about now." Jasmine paused before she said, "Maybe you can help me."

"How?"

"I don't know. I haven't figured out a full plan yet, but I'm going to need some help."

"I agree, but the kind of help you need can't come from me. Only God can give you that."

Jasmine rolled her eyes. "I don't feel like hearing a sermon right now."

"Good, 'cause I'm not preaching. But I'm a bit surprised. Jasmine, you've been spending all of this time with Hosea, all of this time in church. And you haven't figured out that a relationship with God is really all you need?"

"I'm just talking about getting my husband back."

"I'm telling you how to do that." She paused. "You need to get rid of all of these lies and plans, and just depend on God, Jasmine." She paused. "I would think that by now you would understand this. It's like you prayed the Sinner's Prayer, asked Jesus into your heart, and stopped right there. I don't want to be harsh, but maybe you and Hosea needed to break up."

"What!"

"Your husband's a minister, yet you're still hanging out on the fringes of God."

"That's not what I'm doing. It's just that you want to turn every situation into something about God."

"Well, every situation is about God."

"No it's not. Not everything in this world is so deep."

"I don't know anything deeper than being married to one man and giving birth to another man's child."

Jasmine pursed her lips, folded her arms.

Serena said, "Jas, with all my heart, I want to see you and

Hosea back together, but this is not going to be easy. You didn't just have an affair; you're asking Hosea to live with and love the proof of your infidelity. Even if he loves Jacqueline, she will always remind him. Unless—" She paused. "Hosea has a change of heart. And that can only come from God. So, He's the one you need to be discussing this situation with."

This time, it was a full wail that came from the bassinet, but before Jasmine could move, Serena said, "Let me get her. I want some time with my niece." As she lifted the baby, she added, "I'm going to take her into the bedroom so you can think about what I said."

Without a word, Jasmine watched her sister. She wanted God's help, but Serena didn't understand. With all that she'd done, there was no way that God would help her. Clearly, she was on her own.

Chapter 52

Hosea was calling.

"Jasmine, Jasmine, wake up."

She opened her eyes with a smile. Serena smiled back.

"Let me take Jacqueline. Both of you fell asleep."

She handed her baby to her sister, then sighed. She was so sure it was Hosea's voice she heard. It was like she couldn't get the sound of him from her mind. Nor could she forget his touch, his smell. Every part of him was still with her, even after a week.

Since he'd walked out of the hospital room, she'd done all she could, but it was difficult when she couldn't reach him. All she could do was flood his cell with messages. She begged, pleaded, told him that Jacqueline needed him, reminded him how much she loved him. Sometimes she was contrite, nonchalant, even angry that he wouldn't give her a chance. But most often on the phone, she'd cried, hoping he could feel her pain.

Still, there was not a word from him.

"I think I'm going to take Jacqueline out today," Serena said. "She's been cooped up without any sunshine."

"Isn't it too cold to take out a newborn?"

"No, it's a pretty warm today, and I'm going to bundle my niece up," she said, cooing at the baby. "We'll only stay out for about ten minutes." She turned toward the baby's room. "Go on, get dressed."

"I'm not going," Jasmine said. "I'm still a bit sore."

"Walking will help."

Jasmine declined, and in less than an hour, Serena and Jacqueline were wrapped to go.

"Take care of my baby," Jasmine said as she kissed Jacqueline's eyelids, the only part of her that wasn't covered.

The moment she closed the door, she wanted to rush behind Serena. It wasn't until that second that she realized she hadn't been apart from Jacqueline since they'd come home.

"It'll just be ten minutes, Jasmine," she told herself.

She sat and waited. And the thought came back. The thought that had been rolling over in her mind for a week. The thought that had first come when she'd taken Serena's advice and began talking to God.

She shook her head. She couldn't do it. She stood, paced, but the idea followed her.

Before she could change her mind, she grabbed the telephone, dialed, and willed herself not to hang up.

"Reverend Bush's office."

Mrs. Whittingham's voice made her cringe. "May I speak to Reverend Bush, please?"

There was a pause. "Who's speaking?"

Jasmine was sure the woman already knew the answer. "Jasmine Bush."

Her smirk came through the phone. "I'll see if the reverend is in, for you."

As she waited, she perused the options in her mind. She could tell him that Jacqueline was very sick, or that they had been robbed. Or maybe even that she had been attacked. Somehow, she'd convince him that she needed his son.

"Hello, Jasmine, how may I help you?"

She opened her mouth. *Get rid of all of these lies and plans, and just depend on God.* Jasmine said, "I've been trying to reach Hosea . . . and . . . he won't return . . . he won't call me back."

"I'm sorry, Jasmine, but I don't know what I can do about that."

I should have lied. "I was hoping, praying that you would talk to him. Reverend Bush, I just want the chance to talk to Hosea."

Several beats passed before he said, "Jasmine, I don't want to get involved."

"But you are involved. You're his father and he respects you." She sighed. "I wouldn't have called if I had any other choice."

Again, there was a pause. "I can't make any promises—"

"That's fine," she said with hope in her voice. "I was just . . . praying that you would at least listen to me. And you've done that. So, thank you."

More time passed. "Have a good day, Jasmine." Before she hung up, she heard him call her name. "How's Jacqueline?" he asked.

Jasmine half-smiled. "She's wonderful, Reverend Bush." Then he hung up.

She stood in the same place for minutes, going over the reverend's words. Serena was right—it was better, without the lie.

She returned the phone to the cradle and dropped to her knees. Talking to God seemed to be working. There was no need to stop now.

Chapter 53

S he sure is beautiful," Mae Frances said.

Jasmine handed Jacqueline back to her sister.

Serena said, "I'll be in her bedroom. It was nice meeting you, Mae Frances."

"So," Mae Frances began once they were alone, "have you heard anything from the preacher man?"

Jasmine shook her head. Thought about the call she'd made to Reverend Bush days ago.

Mae Frances said, "That's good."

"Why do you—" She stopped. Held up her hand. "We need to change the subject."

Mae Frances shrugged. "It's amazing how you don't want to talk about the truth."

Jasmine shifted on the couch so that she faced her neighbor. "You want to talk about the truth? Then, tell me the truth about Dr. Edmonds."

Mae Frances sat higher. "Jasmine Larson, you are always in my business."

Jasmine could not believe her neighbor's words. But with her stare, she told Mae Frances that she refused to let the subject go.

"All right. Jeremy is a good friend of mine. Has been for years."

"How good?"

Mae Frances raised her eyebrows.

Jasmine leaned forward. "I want to know. Are you two knocking boots?"

Slowly, Mae Frances rose from the couch. Looked at Jasmine as if she'd never been so insulted, and then she smiled. "Can't say that we've . . . knocked boots . . . for a while. Can say that we used to."

"I knew it," Jasmine exclaimed. "So, he's been keeping you company since your husband left."

"He's the reason my husband left."

Jasmine's mouth was shaped into a wide *O*. "He's the one? The affair?"

Mae Frances nodded.

"Wow, so you're not involved and he still comes around?"

"We were always friends," Mae Frances said, sitting down. "In fact, Elijah Van Dorn introduced us. It wasn't long after we met that we had that fling, though it was shortened by my husband's father." She sighed. "I ended up being divorced and Jeremy didn't."

"He's married?"

She nodded again. "Still is. His wife didn't leave him." She chuckled. "I guess she's not a Christian."

"Mae Frances, why do you keep blaming your divorce on your in-laws being Christian? You had an affair. If they had been atheists, I think the reaction would have been the same."

"Maybe, but my problem with Christians is what they claim to be."

"Okay, I've known a few like that too. But I just get mad at them, not at God."

"Never said I was mad at God. Can't be mad at something I don't believe in."

"Did you ever believe in God?"

"As much as I believed in Santa Claus and the Tooth Fairy. But then I grew up and I discovered which parts of life were real and which parts were fairy tales."

Jasmine shook her head. "I'm the first one to admit that I don't do everything right by God. But I really feel sorry for you. I can't imagine living without faith."

"Don't feel sorry for me. I've got plenty of faith, it's just not misplaced. I have faith in myself."

Jasmine wanted to ask where her faith had led her.

Mae Frances stood. "If you're finished trying to recruit me to your side, I have some things to do. Just wanted to check on you and the baby."

Even after Mae Frances was gone, Jasmine sat. She'd been able to buy her neighbor food; she wished she could buy her real faith.

"Well, well." Serena came into the living room and handed Jacqueline to her sister. "Never thought I'd hear my sister witnessing."

"That's not what I was doing. I was just talking. Mae Frances is really lost." Then she asked, "If you heard, why didn't you come out here and help?"

Serena shook her head. "You can't argue anyone into believing in God. I stay away from that. Just try to let my life be a testimony."

"My life isn't much of a testimony right now."

"Yes, it is. The way you're standing, the way you're believing, the way you're praying. Mae Frances will see that, and who knows?"

Jasmine shook her head. She was sure of it now. Mae Frances and God? That would never happen.

Chapter 54

J acqueline wailed.

"Are you sure there's nothing wrong with her?" Jasmine asked as she rocked her baby.

Serena chuckled, but continued folding the clothes into her suitcase. "There's nothing wrong with Missy. She's changed, she doesn't want her bottle. She's just being fussy. Has an attitude about something."

Jasmine nodded and walked some more; still, Jacqueline cried. As she cradled her baby and watched her sister pack, Jasmine felt like joining her daughter. Even after two weeks, she couldn't believe Serena was leaving.

"Maybe I should go with you," Jasmine said suddenly.

Serena paused, faced her sister. "Go with me where?"

"To Florida."

"That doesn't make sense. We just hired Mrs. Sloss and as many women as we had to go through, that woman is going to be a nanny for Jacqueline." Serena turned back to her suitcase.

"But I'm thinking, there's nothing keeping me here."

Serena sighed. "Jasmine, you're just scared, but you're going to be fine. Mrs. Sloss will help you take care of Jacqueline. And in a couple of weeks, you'll be back at work. But the most important reason for you to stay," she walked to where her sister stood, "is that you and Jacqueline need to wait here for Hosea."

Serena's words seemed to soothe Jacqueline. Her whimpers stopped, just as Jasmine's tears began.

"This isn't like you," Serena said. "What happened to the woman who refuses to be denied?"

"This time, it's not going to happen, Serena. I gave up the lies. Gave up the plan, like you said. And I've been praying every day. But still, not a word from Hosea. He's never coming back," she whispered.

A knock interrupted Serena's response.

Jasmine said, "That's just Mae Frances. I don't feel like dealing with her right now."

"I'll tell her you're resting."

Jasmine closed the bedroom door behind Serena and sat in the rocker. She hadn't considered going back to Florida until now, but maybe she should. Being a single mother was not how she imagined life in New York.

Jasmine sighed. A week ago, she'd had hope. But as each day passed she was beginning to accept that she couldn't fight this.

"You'll be warmer in Florida," she said to Jacqueline. "You'll have your auntie, and your cousins." The thought that she couldn't tell her daughter that she'd have her father brought back her tears.

"Jasmine," Serena called, "can you come out here?"

She sucked her teeth. She'd told Serena that she couldn't deal with Mae Frances right now.

She stood, wiped her tears away, then marched toward the door. "Mae Frances," she said, whipping open the door. She stopped. "Hosea."

He stood next to Serena, shifting from one foot to the next, as if he didn't belong—or didn't want to be—there.

"Let me take the baby," Serena said.

As she pulled Jacqueline from Jasmine's arms, Hosea said, "Serena, can I—"

"Sure," she responded before he finished.

As her sister took Jacqueline to Hosea, Jasmine stood still, fearing any move might drive him away.

It had been two weeks since she'd seen him, but a lifetime had passed. She wanted to rush to him, hold him, beg him to stay.

He peered at Jacqueline. "How're you doing, little one?"

Even from across the room, she could see their baby wiggle at the sound of Hosea's voice.

"Yes, I'm here," he said.

She belongs to you, she said inside. *Just like I do.*

It wasn't until Serena took Jacqueline into her room that Hosea looked at Jasmine.

"She's gotten bigger," he said. "I didn't expect that."

Jasmine searched his eyes for the love she hoped was still there. But when he looked at her, she saw nothing. She said, "It's good to see you." She motioned toward the couch and he followed her. When she sat on one end, he sat on the other.

"I'm glad you came over—"

He held up his hand. "Jasmine," he began with his eyes away from her. "I can't even explain why I'm here. But there are some things I need to know."

No lies, she thought as she nodded.

"When I look back, there were so many signs. I mean, you were pregnant so soon," he said as if that sounded stupid to him now. "I guess love *is* blind. Makes you believe the ridiculous."

"I'm so sorry."

"When did you know you were pregnant?" he asked as if he hadn't heard her apology.

She swallowed, thought about editing her words to keep hurt far from him. "I suspected the night before our wedding."

He flinched. "You walked down that aisle knowing you were pregnant."

She shook her head. "I wasn't sure and I was praying it wasn't true because I loved you so much. Just as I do now."

This time, it was her words of love that he ignored. "So, when—"

"The day you overheard me talking to the doctor." She answered before he could ask.

"Why didn't you tell me then?"

"The look on your face when you thought the baby was . . . ours. I couldn't. I did try once," she added. "I didn't want this lie between us anymore. But when you came home and talked about cheaters— I couldn't do it. I didn't want to lose you."

"You were going to let me believe forever that Jacqueline was my daughter."

"Hosea, she is."

"No, she's not."

"She is in every way that counts. You took care of me, of her. You loved her every day. And I came to believe she was your baby."

"Stop saying that," he said slowly. "She's not mine, and saying she is won't make it so." He paused. "I just want to know why?"

She swallowed again. "It had absolutely nothing to do with you. Every time it happened," she paused as his hands balled into fists, "I wondered why it did because all I could think of was how I was falling in love with you."

"So this was going on all that time. Behind my back."

"No, it was only a few times. And I never sought him out. He came after me and . . . I was weak. It was hard for me with you, and no sex. I tried to talk to you about that—"

His head turned slowly until his eyes held hers. With his eyebrows raised, he said, "So, this is my fault?" She shook her head, but he continued. "You slept with some man, carried his baby, and then tried to pass her off as mine, all because I wanted a relationship where I honored you and honored God?"

"No. You asked me why and I'm doing the best I can to explain. My relationship with you was different, and that's why I knew my love for you was different as well. Hosea, you're the first man I ever really loved."

"But you didn't love me enough to stay out of some other man's bed."

She didn't let the sting of his words deter her. "I wanted the intimacy of sex from you, but—"

He held up his hand and stood. "Don't say it again. Don't even think about blaming me."

She stood with him. "I'm not. This is my fault, my mistake, one that I will regret forever." She paused, and thought of her baby. She didn't regret Jacqueline, but she kept that thought inside. "I love you and don't want to lose you."

He looked at her as if he didn't believe a word she said, as if he never would.

"Hosea, please." She reached for him, but he stepped away from her grasp. "I'm sorry, but you've got to believe that I love you."

His eyes held the same disdain that he'd entered with. "I have one more question, and don't lie, Jasmine."

She nodded.

"Were you ever with him once we were married?"

"No!" she exclaimed, relieved that was the truth. "Not even once we were engaged."

He grabbed his jacket.

"Hosea, I know we can work this out."

He shook his head. "I didn't come over here for that."

It was only instinct that made her back away and she watched as he stepped toward the door. She followed him with her eyes only. But the moment he put his hand on the door-knob, he said, "Would you mind if I saw Jacqueline again?"

"Of course not." She turned, but he held up his hand and then disappeared into their baby's room.

Jasmine stood outside the bedroom, away from his sight.

"Isn't she a cutey?" she heard Serena say.

"Yeah."

Jasmine smiled because she could hear his smile.

"Sit over here while you hold her," Serena said.

Time passed until Serena stepped into the hallway.

"What are you doing?" she whispered when she bumped into Jasmine.

Jasmine held her finger to her lips and pressed closer to the door. The rocker creaked as Hosea moved back and forth, and Jasmine could imagine his eyes—loving, caring—as he looked at their daughter.

The sisters heard Hosea say, "I loved you even before you were born."

Jasmine pressed closer; peeked around the opening and watched Hosea kiss their daughter. She rushed into the kitchen.

"Yes," Jasmine cheered as softly as she could.

"I told you!" Serena whispered, following her sister.

A moment later, Hosea called Serena. When he came out of the bedroom he thanked Jasmine.

"You can see her any time." She added, "She's your daughter and she needs you."

He almost nodded; he almost agreed.

The moment he left, Serena came into the living room holding Jacqueline. "Now what were you saying about moving to Florida?"

Chapter 55

ae Frances," Jasmine said the moment her neighbor opened the door. "Don't say anything." She stomped past her into the apartment. "This is not charity," she said, holding up two shopping bags.

Mae Frances frowned. Her back stiffened. Her shoulders straightened.

"My sister went shopping before she left and the way she shops you would think there are ten people living with me. Jacqueline and I are never going to use all of this stuff." She placed the bags on the table. "So, here. You can pay me back later."

Mae Frances eyed the bag's contents, looked at Jasmine again, finally smiled. "Thank you, Jasmine Larson." Her smile went away. "What has you so chipper?"

Jasmine plopped onto the couch. "I think Hosea's coming back."

Mae Frances raised one eyebrow before she sat next to Jasmine. "When did this happen?"

"Yesterday. Nothing's definite. But I know he loves me. And he loves the baby."

Mae Frances smirked. "Did he *say* he was coming back?"

Jasmine held up her hand. "I'm not going to let you bring me down, Mae Frances. This is the first time I've had hope."

"Hmph, I'm just trying to help so you won't be disappointed. That man ain't never coming back."

Jasmine chuckled, shook her head.

"I'm just speaking from experience."

"And I'm speaking from mine. You know what's helped me?" She paused. "Prayer."

"Oh, brother."

"My sister told me to start praying," Jasmine explained, ignoring the grimace on her friend's face. "I did. And the next thing I knew, Hosea was there, willing to talk."

"You think prayer did that?"

"Yeah." She paused. "You should try it sometime."

Mae Frances laughed. "That won't ever happen."

"Oh yeah?" Jasmine turned toward her. "So you really don't think Hosea will come back?"

"Never. I know men."

"And I'm beginning to really know God." She'd just bought Mae Frances two bags of food. Maybe now, she could bring her some faith. "Let's make a deal. Remember that Bible I gave you?"

Mae Frances's eyes narrowed. "Yes."

"If Hosea comes back, I want you to take the Bible."

"Oh, please."

"What are you worried about? If you're right, that Bible will stay in my apartment."

Mae Frances folded her arms.

"You're scared?" Jasmine teased.

"You think you're so smart. All right. I'll accept, and I'll raise you one better. The preacher man comes back, I'll take the Bible and I'll go to church with you."

Jasmine grinned. "For a year."

"Why that long?" Mae Frances said grumpily.

"What are you afraid of?"

"Absolutely nothing." Mae Frances rocked as she sat. "I won't be going to no church."

Jasmine held out her hand and it took a moment for Mae Frances to shake, sealing their agreement. Then she laughed. "Next thing you know, Mae Frances, you're going to be saved."

Her neighbor frowned; did not laugh with her.

"Well, let me get back to Jacqueline. I wanted to give her a little time with the nanny." As she headed toward the door, she yelled over her shoulder, "Get your Sunday clothes ready, Mae Frances, 'cause you are going to church!"

Chapter 56

ope had her on an emotional roller coaster.

After Hosea's visit, Jasmine had done all she could to prepare for her husband's homecoming. She didn't know when it would happen; she was just sure that it would. The picture of him holding Jacqueline, talking to her, kissing her, had Jasmine's confidence high.

Each day she waited for Hosea to call, carrying both her cell and the cordless phone from room to room. Each night, she slept with both phones in her bed near her ear. Each morning, she determined that today would be the day when her family would come together. Each evening she prayed, trying to hold on to hope and faith.

Now, as she stood at the window of her office, she marveled at the clearness of the night. The stars were rhinestones against the blackened sky, glittering as bright as her wedding ring.

She glanced at the diamond on her hand. It had been four weeks since Hosea stopped by, and it had taken that long for all hope to be gone. She took off her ring, slipped it into her suit pocket.

"Knock, knock," Malik said as he entered. "How was your first day back?"

"Long, tiring," she said returning to her desk. "And I can't wait to get home to Jacqueline."

"So, do you think you'll be able to do this woman-of-the-new-millennium thing? Can you handle this high-powered job and be a mother too?"

She shook her head. "Only a man would ask that. Women have been doing this new millennium thing for decades. I love Jacqueline and I'll be eager to see her every night, but it sure feels good to talk to adults about something other than the newest formula, or the latest infant fashions."

Malik chuckled, but then his expression became serious. "So—"

She raised her hand, stopping his question. "I haven't heard from Hosea." She fingered the diamond key around her neck. Soon, this would have to go too.

"I'm sorry, Jasmine. I really thought he would find some way to handle this."

Jasmine shrugged. "Like you said, this is a big deal. He'd have to accept Jacqueline and realistically, would any man be able to accept another man's child?"

"You're putting all men into one category. Yes, there are men who could accept Jacqueline. Men raise stepdaughters all the time. And I would have bet all kinds of money that Hosea would have been one of them."

"I'm glad you kept your bank account intact." She stuffed papers inside of her briefcase and stood.

"Just know that I'm here. In any way, okay?"

She smiled. "I know." But she walked out of the office without giving Malik the one thing she was sure he wanted. She could see it in his eyes every time she saw him—he was waiting for her to say that she didn't blame him for having that conversation in the hospital. But she couldn't say those words. Not yet.

By the time she entered her building, she barely had a nod for Henrikas. All she wanted was to get into her apartment, hold Jacqueline until she settled down, and then let unconsciousness take her away from the pressures of this life.

"Mrs. Sloss," she yelled the moment she stepped inside, and then she stopped. Reverend Bush sat on the couch, holding Jacqueline.

"Jasmine," he said before he handed the baby to Mrs. Sloss. "I hope you don't mind. I stopped by to see you and the baby, and Mrs. Sloss said you'd returned to work today."

"Yes," she said, the frown still etched on her face.

"Don't worry. Your doorman assured Mrs. Sloss that I was who I said I was. And I showed her the wedding pictures." He pointed to the mantel.

"No, it's okay," she said. "I'm just surprised."

"Let's sit down," he said as if this was his apartment. When Mrs. Sloss took Jacqueline into the bedroom, Reverend Bush said, "She's something. Getting so big. She's six weeks, right?"

Jasmine nodded, but didn't say anything. She was waiting for the news. Surely, he had a message from Hosea.

There was a bit of silence and then, "So, how are you?"

"I'm fine. Reverend Bush, I want to thank you for listening to me when I called. Hosea did come by."

He nodded. "I know, we've talked."

There was no hope in his tone.

Reverend Bush said, "I asked Hosea to talk to you. I wanted the two of you . . . to find a way to work this out."

It took seconds for his words to make sense. She wanted to jump up, slap him, do something. "If you wanted us to work this out, then why did you give me that ultimatum? Why did you tell me that I had to tell Hosea?"

"Because a marriage cannot survive on lies."

"But you knew what this would do to us. You knew Hosea couldn't handle this. No man could."

The reverend shook his head. "I wouldn't say that. I know plenty of men who could make this work."

Jasmine folded her arms.

He said, "It wouldn't be easy, but you see, there's one thing I know. When you've tasted even just a bit of the mercy of

God, it's a lot easier to have a forgiving heart and do things you'd never thought you'd do."

"So you told Hosea that we should work this out?"

"Yes. But like he—and you—told me a long time ago, Hosea's grown."

Jasmine stood, paced. Her thoughts were a ball of confusion bouncing inside her head. "I don't get this, Reverend Bush. Now you're for me and Hosea's against me."

"He's not against you, Jasmine. He's just hurt. But I told him that he could get past this. Because if God told Hosea to marry you, then he has to do it without compromise, and without conditions. He has to do it for a lifetime, not a limited time, no matter what's going on."

"You really believe that? Even with what I did?"

"What you did was beyond—" Reverend Bush shook his head. "But even with that I'm looking at this through God's eyes. Just because something doesn't look good to us, doesn't mean it doesn't look good to God. All of this may have happened just so Jacqueline could be here."

"Reverend Bush, I feel that too." She paused, trying to find the courage to ask, "You think Hosea can eventually accept Jacqueline?"

"Oh, he's already accepted Jacqueline. She's not the problem."

That good news didn't make her feel better. "I am," she whispered.

He didn't respond.

"Reverend Bush, I don't know what more I can do."

"Have you asked Hosea to forgive you?"

She threw her hands in the air. "I've told him over and over that I was sorry."

"That's not the same thing. You need to ask Hosea to forgive you."

She frowned.

"You know one of the things that made a difference with

me is that you asked me to forgive you. That's what touched my heart, Jasmine. I wasn't sure if you were really going to tell Hosea everything that had happened before, but that was between you and God. Forgiveness, that was my job. And since I ask the Lord to forgive me every day, I knew I could forgive you."

"So, all I have to do is ask Hosea to forgive me and he'll come back?"

"I'm not saying that. I don't know." The reverend stood, grabbed his coat. "But I do know that this is where I bow out. I've spoken to Hosea, and to you. Now it's up to you, Hosea, and God. No one else needs to be involved."

She followed him to the door.

He paused. "I've missed you in church."

She folded her arms. "I can't come there . . . not with Jacqueline."

"I hope you're still being fed spiritually."

"I haven't joined another church, but I've been reading my Bible more than I ever have. And, I've been praying. I've really tried to make God a part of my life."

His smile was slight. "Good. But if you don't mind, this advice Jasmine: Instead of having the Lord as just a part of your life, why not make Him the center? Let Jesus take the wheel."

Without another word, he hugged her and then he was out the door.

Chapter 57

O kay," Jasmine said as she hung up the telephone. It was done—she'd taken the first step in this new life.

She entered the appointment into her PDA, then rushed into the bedroom to check on Jacqueline. She smiled as her daughter slept. She couldn't believe how she'd grown. Each week, there was something new, and Jasmine lived just to see what her daughter would do next.

But at the same time, each passing week expanded the bridge between her and Hosea. It had been ten weeks now, and she'd seen him just once.

Although he hadn't yet sent any divorce papers, she felt those were on the way. She needed to be prepared for them; she needed to move on.

She'd take that first step tomorrow. The broker said there were several apartments he wanted her to see. By next weekend, she and Jacqueline could be making plans to be in their new place.

She adjusted the blanket over her daughter, then glanced at her watch. Jacqueline would be up in an hour or so. She still had time to do what she'd come to enjoy doing on Sunday evenings.

When she picked up the Bible, an index card fell from the front pages.

Let Jesus take the wheel.

She'd written those words right after Reverend Bush had spoken them. Each morning she repeated them before and after she read her Bible. And she included the phrase in her prayers. She wasn't sure exactly what those words meant, but she could feel peace at the center of her life. She found herself smiling, and enjoying Jacqueline. She let go of the urge to somehow coerce Hosea into coming home. This was not the life she would have chosen for her and Jacqueline, but she was coming to accept it. With a healthy daughter, and a six-figure income, she was wearing shoes that many would pay a high price to step into. Praying, and talking to Serena daily, helped her to recognize her blessings and turn the rest over to God.

Just as she opened the Bible, the telephone rang.

"Jasmine, this is Reverend Bush. How're you?"

"I'm fine." It surprised her, how hearing his voice pleased her. It almost felt as if he were her friend.

"And, how's my—how's Jacqueline?"

"She's fine," she said, matching the sadness that she heard in his voice. He'd never be able to call her his granddaughter. "She's getting big."

"I can imagine. I'm sorry I haven't been by, but I'm always thinking about and praying for you two."

She thanked him and he asked, "Jasmine, have you thought about Jacqueline's dedication?"

She frowned. "Dedication?"

"Some churches call it a christening. But at City of Lights we dedicate the baby to God until she's able to accept Jesus on her own."

"No, I haven't thought about that."

"Well, I'd be honored if you allowed me to perform the service. We're doing a few baby dedications next Sunday."

Next Sunday? At City of Lights? In front of all those people—Brother Hill, Mrs. Whittingham, and a host of other gossipers and naysayers who were probably rejoicing in her misery?

"Reverend Bush, thank you, but I can't do that—" She left it there, hoping he wouldn't ask for her reasons.

After a moment, he said, "I understand. Still . . ."

She wasn't going to be talked into it. Even now, she could hear the snickers, see the smirks.

He said, "I may have a solution." He paused. "The most important thing is that we do this for Jacqueline. The time doesn't matter, the people don't matter. Really, only you, Jacqueline, and I need to be there. So, we won't do it on Sunday. What's another day that's good for you and I'll close the church."

"I don't know," she said, trying to imagine the sight. The two-thousand-seat cathedral closed and only the three of them standing, at the altar. "Have you ever closed the church before?"

"No, but that has nothing to do with my wanting to do it now."

A dedication to God, for Jacqueline. Something she hadn't considered, but maybe with God in her life, Jacqueline wouldn't grow up making the mistakes she had.

"Okay," she said. "Do you have any time available this week?"

"I do, but let's do it next week. This way, you'll have some time to invite people to stand with you. I know Serena may not be able to make it, but Malik, any other friends."

She held her breath, waiting for him to mention his son.

He continued, "I want you to have people there who will pledge to stand by and help you raise Jacqueline in the Lord."

"That's a good idea," she said, trying to keep the sorrow from her voice.

They made plans for the following Thursday. At seven o'clock her daughter would be dedicated to God, behind the closed doors of City of Lights.

Jasmine sighed as she hung up the phone, but the moment she heard Jacqueline's cries, she wiped away her tears. She needed to push sadness away.

Chapter 58

M ae Frances, I can't let you do this," Jasmine said as she held up the silk christening gown.

"You don't like it?" Mae Frances said with her hands folded in her lap.

"I love it, it's just that—" She stopped. She'd known her neighbor for more than a year and she still couldn't figure this out. She glanced at Mae Frances, covered in one of the three dresses she'd always seen her in, yet she'd just handed Jasmine a gown for Jacqueline that could have cost almost one hundred dollars.

"So, why can't you accept this, Jasmine Larson?"

"It's so . . ."

When Mae Frances raised one of her penciled eyebrows, Jasmine took a breath and said, "Thank you." She lowered her eyes. "Mae Frances, do you think there is any way you can come—"

"No way," she interrupted Jasmine. "I don't know how many times I have to tell you that I don't go into anybody's church."

Jasmine waited for Mae Frances's punch line, her reminder of their bet that Jasmine lost.

"Well, before we leave tomorrow, come over, and we'll take pictures with you and Jacqueline."

Mae Frances smiled. "That'll be nice. So, who's going to the church with you?"

"Just Malik and Mrs. Sloss."

"Good. You've given up on the preacher man."

Jasmine sighed. Guess her neighbor couldn't walk away without saying anything. "Yes, Mae Frances. I've given up." Jasmine sank back onto the couch. "I know this story isn't going to have a happy ending."

The knock made Mae Frances stand. "I'll get that for you." She opened the door. Gasped, then said, "What do you want?"

Jasmine turned and her mouth opened wide. "Hosea, come in," she said, dropping the christening gown to the couch.

Mae Frances stood next to the door, her arms folded as if she had no plans to leave.

Jasmine said, "I'll see you tomorrow, Mae Frances," then escorted her into the hallway. She closed the door, turned to Hosea, and said, "This is a surprise."

"How's Jacqueline?"

"She's fine. She's in the bedroom with Mrs. Sloss."

"Oh." His eyes showed his disappointment.

"You can see her."

"I want to, but actually I wanted to talk to you."

"That's great." She motioned toward the couch.

"I think we should talk in private." He paused. "Do you feel comfortable leaving her alone?"

"Sure, I do it everyday." She called Mrs. Sloss and when the nanny walked into the living room, Jasmine made the introduction. "Mrs. Sloss, this is Jacqueline's . . . this is my . . . this is Hosea Bush." As she slipped into her coat, she added, "I'm going out for just a bit."

"That's fine, Mrs. Bush."

The moment they stepped into the hallway, Mae Frances's door swung open. She glared at Hosea, her face scrunched in disapproval, but Jasmine moved past her neighbor without a word.

In the elevator, it took total control to keep her focus on the doors, rather than on the way his arm brushed against hers. Or the way his fragrance filled her nostrils. Or the way she yearned to touch him, kiss him, love him.

"Let's head over to the park," Hosea said once they stepped outside.

Jasmine was grateful for the lamb-end of March as they strolled the blocks to Central Park. Once Hosea motioned toward a bench, they sat in silence, as cars and pedestrians rushed by at a New York City pace.

Finally Hosea pulled an envelope from his briefcase. He turned the legal size envelope over in his hands.

"My plan had been to give you this."

She didn't need X-ray vision to know the package didn't contain good news.

"But I can't give it to you. Not right now. Not yet."

"Hosea," she said, knowing she needed to speak quickly. "I wish I could make you believe how much I love you. Make you know just how sorry I am. How much I've prayed that you'll forgive me."

He nodded, said nothing.

She stared at the envelope. "What's that?" she asked, feeling as if a stone sat in her throat.

"Divorce papers."

She nodded; she'd known.

"I was actually trying to get our marriage annulled," he said matter-of-factly.

Annulled. As if she, their marriage, never existed. Tears came with that thought, but she pressed the emotional water back inside. Emotions would get in the way of her fight.

"I don't want a divorce," she said.

"Why would you?" he asked as if he thought her statement made no sense. "I haven't given you a reason to want one."

"I know I've given you reasons to leave, but I've also given you reasons to stay." Tentatively, she reached across the bench, touched his arm. He didn't look at her, but he didn't push away either. "I love you," she said softly. "That's one reason. And another is I think, I pray, that you still love me." He said nothing.

"And another is that in the midst of this horror, we have a beautiful baby girl."

He nodded, let moments go by. "That's why I'm having such a hard time with this. Because of her . . . and because of God." He shook his head as if God were having a conversation with him at that moment.

She wanted to throw her arms around him, kiss him, and make him remember the way they were.

"Jasmine, if we—"

"I will do anything," she said.

It was the first time he looked at her. "I need something from you."

"Whatever you need."

"I need—"

"Anything."

"I need the truth. I need to know if there are any other lies."

His question sucked the air from her.

He continued. "Because if we are going to make this work, I have to know." He leaned back, as if he were trying to get a better look, trying to see inside of her. "Jasmine, is there anything else I should know? Are there any other secrets? Any other lies?"

Her mind scrolled through the stories she'd told. How he thought she was thirty-five instead of forty. How she was a woman who had never been married and not a divorcée.

Oh, God, she thought. *You've given me this chance to get Hosea back.* But confessing to more lies would push him away forever.

She looked at the divorce papers he held in his hand.

Thought about Reverend Bush's words: *Just let Jesus take the wheel.*

Thought about Serena's words: *Get rid of all of these lies and plans, and just depend on God.*

Her eyes returned to the envelope that could take away all

that she loved. She glanced at her husband. He looked at her with hope in his eyes. Hope for a future.

"Jasmine?"

"Are you saying you want to work this out?" Her voice trembled.

"I'm saying that I need to know the answer to this question."

She swallowed, took a breath. *God, please, please forgive me.* "No, Hosea, there are no more lies," she said with strength.

He exhaled relief for knowing that truth.

She inhaled regret for telling that lie.

"Okay," he said with just a bit of buoyancy. "There's just one more thing."

Jasmine nodded. Nothing could be as bad as what he'd just asked. Nothing could be as bad as what she'd just done. But she kept her focus on her objective and her eyes on the envelope. She asked, "What else do you want to know?"

He took a breath. Shifted on the bench. Held the envelope tighter between his fingers. "Jacqueline's father," he finally said, "Who is he?"

She waited a moment, fighting back the tears that hovered beneath her lashes. "Brian. Brian Lewis."

He frowned, squinted, as if the name was familiar. Then, his eyes widened, his mouth opened. "Brian. From California," he spoke as if he were reading a résumé. "The one who was sitting at our table when you fainted. The one who helped me get you into the ambulance. The one who said he'd come from California to New York to see you."

"No!" She shook her head. "I didn't know he was going to be there. I hadn't seen him since the day . . . since before we were engaged." When he looked at her through thin eyes, she said, "Hosea, he doesn't even know he's her father, because to me, you are."

He shook his head. Looked straight at her. "Brian. Brian Lewis." And then he laughed. Threw his head back and guffawed as if he had never heard anything so ridiculous. "I can't believe this mess." Suddenly, the laughter stopped. "You made a big mistake, Jasmine." His tone was ominous. "You got it twisted. Confused my compassion and morals for being soft."

"No, I never thought—"

He spoke over her words. "You must have thought that because I wanted to be celibate, I wasn't a real man."

"No," she cried, even as passing pedestrians slowed to view the unfolding drama.

He stood, towered over her. "Jasmine, let me ask you this, what do you call a woman who marries one man while carrying the child of another?"

She sobbed.

He looked at her as if he were repulsed by all that he saw. Then, he backed away. Tossed the enveloped toward her and without another word, walked up Central Park West.

Jasmine was bolted to the bench, her tears falling freely now. She stayed as he moved, stayed as he never looked back, stayed as he walked farther and farther until she could see him no more.

She looked down at the envelope that was now wet with her tears.

This was worse than her dream.

Chapter 59

"Come on in, Jasmine," Reverend Bush greeted her as she stepped into the office. "Where's Jacqueline?"

"She's with Mrs. Sloss and Malik. They'll be here in about fifteen minutes. I thought it best if she came right before the ceremony; they're trying to get her to sleep because if she doesn't, I don't know what she'll do."

Reverend Bush motioned for Jasmine to have a seat. "It won't matter what she does. That's what's so wonderful about baby dedications. It's where the sacred and the mundane collide."

Jasmine tried to chuckle, but her eyes roamed to the package she held. "Reverend Bush, before we get started, I saw Hosea last night." She paused, tried to squeeze from her mind the vision of the way he looked at her. "He gave me this."

Reverend Bush nodded as he took the package. As if he already knew the contents. "I'm sorry, Jasmine," and he sounded as if he really was. "I was hoping Hosea could find a way—"

"But he couldn't." Her heart still cried, but her eyes didn't. There were no tears left. She'd cried them all yesterday as she sat on the park bench long after Hosea had gone, and the tears were still with her when she rushed back into her apartment. Mrs. Sloss had wrung her hands, not knowing if she should comfort Jasmine or Jacqueline.

Through the night, and into this morning, her cries continued. The emotional water didn't stop until noon—didn't stop until she accepted that she was going to be a divorced woman—once more.

"I'm sorry, Jasmine," the reverend said again, as if he couldn't think of anything else to say.

She nodded. "There's one thing. Today, in the ceremony," she swallowed, "please call the baby, Jacqueline . . . Larson." She took a deep breath. "Her name has to be Jacqueline Elizabeth Larson."

The reverend frowned.

"In those papers," she nodded toward the envelope, "Hosea says that he wants no legal or financial responsibility for her." She paused as tears that she was sure were no longer there pressed toward her eyes. "So, I'm going to have her name changed to Larson. And mine, as well."

The reverend sighed. "I want you to know that I will do everything I can for you and Jacqueline." He added, "Maybe in time, you'll even come back to services here."

Jasmine smiled, although she knew she wouldn't be doing that. "I appreciate all you've done, Reverend Bush. Especially after all of this."

The reverend held up his hands. "You know, one of my favorite sermons is about grace and mercy and how we all survive in this world only because God has decided to give them both to us. I can't say you were my favorite person in the beginning. But God helped me to see the better parts of you." He shrugged. "If we all did that—just searched for the good, instead of expecting the bad—this world would be a much better place. People rise to expectations, Jasmine, and I think that's what you're doing."

"Thank you."

"Well," the reverend began, slapping his thighs, "this is not a sad occasion. So, let's get on with the business of getting this little girl dedicated." He went around the desk and took out the certificate. "One of the things I always say to parents is that this is a good time to look at your relationship with God."

Jasmine thought about how far she'd come. She prayed and read her Bible daily. Even knew a few scriptures. She'd be the first to admit that she still had a long way to go. She recalled the lies she'd told Hosea yesterday and regretted that she didn't have the faith to tell the truth. But that was the only good thing about this situation—at least she wouldn't have to live under those lies.

"Now, I will be standing at the altar with you in front of me. Will Malik be standing in as her godfather?"

Jasmine nodded. Malik had asked if she wanted him to stand in as Jacqueline's father, but she declined. She was Jacqueline's mother, and for now, she'd walk in the shoes of her father as well.

"There is a point in the ceremony, Jasmine, where I'm going to ask who gives this child to be dedicated." He paused, shook his head.

"Is something wrong?"

"No, that's just the point where the father . . ." His voice trailed off. "Well, I think that's it." He stood. "I'm sure they're here by now. Why don't you go into the sanctuary and I'll be right there."

She nodded, but before she took a step, she said, "I'm really sorry the way this worked out, because Jacqueline would have been blessed to have you as a grandfather."

He hugged her before she left the room.

They stood in the same spot where Jasmine had promised to love Hosea until death.

"I count it an honor and a privilege to stand with you as we come together to thank God for the gift that He's given us in Jacqueline Elizabeth—" Reverend Bush paused. "Jacqueline Elizabeth Larson."

The reverend cleared his throat and continued. "Dedicat

ing a child to God acknowledges the Lord's sovereignty. And so we stand before God tonight, together, to pray for His grace and wisdom in carrying out our responsibilities."

Jacqueline wiggled and Jasmine held her tighter. To her right, Malik stood, smiled.

"As believers, we recognize that children belong to the Lord."

Jacqueline gurgled her agreement, and they all chuckled.

As the ceremony continued, Jasmine quickly glanced around the church. The lights had been dimmed so that the spotlight was on just the four of them at the altar—she, Malik, Mrs. Sloss, and Reverend Bush—standing for Jacqueline Elizabeth. It was almost pathetic, the absence of people in her life, and therefore missing from her daughter's. She'd made Hosea and work her priorities. Maybe that would change; maybe not. She was fine with it being all about Jacqueline, for now.

It was difficult, though, to keep sadness at bay. This was a special moment, meant to be shared by her and Hosea with their daughter. And it was even sadder that she'd never be able to tell Jacqueline wonderful stories about how her father wanted her, loved her while she was still in the womb.

"As her mother," the reverend said, dragging Jasmine from her thoughts, "it is important for you to love God with every ounce of your being and teach Jacqueline to do the same."

Jasmine nodded. Jacqueline would know the love of God. Between His love and hers, she'd make sure that her daughter never felt that there was anything missing.

"Who gives this child to be dedicated to the Lord?" Reverend Bush asked.

Jasmine took a breath, lifted Jacqueline toward the reverend.

"I do."

The voice came from the back of the church. They all turned, peered through the darkness, until Hosea stepped into the light. Slowly, he moved with steps that seemed forced, as if he were not coming on his own accord. Yet, he wore a smile.

He walked straight to Jasmine, and gently lifted Jacqueline from her arms. He held their baby, looked at her as if he adored her. Then, he said, "Reverend Bush, you asked who gives this child to be dedicated to the Lord." He paused, looked at Jasmine, said, "Her mother and I do."

They were all silent with shock, stared at Hosea as if he were the one being dedicated to God.

Hosea's eyes moved from Jasmine to his father, to Malik, back to Jasmine.

"Well," he began, "are we going to do my daughter's dedication or not?"

Reverend Bush's smile was wide as he took the baby from his son's arms. Jasmine stood stiff, afraid that if she even blinked, Hosea would go away.

Hosea took her hand and squeezed it, and she started breathing again. *Amen and amen.*

With Jacqueline in his arms, the reverend said, "Hosea and Jasmine," he paused. "By coming forward before God, do you declare your desire to dedicate yourselves and your daughter, Jacqueline Elizabeth . . . Bush to the Lord?"

Hosea looked at Jasmine and he nodded slightly. Together, they said, "We do."

Reverend Bush raised a wiggling Jacqueline above his head. "In the name of the Father, the Son, and the Holy Spirit, I present to you Jacqueline Elizabeth Bush." He paused and then added with a laugh, "My granddaughter."

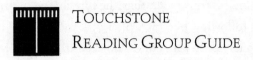

TOUCHSTONE
READING GROUP GUIDE

A Sin and a Shame

DISCUSSION POINTS

1. Serena tells Jasmine that "there are plenty of unsaved folks parked in the pews all across America." What does she mean by this?

2. Jasmine thinks her father's insurance money is being used well to put her in a fancy Manhattan condo and a mink coat, all so that she can snag a rich husband. If you suddenly inherited a few hundred thousand dollars, what changes would you make in your lifestyle?

3. Malik thinks that Jasmine seems "obsessed . . . again" with Reverend Bush. What about her behavior is obsessive and what is just aggressive? Where do you think the line is between an ambitious woman going after what she wants and a stalker? Is this line different for men?

4. If you've read *Temptation*, the first of Murray's novels in which Jasmine appears, do you agree with Jasmine—

that she's changed and come a long way since being "saved"? Why or why not?

5. Jasmine often repeats that she's in charge, it's her game, she's following her own plan . . . and yet the man who awakens her heart is one who takes the control right out of her hands. What does this say about Jasmine? How does her need for control relate to her views about and use of sex?

6. Why is Jasmine so upset to learn that Hosea won't have sex with her? Why do you suspect Jasmine doesn't agree with celibacy?

7. Jasmine loves Hosea. But she can't resist Brian. Have you ever wanted something you knew wasn't good for you? How did you handle the situation?

8. Reverend Bush preaches about being an example to others, but Jasmine feels she's failed when Mae Frances catches her with both Brian and Hosea. How do you feel about the concept of being responsible as a monument to God's love every day? How do you try to live by example?

9. Jasmine unhappily muses that she was happy with the way Hosea loved her, so why was she lusting after a man she almost despised? What would you tell Jasmine if she asked you this question?

10. How do you feel about the pervasive belief that "all men cheat"?

11. Jasmine realizes that she and Mae Frances are the

same—both women just taking care of themselves. What else makes them similar? Why do you think the author created Mae Frances as she did?

12. Jasmine's experience is the perfect example of how easily "God's word" can be twisted and manipulated to fit people's needs. For example, when she is about to come clean to Hosea about her affair with Brian, and Hosea begins to tell her about the terrible day he's had discussing cheaters, Jasmine takes it as a sign from God not to tell Hosea the truth. How do you distinguish between signs from God and coincidence in your own life?

13. Are you satisfied by the novel's ending? Do you think Jasmine will ever come completely clean with Hosea? Should she?

Enhance Your Book Club Experience

1. Read the biblical passages on Hosea and the whore he took for a wife, per God's instructions. Consider how it relates to the themes in *A Sin and a Shame*.

2. Jasmine is often blinded by the glitter of the "high life," which leaves her doing almost anything to achieve the lifestyle she thinks she deserves. Get a taste of Jasmine's temptation by taking your club on the road to the swankiest restaurant or nightclub in town. Try searching on www.citysearch.com or www.zagats.com for the right place, make a reservation, don your hottest outfit, and have fun.

3. Several characters in the novel refer to "witnessing," which is when Christians tell stories about their experiences with God, often in order to convince others to open their hearts to His love. At your next book club meeting, go around the circle and share your own stories about the moments when you've felt God's presence in your life.

4. Take some time to visit and browse the author's website at victoriachristophermurray.com.

Author Q&A

1. What made you decide to write a follow-up novel to *Temptation* focused solely on Jasmine?

   I received hundreds of letters from readers asking what happened to Jasmine. I had no plans to ever write a sequel; however when I came up with the story line for *A Sin and a Shame*, I decided this plot was perfect for Jasmine Larson.

2. When we first meet up with Jasmine and Serena, they are recovering from the tragic loss of their father. You also lost your father during the writing of *A Sin and a Shame*. How did your experience influence this story?

   Interestingly, my father passed away several months after I wrote the scene where Jasmine and Serena talk about their father. I was more than halfway through the book when I lost my father. So, his passing didn't really influence the book at all. (Except that this book was difficult to complete because my father was the person that I discussed my books with as I was writing. I missed that a lot with *A Sin and a Shame*.)

3. It seems that Jasmine is often the subtle butt of a joke in *A Sin and a Shame*, particularly because she doesn't get what it really means to live a Christian life. What were you trying to do by portraying Jasmine in this way?

   I didn't mean to write Jasmine as the butt of a joke at all. What I was trying to show is that there are many Christians like Jasmine—people who have prayed the Sinner's Prayer and then they stopped right there. I don't believe there is "a Christian life." I think being saved is a journey—where we all walk into this life at different stages, but wherever we come in, we should continue to strive and grow. Jasmine came into this life as a baby Christian, and she continued to take baby steps. She is still not perfect, but she is trying.

4. You're the author of several African American novels that preach God's love. Do you consider your work Christian fiction? Why or why not?

   I hope that no one reads any kind of preaching into my work. I don't want to preach a thing. But, I do want to show the message of God's love. When I wrote my first novel, I didn't even know there was such a thing as Christian fiction. So, I couldn't write to a genre that I didn't know existed. Other people called me a Christian fiction writer. I've learned to accept that label, although it is a difficult label to wear. Once a reader hears "Christian fiction," certain assumptions are made—my characters are held to a certain standard, people expect me to behave a certain way . . . it adds more pressure in the way of criticism and critiques that I'm sure other writers don't have to endure. But the good thing is that I don't have to answer to anyone—except for God. So, I will continue to write what He puts on my heart and hope that the readers who are supposed to "get it," get it.

5. Do you think non–African American, non-Christian readers can still glean something profound from your novels?

I don't know if any reader will glean anything profound from my work. I'm really not trying to be a profound writer. I'm trying to just tell a good story and if a reader can relate or get something out of it, that's extra for me. I want my characters to be universal. My characters just happen to be African American; but I could write an entire book and never mention the characters' race because that's not what's important. What's meaningful to me is the message of the books—that any one of us can get through anything with the power and love of God.

6. Reverend Bush tells Jasmine that when she asked for forgiveness he was able to open his heart to her. He en-

courages her to ask for forgiveness from Hosea as well. What do you think the real "power of forgiveness" is?

The entire Christian doctrine is based on forgiveness. God forgives us every minute of every day for all the things we do. It is the basis of our salvation. Therefore, I cannot write a book about God's love without connecting it to forgiveness. We have to follow Him and forgive others as He asks us to.

7. Many first-time authors write semiautobiographical novels. Now that you've written several, how much of your own life still ends up in your novels?

I haven't yet written a book about my life; I'm much too private a person to have any part of my life end up in my novels. However, I did pull on some personal experiences in *Grown Folks Business*. (No, my husband is not/was not gay.) But, the family structure in *Grown Folks Business* is very similar to my own.

8. Jasmine gets to do things that the rest of us only daydream about, but would never do, whether out of fear or conscience! Did you get to live out any deep, dark fantasies through Jasmine in either *Temptation* or *A Sin and a Shame?*

I get to live out all of my deep, dark fantasies whenever I'm writing about a "bad" character. I think all writers do. Just like I get to live out my "good girl" fantasies whenever I'm writing about someone good. (I would love to live like Serena.) However, my favorite characters to write are the "bad guys." There are no limits.

9. Even though Jasmine tells some truly horrible lies and hurts a lot of people in this novel, she still ends up with everything she ever wanted. Why should readers be glad for her?

I don't know if Jasmine ends up with everything she wanted. She has to live with the fact that she still has lies hanging over her head. And she has to live with these lies with the first man that she has ever loved. And, I don't think Jasmine hurt a lot of people in the novel (at least I didn't mean for her to). I think Jasmine always does the greatest damage to herself. But as far as readers feeling glad for her—I don't know if someone should feel glad, but a reader can test their "forgiveness radar" by just how much they decide to forgive Jasmine. Because after all, none of us is perfect.

10. In the novel, Mae Frances seems to be the mouthpiece for all nonbelievers, while Jasmine stands as testament to the misled and confused. What character or characters represent your own opinions?

In all of my novels, I spread my beliefs among all of the characters. Mae Frances says some things that I believe . . . so does Jasmine, Reverend Bush, Hosea, and even Brian.

11. *A Sin and a Shame* takes place primarily in New York City among the upper class . . . hot clubs, fancy restaurants, and designer clothes abound. Have you spent a lot of time in New York cruising this scene, or did you have to do research to create the authentic feel of the novel?

I was born and raised in New York and when I attended graduate school, I lived in Manhattan—first downtown in Stuyvesant Town on Fourteenth and First and then on Central Park West and Ninety-sixth Street. I didn't "cruise" this scene. I just really wanted to make Manhattan (my favorite place in the world) a character in this novel.

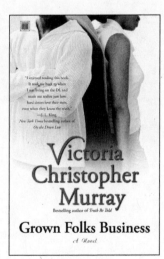